D0843032

DISCARD

The WOW Factor
The Art of Writing a Novel

By
Robert C. Powers, Ph.D.

Explore how to write a novel... while writing one!

Powerful **P**ublisher LLC
Virginia Beach, Virginia

Published by:
Powerful Publishers LLC
2317 Broad Bay Road, Suite 17
Virginia Beach, Virginia 23451

Library of Congress Control Number: 2006902807

International Standard Book Number (ISBN):
0-9769773-3-8

Printed in the United States of America
1st Printing

Preface

After writing eight novels and four screen plays, it occurred to me that I have learned a lot about writing. I looked at many of the books that are available about writing a novel and concluded that I have a different approach to offer that many will find interesting, entertaining and useful.

I use a different methodology than most. I believe it is very instructive. I provide information and thoughts about how to write a novel in an artistic and freeform style. Then I begin writing a novel along with the Reader. The examples I use are spontaneous as I think about a new novel I plan to write.

I have researched the Chesapeake Native Americans who are the subject of the "example" Rough-Through of the novel that I use. There is not a lot of information about this tribe which disappeared during the Seventeenth Century, though the Bay keeps their name alive (The Chesapeake Bay).

There are several very good books about the Powhatan Federation of 1607 of which the Chesapeake were a part, though they focus primarily on the inland tribes. The language of the Powhatan Federation is partially documented, though not specific to the Chesapeake.

The Algonquian Lenape language is similar to the Powhatan, though deriving from Tribes north of Virginia. Where I use Native American Language in the novel The Unknown Horizon, it is from one of these sources. In some cases the word I use has a "sound" or "root" of a word from one of these sources, though not necessarily the actual Chesapeake word (the Chesapeake language is partially lost).

I also use examples from some of my other manuscripts and from several classic Authors. I guide the Reader through writing chapters and scenes similar to the examples I provide. It's a lot of fun for the Reader... and for me!

Robert C. Powers
Author

Dedicated to
My Father
Robert Davis Powers, Jr.
Who Always Wanted to Write a Novel

Novels by Robert C. Powers

Quester, A Story of the River Warriors
The Mud Fox, Ghost of the Jungle
Black Dragon, Further Adventures of Quester and the
Mud Fox
The Wara Wa, The Ultimate Campfire Story
Old House on the Island, A Traditional Family With a
Dark Secret
The Perfect Season, A Story of the High School Gridiron
Unleash the Eagle, After 9/11, the Search for Usama
Trail of the Scorpion, The Search for Weapons of Mass
Destruction

Screenplays by Robert C. Powers

River Wars (Based on the Novel "Quester")
Ghost of the Jungle (Based on the Novel "The Mud Fox")
Old House on Haunted Island (Based on the Novel "Old
House on the Island")
Curse of the Were (Based on the Novel "The Wara Wa")

Contents

Chapter	Title	Page
1.	The Art of Writing a Novel	11
2.	The Experience of Writing a Novel	17
3.	The Seminal Idea for a Story	25
4.	Story Development	33
5.	Choice of Characters	47
6.	Character Development	59
7.	The Storyteller's Direction	75
8.	Scenario Development	83
9.	Plot Development	91
10.	Logic, Flow, Tempo and Timing	103
11.	Creation of Dialogue	111
12.	Creation of Description and Action	119
13.	The Structure of a Novel	133
14.	Perspective and Tense	143
15.	Inside the Creative Cave	153
16.	Action and Emotional Scenes	163
17.	Humorous and Mystery Scenes	173
18.	Romantic and Sex Scenes	183
19.	Innovative and Highly Dramatic Scenes	195
20.	Battle and Mourning Scenes	207
21.	Storm and Fantasy Scenes	223
22.	Peril and Extreme Peril Scenes	233
23.	Turning Point and Multi-perspective Scenes	243
24.	Defining and Triumphant Scenes	257
25.	Endings	271
26.	The Rough-Through and the Creative Reviews	277
27.	Getting Published	287
28.	After Publishing	301
Appendices		
a.	Book Coaching for Authors	313
b.	Map Supporting "The Unknown Horizon"	317
c.	Bibliography	319

Chapter One
The Art of Writing a Novel

What, you say, is a WOW Factor? It is what the Author injects into a story that will make the Reader say "WOW" over and over again! In a WOW novel, when the Reader finishes, he/she will sit back and savor a real experience, one that stirred the emotions and will never be forgotten. This book is about how to write a WOW novel and the experience of writing one! You don't need an outline to START! There is no need for a formula or step by step approach!

Writing a novel is "freeform art".

The Seminal Idea

This is the "seed" that is planted to grow into a novel. It is "in your head", almost to the point of obsession. You wish you had the time and knowledge to get it out of your head and onto paper.

This "seed" seems a crazy idea at first... but now that I've had time to think about it, it might work!

The seminal idea may revolve around people you know. How, you ask, will I ever be able to write about "that" without embarrassing myself and other people? Write it down anyway!

Perhaps you don't have a good seminal idea. You want to write a novel, so you'll need to search around for an idea that would make a great novel.

The Title

It may be crystal clear to you what the title of your novel should be, based on your seminal idea. Or, the title may not be clear. Pick out a title and use it until the title you really want becomes clear. Your writings will eventually suggest to you the best title.

Choosing a title is very important. You want a title that is descriptive of the novel, focusing on the characters, the plot, the scenario or all of these. It should be as short as you can make it. It should have a high "WOW!" factor, that is, it should be something that will grab a potential Reader's eye if seen on a book shelf.

Paint and Canvas

What do I use to create a novel? If writing a novel is freeform art, what paint and canvas do I use? I will provide and describe six primary concepts that you will use to paint your picture… write your novel. They are:
1. The Tools of the Author
2. The WOW Factors
3. The Story Events
4. The Creative Principles
5. The Rough-Through
6. The Creative Reviews

We are going to have an adventure together… exploring how to write a novel… while writing one! We'll use the paint and canvas noted above to write the "Rough-Through" of a novel called "The Unknown Horizon"!

The Tools of the Author

These are the tools you will use:
1. Storytelling
2. Description
3. Action
4. Dialogue.

Everything you write will fit into one of these categories.

The WOW Factors

The WOW Factors are, in the approximate order of importance:
1. Emotion

2. Suspense
3. Conflict
4. Action
5. Surprise
6. Romance
7. Mystery
8. Heroism
9. Humor
10. Pizzazz.

We will talk about these and use them as we write our Rough-Through.

The Story Events

How do you take the seminal idea and transform it into a story? We will look at a sequence of "story events" as a guide for developing a successful story.

The Creative Principles

We will examine some basic creative principles that will prepare you to START writing. They are:
1. Story Development.
2. Choice of Characters.
3. Character Development.
4. The Direction.
5. Scenario Development.
6. Plot Development.
7. Logic.
8. Flow, Tempo and Timing.
9. Creation of Dialogue.
10. Creation of Description.
11. The Structure of a Novel.
12. Perspective and Tense.

The Rough - Through

But, you say, if I don't need an outline, and there is no need for a formula or step by step approach... how do I start?

13

Well, what we are going to do I call a "Rough-Through". The Rough-Through is just what it says... the pouring out of the author's mind onto paper to create a rough novel.

The Rough-Through is a "controlled rush" to get about 80,000 words (or so) on paper.

After the Rough-Through is completed, we will have something to work on... the rough "block of granite" that is ready for the sculptor's tool... the "lump of coal" that can be polished to a diamond!

The Creative Review

Once we have the Rough-Through, we will conduct Creative Reviews, going back over the Rough-Through many times, each time with a "focus" on some WOW Factor or Creative Principle. Each Creative Review is a complete, focused reading of the entire Rough-Through... word by word. During each Creative Review, we will make changes to the Rough-Through that organize and enhance it.

The Whole Story

It is hard to write the story until you know the whole story in some detail! Let me say that again, as it is very important:

It is hard to write the story until you know the whole story in some detail!

Think about that! For example, if you are writing in Chapter Three about a character and you still don't fully understand (yet) what's going to happen to that character in the end... and what personality traits, etc. match his ending... you cannot write about him/her with great authority.

You will write the story as you do the Rough-Through. You know roughly where and how to START, but you don't necessarily now where you will end. You don't have some fixed "grand outline". Keep in mind that you are engaged in an art form! You are not turning the crank of a "novel machine".

> **In writing a novel, you are conducting a symphony orchestra of literary instruments, blending the harmony of plot and subplot; a kaleidoscope of actions, thoughts, dialogues and descriptions that all function together in perfect harmony to tell an emotional and exciting story.**

The Conceptual Framework

the Author needs a "Conceptual Framework" to which he or she can refer as a guideline for artistic actions. Such a "Conceptual Framework" is suggested in Figure 1-1.

Figure 1-1

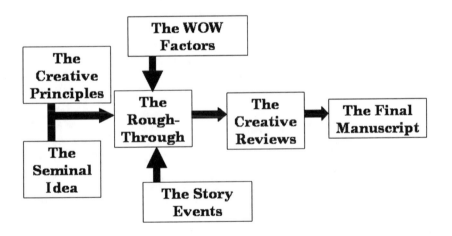

The Art of Writing A Novel
Not a Formula or "Step by Step" Process

You have (or develop) a "seminal idea" for a novel. You understand some "Creative Principles" as a guideline for writing this novel. You use the WOW Factors and Story Events as a guide in writing the Rough-Through. You "rough through" the first writing of your novel. You take the "Rough-Through" and subject it to a number of "Creative Reviews" that embellish and polish the novel. Through this series of creative actions, you evolve and produce the final manuscript.

****

Chapter Two
The Experience of Writing a Novel

Writing a novel is as easy as just sitting down and doing it! Right? The story runs through your mind all the time! The only reason you haven't done it is... well, you just don't have the time!

Writing a novel begins with finding the time to do it!

Writing a novel may look like an insurmountable task if you don't yet have the experience of writing one... or attempting to write one. You find that out once you sit down and START!

The most important thing you can do to fulfill your dream is... START! After you read this book, sit down and start writing! It doesn't matter where you start... not at first. We'll see as we go along that how you begin the novel is very important... but it doesn't matter how or "where" you "START"! Just do it!

Who Are You, the Novelist?

There is a story in each of us. Indeed, we all live our own story. Most people never get their story "out". You want to write a novel. You are therefore a person who wants to get it "out". You believe you can do it. You have a passion to do it! You are likely to be a person for whom creativity is a "high". You are happiest when you are creating.

You want to be recognized for your creativity. You read a lot, and enjoy a good novel. You are constantly seeking a novel that raises your emotions to a high level and takes you away from the dullness of reality (a high WOW Factor)! You like to write and may have written short stories, poems and even been published in school magazines... even commercial magazines. Or, perhaps, you have never written anything and want to start with "your novel".

The Author's Perspective

You have an idea for a novel! It may be based on some personal experience. If so, that's good! Novels based on personal experiences are always the best, because you are closer to it… you know it… you can describe it with passion. But, as we shall see, a novel based on your personal experience is not necessarily a novel "about" your personal experience. The experience can form the idea for the novel, but after that, the whole universe of literary expression is open to you… unless you choose to restrict it by making the story "personal".

You, the Author, are a nice person. You are likely a moral person. You don't particularly enjoy conflict, either between persons or in the broader, more violent sense. But…

Good novels are mostly about conflict!

Stories are based to a large degree on conflict of all kinds… personal conflict, romantic conflict, violent conflict, professional conflict… and how the heroes and heroines of your book deal with the conflicts and surmount them. Your hero/heroine must experience external conflict (conflict with his/her external world) and internal conflict (conflict with his/her internal feelings, doubts and desires). Most likely, you are not used to dealing with the amount of conflict you need in a good novel… except when you are reading a good novel!

To be a successful Author of novels, you need to start thinking about how to create and manage conflict in your writings… and share the emotions of those in conflict. You should include romance in your novel, and it should be filled with emotional content. You have had romantic and sexual experiences, but you are a bit shy about them. You will learn herein that an author cannot afford to be bashful.

And yes, you may have some sex in the novel, but it doesn't have to be graphic or vulgar to be interesting and exciting. The most effective treatment of sex in a novel is not the mechanics of it, but creating "sexual tension" between your characters and placing them in "sexy" situations. The chase is usually more interesting than the climax... at least for the Reader!

The traits you most likely lack for an Author are patience and persistence. Do you have the patience to learn how to write a novel... to finish a novel? To get an Agent? To get a Publisher? Do you have the persistence to confront problem after problem and take the time to learn in each instance what you need to do to solve them? You can discipline yourself to have patience and persistence. Will you?

Narratives, Sermons and Stories

What is it you are going to write? Many new Authors begin writing, and it turns out to be a "narrative", or a "sermon", not a story. What's the difference?

A Narrative: A narrative is "what happened", in approximate chronological order. The Author attempts to "tell it all". A narrative is a number of events (perhaps interesting and exciting) in which the hero is just a hero... not a person with a goal who transforms and becomes a new, better person. Some of the macho soldier type books follow this pattern. The emphasis is on how tough the guy is in a number of related events. But, he doesn't always "grow".

A Sermon: A sermon is the Author chasing a "cause". When an Author writes a sermon, all the good guys are "really good" and all the bad guys are "really bad" and neither group changes much as in a real story. The Author becomes preoccupied with the message in his/her "sermon" (social drama) and fails to tell a story. Beware of this, as it is a natural tendency, since we all have strong beliefs. A good Author will present both sides of an argument and have his characters torn between the two and transformed as events transpire.

A Story (Novel): Events that relate to a story theme that follow a logical pattern (but not "everything"). The Author structures a story by engaging in "storytelling". It may be based on true events, but Author's license is exercised to modify or change things (a little or radically, it doesn't matter), and attention is paid to the proper structure of a story. The hero/heroine achieves a tough goal and "grows".

The Author's Time and Effort

You should recognize that writing a novel is an undertaking of some length. This is particularly so if you are learning by writing your first novel. Many people think they can write... but like anything else, you must learn how to do it right. You don't do it overnight. Nor do you do it in a few weeks, or a few months! It took me over two years to write my first novel, learning as I went. Now, I can do it in six to twelve months, depending on the nature of the novel and how much research is required. If you have never written a novel, you should plan on at least a year long effort... as a trial. During this time, you should plan to spend your time at 2-4 writing sessions per week, each 3-6 hours in length (6-24 hours a week if you also work for a living... 24-30 hours a week if you pursue it mostly full time).

At the end of six months you will have a feel for whether your novel is going to "make it" and whether or not you are enjoying the process. You need to have someone else read what you have done. It can be an associate or friend, but that usually does not produce the most benefit for you. You need to have someone who knows how to write a novel read it (See Appendix A: Book Coaching for Authors).

If you are not enjoying writing your novel, stop. You'll never get to the end if you are not enjoying it! If you are enjoying it, but you're not sure of what you have produced so far, keep going! If, at the end of a year, you are frustrated and haven't produced something you like, it's time to go get your golf clubs, fishing rods or whatever!

Writing a novel can be one of the most enjoyable things you have ever done! You will live and relive every exciting moment of each character you develop. You will create "your own universe", your own environment... and give birth to exciting characters that exist at first only in your imagination! You will come to know the characters you develop as if they were intimate friends of yours… or perhaps ultimate enemies. They will become a part of you, forever!

The Author's Place

Create your own "Author's Place". It should be a place you enjoy where you can relax and be creative. It should be, to the degree that you can accomplish it, "closed off" from the rest of your house… your world. It should be a special place where you can drink a good cup of coffee (or whatever) and enter the "Creative Cave".

We all think about that magic and romantic place where we sit in "Author attire" and are inspired by a sweeping view of a mountain lake, or the seashore, or canyons and big sky. As we sit there amid stacks of paper, scribbled notes and stained coffee cups, great thoughts come to us and we are able to write beautiful, emotional and exciting passages. Well, maybe you have such a place. If you do, use it! If you don't, create your own place where you like to be.

Go to your "Author's Place". It has to be a "special" place. The family (or whoever) has to know it exists and allow it to exist. The dining room table doesn't qualify. Use a spare bedroom. Put up some pictures with sweeping views. Make sure a coffee (or tea, or something) pot is near. Get a desk from the local office store upon which you can spread out your "stuff". Rig a computer with a printer, preferably a laser printer (they don't cost that much any more).

Sit in your "Author's Place", play solitaire on the computer, surf the web and convince yourself that you like it. You may spend a lot of time there! Now, surf the web randomly and see what catalyzes your most interesting thoughts. Get "in the mood"!

The Creative Cave

The "Creative Cave" is not a place, but a state of mind. You must learn to enter the "Creative Cave" every time you sit down to write. It usually takes thirty or more minutes after you sit down in your "Author's Place" to enter, or reenter the Creative Cave.

You may find yourself in the Creative Cave in places other than the Author's Place. For example, you may find yourself in the Creative Cave with a head full of ideas while driving a long distance. That's good, but... you are not well equipped behind the wheel to capture your ideas. Stop for gas and scribble a few notes to remind you of your thoughts. Those thoughts will surely escape you if you don't do this!

You need a catalyst to enter the Creative Cave... such as rereading the last several scenes you have written... or doing some spot research on something that will inspire you (the internet is great for this! Just type a key word related to your story into "search" and see what pops up!)

Once in the Cave, you are oblivious to all things around you except for the manuscript you are working on and the characters and situations you are creating. Any interruption will likely take you out of the Creative Cave and cause you to lose the emotion and continuity of that which you write. Then, you will have to go through the process again of entering the Creative Cave.

Spouses (and children) seldom understand the Creative Cave, even if they claim to. They also become impatient. They have lost you to the Creative Cave, and there is no room for them therein. My wife will tolerate my presence in the Creative Cave for 4-6 hours, and then the question comes in impatient tones, "Are you still typing?"

"No," I reply, "I'm creating!"

"Well, come out of there and let's create something together!"

I know then that my session in the Creative Cave is ended for the day and I return to the world I share with my spouse, which isn't so bad. I understand her feelings... and I am glad to come out of the Creative Cave for awhile... and give my brain a rest. But the characters, situations and myriad options for my story in the secret universe I have created still dance in my head.

You will know you have entered the Creative Cave when your mind shifts into overdrive and your fingers start to move over the keys at a speed you never before understood. Ideas will flow... not all good ones... but they will flow. You will be sorting them out... but don't lose them. Just write!

Any idea that is spawned within the Creative Cave is worth considering. It may not be clear at first how to use it... but write it down... devote some time to developing it. You will be grateful later that you did. You will come to a point in the manuscript where there is an obvious use for the little excerpt you created several Caves ago.

Once in the Creative Cave, you will not want to leave, for it is an emotional high. You will feel enlightened and your mind will race. All of your experience will become focused and you will use the parts of that experience you need to create your novel. Your creative juices will flow! But beware! There comes a point where fatigue will edge into the Creative Cave. You are still enjoying the Cave, but your mind has been running at full speed for awhile now and must rest. This is the "Doldrums Period". You are having fun but what you are producing is likely of inferior quality due to fatigue.

There will be interruptions. You will be in the middle of a complex brain exercise in character development and linking events chapter to chapter when you suddenly realize you have to stop to attend a family function. Okay. Stop. Don't let your obsession with the novel ruin your family life.

Yes, working on a novel can become an obsession. It needs to become an obsession! Be obsessed, yes... but do it in a controlled way that doesn't allow your fictional universe to take you over!

People differ in their ability to remain productively in the Creative Cave. For me, it is 4-6 hours at a time. After that I must rest. My wife is thankful as I emerge from the Creative Cave and become available to do all those things she has thought up for me to do while I was within the magical shrouds of the Creative Cave!

Just because you go to your Author's Place, sit down and attempt to enter the Creative Cave does not mean that you will get there. Sometimes, you won't. You may just not be in the mood. Something is distracting you. Be sure you are capable of recognizing this situation! When it occurs, put the Creative Cave aside for another day and go do something else. Trying to write fiction while you are not in the Creative Cave is like swimming without water; much effort and no progress!

The Highest Art Form

Writing a fictional novel is among the highest art forms. Think about the magnitude of it! You are creating a "universe" that hasn't existed until you touched it. It rises high above nonfictional writing in which accurate research, clarity and logic are dominant. Many of the principles of writing a novel apply to writing nonfiction as well, but the novel is by far the most noble... a true art form!

Painting, music and sculpture are all high forms of art and can rise to the highest plateaus of achievement. The novelist can rise the highest if he/she masters the Creative Principles and applies them at the highest level.

Writing a novel requires skills in expression and writing, a decent vocabulary and a high degree of vision... the ability to create a fictional universe, populate it with interesting characters and cause these characters to interact with situations the author creates in a way that is interesting, exciting and absorbing to a Reader. It is the most complex of all the arts in that it creates and deals with many more things... not a single piece of music, not a single painting, not a single sculpture... but a whole, new, fictional universe totally created and managed by the author!

Writing a novel is not reality... reality is often boring.
The reason people read novels is to escape reality!

****

Chapter Three
The Seminal Idea for a Story

The "Seminal Idea" is the "idea" that you think "would make a good novel". It can derive from many sources. Some of these sources are suggested as follows:

1. An exciting experience of the Author.
2. A unique character known to the Author.
3. A unique geographical location with exciting scenery known to the Author.
4. An overheard dialogue that stirred interest.
5. A spin-off of a "WOW!" novel (be careful here).
6. A Sequel.
7. A newspaper story about an exciting character or event.
8. Market research conducted by the author; what kind of book is currently in demand?

An Experience

Many people have experiences that to them were inspiring, exciting, frightening, beautiful, emotional, dramatic, tranquil, or combinations of these. Do you have a Seminal Idea for a novel based on such an experience?

Perhaps, the Seminal Idea is based on an experience in a war time situation while you were in the service. Or, perhaps it is one of those unique experiences that happen once or twice in a lifetime… that time in the airport when…that time at camp while riding horseback that… the time while sitting on your grandparent's front porch with them that the thunderstorm came and…

You need to pick a time when you can "day-dream" uninterrupted. What could be the Seminal Idea for a good novel? How would it translate into a novel? Who would the lead character be? Was the experience inspiring, exciting, emotional, etc.?

A Unique Character

How many times have you met someone that impressed you and said "there ought to be a book about that person!" Well, why not write the book... the novel? The character you met may have impressed you in a variety of ways, such as the person's intellect, the person's beauty, the person's related experiences, the person's bravery, the person's villainy, the repulsive nature of the person, and others, or combinations of these.

A Geographical Location

In your travels there is most assuredly a place that sticks in your mind. Why does it stick there? Is it because of its beauty? Or tranquility? Perhaps it is because it was a frightening place. Or, was it because of the things you witnessed there?

If a "location" is the basis for your Seminal Idea, how would you use this location as the basis for a novel? If the location was a furious ocean that you witnessed from the decks of a cruise ship, how could you use the fury of the sea?

An Overheard Dialogue

On numerous occasions you have participated in a dialogue among people you know, or perhaps overheard a dialogue between people in which you were not a participant. Something about the dialogue stuck in your mind. What was it? Was it something about a mysterious occurrence? Was it a reference to a tragic sequence of events? How can this overheard dialogue form the Seminal Idea for a novel?

A Spin-Off

Many good novels are the result of an Author reading a WOW novel and deciding to write one in the same genre in a similar, but different way. The key word is "different". You can't just change the names and places and follow the same pattern of the WOW book. That's called plagiarism, and it's not for you!

A Sequel

If you have written a book, even if it is not yet published, you can write a sequel to it (a story that uses the same characters and "moves on"), or a prequel (a story that precedes the one you wrote). They are "your "characters"... you already know them. What would happen next in their lives that would make an interesting story?

A Newspaper Story

The newspapers and magazines are filled with reports of real life events and characters that could be the basis for a novel. Reality contains many stories... but they cannot be "told" as reality to make a good novel. They must be fictionalized and told with the rapid pace and emotional punctuation of a novel! Have you come across a good one lately? Is there a Seminal Idea there for a novel?

Market Research

The novel you want to write may not be the novel the public wants to read. So, it is always wise to conduct a little market research. However, don't let this hold you up in writing the novel you want to write. As I have said, there are many, many "excuses" that can be used for not STARTING. You need to START! However, a look at "what's selling" can give you a good Seminal Idea for a novel. What's on the best seller list? Read a best seller or two and see what Seminal Ideas they produce for you. Are books about sports selling well? What about war books? Spy books? Historical romances? Catalyze your thought about a seminal idea for a novel using market research.

The Story and the Plot

The Seminal Idea leads to the beginnings of a "story". You will develop a "plot" that tells the story in a WOW way.

The story is about some primary character and how he/she seeks a goal and is transformed by the experience.
The plot is how you tell the story.

You may have a good, solid Seminal Idea for a story but not yet know what the plot is. That's okay. It will come to you as we proceed.

The Seminal Idea Experience

How does one go about getting a Seminal Idea? Most folks who want to write a novel already have one, but not always. And, the idea they have may not "work". You get a Seminal Idea by knowing that you want one and keeping your eyes and ears open. If you know you want one, it will come.

Example of a Seminal Idea Experience;
You visited a Native American Reservation in Virginia and you met an interesting young man who lived there. He told you about Native Americans who used to live near the Chesapeake Bay and the Atlantic Ocean long ago, before the European explorers arrived. The young man impressed you. The scenario of Native Americans along the sea shore (as opposed to the usual Western Plains Native Americans) intrigued you.

Translating the Experience Into The Seminal Idea:
A young Chesapeake Native American has great adventures along the sea shore and in the ocean, set in a scenario before the European explorers arrive. Upon further thought, it may involve the arrival of the Europeans. This young Native American has a great ambition and a great love, a Native American maiden to whom he must prove himself.

Taking it Further:

The young Chesapeake Native American wonders what is over the unknown horizon as he stares eastward into the ocean. Perhaps the plot may involve him trying to find out what is over the unknown horizon. Perhaps that is his great ambition. He may meet the English Explorers there!

This is not a story! But it is the beginning of one. We don't have to have a fully thought out "story" to START! In fact, we may not know the whole story until we are near completion of the manuscript.

Take your seminal idea and think about how to translate it into the beginning of a story. What is the plot (how to tell the story)? Stick with me, and you'll see how the plot develops the story... and vice versa.

Author's License

A little bit about "Author's License" is appropriate at this point.

Author's License is the artistic right of an Author of fiction to write in a way that "represents" reality in a story, but does not submit to the humdrum events that make up day to day reality.

This means that an Author may take certain liberties with reality to benefit the "flow" of the novel. You may have in mind a certain reality that is the basis for your seminal idea, but to describe it all in detail would destroy the "flow" of the novel. You don't have to be accurate in "quoting" characters that resemble the real people of the reality upon which the story is based. A responsible Author will, instead, capture the "essence" of the situation and use action and dialogue that represents the reality... not duplicates it.

We have in our pocket a seminal idea. Where do we go now?

The Unknown Horizon

As we write the Rough-Through, I am going to provide examples from a novel I am working on, "The Unknown Horizon" which is based on the seminal experience described in the previous paragraph.

The complete "Rough-Through" is not contained in this book.

The novel is about a young Native American of the Chesapeake Tribe in the early Seventeenth Century. The Chesapeake Tribe lived in the area now known as Cape Henry in Virginia Beach, Virginia, where the Chesapeake Bay joins the Atlantic Ocean. They lived in a village they called Chesepiooc, "the place of great shellfish-water people".

The Chesapeake Villages were circular in shape, surrounded by high poles in a sort of palisade. Inside were the Lodge of the Braves Council, the Lodge of the Chief (Sachem), the Temple of the Priest (Periku) and other single room lodges each with 20 or more people. The lodges were long, built with bent saplings covered with mats made of reeds. Fires smoldered inside the lodges, even in the summer when the smoke helped to drive out the mosquitoes. Around the edge of the lodge were bunks made of mats, lashed to stakes raised from the ground and covered with deer and other hides. There were stumps for sitting and working.

The lodges of the Sachem and the Periku were also covered with bark. Around the camp were several cooking fires, shared by the lodges. Cooking racks, made from strips of wood lashed to poles stood over some of the fires. These were used to roast fish and other meat. Nearby were "sitting shelters", lean-tos with open sides containing stumps for sitting. In the Center of the Village, in front of the Lodge of the Braves Council, was the Council Campfire where the Council of Braves met.

The village of Chesepiooc was near the current First Landing State Park about a mile from Cape Henry, Virginia, at the mouth of the Broad Waters (Chesapeake Bay) where it meets the Water-That-Never-Ends (Atlantic Ocean). There were smaller villages of the Chesapeake nearby on the shores of the Lynnhaven River (River-Where-Swift-Waters-Flow) and on small islands that dotted a shallow inland bay, Bay-of-the-Great-White-Bird (Lynnhaven Bay).

The Chesapeake were part of the Algonquian speaking Powhatan Federation headed by Wahunsonacock, who the English later called Powhatan. Wahunsonacock came from the village of Powhatan near the source of the James River. He was a member of the Pamunkey Tribe, the largest of the Powhatan Federation. At the time of the story in "The Unknown Horizon", Powhatan lived in Werocomoco on the left bank of the York River near the current Yorktown, about forty miles from Chesepiooc. Under him were several hundred tribes whose location ranged from the Tidewater area of what is now Virginia to the Potomac River region.

The Chesapeake tribe numbered some 300 people. In addition to the Sachem, there was a Werowance (War Leader), and a Council of Braves. The Chesapeake had about eighty Braves. A boy was eligible to become a Brave soon after puberty (age 15-16). To become a Brave, he was subjected to passing rigid tests of the Council.

The Chesapeake worshipped Okee (called Ahone in some references), a single God who saw over Quiacosough (The Goodness) and Tagkanysough (The Evil, referred to as Oke in some references) and dealt justly with the people. They lived in a rich land where sea food, especially shellfish, was plentiful, including oysters, clams, crabs and turtles. The fish included the striped bass, shad, herring and sturgeon. The Chesapeake built large canoes and fished in the rivers, the bay and the ocean, using hooks from bone and crabs as bait. They used nets woven from reeds, grasses, animal hides and sinew. The great enemy of the shellfish-water people in the bay and ocean were the sharks that imperiled the fishermen in their canoes made of hollowed out logs.

The Chesapeake grew beans and maize (corn), squash, sunflowers, potato, and various green plants. They foraged for roots, berries and plants in the thick forests around Chesepiooc. The forests had abundant game, including deer, black bear, turkey, rabbit and water fowl.

The Chesapeake disappeared during the Seventeenth Century and research reveals that little is known about them. What happened to them? No one really knows. The novel we are going to write suggests a fictional answer.

The main character is a young Chesapeake called Chataqua who is near the age where he must become a Brave. He is known as a "bright" but meddlesome young man who is always in search of new ideas. The Villain is an older Brave (about four years older), Malapok, who resents Chataqua's ramblings about what he will discover and what he will make happen. They are both in love with Alanoas, a beautiful young girl of the tribe who has not yet "come of age". Chesapeake girls "came of age" a few years after puberty (age 14-15).

Wahunsonacock was ruler of the Powhatan Federation. Opechanocock, the brother of Wahunsonacock, was the Sachem of the Pamunkey Tribe located along the shores of the York River and its tributary, the Pamunkey River. I use a fictitious tribe, the Wepeneooc, as the enemies of the Chesapeake, with Opectanotak as its Sachem.

I made up "Chataqua" as the hero's name. We want our hero to have a name that helps the Reader to identify with him as the hero... we don't want to name him "Uglabanotok".

Note:
The examples from *The Unknown Horizon* are proprietary.
There are excerpts from some of my other novels and manuscripts herein, which are also proprietary.

****

Chapter Four
Story Development

The Premise

The premise is a short statement that captures the nature of the hero/heroine and his/her goal.

The Premise is your story stated in one sentence. No more!

Take your seminal idea and try to state what the story is all about in a few sentences. Then reduce it to one sentence (not too long, and not a string of awkward statements), being sure to capture the "essence" of the story.

Novel Example, The premise for "Gone With The Wind";

What if a beautiful southern girl's life is destroyed by events in the War Between the States and she vows to "never be hungry again"?

Screenplay Example, The premise for "The Graduate";

What if a new college graduate, confused about his future, is seduced by the wife of his father's friend and falls in love with her daughter?

The initial premise for "The Unknown Horizon" could be;

What if a young Chesapeake Indian seeks to become a hero of the tribe by canoeing beyond the unknown horizon to the east to discover the Land-Where-The-Sun-Is-Born?

Premise is the inspiration that inspires you as you write. It captures the "conflict" in the story. You have to believe that your premise will be the "hook" that catches thousands of readers!

The Controlling Idea (Theme)

The controlling idea, or theme, is the thread that runs through the story. It helps you, the Author, to know your story and keep your eyes on the "story ball". When we get to the ending, you and the reader should fully know and understand the theme.

The controlling idea of our story may be:
Courage and a willingness to take risks leads to hardships and challenges larger then life, but if one perseveres and survives, one becomes a leader.

In defining your controlling idea, you are setting up choices for the hero that take place throughout the story. Think of them as "pro" and "con". In some circumstance, will our hero have courage and takes risks (the "pro" choice with respect to the controlling idea), or will he choose a course of action more in keeping with a cautious and "normal" life (the "con" choice with respect to the controlling idea)?

You may not fully understand what your premise or controlling idea are as you write your "Rough-Through". One of the purposes of beginning with a "free form art" Rough-Through is to get your thoughts about your story down on paper where you can study, understand and shape them. As you do, your premise and controlling idea will form. When you start your Creative Reviews, they should be mostly formed... and pasted where you can see them!

The Synopsis

The synopsis is an expansion of the premise. While the premise is only one sentence, the synopsis is one to two pages. A "capsule synopsis" is a third of a page. When you are finished with your novel, you will write a synopsis to use as a marketing tool with agents and publishers.

The Essence of the Story

Which comes first... the idea for a story, or the idea for a character around which you want to build a story? It can be either... but you have to have an idea about a few characters in order to START. Let's rough out a set of initial characters to get the Rough-Through started. We don't fully understand these characters yet. We will develop them as we write.

Primary Characters:
  1. *Hero (Main Character): Chataqua is a boy of the Chesapeake Tribe in the year 1607. He is on the edge of manhood and will soon try to become a Brave.*
  2. *Villain: Malapok, a stronger, older Brave, was at first a friend and mentor of Chataqua, but has come to resent him. He loves Alanoas, as does Chataqua.*
  3. *Romantic Interest: Alanoas is a maiden of the Chesapeake. She is submissive like all good Chesapeake women, but can be strong and resolute when she needs to be. She resists Malapok and yearns for Chataqua.*

Secondary Characters:
  1. *Mentor: Benatagua is Chataqua's father and initial mentor.*
  2. *Best Friend: Manatapac is Chataqua's best friend. He is slightly older than Chataqua.*
  3. *Chief: Chesapian is the Sachem (Chief) of the Chesapeake Nation.*

The Tools for Writing a Novel

As mentioned before, the tools you will use in writing your novel are:
  1. Storytelling.
  2. Description.
  3. Action.
  4. Dialogue.

"Storytelling" is what the Author does to tell the story.

Example, Storytelling;
Once upon a time, there was a Prince and a Princess...

Description is when the Author uses prose to describe something or someone.

Example, Description;
The Prince was a handsome fellow...

Action is when the Author uses prose to describe what something or someone is "doing".

Example, Action;
The Prince jumped onto his great white stallion...

Dialogue is when the Author puts words or sounds into the mouth of something or someone... it is what is "said".

Example, Dialogue;
"Come with me, my love," said the Prince.

Dialogue sometimes has a "dialogue tag" that contains description or action.

Example, Dialogue Tag;
"Come with me, my love," said the Prince warmly as he opened the door.

Don't confuse the Storyteller with the Author. The Storyteller is a tool the Author uses... an omniscient being in the novel used to "progress the story". Storytelling is the glue that holds the others together. It is a form of description... but not exactly.

The Story Events

Most good novels have some or all of the events shown in Figure 4-1 in the approximate order shown.

Figure 4-1

The Story Events

Part I	Part III
The Status Quo	The Reckoning
The Mentor	The Transformation
The Bonding	The Transformed
The Goal	World
The Catalyst	The Goal Won
The Decision	

Part II
The Climax
The Ordeal
The Resulting Situation
The Testing
The New World

Your story does not have to follow the sequence of the "events" shown. The sequence is the Author's choice. For example, in my novel "The Mud Fox", the hero, Allman Buddinger (alias The Mud Fox) is a SEAL in Vietnam who is AWOL (away without leave) and fighting his own war against the Viet Cong. His goal is unique... to find an "honorable way to die". He has a death wish that derives from feeling responsible for the death of his Lieutenant and a feeling that there is nothing "back in The World" for him. His goal is dramatically altered when he meets Brenda McAllister, a beautiful woman with a background as tragic as his own. And so, he enters a "whole new world" in which he wants "life and love" but must endure the dangers in which he has immersed himself and fulfill the commitments he made before he met Brenda. Thus the hero's "goal" to seek "life and love" is an altered goal that emerges midway in the story.

What follows is a summary of "Story Events" in our story "The Unknown Horizon". When I STARTED I only had a good understanding of the first two events in my head.

When you START, you need only to understand the first several "Story Events".

1. The Status Quo Event(s)

The hero/heroine exists in some status quo world. He/She is in a comfortable situation but is, for some reason, discontent with his/her life.

Chataqua and his Father, Benatagua, are happy in the status quo world we will describe in the first scene in which they are canoeing together near Point-Where-Great-Waters-Meet. But, Chataqua is growing up and must soon assume great responsibilities. Benatagua has a vision of what lies ahead for Chataqua. He knows that the Sachem, Chesapian, has Chataqua in mind as the future Sachem. Chataqua is uneasy because he knows that he soon faces decisions that will influence his entire life.

2. The Mentor Event(s)

The hero/heroine seeks out or encounters a person who "mentors" him/her. This mentor can take many forms. For example, it can be the wise older person, or a best friend. In this event, the Mentor aids the hero/heroine in making a decision to pursue his/her goal and accept the associated risk.

Chataqua has a Mentor in his Father in the first scene. Benatagua tells him his vision of the young man's future. He tells him stories about his expedition to the Land-Where-The-Cold-Wind-Blows and his encounter with the great sea beast Gitsche Kakapa.
Chataqua had a Mentor in the older Brave Malapok. But as they grew up, they drew apart and Malapok came to hate Chataqua because of their rivalry for the affections of Alanoas.

Chataqua also has a mentor in his best friend Manatapac. Chataqua has "long talks" with Manatapac, who encourages the young man's ideas even though they seem strange and radical to him.

3. The Bonding Event(s)

The hero/heroine has close friends with whom he/she bonds. These friends will play a part in his story. In this event, we show evidence of previous bonding or show how the bonding takes place.

Chataqua's close friends, as we shall see, are Manatapac, Chalapow and Rowhatan. When we come to the chapters on "creating scenes", we will see how these characters "bond" with Chataqua and become his allies. There is also a "bond" with Malapok, one that changes from friendship to association to enemy. We shall also see how and why this relationship transforms.

4. The Goal Event(s)

The hero/heroine meets a person or encounters a situation that provides him/her with a new goal, one that will resolve his/her discontent with the Status Quo.

In our novel, the new goal is suggested to Chataqua by his father Benatagua in the opening scene. He reveals that the Sachem (Chief) has confided in him that be believes Chataqua can be the next Chief. Chataqua doubts his ability to fulfill that promise. He must first be accepted as a Brave. He wants to exceed his Father's deed of canoeing to the Land-Where-The-Cold-Wind-Blows (Cape Charles) by canoeing east to the Land-Where-The-Sun-Is-Born (open ocean).

Chataqua faces the world that is confronting him. He sets a goal to become a Brave and to exceed that by matching his Father's deed of canoeing into the unknown to find the Land-Where-The-Cold-Wind-Blows. He decides to build a new canoe and take it to the east and find the Land-Where-The-Sun-Is-Born.

Chataqua is faced by his inner conflict, a dilemma in that he feels he can not ask for Alanoas as wife until he has completed these goals, proving his courage and also showing that he is a man of great deeds like his Father. He also has inner conflict in that he does not believe that he has the wisdom to become Sachem as his father has predicted will occur. Chataqua's goals will transform as events take place, as will he.

5. The Catalyst Event(s)

The hero/heroine is reluctant to pursue the goal because he/she is "comfortable" with the status quo. To achieve the new goal involves a risk and/or danger that is formidable (little risks don't make good stories). Some big event catalyzes and influences the hero/heroine's decision.

Chataqua and his friends discover strange pieces of wood and cloth on the beach. Chataqua believes the wood and cloth are from a "great canoe" that has come from the Land-Where-The-Sun-Is-Born and been wrecked in a storm. His belief that there is a land beyond the unknown horizon to the east is reinforced. His determination to go there and become a great discoverer like his father gains momentum.
Chataqua has several confrontations with Malapok. He doubts his ability to overcome him during the Tests of the Brave. This makes him even more doubtful about his ability to become Sachem. He is reluctant to face Malapok. During the Tests of the Brave, he uses his wits to overcome Malapok. He becomes a Brave. He now has the confidence to resolve his doubts and consider his goals.

6. The Decision Event(s)

The hero/heroine is placed in a situation that forces a decision with respect to his/her goals. Usually a time factor is introduced by an event that makes the choice a pressing matter. He/she crosses a threshold into a new set of conditions based on the decision to achieve his/her goal and resolve his/her discontent.

Chataqua participates in a battle with the rival Wepeneooc Tribe and distinguishes himself. His confidence is bolstered. However, his Father is killed in the battle and he is cast into despair. He decides to pursue his dream to sail to the unknown horizon to honor his father and resolve his own doubts. He proceeds to design and build a new type of canoe to go to the Land-Where-The-Sun-Is-Born. He tells Alanoas that he will ask for her as wife as soon as he comes back and she comes of age. Chataqua has made the difficult decision to pursue his goals, where before he had "held back".

7. The New World Event(s)

As a result of the decision, the hero/heroine experiences an event(s) that takes him/her to "a whole new world" to which he/she is not accustomed. He/she experiences doubt as to whether the goal can be achieved.

Chataqua sets forth in his new canoe to seek the Land-Where-The-Sun-Is-Born. It takes him immediately into an entirely new situation fraught with danger. He pursues his goal of performing a deed to equal that of his Father.

8. The Testing Event(s)

The hero/heroine experiences one or more big events in the "new world" that severely tests him/her. The hero does/ does not pass these tests and his/her situation is changed again (there may be more than one "Test").

Test 1: Chataqua is tested by a storm at sea that wrecks his canoe.

Test 2: He is tested by an encounter with a marauding pack of kakapa (sharks). He is saved by his friend Calypo-Ma (the dolphin he once saved and befriended).

Test 3: After two days in the ocean without seeing land, and acknowledging his wrecked canoe, he is despondent and feels he must return to the tribe in failure.

Test 4: He is tested by an encounter with the great sea beast Gitsche Kakapa (the great white shark).

Test 5: He is rescued from Gitsche Kakapa by pale white men in a strange canoe with wings. He fears that these strangers will enslave him or eat him.

9. The Resulting Situation Event(s)

As a result of the hero/heroine succeeding/not succeeding in the Test Event(s), a "Resulting Situation" comes about. The new world becomes even stranger and the hero/heroine must deal with it.

Created Situation 1: Chataqua is taken aboard the canoe with wings (The English Explorer's ship "Discovery"). He encounters strange and fierce looking men. One of them (Nathan Smythe) treats him well and they become friends. To Chataqua's surprise, the people from the Land-Where-The-Sun-Is-Born take him back to the Broad Waters and release him to his people.

Created Situation 2: The Ingelesez (English) come ashore to replenish their supplies. They are greeted by the Chesapeake with caution. Chataqua is hailed as a hero of the tribe for discovering the people from the Land-Where-The-Sun-Is-Born.

Created Situation 3: The Periku, Maltakak, uses the presence of the Ingelesez to foster discontent with the Sachem, Chesapian.

Created Situation 4: Chataqua and Malapok confront each other regarding Alanoas.

This is as far as I take the story in my examples. I don't want to give it away. I want you to read it! So, the remaining events depend on which of several endings is chosen. This is discussed at the end of the book.

10. The Ordeal Event(s)

The hero/heroine must endure an ordeal that tests him/her in a most dramatic and difficult way. This is the "low point" for the hero/heroine. All seems lost.

11. The Climax Event(s)

The hero/heroine rises from the despair of the Ordeal Event and battles his opponents(s) in a dramatic and cataclysmic event. The battle is one in which the hero/heroine's goals at are at stake. It must be won or the hero/heroine will fail and/or be killed.

12. The Goal Won Event(s)

The hero/heroine, through his/her cunning and abilities achieves his/her goal in the face of overwhelming odds. This event usually involves the difficult and dramatic death or demise of the villain/villainess. The hero's/heroine's romantic interest is won/lost and they prevail/despair.

13. The Transformed World Event(s)

As a result of the achievement of the goal, there is an event in which it becomes clear that a "new world" is created for the hero/heroine. The hero/heroine is factually or spiritually "reborn".

14. The Transformation Event(s)

As a result of the experiences in achieving the goal, the hero/heroine is transformed, changed forever (usually in a positive way). There is an event that makes this transformation clear. Where there is a romance, this transformation may include the "romantic climax" that transforms the parties involved.

15. The Reckoning Event(s)

The hero/heroine participates in an event where "all the loose ends" are wrapped up (or in some cases, purposefully left unresolved).

The Story Events should be used as a way to think about your story, not as a formula or outline. START writing and they will come. They will come in an order that builds your story.

The Back Story

There is always a "back-story". The back story is that which occurred before the present story that is pertinent to the present story.

Initial back-story events for "The Unknown Horizon" are:

1. Chataqua's Father, Benatagua canoed to the Land-Were-The-Cold-Wind-Blows, discovered new lands and was recognized by the Tribe as hero.
2. The Sachem, Chesapian, had a son but he died in his early youth of a chest clogging disease.
3. The Periku, Maltakak, has long been a rival of Chesapian and when they were young challenged him to become Sachem.

There are different ways of getting the back-story out. It is best accomplished in dialogue as someone tells of these events. A common way of doing this is to have the Mentor tell the stories to the hero. Another method is a "flashback" that goes back in time to create a scene about the back-story events. This is a useful method if not used too frequently.

You don't need to tell the entire "back story" or go into great detail. You need to expose events of the back story that pertain to your story.

Action Under Cover

Another important part of the story is what I call "action under cover"... action the character in the story cannot see, but action that nevertheless is a part of the story. The character in the story sees only "evidence" of the "action under cover".

For example, if the story is about fishing, there are fish under the water that the character cannot see. The Author must know what the fish "are doing" to adequately describe "what the character sees" to successfully describe fishing.

Another example: An enemy is coming through the forest to attack a village. We are describing the event from the perspective of the Native Americans Braves defending the village. We want to describe what they see, what they hear. To do this, we must as a Storyteller, know what the enemy is doing... his strategy over time. That is the "action under cover". But we want to only reveal as much of it as the defending Braves would "see" or "hear".

Scope of the Story

The scope of the story refers to how you, as an Author, limit the "size" of the story. You may have a story in a "grand setting", a wide scope, scenic background of places and events. Or, the story may be set with a modest small town "log cabin" background. In either case, the story you tell is about a limited number of primary and secondary characters against some background. The number of characters you have determines largely the "scope" of your story. It must be a number that you (and the Reader) can "manage" within the fictional universe you create.

The fictional world you are going to create is "small" when compared to the reality you know. It has to be. If it isn't, you can't write it and your Reader can't read it! You must learn how to limit the way the story is told using only the characters that are essential and only the events that are directly related to your "story line". Your story line is not every detail of what might transpire in reality. You limit your fictional world by using scenes and events that "make a point" in the story. "It's a small world after all", or so says the song. Your story is "small" compared to the actual universe. But, it should be "large" with regard to the emotion and impact it has on the reader (the WOW Factor).

Put a lot of thought into the scope of your story. Start small and expand. If you start large, you will run into difficulty quickly.

****

Chapter Five
Choice of Characters

Characters have to be chosen in a way that sets them firmly in the Reader's mind. The Reader must be able to understand each character, what motivates the character and why. They should be "fascinating" characters that will capture the Reader's attention.

The characters are the most interesting part of a novel.

Primary Characters

Success in a novel depends very heavily on whether or not you can cause the Readers to "identify" with the main character(s). Typically the primary characters are:
1. The hero/heroine (main character).
    The "main character" about whom the story revolves.
2. The hero's/ heroine's romantic interest.
    The character that supports a romantic plot or sub-plot.
3. The villain/villainess.
    This character is sometimes called "the opponent". He/she is the character who opposes the hero/heroine in achieving his/her goal.

All of these characters have "goals", though the "goal" the story is about is that of the main character. Think about it this way;

Each character is "living his/her own story" within the story we are telling.
The story we are telling is about the hero/heroine!

The goals and motivations of all the characters influence our story. We will concentrate on the hero's/heroine's goal/story and we will tell the stories of the other characters in so far as they "play" in our story.

Secondary Characters

Examples of secondary characters the Author may choose to use are:

1. The hero's rival.
   Usually the villain, but could also be a romantic rival, a rival in business, etc.
2. The hero's/heroine's "buddy".
   The buddy may be an equal, a junior or a superior, but for some reason there is a close bond between the two. He/she is not constantly by the side of the hero/heroine as is the "sidekick", but is essential to the hero/heroine for some reason.
3. The hero's/heroine's "sidekick".
   The sidekick may be a "buddy", but is usually inferior to the hero/heroine and is someone who is constantly at his/her side. The hero/heroine may "need' the sidekick for some reason. The sidekick may be the "humorous" character.
4. The hero's/heroine's Mentor.
   The Mentor is usually a wise, older person who plays a role in offering advice and motivation that influences the hero's/heroine's decision to take some action. It can be a younger person, a buddy, even an animal or "wizard" character in a fantasy.
5. The hero's/heroine's allies.
   The ally is a strong character, not necessarily a friend, who in some way helps the hero.
6. The villain's/villainess' allies.
   The villain/villainess also has allies.
7. Friends of the hero/heroine.
   The hero has friends that help him. These are people who are close to the hero/heroine.
8. Friends of the villain/villainess.
   The villain/villainess also has friends.
9. The humorous character.
   This is a special character not always used. It can be a friend, buddy or sidekick. Or someone else. This character is designed to inject humor into dramatic situations.

Supporting Characters

Supporting characters are those you need to "make a scene work". They may appear in more than one scene, but they are never "in the forefront". Examples are:

1. Waitresses in a restaurant (restaurant scene).
2. Conductors on a train (train scene).
3. Soldiers in a fight (battle scene).

The degree to which you describe the supporting characters and have them do anything other than their "function" (serving dinner, taking tickets, fighting battles, etc.) depends on the story. If a supporting character plays an important role in a scene, or appears in many scenes, you should describe him/her more.

Character Traits and Habits

All of our characters should have various traits that support their role in the story. They may be heroic, straightforward, truthful, kind, trustworthy and beautiful. Or they may be cowardly, tricky, deceitful, unkind, devious and ugly. They may confront their problem with boldness or be more cautious. They may have "habits" that enhance their character or help to identify them.

Examples of "habits" are; smoking cigars, running fingers through their hair when nervous, lifting an eyebrow when in doubt, giggling, wrinkling their nose, etc. Use "body language" effectively.

Choose these traits carefully. Use them and the character's actions to make the character have a "distinctive voice" that immediately conjures an image and the sound of a voice in the mind of the Reader.

The Number of Characters

The primary characters are the ones most used to "tell the story". They are the ones you will spend the most time (and words) developing. They are the ones you want the Reader to best understand and identify with. Resist the temptation to have more than one hero/heroine (main character). You need to focus on one. He or she is the one you most want the Reader to identify with... the one the story is "about". He or she must be a WOW character, with characteristics that make him/her stand out from the crowd. Characters in a novel are not like reality characters... they have "larger than life characteristics".

The number of primary characters is important. A good novel will have three primary characters; the main character (hero/heroine), one romantic interest, and one villain/villainess. Up to six primary characters are workable. More than that leads to trouble.

If you are trying to write "reality", the number of characters immediately gets you into trouble. There are too many characters in reality. To write a good novel, you must be able to pick out the primary and secondary characters of your story (not a narrative) and manage their numbers.

Invent Your Characters

When you START, you can go merrily on your way using the characters that are a part of your seminal idea. As you proceed, your story will demand that you "invent" new characters. Go ahead... invent them. Don't worry about it for awhile. At some point, you will have enough characters that you need to jot them down so that you don't lose track of them. Jot down the basic characteristics you assign to each character. Their roles will evolve as you write.

The Character "Model"

Is it a good idea to "model" some of your characters after someone you know well? How about modeling the character after some famous person who has "amplified characteristics"? Well, yes and no.

Having someone "in mind" as you describe your character is very helpful. What is it about that guy that sets him apart? I know... it's the purely athletic body that seems to just flow through any movement. Now I have something I can describe! What is it about that gal that really turns the guys on? The body… it's great, but that isn't "it". It's the smile… that half giggle, half flirtatious, partly cynical smile that suggests nothing and everything at the same time! I can describe that! But can a smile make such a difference? Well, if it weren't for the subtle smile and the twinkling of the eye the Mona Lisa would be just another painting!

Now if the person you are thinking about as a "character model" is an actor or actress who is "in the public domain", it works well to use him/her. Is my character a John Wayne type? Or is he an Andy Griffith type? A Brad Pitt? Go ahead and use such a character model, but be careful not to make the model so transparent that it is obvious. Think of the model's "type", not the model him/her self. You want your character to be "new"! It's better at times to use a "blend" of character models.

If the person you are thinking about as a character model is someone you know, someone not in the public domain, be more careful. You don't want this person, perhaps a friend, to later accuse you of creating a character "just like him/her".

Your intent is always to create fictional characters. Whatever you do, remember that the characters you create are fictional and that they must meet the test of the statement at the beginning of your novel:

This novel is a work of fiction. All characters and events in this novel are fictional, and any resemblance to real people or events is coincidental.

Multi-dimensional Characters

Your main characters have to be multi-dimensional. "Flat" characters will never take a novel to the point of being publishable. What do I mean by multi-dimensional? They must be interesting for some very specific reasons: they were grossly disfigured in a war; they are Type A business people without conscience; they are bold adventurers with a passion for the mountains; they are meek, secretive people whose hidden personal lives are bizarre! You've got to come up with something that gives your characters dimensions that are extremely interesting and sometimes bizarre!

Avoiding "flat" characters is a stretch for the new Author, who considers himself/herself a "normal" person (does that mean "flat"... well, maybe). Most of the people he/she has contact with are "normal". But are they really? Dig a little bit and you'll find that all of us are multi-dimensional, some more so than others. Find those dimensions and amplify them for your characters! Yes... amplify them. Your fictional characters have to stand out from normal people! They must be super-interesting! They are not reality... though they must represent it. Reality seems sometimes "flat"... but never fiction.

Expressing Emotion Through Characters

A WOW novel by definition contains a lot of emotion. The component of our novel that creates the most emotion are our characters. We should seize every opportunity to have our characters feel and express strong emotion.

As the characters confront their problems, battle their demons and pursue their romantic interests, it is the EMOTION that captures the Reader.

A character's emotions can be expressed through description, action and dialogue, and you should use all of these methods in a balanced way. Avoid "flat dialogue" by putting emotion into it. Some characters are openly emotional. Others hide their emotions. But, they are all emotional!

Naming Your Characters

How do you name your characters? The answer is... anyway you want to. Throw darts at the pages of a telephone book... or whatever. You own this universe... this fictional world you are creating, so don't get hung up on naming characters... or for that matter, naming "things".

You should ensure that the name fits the environment you are creating. You don't want to name your Native American hero McGrady! As for "things".... if you need a "thing" and it doesn't have a good name, think up a name that fits. If the novel is about Native Americans then "Cape Henry" at the mouth of the Chesapeake Bay might be "Point-Where-Great-Waters-Meet".

Character names can also imply the nature of the character, particularly nick names. If a character is nick-named "Young Squirrel", he is certainly different from one whose nick name is "Bad Bear". Proper names can also suggest character. "Chataqua" has the ring of the forest about it. "Malapok" uses the root "mal" which in many languages means "bad" or "evil". Words and names and the "sound" of them have great suggestive power! Learn to use that power!

The Character's Problem

The next most interesting part of the novel is what the characters do to solve the problem you pose for them. Let's try an opening scene where Chataqua's problem is set forth.

Example, Posing the Problem;
"I have waited until this time, when you are to become a Brave, to tell you something very important," said Benatagua slowly in a deep voice.
"What is it, Father?" asked Chataqua.
"The Sachem, Chesapian, is as you know a friend and a wise man."
Chataqua nods. "Yes, I have seen that."
"When you were a small child, Chesapian also had a son," said Benatagua. "His son died of an evil clogging of the chest when he became a small boy."
"I am sorry for Chesapian," said Chataqua.
"As you grew, Chesapian watched you closely. He told me that he expects you to one day become Sachem."

Now a goal for Chataqua is exposed. It becomes his "problem". He expresses doubt.

Chataqua stops paddling and looks back at his Father. "How could I become Sachem?" he asked in an astounded voice.

The Sachem was to Chataqua something that always existed, a pillar of strength upon which all could rely. The thought of becoming that pillar of strength overwhelmed him.

Motivation

Every character in a story has some motivation, some "goal" that causes him/her to be the way he/she is, to do and say the things that he/she does and says.

Example, Developing Motivation;
Alanoas' mind cowered as she remembered the time the Brave Malapok came upon her at this place in the Grand-Salt-Water-Swamp. He embraced her and tried to persuade her to come with him along the path to the Place-of-Many-Islands. He held her hand tightly, but she broke away and ran down the path to Chesepiooc.

Here we see one of the motivations of the Brave Malapok through the eyes of Alanoas. He obviously has a crush on Alanoas... or maybe he just chases all the Native American Maidens that way! Malapok's motivation is to be Alanoas' lover... for whatever reason. Alanoas sees Malapok as a bad guy here. And since, Alanoas is clearly the heroine, the Reader will tend to identify with her and see Malapok in the same way.

Malapok is motivated to oppose Chataqua in his quest to become a Brave.

Example, Malapok's Motivation;
"She has been on the beach with that Young Squirrel, Chataqua," said Malapok. "I must talk to her soon."

Here we see that Malapok doesn't think much of Chataqua, even though they were friends in their childhood. He realizes that Chataqua stands between him and Alanoas. Be careful to always paint a complete logic train between the character's motivation and what the character says and does.

Consistency of Characters

Many times an Author will establish a character's "motivation" early in the story and then, later, have the character do or say something that is totally "out of character" without explanation. The Author simply forgot the "character of the character". Be consistent!

Always Be Sure That the Character Is "In Character"

When you place a character in a situation (in a scene), he/she must speak, act and interact with others completely according to the way the character has been portrayed. Or, if not, there must have been some "happening" that caused the character to transition to a new set of motivations and/or characteristics. Indeed, the transition of a character's "character" may be the essence of the story.

Humanizing Characters

You have to make your characters "human". You do that by assigning them characteristics that the Reader may have... creating instant identification with the character. The character may hate mosquitoes. "Darn things... me too!" thinks the Reader. The character has to have inner worries and fears... just like the Reader. He fears heights. "Yeah," thinks the Reader, "this guy is like me!"

The characters also have to be human enough to make mistakes, feel lust, greed and be tempted by all the things that tempt us. Your character may (or may not) really be a "good guy" and overcome some of the more base feelings... but he/she must feel them, as we all do.

I recently had a call from one of my Readers about my novel "The Perfect Season, A Story of the High School Gridiron". He said:

Bob, I really liked your book, The Perfect Season! You captured the character of the tough-as-nails coach exactly, but the character I really liked was the "new guy" football player,

Harry Quester. You did a super job with him. I felt like I was in Harry's skin all the way through the book."

That's the way you want your Readers to feel! That's a WOW book! You want the Reader to experience the story as if he/she were the main character, feeling his/her emotions, experiencing the ups and downs, the physical exhaustion, the emotional highs… feeling the hits from the other team!

The Author as a Character in Fiction

In a fictional novel, you the Author can not be a "character" in the novel. Even if it's a story based almost entirely on your own experiences, you can not be "the character".

If, as you are writing, you think of the character as "you", you are unnecessarily limiting yourself in writing the novel. You become "too close" to it.

Your character suddenly becomes limited by what "you" might do or say. He/she is limited by your morals, your values, your culture and so forth. Stay away from this! Write about somebody, some fictional somebody who is not you! Maintain yourself as the Author, a person set aside telling the story from a detached perspective. Even if you are telling the fictional story in the first person, that first person in most cases should not be "you"!

The Author as a Character in Non-Fiction

Only in a non-fictional book can you think of "yourself" as a character. It has to be a true story about you, and defined as such, limited by the bounds of reality. Then you need to be "you". You also need to be accurate and not embellish and expand the story as you would were it fiction.

The Choice: Fiction or Non-Fiction

If the novel you want to write is based on a personal story, you have a choice:

1. A non-fiction book that recounts your story (reality).
2. A fictional treatment in which your story is the "basis" for the novel, but expands beyond reality into fiction (usually using characters with names different from those of the actual people in order to preserve the fictional nature of the work).

In a non-fiction book, you are locked to reality, which is often boring. It is hard to "pace" a true story (there are notable exceptions). It tends to become a "narrative" rather than a story. Your development of characters and dialogue is limited by your recollection of "how it was". You become overly concerned about "not offending someone" and the story may be limited as a result.

In a fictional book, you have far greater flexibility in character development, dialogue, plot and how you pace the book to make it a WOW novel (even if it's "based" on a story in which you were involved). Your story is the Seminal Idea. It is not the entire story in your novel.

I recommend the second alternative (fiction). Non fiction books are normally written that way because the Author wants an "exposé" of something in his/her past. If that is what the Author wants, then write it as non-fiction. But be careful; it may become a "sermon" or a narrative, not a story.

There are many "true to life" stories that make compelling books. Some of them are written by a participant in the story. Most are written by an Author to whom the story is told (who has more flexibility than one of the participants).

Try to avoid the pitfalls of the "narrative" and give your book as many "novel-like" characteristics as you can. Writing a narrative is fairly simple. Writing a novel is an art.

Writing a Fictional Novel Based on Real Life Experiences

You will use the characteristics of everyone you have ever met to help you think about "who" each character should be. Each character will, whether you choose it or not, be a creature of your own experience.

In my fictional novel "The Perfect Season", based on the championship high school football team that I played on, I thought about how to approach development of the characters a long time. I decided that I had to have several characters that were purely fictional and not based on any "character model" of the actual team members or coaches.

When I referred to a character who was "the left guard"... or whatever position, I made him some combination of a lot of folks I have known, perhaps even some of the actual left guard. I wrote from the perspective of the "detached storyteller" in the third person and worked hard not to interject myself as "one of the characters" (though I was very close to the story). I also put in situations and characters I needed to build an interesting story... that were beyond "reality".

At our annual reunion, everyone wanted to know "is so-and-so in the book you?" Or, "is so-and-so in the book me?" I carefully answered each question "All the characters are fictional... yes, all of them!"

****

Chapter Six
Character Development

What is "character development"? In short, it is what the Author does over time in the novel to make each character interesting. It is critical talent for a WOW book Author.

The development of characters can not take place all at once. It has to occur as the story unfolds. It is important to get the basic characteristics of the primary characters firmly in the Reader's mind within the first several chapters.

Keep these five things in mind:

1. The Author can describe the character in storytelling. Some of this is okay... but not too much.

2. What the character says (dialogue) and how he/she says it are part of character development. This is a very effective way of developing a character and should be used as much as possible.

3. What the character thinks (a form of dialogue posing as description) is part of character development. The storyteller can use description to describe what the character is "thinking". For example; *Chataqua thought long and hard before he made the decision to fight Malapok*. You can also use "body language". For example; *Chataqua clenched his fist at the mention of Malapok*. And then, there's the direct approach in dialogue. For example; *"I don't think you can beat me, Malapok. I'll fight you!" said Chataqua*.

4. What the character does and how he/she does it are part of character development. This is a very effective way of developing a character and should be used as much as possible. For example; does the character *"walk quickly"* or does he/she *"amble along"*.

5. How the character interacts with other characters is a very important part of character development. It defines the relationship as well as part of each character's "character".

To give you a "feel" for it, of the five methods above, I recommend approximate usage as follows:

1. Storytelling   5%
2. Description: 20%
3. Speaking dialogue: 35%
4. Action: 30%
5. Interaction: 10%

Primary Factors in Character Development

The primary factors in character development are: description; background; relationships, how the character addresses his/her problem; interactions.

Description

The author must provide sufficient information about the character's physical appearance to allow the Reader to conjure up a picture in his/her mind. A complete physical description is not necessary... in fact, seldom do you want to do that. Use the imagination of the Reader to your advantage!

Remember that in describing a character, you are not just defining his/her appearance. By defining his/her appearance, you are also building in the mind of the Reader a feeling for just what kind of person the character is. Sometimes bad guys look like good guys... but often bad guys have a physical characteristic that gives the Reader the image of a bad guy.

Example, Using Description to Suggest Character;
Malapok was a tall, strong Brave with intense, darting eyes that constantly searched around him as if always looking for trouble. Some said he had scary eyes and avoided meeting his stare.

Intense, darting eyes don't necessarily define a bad guy... but they can be an indicator. Scary eyes take it a bit further. This description has planted the seeds of an image of Malapok in the Reader's mind. If other indicators of character point in the direction of "bad guy", the Reader's picture of Malapok will become clearer.

A trick of the Author is to make a character seem bad...
but in the end he/she turns out to be good. There is a
"transformation" of the villain/villainess. Or, in some case a
transformation of the allies of the villain/villainess to the
"side of good" (which can be an important element in the
plot).

You can use description to show the bad character to have
"good" leanings.

Example, A Bad-Good character;
    *Stakto winced as he listened to Malapok talk about how he
was going to trick Chataqua.*

In this description, we see Malapok's friend, Stakto,
wincing at Malapok's plans, an indication that he does not
agree, or is uncomfortable using his own standards.

Then there is the good guy, rogue type of character... a
hero who has many of the characteristics of a villain, but
people love him for it! We have all known a person like that
at one time or another! In my novel "The Mud Fox", the main
character, Allman Buddinger, is such a person. He does
things normal people could never get away with but
somehow does... and people love him!

There is also the inverse of the rogue character... the
seemingly good person who for some reason does a bad thing
or betrays the hero/heroine. You can describe such a person
as "good" but show tendencies to weakness.

Example, Tendencies to Weakness;
    *Nathan stood firmly beside Chataqua as they faced the
Ingelesez Leader, though he cast uneasy glances at the
Ingelesez men around them.*

You want to provide your characters with physical
characteristics that help make them fascinating. Straight
"average Joe/Jane" characters are seldom fascinating. Does
your character have an eye twitch? Why? Has one of your
characters lost one of his/her ears? How was it lost? Does one
of your characters speak with a snarl? What is the effect?

These are the kind of "amplified characteristics" that will help you in character development.

It is useful to have a character have a distinguishing "mark" (such as lack of an ear) as well as a distinguishing "action". But, don't overuse the action! In one of my recent novels, I gave a character a "big toothy grin". One of my Test Readers told me that I had overdone the "big toothy grin", and that he was sick of reading about it! So, I went back, did a word search for "big toothy grin" and modified my usage of it. Balance this with the need to contantly refresh a character's image in the mind of the Reader.

The Need For New Characters

You will come to points in your story where it becomes apparent that you "need" a new character. When Chataqua stands to become a Brave, he needs a friend to stand with him. There is a temptation to "stick in a character" at this point rather than developing a character from an earlier point in the book. Watch out for this!

When I came to this point in the first Rough-Through, I had not thought of or developed Manatapac, Chataqua's best friend. I had concentrated on Chataqua's relationship with Alanoas and Malapok. Rather than "sticking" a character in, I went back and developed Manatapac in earlier events and scenes.

What would it look like if we took the "easy way" and "stuck in" a character called Manatapac, a friend of Chataqua.

Example, Taking the Short Cut by "Sticking In" a Character;
Chataqua was thankful for his friend Manatapac. Manatapac was older and had grown up with Chataqua, becoming a Brave two years ago.

But, this is the wrong way to approach it! The Reader says "Whoa! Where did this Manatapac guy come from all of a sudden (assuming we had not developed Manatapac earlier)? If he's such a good friend of Chataqua, why don't I know more about him? It's much better to have made some mention of Manatapac earlier in the manuscript, as well as provide some background on this important supporting character.

Example, Going Back and Developing the Character "Right";
  Chataqua ran through the Grand-Salt-Water-Swamp toward Point-Where-Great-Waters-Meet. He hoped Manatapac would meet him there. He had grown up with Manatapac, who was two years older than Chataqua and his best friend. He heard footsteps running behind him and turned. Manatapac ran up beside him, a tall Brave with a wiry frame, a broad face and muscular arms.
  "Where do you go in such a hurry?" grinned Manatapac.
  "To meet you, of course," said Chataqua, happy to see his friend.
  They ran on together and soon emerged onto the white beach at Point-Where-Great-Waters-Meet. They slowed to a walk and strolled along the beach watching the sea birds search for fish in the waves. Small white crabs scuttled into their holes as they approached and poked round black eyes out of their burrows to watch the intruders suspiciously.
  "So, you want to have another of your long talks!" exclaimed Manatapac. "You, the one with all the ideas and dreams!"
  "Yes," said Chataqua. "Who else can I talk to about the things that obsess me if I do not talk to you?"

Background

How did a character get to be the way he/she is? What things happened that caused the character to be motivated in the way he/she is? What are his/her standards and "belief systems"? This is a dangerous area for the Author. It is too easy to engage in long digressions providing background on characters that does not contribute to the main story. Every character has a story, but...

The story of every character is not the story you are telling.

You are telling the story of the main character. The primary, secondary and supporting characters are there because they are a part of that story. Don't digress too much trying to tell their story. Some background on the primary characters is necessary. The background of most secondary and supporting characters can be treated with a "hint". Give the Reader a "hint" as to what caused the character to have his/her motivation... and let the Reader fill in the rest in his/her mind.

Example, Showing Character Background With a Hint;
"Why do you seek this Maiden, Malapok?" asked Stakto.
"Because Chataqua seeks her," said Malapok darkly.
"I don't understand," said Stakto.
"Chataqua's father Benatagua opposed me for Brave," said Malapok sullenly. "He has hated my father and my family... and I will not let Chataqua treat me in that way."
"So you don't seek Alanoas for her beauty?" asked Stakto in surprise.
Malapok grinned lasciviously and his eyes darted about the swamp. "Oh... that too," he said. "She has a flower that yearns to be plucked!"
"When will you ask her father, Masonnacok, to let you pluck this flower?" grinned Stakto.
"Soon," said Malapok with a confident nod. "When she comes of age in the Time-of-the-Hot-Sun."

Relationships

The relationships between characters is an important factor in defining each character. Using a discussion between Manatapac and Chataqua provides a good example.

Example, Character Development Using Dialogue;
"I used to help my Mother with the building of our lodges in Chesepiooc," said Chataqua. "I still do."
"Ahhh..." said Manatapac, "you should be careful about that. If Malapok saw you building lodges he would call you a woman... and you would have to fight him!"

"I would not like that," said Chataqua, "but I enjoy building things."

"You and Malapok were once friends," said Manatapac. "Now, it seems you're not. Why is that?"

"I do not know... I was never sure he was a friend, though we did things together," said Chataqua. "He somehow resents me now... calls me Young Squirrel!"

Manatapac grinned. "That is because you are always busy...running about as a squirrel!"

"He does it to make me mad" said Chataqua, shaking his head. "But I just laugh at him when he does it!"

"He never joined us... you, me, Rowhatan and Chalapo...along the beaches and in the water."

"He does not enjoy the water as we do," said Chataqua. "He prefers the forests!"

Here we see that Chataqua and Manatapac are completely at ease with each other. Chataqua is honest and open about his problem with Malapok. Manatapac is a good listener, a prime characteristic of a Mentor.

There has to be more background to the relationship between Chataqua and Malapok than just their rivalry for the love of Alanoas. Using the conversation with Manatapac, we can develop this interaction.

Example, Developing the Relationship Between Characters;

"Remember the time when we were boys that the small kakapa bit Malapok's leg?" asked Manatapac.

"Yes," said Chataqua, "but he does not remember that it was I who pulled the kakapa away from him."

Manatapac laughed. "You have no sense! I remember I ran to the beach!"

"You were already on the beach," said Chataqua modestly.

"Then I remember that you beat Malapok when we swam a race here along the beach!"

"He did not like that... we embarrassed him into getting into the water... he didn't like that either."

"He is older than you and unable to accept competition," observed Manatapac. "He must win... or he sulks and moans!"

"I did not mean to shame him. It is no shame to lose a race among friends."

"I know that. But he fears the water... and he is not a friend," said Manatapac. "He is like a woman in the water!"

Chataqua grimaced. "He does not come here to the beach very much. I like the beach... it is a place to stare at the Water-That-Never-Ends and think... think about everything!"

"He does not like it either that you are smarter than he!' said Manatapac.

"I don't pretend to be smart!" said Chataqua, embarrassed.

What is the relationship between Chataqua and Manatapac? It isn't enough to just say that they are "friends". This is a very important relationship and we must develop it in more depth.

Example, Developing a Relationship in Depth;
"Ahh... but you have a quick tongue and a head that is filled with ideas," said Manatapac leaning over, picking up some sand and throwing it into the wind as they walked along.

"And you?" asked Chataqua, "Do you think I am smarter than you?"

"If you are, it is alright by me," grinned Manatapac. "I need smart friends!"

"I am glad that you are my friend!"

"You are to become a Brave soon," said Manatapac. "Your time of helping your Mother cook, plant maize, make mats and build lodges must be put behind you. You will become a hunter... a fisher and you will train to defend Chesepiooc as a warrior."

"But now you are a Brave, and I am still but a boy."

Manatapac laughed and pushed Chataqua playfully. "You haven't been a boy for a long time," he said. "You of the big ideas and strong body... and soon you will be a Brave."

Chataqua grinned. He was used to the comments about his ideas from Manatapac. He joked about them with Manatapac. Manatapac always listened, and Chataqua could depend on him for sound critique. He needed that.

"I am going to canoe to the Land-Where-The-Sun-Is-Born," said Chataqua looking out at the blue horizon of the Water-That-Never-Ends.

Manatapac looked out to sea and thought for a moment. "You believe there is a land there?"

"Yes."

"You do not know that there is... there is nothing there but blue water."

"My father did not know there was a land when he canoed to the Land-Where-The-Cold-Wind-Blows."

"It is true," mused Manatapac. "That is why he is the honored one... Honokaa Tu!"

"Benatagua wears the cape of Honokaa Tu with great humility," said Chataqua.

"As a great man should," said Manatapac. "Perhaps I can go with you on this adventure."

"No... it is something I must do alone," said Chataqua gazing at the Water-That-Never-Ends. "Quiacosough will guide me! Okee will protect me!"

"First you must canoe to the same shore as did your Father," said Manatapac, looking worriedly at his friend "and you will learn that which you need to know!"

Note that I have used this sequence of scene excerpts to introduce a bit of Chesapeake culture...the women built the lodges. The men were not builders, except for their canoes and weapons. They were hunters, fishermen and protectors. This is called "color" or "pizzazz".

How the Character Addresses the Problem

The "problem" helps to define the character. In the novel "The Unknown Horizon", the hero, Chataqua has a problem in that he must live up to his father's reputation by performing some great deed. To do this, he must first become a Brave of the Chesapeake Tribe, a feat complicated by the opposition of the Brave Malapok. He knows that the Sachem, Chesapian, has tagged him to become Sachem, and he is under pressure to live up to that expectation. He fears the distraction of falling in love with Alanoas. Somehow, he must solve his problem and take Alanoas as his bride.

We use the solving of this problem to shape the character of Chataqua, showing how he is "transformed". Later, Chataqua's problem is compounded by the arrival of the English explorers. Thus, we have an "expanding" problem. This is the best type of problem for a novel in that it starts off fairly well defined, is almost solved and then...

Wham! The problem is compounded and expanded.

...which plunges the hero into despair just as the solution to the problem was in his/her grasp. Now he/she must gather his/her resolve and solve the expanded problem! What is there in his/her character that allows him/her to succeed? Good grist for the novel mill!

Interactions

How a character interacts with characters in the presence of other characters is an important part of defining each character. Each character is different, and so, the main character will interact with them in different ways.

Example, Interaction of Chataqua, Manatapac and Malapok;
Chesapian, Sachem of the Chesapeake, was an impressive figure as he stood on the sandy beach in front of Chataqua, the five eagle feathers of the Sachem bright in the morning sun. Benatagua, Werowance and First Among Braves stood next to him wearing the four eagle feathers of his rank. Behind him were the Braves of the Chesapeake, their arms folded over their chests, their faces stoic and judgmental. Chataqua looked straight ahead, avoiding the cold stare of Malapok.

"Who speaks for Chataqua?" asked Chesapian.

"I speak for Chataqua," said the Brave Manatapac. "He is courageous and will accept and conquer all challenges."

"Who speaks against Chataqua?" came the booming voice of Chesapian.

"I speak against Chataqua!" said Malapok. "He is weak and will not conquer the important challenges. His mind is occupied with foolish ideas... not the tasks of a Brave!"

"So Chataqua has his Champion and his Opponent as the Laws of the Chesapeake require," said Chesapian. "Each will choose from the ten challenges until six have been conquered. None may be lost if Chataqua is to become a Brave. What is your word, Chataqua?"

Chataqua trembled inside. He knew what he must do and steeled himself to do it. He feared Malapok, but he must not show it.

Our hero must make an important decision regarding his goals. We put him in a situation where he is under great pressure to make a decision he fears.

"I will conquer all challenges as Manatapac says," said Chataqua in a voice he hoped sounded strong. He turned and faced Malapok directly. "I will conquer all the challenges of Malapok!"

Malapok smirked and shook his head negatively.

"The challenges are of the Broad Waters, of the forest, of the bow, of the knife, of the fire, of the body, of the cunning, of the brave, of the mind, of the welfare of the tribe... which do you choose for Chataqua, Manatapac?" asked Chesapian.

"I choose the challenge of the Broad Waters for Chataqua," said Manatapac. "He must accomplish the feat of his father and canoe to the Land-Where-The-Cold-Wind-Blows."

"Which do you choose for Chataqua, Malapok?" asked the Sachem.

"I choose the challenge of the brave," said Malapok in a snarling voice. "Chataqua must fight me with his hands and body and not surrender for the time between sunrise and the heat of the morning."

Chataqua tightened his fists. He knew Malapok would choose to fight him. The challenge of the Broad Waters did not frighten him. Fighting the older, stronger Brave Malapok, even if all he had to do was stay in the fight from sunrise to the time before the sun began to fall, put fear in his heart.

Here, the interaction between Chataqua and Malapok becomes clearer. It becomes an interaction of pure hostility on the part of Malapok. From Chataqua's perspective, it is one of trepidation and lack of confidence. What will he have to do to survive a fight during the morning hours with Malapok?

A partial list of the relationship between characters is: loving, neutral, comic, trusting, suspicious, dominant, submissive. There should be no "neutral" (flat) relationships. The relationships must become clear to the Reader. The Author should develop and understand the relationship between all characters. And, as we have said, the relationships that form interactions between characters can "transform" if the Author provides the reason... the basis for the transformation.

Designing Characters Into a Scene

Selection of characters for a scene need only start with one or two. As the scene progresses, the need for additional characters to make the "point" of the scene will become apparent. Introduce them at the right time.

The interactions between characters are what provide the "emotion" of the scene. The emotion generated by the scene is a very important WOW Factor. So, we must work hard to put heart rending emotion into the interaction between characters where we can.

Some of the interactions between characters are suggested by Figure 6-1.

Figure 6-1

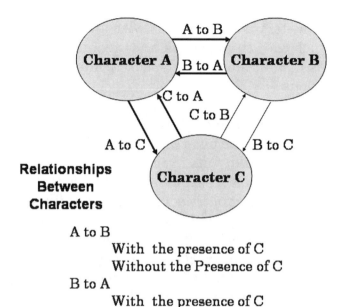

Relationships
Between
Characters

A to B
    With the presence of C
    Without the Presence of C
B to A
    With the presence of C
    Without the Presence of C, Etc.

The more characters you put in a scene, the more possible interactions you create.... the more complex the scene. You don't have to deal with them all. Use the interactions you need to get the most emotion and make the scene's "point".

Animal Characters

Richard Bach's novel *Jonathon Livingston Seagull* is a book all about sea birds. The sea birds think, speak and emote.

Excerpt;
Jonathan circled slowly over the Far Cliffs, watching. This rough young Fletcher Gull was very nearly a perfect flight-student. He was strong and light and quick in the air, but far and away more important, he had a blazing drive to learn to fly. Here he came this minute, a blurred gray shape roaring out of a dive, flashing one hundred fifty miles per hour past

his instructor. He pulled abruptly into another try at a sixteen point vertical slow roll, calling the points out loud.

You can write a story about animals with animal characters in which they think, speak and emote... or you can have animals in your story who "speak" primarily through their actions.

Example, Introducing an Animal Character;
Chataqua and Manatapac put aside their fish net and their clothes. They swam playfully in the surf near Point-Where-Great-Waters-Meet. It was a windy day with multi-shaped clouds that floated rapidly across the light blue sky. They had mastered the art of catching the cresting wave at just the right moment and riding it to the sand shore. They paddled furiously to get to the crest of the wave and dashed along with the momentum of the rushing water. The taste of the salty water was in their mouths, and then the wave would break and hurl them and hundreds of little seashells onto the beach.

"That was a good one!" shouted Manatapac rising from the surf which now rushed back into the sea, his body glistening wet.

"You got ahead of me on that one," shouted Chataqua, rising and joining Manatapac to search for the next big wave.

They waded back into the water until it was almost over their heads and waited. Suddenly, they saw a fin emerge from the water only a few arm lengths from where they stood. Manatapac started, fearing it was Kakapa, the Fish-That-Eats-Men.

"Look out!" exclaimed Manatapac. "It is Kakapa!"

"No!" shouted Chataqua, who knew all the fish and sea creatures better than any Chesapeake. "It is calypo! The sea-creature-that-smiles!"

The fin swam toward them. It leaned over at a crazy angle.

"Look!" said Chataqua. "There is blood!"

"Kakapa is near!" shouted Manatapac in alarm.

We take this opportunity to create the suspense of being in the water with sharks nearby. It also anticipates "events to come".

Chataqua swam to the calypo. The large mammal was bleeding from a wound near its tail. Chataqua heard a high pitched call, as if in distress. He guided the calypo toward the shore.

"What are you doing?" exclaimed Manatapac.

"The calypo is hurt!" exclaimed Chataqua. "We must help him!"

They pulled the calypo to the beach. The mammal lay on its side, exhausted. They pulled it over the beach and into a deep tidal pool that was about ten paces away from the surf. The Calypo lay on its side and blew a stream of spray from the blow hole in the top of its head. He was dark gray on the top with a lighter gray belly. His long snout held a grinning mouth lined with small, sharp teeth. Chataqua ran to his clothes and retrieved his buckskin shirt. He put the shirt on calypo's wound to stem the flow of blood. He whistled at the calypo and was surprised to hear it squeak in return.

Supernatural Characters

You would expect a supernatural character to appear in a book about supernaturals... but they need not be limited to that type of book. Supernatural characters can include: super heroes; mythic beasts; mythic gods; ghosts of people and beasts past; classic monsters (vampires, werewolves, etc.); characters from legend; your own creation.

These supernatural characters can be friendly or not, and like your human characters, may "transition" during the story from good to bad or vice versa. They can be main characters, primary characters, secondary characters or supporting characters. Many times they are a type of "Mentor". They can be people, gods, demons or beasts. They can appear on and off throughout the story, or be used for special purposes.

In my fantasy novel "The Wara Wa", the hero, Beau Hunter, goes through an amazing transformation. The novel is about the "Wara" who, as decreed by the Great Spirit, exist to counter the evil of the Great Demon and his henchmen the Were (Werewolves) who haunt a boy's camp (Camp Chicawa) in a small southern town.

Example, A Supernatural Character;

Beau reached down and loosed the piece of rawhide that bound the loincloth to him. He knelt naked beneath the vine covered rock formation, his muscled body glistening in the moonlight. He felt trapped, and fear set into his mind. If he could not transform, he would be killed! He flexed each muscle in his body one by one, sending the signal along the nerves from his brain, until, in his mind, he encountered a nerve connection that seemed new. Beau cautiously sent a signal along the new nerve connection, and felt a sense of peace and pleasure sweep over his body. The transformation began in the legs and arms, and quickly spread to the body and head. Beau was willing each cell in his body to transform. The Wara Za watched Beau intently. The transformation seemed to take a long time. Beau saw the Wara Za staring at him strangely. He looked down at his arms and saw that he was standing on wolf legs. But had he completely transformed?

"Wara Za?" asked Beau. "Is it complete?"

The Wara Za walked around him, staring at him with intense eyes. "You have transformed in a most unusual way," said the Wara Za.

Obviously, "The Wara Wa" is a novel with a setting in the supernatural. If you include a supernatural character in a story that is not primarily "about" supernaturals, be careful. It must make sense to the Reader, and there should be some plausible explanation regarding how the supernatural character appears… such as a hallucination under stress, dreams, etc.

****

Chapter Seven
The Storyteller's Direction

The "Storyteller's Direction" is the pattern of how to progress the novel using the plot. It defines the main characters, a beginning point, "events along the way", a possible ending point, and presents rough ideas on how to get from beginning to end. It is a guide for the Rough-Through, as shown in Figure 7-1.

Figure 7-1

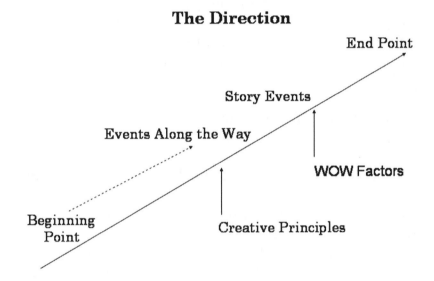

The Direction

The Direction may exist in your mind or be in some written form for referral. It is not a long "document" over which you should labor. Indeed, it may be only a diagram with some scribbled notes. It may only go "a few scenes ahead" as you write.

I recommend that you address the following in establishing your first "Direction".

1. The Title.

Pick one out. You'll have more ideas as you write.
2. The Story.
Jot down a few initial story events.
3. Initial Characters.
Who are they? What are their names?
4. Beginning Point.
How do you start the story?
5. Events along the Way.
"Events Along The Way" are events in more detail than Story Events. What events happen in the first scenes? You need only a few to START.
6. End Point.
Where do you think the story will end? (The Rough-Through goal). This will change as you write, but have an initial "direction" in mind... or several. The ending that best fits will become clearer as you write.

Storytelling

You use "storytelling" throughout the novel to maintain "the Direction".

"Storytelling" is what the Author does to tell the story.

Story telling is not description, action or dialogue. It may have the characteristics of description, or action, but it "stands apart". It is the part of the text in which the Storyteller (whoever that may be) exercises his/her authority to "progress the story".

"Once upon a time" is a simple but illustrative example of storytelling. Nothing is being described except the story. No action is taking place except the progression of the story. No character is saying anything.

Another example: "A year passed". The Storyteller is exercising his/her authority to manage the time perspective of the Reader. The Storyteller is "speaking" to the Reader outside the context of the setting and characters of the novel.

Another example: "The war began the following week." The Storyteller steps outside of the story briefly to talk to the Reader and inform him/her of a major event in the story.

You must understand how to use, but not overuse, the Storyteller in our novel. It is a very important tool!

Imagination, Dreams and Ideas

Where do "events along the way", scenes and scene elements come from? They come from the Author's head... his/her imagination, dreams and ideas.

Authors typically have a lot of experience to draw on. That doesn't mean that a young person cannot be an Author. But, the more one experiences life, the more experience there is to draw upon.

Authors seek out activities that will provide them with experience. Authors read a lot. They read things that interest them and also things beyond their normal range of interests. Authors listen. They listen to the world around them and observe everything. Authors have wild fantasies. They day dream a lot. They are always tossing some new (or old) idea around in their head. Occasionally, Authors even do research. Delving deep into some subject will always catalyze ideas for a story... a novel.

So, as you begin to write, adopt the habits of Authors. Write your ideas down (scribble on the back of a napkin... or wherever)!

The half life of an idea is only the time until the next distraction.

The Title

We have one... "The Unknown Horizon". It may change, but for now it is descriptive of the intended content of our novel.

The Story

We have a good initial premise. We have an idea of how to approach each of the story events. We only need a few story events to START, so we're in good shape.

Initial Characters

To START, it helps to "flesh out" your list of initial characters. You'll find that their character will grow and change as you write. That's okay. But you need to have some idea of the characteristics of the initial characters.

The way you "set up" your main characters not only supports your ideas for a story... it also gives you ideas for how to START.

There aren't many new stories, but there are a million ways to tell them, and a million interesting characters with which to populate them!

The Beginning Point

We know where we want to start.

Example, The Beginning Point:
Chataqua and his father, Benatagua, paddled a long canoe with fish and sea birds carved on its sides near Point-Where-Great-Waters-Meet. Chataqua sat in the front, his father at the rear. Both were bare of chest and wore only a loin cloth. It was a clear day in the Time-When-The-Trees-Bring-Leaves. The morning sun shown warmly.

"Chataqua, you will soon be a man and seek to be a Brave," said Benatagua in his deep voice. "You paddle well and have a strong body... you will honor our family!"

Events Along the Way

We have our beginning point. Now we must rough out a series of "events along the way" that follow the story events. Try to stay a scene or two ahead of where you are and think through "what comes next". The events are not sacrosanct. You may change them or modify them as you go... and you will find that you need to. Remember, this is an art form, not a "formula".

Sample Events Along the Way:

1. *Chataqua learns from his father of the desire of Sachem Chesapian to have Chataqua groomed as the future chief.*

2. *Benatagua warns Chataqua of the evil intent of the Periku to become Sachem.*

3. *Chataqua yearns to canoe to the unknown horizon to find the land-where-the-sun-is-born and find unknown lands as did his father.*

4. *Chataqua saves a sick dolphin from sharks and befriends it. He names the dolphin Calypo-Ma, Creature-of-the-Sea-That-Smiles-My-Friend.*

5. *Chataqua becomes a Brave, though he is opposed by Malapok.*

6. *Chataqua loves Alanoas but is obsessed with canoeing to the land-where-the sun-is-born. He says he can not ask for her until he has proven his worth by doing this.*

That's enough to establish your initial direction and get you STARTED. What Story Events are these? They contain elements of The Status Quo Event and the Mentor Event. We didn't "try" to write those events. We wrote in freeform art and discovered that we have the essence of those events. If we find that what we have written does not "capture" some of the first Story Events, we should go back, ask why we haven't, accept it for good reason or try again. As you approach number six above, you will want to revisit your Events Along the Way and take your direction further.

The End Point

Once we complete the Rough-Through, we'll have a better idea of how to build to a climax and end the novel successfully. It is useful as you proceed to keep thinking abut an "End Point". How do I know how to end this novel? I haven't written much yet!

Don't worry… the End Point you select now probably won't be where you end up… but it might be! Establishing a goal "End Point" basically sets the initial "direction" in which you will write. One begins at the Beginning Point and moves through Story Events and Events Along the Way towards the End Point… that's the "Direction". It is useful to always have a Direction… even if you wander artistically toward it.

Sample End Point, Possible Events of the Ending:
1. *Time of the Year: The novel ends in the fall of the year after it began it began (about a 14 month time span for the novel).*
2. *Benatagua was killed by a rival tribe at the order of Powhatan.*
3. *Chesapian was killed by the English explorers when they first landed at Point-Where-Great-Waters-Meet.*
4. *The Periku assumes Sachem.*
5. *Chataqua escapes with Alanoas to Teme Forest, Chataqua tries to position to become Sachem.*
6. *Powhatan sends his brother, Opectanotak, Chief of the Wepeneooc to force the Chesapeake to pay tribute. They are armed with sticks-that-make-fire, obtained from the Ingelesez. Some of the Ingelesez, now allied with Powhatan, aid the Wepeneooc.*
7. *Climax Scene: A great battle occurs between the Wepeneooc, the Ingelesez and the Chesapeake. Chataqua saves the day and Malapok is killed.*
8. *The Wepeneooc return. Chataqua leads the Chesapeake Braves and they fight with great courage, but are overwhelmed.*
9. *Chataqua, Alanoas and some of the Chesapeake escape in canoes and canoe to the Land-Where-The-Cold-Wind-Blows, the land discovered by Benatagua. There, Chataqua leads them in seeking a new life (explaining the disappearance of the Chesapeake Nation).*

Notes

I recommend that you create a "NOTES" file and type in your rough Beginning Point, Events Along the Way and End Point. Put your list of characters in your "NOTES". Put in anything you want to have as ready reference that will allow you to maintain continuity.

Getting to the End Point

Now you know who your main characters are... at least, the first cut at it. You have sketched out the Beginning Point and the End Point of your novel... using these characters. You have gone into "full imagination scan" and come up with a "head full" of events that will help to tell your story.

You are frustrated that you can not do a "memory dump" and immediately get all of those ideas on paper. That's okay! Allow the frustration, but keep in mind that now you will embark on the Rough-Through in earnest, using all the Building Blocks and Creative Principles. Each chapter, each scene, each element of the scene is a creative project that takes time and artistic talent! Take them one at a time!

Be patient! You won't get to the end until you get to the end!

You must enter the Creative Cave and spend time on every building block. Keep the "big picture" of your novel in mind... the Storyteller's Direction. But, be able to treat each scene as a "work of art" that requires your time and attention. If you complete one good scene in a day, you are doing well.

Spend enough time on the Rough-Through to allow you to create a stone that can be sculpted! I spend three to five months on a Rough–Through, depending on the nature of the novel, sometimes longer. For my first novel, it was twice that amount of time.

In the mechanical "step by step approach" (which I do not recommend), the Direction takes the form of a formal outline, chapter by chapter, scene by scene. The assumption is made that the Author already knows the story and its flow well enough to make an outline that will stand the test of writing it out. This is usually a fallacious assumption.

The mechanical approach compared to the Rough-Through approach is suggested in Figure 7-2. I recommend the "art form approach". It is the most difficult approach... because it is the best.

Figure 7-2

The "Step By Step" Mechanical Approach

The Novel

The Art Form Approach: The Rough - Through

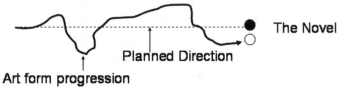

The Novel

Planned Direction

Art form progression

The Art Form Approach: The Creative Reviews

The Novel

You won't know the whole story until you get to the end!

By the time you complete the Rough-Through, you will know the whole story... mostly. The "wandering" means you are not following a rigidly planned format toward the end point; rather you are following a rough "direction" that leads to an end point; not necessarily "the" end point.

Do not fear the Re-Write!

****

Chapter Eight
Scenario Development

The term "scenario" has several meanings in structuring a novel: an outline of the plot of a dramatic or literary work; or, the setting in which the plot of a dramatic or literary work takes place. I use the term "scenario" more in the sense of "the setting", though obviously, the setting is closely related to the plot and the characters. When determining the "setting". You should ask the following types of questions:

1. How do I describe the "where" of the setting?
2. Who are the characters in the setting?
3. How do I describe the physical characteristics of the setting?
4. How do I describe the "when" of the setting?
5. How do I use the setting to aid in character development?
6. How do I use the setting to aid the plot?
7. How much should I describe the setting to hold Reader interest?

There are at least three scenario "levels": the overall scenario (setting) of the novel (a macro view); the scenario (setting) for each chapter; the scenario (setting) for each scene. In general, each "scene" in each chapter should have its own setting. Changing settings within a scene is confusing to the Reader and detracts from the logical "flow" of the novel.

There are two "types" of scenarios:

1. The static scenario.
   The setting is static, that is, it doesn't change. Things may "go through it" dynamically (cars, airplanes, etc.), but the setting itself remains the same. All of the action described occurs in the same setting.
2. The flowing scenario.
   The setting moves with the action. However, the movement has to have continuity. For example, the hero/heroine is running through an urban area which transitions to a rural area as he/she runs. Action

occurs as he/she runs. The continuity necessary to the scene in this case is the running of the hero/heroine, not the static setting. The author should intersperse the action with description of the changing setting. Or even better, create dialogue and action that notes the changing setting.

Example, Flowing Scenario;
Alanoas and Musiasas ran through the Grand-Salt-Water-Swamp toward Chesepiooc Village, jumping over roots and fallen branches in the path.

"I don't think Malapok is watching us!" panted Musiasas as her short legs tried to move as fast along the moist trail as those of Alanoas.

"I have a strange feeling," said Alanoas as they ran up the little hill that led to higher ground.

"What?" asked Musiasas as they passed a murky black lagoon.

"I feel eyes on us," said Alanoas, feeling relieved as she saw the great spreading oak outside Chesepiooc Village ahead of them.

The Scenario

Each chapter may have a static or flowing setting. More common, a chapter is made up of a number of related scenes, each of which have a static or flowing setting.

Examples follow:
Scene 1: A flowing scene in which Chataqua and Benatagua are in a canoe near Point-Where-Great-Waters-Meet.

Scene 2: A static scene that takes place on the beach near the Chesapeake Village of Chesepiooc. Alanoas and Chataqua meet on the beach.

Scene 3: A flowing setting as the heroine Alanoas walks back from the beach to Chesepiooc through the Grand-Salt-Water-Swamp and the cypress and evergreen forest.

Notes like this are useful as a guide, but the scenario and timing of your scenes will be suggested by your artistic need as you tell the story. Don't get locked into any "outline"! Stay one or two scenes ahead of where you are writing to maintain your direction! Then you can end a scene with a logical event leading to the next.

Where Are The Characters?

Right away, the Reader needs to know where the characters that are going to be speaking and taking action in the scene are. Several examples of how to handle this follow:

Example, The "Where" Using Description;
Malapok and his friend Stakto stood hidden in a stand of cypress and pine trees in the Grand-Salt-Water-Swamp near the Point-Where-Great-Waters-Meet. Malapok was a tall, strong Brave with intense, darting eyes. Stakto was shorter and carried more weight than a Brave should have. Tall trees stood majestically around them and blocked out the sun, making the swamp seem gloomy.

Example, The "Where" Using Action;
Malapok ran as fast as he could run through the Grand-Salt-Water-Swamp, his heart bursting with eagerness to see Alanoas. His friend Stakto ran beside him.
"I saw her come into the swamp with the little chubby girl," said Stakto.
"We'll hide here behind these cypress trees," said Malapok, coming to a stop and scanning the mysterious gloom of the swamp.

Example, The "Where" Using Dialogue;
"Be very quiet," whispered Malapok to his friend Stakto. "The Swamp has many echoes."
"I see them coming," whispered Stakto, pointing. "They are beyond those tall cypress and pine trees."
"She has been on the beach with that foolish boy, the Young Squirrel Chataqua," said Malapok. "I must talk to her soon."

"Then why don't you, Malapok?" asked Stakto. "You are foolish to wait."

"The time must be right... she is with the other girl," said Malapok. "I will follow her along the path to the village."

In choosing from the description, action and dialogue methods, use some of each, but err in favor of dialogue punctuated with action.

Describing the Setting

Every setting has its own unique characteristics. A certain amount of experience or research is required to set the scene well. If, like me, you grew up along the coast of Eastern Virginia, the words should flow from that experience. If not, go to the library and get a book that describes your chosen location. Study it. Your description must fit not only the geography, but also the nature of the geography in the time of the scene.

The coastal Virginia setting is much different in the 17th Century than in the 21st. You have to understand the difference made by time in a setting. Get on the internet and type in an inquiry with the right key words, such as "Coastal Virginia 1607". The internet will always turn up something. If your first key words don't work, try something else, such as "History of Virginia Tidelands". The internet will provide you with a description of what you're looking for in most cases.

You want the words you use to describe the setting to be dynamic, beautiful words. Pick out a word and use it. Then go back and use the "find synonym" key (Shift F7 on most word processors) on your computer. See if there's a better word.

Example, Different Ways of Describing:
1. *The Grand-Salt-Water-Swamp was gloomy and mysterious.*
2. *The Grand-Salt-Water-Marsh was dim and mystifying.*
3. *The Immense-Salt-Water-Bog was depressing and weird.*

Which of these is the most dynamic? The most interesting? Which one best sets the mood you want to create in this setting? Is it best expressed using the description, action or dialogue methods?

When Do I Describe the Setting?

You don't have to describe the setting all in the first sentence of the scene. But, you must give the Reader a clue as to "where he/she is" as soon in the scene as possible. Then, you can "build" the description! Give it time. You can describe the setting using an unfolding sequence of description, action and dialogue (use dialogue tags liberally).

As you are writing dialogue, don't forget to think about what the speaking character is "seeing" and use the opportunity to build the setting further.

Example, Using Dialogue Tag to Describe What the Character is Seeing;
"I hope I see you again soon," shouted Chataqua as Alanoas ran behind the sand dune and disappeared among the giant cypress trees of the Grand- Salt-Water-Swamp.

Try starting a scene with dialogue that provides an immediate clue as to where the characters "are".

Example, Starting a Scene with Dialogue;
"I see them!" exclaimed Chataqua staring out at the Broad Waters.
Manatapac raised his head slightly above the reeds on the sand dune. "I see them too!" he exclaimed.

How To Use Setting To Aid Character Development

The way a character "sees" the setting defines what type of person he/she is. Two characters "seeing" the same thing in different ways provides the Reader with a sharp contrast in their personalities.

Example, Seeing With Beauty;

Alanoas walked rapidly through the Grand-Salt-Water-Swamp. She stopped when she saw White-Bird-With-Long-Legs who waded slowly through the glistening, brackish water. She spoke to him gently. "Oh, great bird of the Swamp, you are full of beauty, and your home is so quiet and majestic!"

Example, Seeing With Depression;

Malapok hid behind the cypress tree and stood in the murky, threatening waters up to his knees. He watched Alanoas talking to White-Bird-With-Long-Legs and wished she was talking to him in this depressing swamp instead of the stupid bird.

How To Use Setting To Aid The Plot

The setting makes the plot exciting, as well as helping to define the plot. A scene in a village between Native Americans is probably not as exciting as the meeting of two young lovers against the backdrop of crashing waves and swooping sea birds. So, use the crashing waves and swooping sea birds to suggest romance!

The setting at the edge of the ocean can be used to suggest the theme or premise of the novel; "The Lost Horizon", the far away and mysterious unknown that challenges our young hero, Chataqua. In this way, the setting builds and amplifies the plot.

How To Describe The Setting To Hold Reader Interest

Things that most hold the Reader's interest include:
1. A setting that suggests sex (note that I didn't say that leads to sex. The suggestion of it is much more alluring than the act itself). Two young people alone on a romantic beach can, if handled correctly, get the hook in the Reader's mouth quickly. The hook still needs, however, to be "set".
2. A setting that, by its nature, suggests dynamic action.
3. A setting that suggests strong emotion.

4. A setting that suggests mystery and intrigue.
5. A setting that suggests intense conflict between characters.

As you set the tempo, or pace of the novel, one of these types of scenes, with the appropriate setting, should show up with a high degree of frequency. A novel should be a smoothly flowing sequence of "highs" and "lows" that provide a stimulating sinusoidal pattern.

The Importance of Place

Where your novel takes place defines a large part of how the novel is written. It also mostly defines your market. Readers are interested in "place". They are interested in: places they know a lot about; and, places they don't know much about and consider "exotic".

Many of my novels have a theme or subplot in them that reflect my Virginia heritage. I enjoy writing about Virginia, as I grew up there and have it in my heart... the green forests speckled with the white blooms of dogwood, the myriad winding rivers filled with fish and crabs, the mysterious and strangely beautiful swamps, the misty, dreamy Blue Ridge Mountains, the rolling hills of the Shenandoah Valley, the mighty Chesapeake Bay and its unpredictable waters, the stark beauty of bare trees covered with frost in the winter... just as you have in your heart the place you grew up.

Having spent a career in the U.S. Navy, I also have many vivid scenes in my memory: violent storms at sea with towering waves that toss one around with incredible fury; beautiful brown rivers surrounded by thick, green foliage in Vietnam with danger lurking in the elephant grass around every bend; squalid, trashy slums in Rio De Janeiro against the lush background of the opulent city; the white sands and skimpy bikinis of Copacabana; jungle beaches in Puerto Rico under a palm canopy with splendorous sunsets; bull fights and flamenco dancers in Seville; colorful, noisy birds and pulsing rhythmic calypso music in Trinidad; exciting back alleys in Barcelona where the sounds of flamenco music echo and give rise to a rush of passionate emotions; alluring hotels and bars amidst the bizarre city of Hong Kong with exotic women who beckon with suggestive smiles.

Wow! But there's more; the bustle of traffic, flocking pigeons and sense of history in London's Trafalgar Square; foreboding Samurai Castles in Japan exuding the atmosphere of the Warrior's Code; gooney birds squawking on Midway Island; warm, sunny beaches and tropical waterfalls in Hawaii; lush jungles in the Philippines alive with the noise of strange and mysterious animals; beautiful sunsets at sea with long steaks of blazing color; breathtaking mountainous scenery along the coast near Naples; little sidewalk ristorantes with hanging cloves of garlic and the aromatic smells of clams and pasta; azure seas and green jungles of the Seychelles Islands; great, rocky bluffs at Capetown; the steamy, dusty city of Mombassa with its Elephant Tusk Arch; thick jungles and flamingos in Jamaica; the deep snows and terrifying seas of Argentia in the winter... a whole kaleidoscope of "places".

So I have a lot to choose from in my writings. You should try to experience as many "places" as you can. You will be a better Author for the experience. Readers have "places" in their minds also. Readers want to experience their favorite place in the books they read. They also want to experience the places they would like to go. So, be very aware of choosing the "place" for your novel whether it's one place or a "sweeping" saga that bounces around the globe.

****

Chapter Nine
Plot Development

We think we "sort of" know the whole story... but know that it may change as we think about it more. The question now is, how do we tell the story? What is the plot? In planning a plot, we should us the Story Events as a guide and consider the following:
1. Building drama.
2. Maintaining suspense.
3. Evolving "the problem".
4. Wrestling with "the solution".
5. Framing the romance.
6. Building to the climax.
7. Showing the transformation.
8. Integrating plot and sub-plot.
9. Keeping it "simple".

Building Drama

What is drama? If you use the word not in the sense of a type of theater, it means something striking or forcefully effective (dramatic). But how does one build drama?

You are creating conflict as the basis of a good story. You must also build suspense, or "tension" for the Reader.

Drama is an artful mixture of conflict and suspense.

To build tension you must disclose only part of the problem or its solution as you write. There is a temptation to "get it all out"... to explain everything. Rather than that, keep the Reader in suspense to create tension.

Maintaining Suspense

We know we don't want to tell the Reader everything right away. We want to unfold the story in a way that maintains a "sense of mystery and suspense" that "builds drama". That's the first principle of creating a plot.

Evolving the Problem

The plot must seek to identify the main character's "problem" and the associated "goal" as early in the plot as possible. Yet, it cannot be done hastily… it should be "evolved". The best way to evolve the problem is through action involving the dialogue of characters. The problem shouldn't be just "stated". It must be a part of something else going on, and in some cases, it isn't "stated" at all. It gradually becomes obvious.

What characters are required to evolve Chataqua's problem in our story? What are the implications of the problem? In the example below, Chesapian, the Sachem, and Chataqua's father Benatagua are the ones required. As you write, you will undoubtedly come to chapters and scenes where other characters are required, or will be used to further describe and amplify the problem.

Example, Implications of the Problem;

The Sachem of the Chesapeake, Chesapian, stood at the campfire of the elders as they considered those eligible to become Braves. The fire crackled and cast deep, flickering shadows over the Broad Waters. Chesapian was a tall man with a body weathered by the wind and sun. He wore the traditional cloth of the Chesapeake, a beaded deerskin waist cloth and a cloak of raccoon hides against the cool evening. His head was bald except for a knot of hair pulled up into the center of his head. The five eagle feathers of the Sachem were clustered in the knot. He wore cloth bands around his legs just below the knee, each adorned with dangling, colored threads.

"Benatagua, the Werowance, First Brave of the Chesapeake, canoed many moons ago over the unknown horizon toward the Land-Where-The-Cold-Winds-Blow," intoned Chesapian in a deep voice. "He took me there to speak to the Sachem of the Delaware. We must look for feats such as this in our Braves, who must be able to defend our lands from the Wepeneooc and others who would take our home by the Broad Waters."

Benatagua stood up beside Sachem Chesapian. He was tall and had the broadest shoulders of all the Braves. He wore the four eagle feathers of the Werowance and had a solemn look on his face. He wore the robe of Honokaa Tu, the Honored One, a white tailed deer hide encrusted with colorful shells.

"In our Braves, we must seek those who do not fear an unknown, be it the dark forest, the deep water or an unknown of the mind" said Benatagua. "If that is so, then they will not fear our enemies! Our enemies, the Wepeneooc, two days toward the Land-Where-The-Warm-Wind-Blows, envy us our land near the Broad Waters, and we must always be prepared to repel them! "

Can you "see the scene"? Before you start writing, you should be able to "see" it in your mind... "feel" the atmosphere... immerse yourself in the scene. As you write, the picture becomes more and more clear.

Here, we have further defined the Chief (Sachem) Chesapian as an essential character in creating the main character's problem. Chesapian uses the example of Benatagua's canoe trip to the northern horizon as an example of the kind of deeds required of a Brave. This reinforces Chataqua's need to live up to his father, an essential component of his "problem".

This scene is also used to begin to define the enemy of the Chesapeake, the Wepeneooc (a fictitious tribe for the purposes of this novel whose villages are two days travel to the southwest). The Wepeneooc are an essential part of the plot, and we must begin to show who they are and why they are an enemy of the Chesapeake. For purposes of a fictitious novel, it is best to use a "made-up" name for organizations, tribes, etc. I could have used the Pamunkey Tribe (a real tribe to the southwest of Chesepiooc), but since this is fiction, I want to avoid that association to give me more freedom in writing. And, I don't want to insult anyone of the Pamunkey Tribe.

We use every opportunity to further define and use the scenario, as well as define the appearance and traits of each character. The more this is done, as long as it is not too repetitive, the more the Reader will "feel" the scenario and "identify" with each character.

Framing the Romance

Framing the romance is a tricky matter. You don't want to start right off saying "boy is in love with girl and girl loves boy". That's not a story! How do they fall in love? What events bring them together... or separate them? Is it a rocky process? Do they dislike each other at first for some reason? What makes them fall in love? Does one love the other but the love is not returned? Why isn't it returned? What is the "tension"?

Whatever the reason, how can it be resolved such that each loves the other? You must structure the answer to these questions throughout the novel.

A rather standard pattern for developing a romance is:
1. One loves the other, but love is not returned for some reason.
2. The matter is resolved, and they are both in love.
3. Something occurs to separate them.
4. Both are miserable.
5. In the process of solving "the problem", they are brought back together.
6. They solve "the problem" together.

There are many variations to this pattern, and you, the Author, must decide how to develop the romance and how the romance is going to integrate into solving the main character's "problem" that is the essence of the story.

How should we start to frame the romance between Chataqua and Alanoas in *The Unknown Horizon?*

Example, Framing the Romance;
Chataqua turned and saw Alanoas emerging from behind a sand dune. He was, as always, stunned by her beauty! Her long, dark hair hung below her shoulders and glistened against the shell decorated deerskin hide that she wore. Her intense brown eyes were fixed on him expectantly.
"Alanoas!" exclaimed Chataqua bashfully.

We see that Chataqua is fascinated by Alanoas, but we don't at this introductory stage know that he is "in love" with her. After all, he is at the age of "racing hormones"! We do know that he understands that he should soon seek a wife. We also know that he is obsessed with living up to the image of his father and the upcoming test for new Braves. These may be the things that are inhibiting him from moving along the road to love.

We know early how Alanoas feels about Chataqua. But will she be able to have him return her love? Will she have the patience to wait until his obsession with "The Unknown Horizon" fades? There is always "a problem" associated with the romance. How should we present it in the plot?

Example, Posing the Problems in the Romance;
   Alanoas walked away from the beach wondering if she would ever be able to convince Chataqua that she loved him. He was so bashful and shy that it worried her. And, he seemed obsessed with this idea about some kind of a new canoe that would take him to the Land-Where-The Sun-Is-Born.

Be sure to develop the romance from the perspective of both participants in the love equation. It takes two to tango!

Writing about love among a man and a woman in a Native American Tribe in 1607 is fraught with difficulty. There is a danger in making it seem that the relationship is similar to what we experience today. In researching this, I don't find a lot of information, yet I know that the relationship is "different". There is a traditional difference in the social roles of men and women in the Chesapeake Tribe than that of today. They marry much earlier than in modern society. The emotions, however, are bound to be similar... so I treat them that way. And, when I can, I reflect some of the differences in the roles.

We learn that there is a love triangle. Another man is in love with Alanoas!

Example, Establishing the Love Triangle;
   It was a short walk back to Chesepiooc along a path bordered by Cyprus trees and salt water swamps. Alanoas came to a fork in the path, one side of which went to the

95

*village and the other to the Place-of-Many-Islands. Her mind
cowered as she remembered the time the Brave Malapok had
come upon her at this place. He had embraced her and tried to
persuade her to come with him along the path to the Place-of-
Many-Islands. He held her hand tightly, but she broke away
and ran down the path to Chesepiooc. She looked cautiously
around her, but she was alone except for the White-Bird-With
Long-Legs who waded slowly through the swamp. She walked
quickly toward Chesepiooc, wishing that Chataqua was with
her. She did not see Malapok hiding in the swamp watching
her every move.*

Every romance should involve a triangle; some form of
competition for the love of the other. It makes it all a lot
more interesting… and is among the things that make a good
novel. Chataqua's rival is Malapok. Alanoas' rival is
Chataqua's obsession with his "problems" and sense of
adventure (perhaps the old male commitment problem). We
know from the initial "End Point" how the romance may be
resolved, and how it integrates with "the problem" (at least
for the Rough-Through).

Example, Resolving the Romance (End Point);
*Chataqua and Alanoas, very much in love, escape in their
canoe, once again toward an unknown horizon where they
hope to find love and peace.*

Now the Author must fill in the details of the romance
between START and END POINT in a gripping, tender and
emotion filled manner that will make the Reader say "WOW"
many times.

The Transformation of Characters

Your plot must clearly show how the hero/heroine and
perhaps other characters are "transformed" by the events in
the novel. By "transformed", I mean how the character is
"changed" by the experiences described in the novel. It's not a
good novel unless the experiences were of such magnitude

that they changed the character in his/her capability, attitude, social station, etc.

What were the primary characteristics of Chataqua at the BEGINNING POINT of *The Unknown Horizon*? What were they like at the END POINT? How has Chataqua changed? What experiences in the novel caused him to change? It helps to do an informal "Before and After Summary". This is nothing fancy. Many of mine have been done on the back of a napkin in a Chinese restaurant waiting for my *Moo Goo Gai Pan*. It looks like this:

"Before and After" Summary
Character: XXXX

Characteristic	Before	After	Because
1. x			
2. x			
3. x			

Think about your character and what his/her dominant characteristics are. Jot them down. You don't need more than six or so. Then think through them and jot down the Before and After. Think about how your plot will produce experiences that cause change. List events or things that you think will cause change in the "Because" column.

You may find that there is no change that you can think of for some of the characteristics you listed. If so, eliminate those characteristics. Put only characteristics in the summary that change directly related to the events and experiences in the novel.

The most important change is that which occurs in your main character. You should do a Before and After Summary for each primary character and use it as a guide as you write. When you complete the Rough-Through, you should be able to identify all of the events/experiences in the novel that cause dramatic change in your primary characters.

Every change must have a credible "Because!"

During your "Creative Review" process, you should refer to the Before and After Summary frequently. You may find that an event to produce a change that you thought would occur as you wrote the "Rough-Through" is not in the text, or is poorly defined and needs "tweaking". Go back and insert the event that you need. Make sure it "fits in" with the logic and continuity of the novel.

Example, "Before and After" Summary
Character: Chataqua

Characteristic	Before	After	Because
1. Confidence	Low	High	Canoes north
2. Bravery	Unproven	Proven	Vs. Malapok
3. Maturity	A boy	A man	Fulfills dream, canoes east
4. Self Esteem	Low	High	Banishment but retains self esteem with help of Alanoas
5. Experience	Little	Improved	Canoeing north and east, fighting Wepeneooc and Europeans
6. Capability	Some	Much	Warrior and Seamanship skills
7. Love	No room	Expanded	Loves Alanoas

Integrating Plot and Sub-Plot

When you put it all together, the plot regarding the main character's "problem" and the various sub-plots, such as the romance, must make sense together. What are the key points? Try taking a well known story (one of your favorites) and doing a "Creative Outline" that might have been done by the Author (The Author probably didn't have such an outline right away, but he/she may have had it when the story was complete). Let's take the example of Hemingway's "Old Man and the Sea", a classic short story.

Example, A Creative Outline of The Old Man and the Sea;

1. *A story of friendship between a young boy and an aging fisherman, Santiago, and how Santiago lost and regained his faith and vitality.*
2. *Santiago is adored by a young boy, Manolin.*
3. *Santiago is tormented by weeks of ill luck in his fishing.*
   He is hungry as he has caught no fish.
4. *Santiago was once a strong, proud man, but he is aging.*
   He feels he must come to terms with his failing abilities and age.
5. *For many weeks he returns to his small village with no fish.*
   Problem: Santiago is forced to accept food from other villager's.
6. *For Santiago, this is humiliating.*
   Problem: Santiago must find a way to feed and redeem himself.
6. *He resolves to sail far out to sea in search of a catch that will redeem his self-confidence.*
7. *Early the next morning, he descends to his fishing skiff, and rows out, into the dark sea, saying good-bye to his friend, the small boy, and the safety of the beach, perhaps for the last time.*
   There is a sense of impending danger and doom as he leaves.
8. *Later that day his luck turns and he hooks a giant marlin.*
   The long battle with the fish begins.
   And with himself as well; the battle for his life and his respect, fighting the effects of aging and the sea.
9. *For two days and two nights the marlin pulls him further out to sea.*
   Memories of his youth fill his vision, memories of battles fought and of hurts from which he has recovered. He tires, but convinces himself the battle is

only winnable if he can triumph mentally. Santiago is unable to loosen or even adjust his grip on the line, further tiring him. He fears that the marlin will sense his failing strength.

10. *Santiago is forced into disciplining himself to hold on and not tire until he lands the fish.*
11. *Finally, the fish tires and dies.*
12. *With great effort Santiago pulls the giant fish alongside his small boat and lashes it there (as it is far too big to put in the boat).*
13. *He starts home triumphantly, feeling redeemed and looking forward to the joy and adulation of the boy, Manolin.*
14. *Then the sharks come and begin tearing at the dead marlin.*
15. *Santiago fights off the sharks, endangering his own life, but to no avail.*
16. *By the time he rows into his home port, all that is left of the marlin is a skeleton and shreds of flesh.*
17. *Santiago is sad and feels defeated.*
18. *The young boy and the people of the village welcome him back, hailing his catch as heroic.*
19. *Santiago begins to understand that he has won the mental battle over his bad luck and aging, in spite of the loss of the fish.*
20. *He has had courage in the face of defeat.*
21. *His is a personal triumph won from loss.*
22. *He now has the confidence and vitality to go forth again and catch more and bigger fish.*

This is a simple story with limited scope, yet it has great power and emotion. There is no "romance" as such, except for that between the Old Man and the Sea (great descriptive title). The main character's "problem" that creates the "plot" is that he is growing old, has a streak of bad luck in fishing and must redeem himself to remain "relevant" in his society. A sub-plot is his relationship with Manolin, the boy who adores him and admires him in spite of his age and bad luck. Santiago's "opponent" is the same as his romantic interest... the sea, as suggested by the title. Integrating the plots,

Manolin's confidence in Santiago helps him to defeat his opponent in spite of losing the fish.

Sometimes, the simplest stories are the best when they are told with beauty and emotion. The several simple plots in "The Old Man and the Sea" that are used to tell the story integrate nicely.

The Sub-Plot

What constitutes a "sub-plot"?

A plot is the way you tell a story, so you have a sub-plot whenever you devote more than a little space to tell a story that supports the plot.

Readers can only deal with a limited number of characters before they "lose track"... and you lose them. Similarly, Readers can only deal with a main plot and perhaps two sub-plots at the most. After that, it becomes too confusing, and you lose them. So, work to retain simplicity!

Consider each new character, or new sub-plot, or new scene from the perspective of "do I really need this?" And, does the Reader really need this? A diversion that may interest you greatly may not be "needed" to tell the story you are telling. Don't let your interest for a potential sub-plot sidetrack you! Your sub-plot must contribute directly to your plot.

The Plot Beneath the Plot

As your plot unfolds using description, dialogue and action, there are really two main plots; the one that is being described and the one that is in the characters' minds (their internal conflict and emotions). This is a subtle difference that you must work to capture. For example, a character may say something but what he says is being forced by the circumstances of the scene. It is not what he/she would really like to say.

Or, a character may do something that isn't what he'd really like to do, but he/she does it because it is "the thing to do". You must capture for the Reader both the plot and the "plot beneath the plot".

Don't confuse the "plot beneath the plot" with a "sub-plot". The sub-plot simply means that there is more than one plot. The sub-plot is subordinate to the main plot and in some way linked to it. The "plot beneath the plot" is much more subtle. What does the character really believe and why is he/she doing and saying something different?

Keeping it Simple

Your plot is usually fairly simple when you start. As you go along in your writing, the plot tends to become more complex. You may "invent" more characters that you "need". Ideas occur to you that are "neat" and you want to use. You find that to "explain" things, you need to "make more things happen". It's okay for the plot to become a bit more complex than you originally envisioned. But not too much!

****

Chapter Ten
Logic, Flow, Tempo and Timing

A novel should "flow" from one point to the next in a logical way so that the Reader doesn't suddenly find him/her self in a place or time that makes no sense with what he/she has already read. The novel has to achieve a "tempo" that is neither boring nor so intense that the intensity becomes boring (like some of the wall to wall action flicks you see these days... ho hum!). The timing of events in the novel should be such that they create a sense of "discovery" in the Reader as he/she begins to fully identify with the characters and uncover their secrets.

Logic

Does the story make sense point to point? Can the Reader logically "follow"? Or does it hop from one point to the next without logic? As the story proceeds, each scene must have a logical sequence. Each Chapter must have a logical sequence. If "logic" is lacking, the Reader can only go so far before he/she asks "what does this have to do with what I have read?" That's a question you don't want the Reader to ask, as it's a sure signal that you have lost him/her.

Sometimes, there is dramatic effect to be achieved in "jumping" to a scene or chapter that is a radical departure from what has transpired to that point. That's okay, as long as the Reader can quickly associate the new scene or chapter with the story. "What is this?" asks the Reader. He/she reads on a bit. "Oh!" says the Reader. "I get it!" Now you have stirred the Reader's interest.

Example, Prelude to the "Jump To" Scene;
The Sachem of the Chesapeake, Chesapian, stood at the campfire of the elders as they considered those eligible to become Braves. The fire crackled and cast deep, flickering shadows over the Broad Waters. Chesapian was a tall man with a body weathered by the wind and sun. He wore the traditional cloth of the Chesapeake, a beaded deerskin waist

cloth and a cloak of raccoon hides against the cool evening. His head was bald except for a knot of hair pulled up into the center of his head. Five eagle feathers were clustered in the knot. He wore cloth bands around his legs lust below the knee, each adorned with dangling, colored threads.

Now we go to the "Jump To" scene (Suddenly, defying immediate logic, the scene shifts):

Example, The "Jump To" Scene;
The young gentleman Nathan Smythe watched the blue-green water glide by the ship making frothy white waves that trailed away from the oaken hull. It was a bright morning with calm seas and the salt laden wind felt good on his face. He took a deep breath and looked up at the billowing sails above him. It had been a trying passage for Her Majesty's pinnace "Discovery", experiencing high winds and seas on two occasions. She was the smallest of the three ships in the group sailing to the New World, being only of twenty tons and forty nine feet in length. She sailed beautifully, but the accommodations were cramped and miserable for the three officers, six sailors and twelve passengers. Now, flying fish skipped along the small waves and Nathan felt better than he had on the entire voyage.

"What?" says the Reader. "What is this?" He/she reads on.

Nathan walked to the officer of the watch, Squire Edward Bollingham. Bollingham was an older man with no hope of becoming Master of a Ship. He had a weathered face and gray whiskers that grew from his hairline down the sides of his face. He was rotund, generally sloppy in his appearance and irritable for much of the time. He was a bitter and hardened old seaman who had little use for young gentlemen such as Nathan. Bollingham was talking to Walter Hardgrave, the Boatswain of His Majesty's Ship Discovery, the senior man among the sailors.

New characters are thrust upon the Reader. We have "jumped" from the world to which the reader was accustomed, to a "different world". We had better show why soon, or we will lose the Reader.

Hardgrave was a tough looking seaman with ragged brown hair and a scar on his face that ran from the center of his forehead to the corner of his left eye and to his missing left ear. The sailors called him "Cutlass" as he was known for his proficiency with that weapon... as well as for the missing ear, sliced off by a French cutlass. It was said that he lost the ear boarding a French ship during which he ferociously killed nine French sailors with his cutlass.

"The crew been at sea a long time, Mister Bollingham," said Cutlass in a voice that sounded like the rattle of an anchor chain.*

"Yes," said Bollingham, "I am sure they would like to see the New World."

"After the Canary Islands, Dominica and the Virgin Isles, we need a place that will not roast us in a tropic sun!"

"Yes, yes... and perhaps with savages that are not so savage!"

"I hear the savage's women hereabouts run around with nothing on," said Cutlass. "We'll be glad to see some of 'em! It's been a long time since I had me a woman!"

"Perhaps," grunted Bollingham sensing an impropriety, "but we had best let them be, Mister Hardgrave. We should not want to incite trouble with any Savages we encounter."

"We'll soon be near the Virginias," said Cutlass with a secretive smile, "and we'll see!"

"Oh!" says the Reader. "I get it! The sailing ship 'Discovery' is something beyond Chataqua's 'unknown horizon'! I wonder what will happen!" Now, the Reader understands why the scene has "jumped". His/her logic is restored. His/her interest is peaked! And, we have had the opportunity to introduce new characters important to our story.

Consistency

You will find it difficult to be always consistent as you write the Rough-Through. After all, you are "pushing ahead" to get the story on paper. Does it make a difference that in the beginning you called the Chesapeake Bay "Broad Water" and later called it "Broad Waters"? Well, it doesn't make much difference in the Rough-Through, as long as you, the Author, know what it is. It makes a big difference in the final manuscript! Being consistent is part of being logical. In the Creative Reviews, you must do searches for terms where you may have been inconsistent in the Rough-Through and fix those inconsistencies.

The same is true of descriptions of characters. Don't let blue eyes change to brown eyes... that's a "transformation" you don't want!

Be consistent in your format! You may start off with only a vague idea of format... spacing between scenes, "break" indicators, etc. Develop the format firmly in your mind and in the Creative Reviews, achieve consistency in format.

Be careful to not give a hint of "something to come" and fail to have it come. Be sensitive to this in your Creative Reviews. Achieve consistency in events and characters.

Flow

A novel with good "flow" means that it transitions from point to point smoothly. It is not "jerky", in the writing or in the architecture of the story.

Example, "Jerky" writing;
The Sachem of the Chesapeake, Chesapian, stood at the campfire. The elders stood with him. The men eligible to become Braves stood there too. The fire crackled. Chesapian was a tall man. He had a weathered body. He wore a beaded deerskin waist garment and shawl. He had five eagle feathers in his hair.

Prose should be poetry in loose form. It should have a natural rhythm to it that is pleasing to read... and for listening. It should "flow" like a poem. The flow should have a changing rhythm. Longer sentences should occasionally be interrupted by shorter sentences. The short sentence among the longer more flowing sentences is a way of punctuating... a way of indicating that something different happened, or is happening. Avoid jerky sentencing. Avoid excessive use of colons and semicolons (which produce jerky sentencing).

Example, Smooth Flow;
The Sachem of the Chesapeake, Chesapian, stood at the campfire of the elders as they considered those eligible to become Braves. The fire crackled and cast deep, flickering shadows over the Broad Waters. Chesapian was a tall man with a body weathered by the wind and sun. He wore the traditional cloth of the Chesapeake, beaded deerskin waist garment and shawl, with five eagle feathers clustered in a knot covered with sea shells.

That has a nice "flow" to it. Now let's inject something short to "punctuate" the flow.

Example, Using "Prose Punctuation";
The Sachem of the Chesapeake, Chesapian, stood at the campfire of the elders as they considered those eligible to become Braves. The fire crackled and cast deep, flickering shadows over the Bay of Broad Waters. Chesapian was a tall man with a body weathered by the wind and sun. His face was stern. He wore the traditional cloth of the Chesapeake, beaded wais garment and shawl, with five eagle feathers clustered in a knot covered with sea shells.

Tempo

A Reader will tolerate a "low point" in the tempo for five to ten minutes of reading. After that, the Reader's "reading energy" will decline and he/she will put the book down until the next day when the "reading energy" is refreshed. He/she will read on with faith that a stimulating scene with intense plot action will quickly show up. If it doesn't, you have lost the Reader.

A long period of low "tempo" will lose the Reader!

The "tempo" is a series of "highs", "lows" and "middles" that creates a dynamic flow of the plot. It "picks you up" before things get too routine. See Figure 10-1.

Figure 10-1

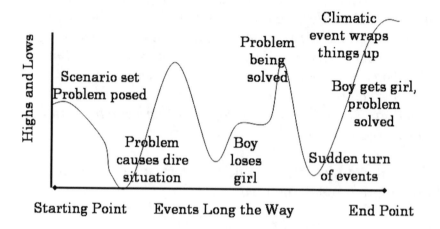

Highs and Lows of the Plot from the perspective of the hero/heroine

Timing

Timing is all important! It relates to the story, as well as the telling of the story. It is different than "tempo" (described above) in that it defines when things happen as opposed to the frequency at which things happen (defined "highs" and "lows"). Two important aspects of timing are:

1. The timing of introduction of characters for the best effect.

2. Hints of what is to come without disclosing the details, maintaining Reader suspense.

The Timing of Introduction of Characters

The timing of character introduction has several purposes:
1. It serves plot development in a logical sequence.
2. The time between new characters being introduced allows the Reader to become acquainted with characters already introduced before having to understand another one.

The Reader encounters Chataqua and Benatagua first. The Author develops their character enough for the Reader to understand who they are and what the "problem" is. Then comes Alanoas, the romantic interest, and her friend Musiasas. Then we encounter the villains for the first time; Maltakak, Malapok and Stakto.

Then we have Sachem Chesapian who holds the key to an essential part of Chataqua's problem; the making of a "Brave". Finally, we get a hint of what's beyond the "unknown horizon" for Chataqua with the introduction of the characters aboard the sailing ship "Discovery". Not much is said about "Discovery"... just enough to set the stage!

Hints of What is to Come

In the draft novel "The Unknown Horizon", hints of "what is to come" are carefully placed to maintain the Reader's interest, such as:

Example, Hints of What Is To Come;
1. *He looked out to sea toward the unknown horizon.*
2. *His father, Benatagua had braved the unknown... he must do the same.*
3. *Alanoas wondered if Chataqua would ever understand her love for him.*
4. *Malapok had embraced Alanoas.*

It is hard to give hints of what is to come if you don't know what is to come!

That's why the initial "direction" and "events along the way" for the novel are so important. You at least have some idea of "what is to come" (it may change as you proceed to write and let the story develop). When you give the Reader a hint of what is to come, make sure it is a "hint", not a disclosure.

Too Many Hints of What Is To Come

As you write the Rough-Through, not knowing the "whole story", you may begin to put words into a character's mouth that "lay out" what is going to happen. In doing this, you are "searching for your story"… laying out the story as you write. It's okay in the Rough-Through. But, it can't be in the final manuscript.

Putting in "too may hints of what is to come" is sometimes called "on the nose exposition". I call it "forecasting". You deliver too much of your plot as characters "talk about their intent" or by having the Storyteller describe their intent. By doing this, you take away the emotional suspense the Reader should have. Beware of this.

The Information Thread

I call revealing an important piece of information without devoting a lot of words in doing it an "information thread". Rather than devoting a scene to the revelation, you have a character "observe that it is so".

Example, Information Thread;
"Chataqua <u>saved Malapok from a kakapa</u>," said Manatapac.

****

Chapter Eleven
Creation of Dialogue

Spoken words are important! The way you say them is important! The words and their tone can make you or break you. They influence what other people think of you. They define your character. The characters in our novel are even more described and affected by the words we put in their mouths than we are in real life. We are limited in the number of words we can use in a novel... thus every word we use must "count"... must contribute to our story!

People are of most interest to the Reader, and the dialogue between people best illuminates them.

Among storytelling, description, action and dialogue, the four primary tools of the Author, dialogue is, in my view, the dominant tool. You will find some Authors who use description more than dialogue, and if that is your nature... have at it! My experience as an Author is that dialogue being dominant produces a novel that will better hold the Reader's interest... providing the dialogue is properly "punctuated " with adequate amounts of description and action. Creation of stimulating dialogue is, many times, the most difficult thing for a new Author to learn. The first time you try to write dialogue, it comes out "stilted"... looks okay in writing but doesn't "sound" like people really talk. Yet, you must learn to write dialogue well to have a WOW novel. A novel that is all description and descriptive action is... booore-ing!

Dialogue starts with the stimulus of the chapter and scene in which the dialogue takes place. That chapter and scene has:

1. A "point" it must make related to the story.
2. A setting or scenario... where it takes place, which includes location, weather, etc.
3. One or more characters who are in the scene for a reason related to it's "point".
4. A "situation" related to the point and involving the characters in the scene.

5. Certain "stimuli" that occur during the scene... a new character, an event, a weather change... something that directs the dialogue toward making the "point".

Once you establish "who" is in the scene, and have the first character "speak", write just as the conversation would progress. Punctuate the dialogue with descriptions of "body language" and action. Use dialogue tags. Understand that different kinds of dialogue should have a distinct rhythm that makes them read as they sound. Real conversation, angry exchange, consoling talk, arrogant pronouncement, etc. all have a different rhythm. Use dialogue to augment description in understanding of the setting. Use the dialogue tag or a direct observation by the character speaking.

Relax and let the dialogue flow naturally based on the characters involved and the situation they are in.

A character having "his/her say" demands a response... which demands a response... and away you go!
1. What would the main character in the scene "say", given the setting, situation and existing stimuli?
2. Who would he/she say it to?
3. How would he/she say it?
4. What would be said in return, and by whom?

The Author has to "know" his characters well enough to create a natural sequence of conversation between the characters. Each character must speak "in character". Once the dialogue is flowing, the place in which to introduce additional stimuli should become apparent. Beware of digressions as you "flow" the dialogue. You want to keep the "point" of the scene firmly in mind. Where do you want the scene to end (where to do a "fade")... and how does dialogue get you there.

As you write the Rough-Through, let your imagination and understanding of the characters take you where it will. In the Creative Reviews, it is likely that you will have to cut some of the dialogue out. Don't worry about it in the Rough-Through. Let the dialogue "flow" as you "hear it".

Punctuating the Dialogue

Be sure to punctuate your dialogue with description and action. The last thing you want is several "talking heads"… "he said this" and "she said that" on and on. Use storytelling and description to allow your character to "think" about what is being said and what is happening. Describe movements or habits of the characters to indicate how they "feel" about what is being said, or what is happening.

Get the "feel" for when there should be a pause in dialogue. Use description or action to create a pause. Write down the dialogue, then go back and "talk through it". I don't mean read it! I mean talk it through out loud with all the intonation, emotion and meaning that your character would use. When you talk through it, does it sound right? Feel right? Does it have the right rhythm? If not, fix it.

Dialogue always "sounds" different that it reads. You want it to sound like real people are talking.

When you punctuate the dialogue with a character's movement or habit, write it down then go back and "do it". I mean, do the motion yourself along with what the character is saying. Does it fit? Do you "feel" the emotion of the character expressed by the gesture or movement?

Example, Punctuating the Dialogue;
Chataqua walked along a sandy path from Chesepiooc to River-Where-Swift-Waters-Flow near the village of Shikiooc.
"I have faith that you will conquer Malapok," said Alanoas confidently.
Chataqua turned and faced her in the shadows of the beach. <u>He clenched his fists against his chest and tightened his lips.</u>
"I… I am building my strength," he said, his voice wavering as the sun began to fall from the sky.

Speak out the conversation. Clench your fists against your chest and tighten your lips! Does it feel like something one would do in telling your girl that you are building your strength? Is it something a Chesapeake Indian would do? Let's do a scene and concentrate on dynamic dialogue!

Example, Dynamic Dialogue;

Chataqua walked along a sandy path from Chesepiooc to River-Where-Swift-Waters-Flow near the village of Shikiooc.

"I have faith that you will conquer Malapok," said Alanoas confidently.

Chataqua turned and faced her in the shadows of the beach. He clenched his fists against his chest and tightened his lips.

"I... I am building my strength," he said.

He looked up, seeing that the sun had begun to fall from the sky.

"Don't be so hesitant!" exclaimed Alanoas with a flash of her brown eyes.

Chataqua was startled by Alanoas' outburst.

"I... I am not hesitant!" he said indignantly.

"You will show your endurance and bravery," said Alanoas in a strong voice. "I know you will."

We see here that Alanoas is strong beneath her beauty and submissiveness.

"I have prepared my mind for it," said Chataqua, staring at the determined face of Alanoas.

Alanoas stood on her toes, held Chataqua by the shoulders and kissed him on the cheek.

"I want to give you strength with my kiss," she said warmly.

Chataqua felt the softness of her kiss and it rushed through him like the wind. "Your kiss makes me weak in the knees!"

Alanoas looked hurt. "I would not want that!" she said.

Chataqua took her in his arms and held her closely. "Alanoas, I...I want your kiss. It does give me strength!"

"You joke with me," said Alanoas with a twinkle in her eye.

"I joke with myself," said Chataqua mischievously. "I want your kiss all the time... but I am afraid of it."

"Why is that?"

"It makes me…. strong, but weak at the same time!"

"Oh! You are fooling me," said Alanoas. "You cannot be weak and strong at the same time!"

"It is possible," said Chataqua. "I know that I have courage…I know that I have strength… but Malapok is older and stronger!"

"You must not fear Malapok," said Alanoas with a distasteful look. "He is all bluster… he is not a man of strength as you are!"

"I do not really fear him… I fear that he will make me look foolish."

Chataqua has the inner strength to achieve his goals. We also see the beginning of how the romance with Alanoas will aid Chataqua.

Hidden Meanings

As characters speak and take actions, they do not always say what they really feel or do things that reflect those feelings. There are often hidden feelings (subtext) lurking there. You can describe the hidden feelings that derive from internal conflicts in your storytelling.

Example, Description to Express Hidden Meaning;

"I have faith that you will conquer Malapok," said Alanoas confidently.

Chataqua turned and faced her in the shadows of the beach. He clenched his fists against his chest and tightened his lips.

"I… I am building my strength," he said.

Chataqua hoped that Alanoas did not detect that he was terrified about the upcoming fight with Malapok.

Sometimes much better than a character's thoughts are "nuances in speech" and/or "body language to indicate his/her feelings.

Example, Nuances in Speech and Body Language to Express Hidden Meaning;

"I have faith that you will conquer Malapok," said Alanoas confidently.

Chataqua turned and faced her in the shadows of the beach. He clenched his fists against his chest and tightened his lips.

"I... I am building my strength," he said, <u>his voice wavering.</u>

<u>*Chataqua looked at the ground and shifted his weight uneasily.*</u>

Dialogue Form

1. In writing dialogue, the most used form is:
"xxxxx xxxxx," said yyy.
    The phrase "said yyy" is a "dialogue tag".

2. A variation is:
"xxxxx xxxxx," said yyy, "and zzzz."
    Use this form for longer dialogue.

3. Dialogue usually stands alone as a paragraph. A variation is:
    [Action or description related to yyy]. "xxxx," said yyy.

Use all of these. In most cases, separate dialogue into its "own" paragraph, apart from paragraphs providing storytelling, description or action (occasional exception is number three above).

Where you can, avoid using "said yyy" all the time. This can be done when: there are only two characters involved in the dialogue; there are only a few characters and the Reader will "know" who's talking by what is said. When you leave out "said yyy", do it for two to four paragraphs, and then reintroduce it, just to provide the Reader with a reassuring frame of reference about who is speaking. Use each set of dialogue as an opportunity to employ an adjective or expression in the dialogue tag that defines the character's mood or appearance at the time.

Example, Using the Dialogue tag;
"I want to give you strength with my kiss," she said <u>*warmly, her face flushed.*</u>

A Reader will get tired of seeing "said Chataqua". It will be possible to refer to every character you create in different ways. Mix it up. Characters may obtain titles, nicknames or pet names in the sequence of events that can be used to identify the speaker. Use these to vary the "he/she said" tag in the dialogue.

Punctuation

This is not an English lesson, so I won't dwell on proper punctuation, except to make a few points:

1. Don't overuse the exclamation point. Many things will seem to need it as you write, but overuse diminishes the impact of when you really need it.
2. You may use the alliteration (...) to indicate a pause longer than a comma, but don't overuse it.
3. You may invoke Author's license to use non-standard punctuation if it fits your style (dashes, serial asterisks, etc.) but don't overuse it.

Using Dialogue for "The Fade"

Sometimes the best kind of "fade" to end the scene is the dialogue of a character. The fade dialogue is like a fade away scene in a movie or TV serial. For example, the TV serial "Law and Order" ends each episode with fade away dialogue.

Example, A Fade "Law and Order" Might Use;
"It turned out that he didn't break the law... but the law broke him," (sarcastically).

Cursing

Should your characters curse? If it fits their character to curse, then they should... to a point. However, the degree to which you use curse words in your novel is a strong factor in defining your book. The use of gore and sex (which we will discuss) has the same amplified effect.

The type of curse words used is important to consider. There are the mild curse words, such as "damn" and "hell". Then there are the harsher curse words, usually associated with sex or other bodily functions. Use the milder curse words if it's "what the character would say". Use them for emphasis and not as routine dialogue. Use the harsher curse words sparingly or not at all. Excess vulgarity will "turn off" many Readers.

Speaking Native American

I have used normal English in creating the dialogue between the Chesapeake Native Americans. I credit the Reader with understanding that they are actually speaking the Chesapeake language.

How do you handle the dialogue when the characters are actually speaking another language in the story? You have them speak intelligently in English just as they would be speaking intelligently in Chesapeake. You can suggest that another language is being used through the use of selected words from that language or a written accent. I use "Sachem" (an actual Algonquian word for "Chief" or "Tribe Leader"). In some cases, use your Author's license to make up a word, such as "kakapa" for "shark" (using three "power" consonants to suggest the nature of the beast).

We will face the situation where we have characters in a scene that speak different languages. You handle that just like you do in real life. You use body language, sign language, pictures and the gradual understanding of some of the words of the other language.

****

Chapter Twelve
Creation of Description and Action

Description and action "go together". The proper blending of the two is necessary to a good novel.

Creation of Description

Description is when the Author uses prose to describe something or someone. Don't confuse description contained in dialogue with "description". The words of the Storyteller are a form of description. As you write description, do not go on too long without interspersing some dialogue. I view description as something that is needed in the right amount, but should be avoided in long passages. Your style may be different, so have at it if that is so.

Good description becomes boring much faster than does interesting dialogue.

Dialogue is from the mouths of the characters. Description is most often from the mouth of the Storyteller... or from whatever perspective the story is being told. Of course, characters may "describe things and people" in their dialogue... and should. The Reader is most interested in the characters as people... and what they are saying... not what the Author is saying!

Description can be used in several ways:
1. Describing the characters.
2. Describing the environment or "things".
3. Describing the action.

Use vivid descriptions! Avoid adjective and metaphor redundancy; for example, the use of the word "vivid" too much. Vary your adjectives and metaphors! Use dialogue to have your characters (rather then the Storyteller) provide dramatic descriptions (which results in more and better dialogue)!

Description of the Characters

Characters are best physically described using dominant characteristics, such as the following:

1. A dominant facial or physical feature: a large nose; hair color; height; dole expression, etc.
2. An indication of physical capability: athletic; slothful; powerful; lazy; talented, etc.
3. An adjective relating to physical nature: fat; skinny; pudgy; beautiful; repugnant, etc.
4. A physical habit: tossing of the hair; lifting an eyebrow; scratching the nose when nervous, etc.
5. A characteristic that is normally unseen but manifests itself through speech and actions; intelligent; stupid; humorous; playful, loyal, noble, ambitious, etc.

Description of the Environment

Many Authors pride themselves in using description to paint glowing pictures of the setting. Older style writing is replete with this. Modern writing uses it much less. My advice is to avoid it except as needed to "set the scene"! Use dialogue where the character speaking observes a characteristic of the environment in preference to the Author's description.

If you want to paint a picture... paint a picture! This is a novel!

Now having warned you away from too much description of the environment, what should you write? What is the environment? Description of the environment involves:

1. The location: country; town; where (train station, tugboat, a green meadow).
2. The dynamics of the setting: dynamic (as in horseback riding through a forest); static (as in sitting in a room).
3. The nature of the setting: rural; urban; beautiful; foreboding, etc.
4. The background: what's going on in the "background"... i.e. the scene behind the scene (the

foreground may be a sword fight between characters, while the background could be a full scale battle... or a cliff above a running river).

5. Physical things important to the scene: stairs with an ornate rail; an old horse munching grass in the field.
6. The weather conditions: bright and sunny day; raining; stormy; bitter cold.
7. The sounds: train whistles in the background; birds singing; owls hooting; brook babbling.
8. The smells: pungent smell of rotting corpses; the perfume of beautiful flowers; the acrid smell of gun smoke.
9. The "feeling": Ominous; Gay (in the traditional sense of that word); Adventurous; Sad; Spooky; Happy.

As you proceed in the scene, you should use description and dialogue (observation of the environment by a character for some reason) employing some or all of these as may suit your purpose.

As you write, one part of you is writing the story, and another part of you is "adding color". Both parts of the Author must be engaged at all times!

Let's look at an excerpt from a Master of Description. The following is an excerpt from Jack London's classic "To Build a Fire":

Example, Master of Description;
Day had broken cold and gray, exceedingly cold and gray, when the man turned aside from the main Yukon trail and climbed the high earth-bank, where a dim and little traveled trail led eastward through the fat spruce timberland. It was a steep bank, and he paused for breath at the top, excusing the act to himself by looking at his watch. It was nine o'clock. There was no sun nor hint of sun, though there was not a cloud in the sky. It was a clear day, and yet there seemed an intangible pall over the face of things, a subtle gloom that made the day dark, and that was due to the absence of sun.

Not only does this passage have many dynamic adjectives and metaphors, it also has a rhythm... a poetic "flow" to the prose. Strive for rhythm and flow.

Louisa May Alcott in her novel "Little Women" written in the early Nineteenth Century starts off in Chapter One with dialogue and then "pauses" to insert a description that also has a rhythm and beauty all its own.

Example, Rhythm and Beauty in Description;

As young Readers like to know "how people look", we will take this moment to give them a little sketch of the four sisters, who sat knitting away in the twilight, while the December snow fell quietly without, and the fire crackled cheerfully within. It was a comfortable room, though the carpet was faded and the furniture very plain, for a good picture or two hung on the walls, books filled the recesses, chrysanthemums and Christmas roses bloomed in the windows, and a pleasant atmosphere of home peace pervaded it.

I don't recommend the "we will take this moment to describe" approach, as description should be blended with action and dialogue. But, it was an accepted method in Alcott's day.

Margaret, the eldest of the four, was sixteen, and very pretty, being plump and fair, with large eyes, plenty of soft brown hair, a sweet mouth, and white hands, of which she was rather vain. Fifteen-year-old Jo was very tall, thin, and brown, and reminded one of a colt, for she never seemed to know what to do with her long limbs, which were very much in her way. She had a decided mouth, a comical nose, and sharp, gray eyes, which appeared to see everything, and were by turns fierce, funny, or thoughtful. Her long, thick hair was her one beauty, but it was usually bundled into a net, to be out of her way. Round shoulders had Jo, big hands and feet, a flyaway look to her clothes, and the uncomfortable appearance of a girl who was rapidly shooting up into a woman and didn't like it.

Elizabeth, or Beth, as everyone called her, was a rosy, smooth-haired, bright-eyed girl of thirteen, with a shy

*manner, a timid voice, and a peaceful expression which was
seldom disturbed. Her father called her "Little Miss
Tranquility", and the name suited her excellently, for she
seemed to live in a happy world of her own, only venturing out
to meet the few whom she trusted and loved. Amy, though the
youngest, was a most important person, in her own opinion at
least. A regular snow maiden, with blue eyes, and yellow hair
curling on her shoulders, pale and slender, and always
carrying herself like a young lady mindful of her manners.*

You can't ask for better or more thorough description. Can
you guess which sister is modeled after Louisa May? For
modern writing it is, in my opinion, a bit too much
description in one place... flowery description structured in
long sentences. But, it is very good description!

One has description of all sorts of things about the
environment in Alcott's text; December snow; crackling fire;
comfortable room; faded carpet; atmosphere of home peace.

There are also ample examples of the descriptions of
people; plump and fair; large eyes; soft brown hair; sweet
mouth; white hands; rosy, smooth haired; bright eyed; shy
and timid; peaceful; tall and thin, sharp gray eyes; comical
nose; decided mouth; snow maiden; yellow hair; pale and
slender. A plethora of vivid adjectives and metaphors!

Beautiful Writing

"Beautiful writing" along with passionate, interesting
characters and a suspenseful plot "makes" a novel. Just what
is "beautiful writing"? Does that mean description of
beautiful things? No, but that's part of it, just as "beautiful"
action and dialogue are. We just observed an example of
"beautiful writing" in the London and Alcott excerpts. Let's
look at an example from Hemingway's Old Man and the Sea.

Example, Beautiful Writing;
   *Just before it was dark, as they passed a great island of
Sargasso weed that heaved and swung in the light sea as
though the ocean were making love with something under a*

yellow blanket, his small line was taken by a dolphin. He saw it first when it jumped in the air, true gold in the last of the sun and bending and flapping wildly in the air.

What characterizes "beautiful writing"?
1. It is a poem without rhyme.
2. It "flows" with a rhythm all its own.
3. It uses "beautiful" words.
4. It has a style all its own (that of the Author).
5. It has "syntax punctuation", that is longer sentences punctuated by shorter, more abrupt sentences.
6. It uses interesting and dynamic metaphors (a figure of speech used to compare an object to some abstract object; an analogy).
7. It uses highly descriptive adjectives.
8. It catalyzes vivid images in the mind of the Reader.
9. It seems to have motion all its own.
10. It causes the Reader to say or think "WOW!"

Can you execute a novel that employs "beautiful writing"? Perhaps. In the Rough-Through, you are setting the stage for that. But your first priority in the Rough-Through is to build a good, logical story. Maybe you write "beautifully" anytime you put a pen to paper, or a finger to the keyboard. If you are like me, your first effort is "okay". Later in the Creative Reviews I will look at everything I have written and see if it can be made "more beautiful". It is an art to do this! It must be done, not in the style of London and Hemingway, but in our own style... a "beautiful" version of our own writing. For example, we have written:

Example, The First Effort;
Chataqua stood gazing at the fast waters as they rushed into the river from the Broad Waters. The sun was falling from the sky. The next sunrise, he must face Malapok and fight him for survival. He must openly demonstrate his endurance and bravery... he knew that. But could he?

Now, let's make it "more beautiful".

Example, After a Focus on Beautiful Writing;

Chataqua stood gazing at the fast waters as they rushed into the river from the Broad Waters, churning and swirling past the poles that held the fish nets like small angry demons intent on becoming whirlpools of destruction. The sun was falling from the sky like a fireball seeking the coolness of the water. It sunk lower and lower over the Land-Where-the-Sun-Sets, purple and orange hues reflecting against long, wispy clouds. The next sunrise, he must face his malevolent enemy, Malapok, and fight him for survival. He must demonstrate his endurance and bravery... he knew that. But could he? He gritted his teeth, picked up a smooth rock and threw it into the churning water. Then he threw another, and another, each time hurling the rock harder as if at the face of the smirking Malapok.

We tried to make the paragraph "more beautiful"... more exciting! We added new adjectives and a dynamic metaphor. We shortened a sentence to gain better rhythm. We added the descriptive "rock throwing" sentence. Is it "more beautiful"? How would you do it?

Beautiful writing may take more words... but don't use too many. Concise beauty has a beauty all its own.

Style

What is your "style"? Have you worked to perfect a certain style, or is your style "what it is"? There are many types of style. Young Authors usually start off with a certain style which then evolves as they continue to write and become more mature. Examples of "styles" are:
1. Abrupt-to the point.
2. Flowery.
3. Descriptive.
4. Action oriented.

Should you have a style model? Should you try to model your style after Hemingway... or whoever? It is helpful to read the modern classics and analyze the style. It helps you mature as an Author. But, I recommend that you not worry about your "style". You should focus on writing a good story and writing it beautifully. Your style is what it is, and it will evolve.

Creation of Action

Action is a coordinated blend of description and dialogue. A modern Reader thrives on action! In a novel, the mix should be about equal between the two. I err in favor of dialogue in a novel. In a screenplay (a visual medium), the emphasis is on the visual... action.

Action is dynamic description of something exciting, such as a battle, a fight, a romantic scene or a confrontation. It often involves some kind of "conflict", either physical or emotional conflict. Action helps the Author establish the tempo of the book. It defines the "highs". How does one best describe it?

1. Action is usually initiated using description, but it can begin with dialogue (and often should).
2. Action should be thoroughly mixed with dialogue.
3. Action should contain vivid description.
4. Action should use dynamic words.
5. Action should be fairly detailed, following the actual movements of the characters closely.
6. Action uses the element of surprise and shock.
7. Action must be realistic enough to "put the Reader into the action".

Initiation of Action

Resist the temptation to begin the scene with a long paragraph describing the setting and what the characters are doing. Start with a short description or brisk dialogue that contains action as well as a hint of where the characters are.

Example, Starting an Action Scene With Description;
Chataqua and Malapok circled each other on the sand of the beach in the morning sun. Chataqua tried to get position on his foe.

Example, Starting an Action Scene With Dialogue;
"We begin the fight, Young Squirrel!" said Malapok, grinning maliciously in the morning sun.
"I am ready!" said Chataqua feeling the sand of the beach between his toes as he tried to get position on his foe.

Action and Dialogue

Use dialogue to describe the action. This can be done inside the dialogue quotations, or in the identifying phrase that accompanies the dialogue (the dialogue tag).

Example, Using the Dialogue Tag to describe Action;
"You are not so quick, Young Squirrel," muttered Malapok, <u>swinging his arms at Chataqua in a series of rapid blows.</u>

Action and Description

Remember that when you use description, you are not just "describing" something. You are doing that, of course, but you are also setting the "mood". Use words that are as powerful as you can (without being trite).

Example, Description That Includes Action;
The sun was low in the sky as Chataqua and Malapok <u>circled </u>each other cautiously on the beach near the Broad Waters. Sea birds <u>glided </u>on a slight breeze that rippled the waters into foam as it lapped at the shore. Chataqua and Malapok were both naked except for loin cloths that held their manhood to them. Suddenly, Malapok <u>darted </u>in and <u>grabbed</u> Chataqua by the leg.

Action and Dynamic Words

Use dynamic words that help to portray action. Verbs are the most dynamic. There can also be dynamic adjectives.

Example, Using Dynamic Words;
Suddenly, Malapok <u>darted </u>in and <u>grabbed</u> Chataqua by the leg. With a strong <u>pull</u>, Malapok <u>flipped</u> Chataqua off his

feet, held his leg and began to drag him through the gritty sand.

There are several dynamic words (verbs) in this example: darted, grabbed, pull, flipped, held, dragged. There are also a few dynamic adjectives: strong, gritty. Generally speaking, dynamic words (verbs and adjectives) tend to begin with the following letters (with word examples):

1. D... darted, damaged, dare, dash, deflect, defy, dilemma
2. F... force, false, feisty, fall, ferocious, festive, fill, flout, flow
3. G... grab, grow, gasp, gird, glutton, goggle, grind, groan, grip
4. H... harbinger, hang, harp, heavy, hirsute, hog, hop
5. J...jam, jangle, jerk, jest, jig, jog, juggle, joy, jump
6. K... keep, kick, kid, kill, kindle, knock, knot, knuckle
7. P...pad, pack, panic, parachute, parley, pass, pen, punch
8. R...rabble, radiate, rail, rat, ransom, razz, retract, regress

These letters are dynamic because they have an "explosive" pronunciation. Other words are dynamic because of the picture they conjure in the Reader's mind, such as "strong". Alliterations are powerful if not used too much. An alliteration is a technique in which successive words (or nearly successive words) begin with the same consonant sound or letter.

Examples, Using an Alliteration;
1. *Chataqua punched powerfully at the retreating Malapok...*
2. *Chataqua pulled and punched powerfully at the retreating Malapok...*

Try saying these with an explosive "p".

Action and Detail

Do not be afraid to provide more detail in an action scene than in other parts of your novel. You should be able to "see" what is happening in your head and describe it in sufficient detail that the Reader will also "see" it.

Example, Detail in an Action Scene;
Chataqua rolled over and broke Malapok's grip on his leg. He jumped to his feet, covered with sand. As he turned to Malapok, the older Brave slapped him in the face with an open palm that humiliated more than it stung. Chataqua raised his hands in defense and turned away another slap, feeling anger rise in him like a mighty storm.

Here the continuity of action is provided in some detail so that the Reader can follow: *rolled over, broke Malapok's grip, jumped to his feet, turned to Malapok, slapped him in the face, raised his hands in defense,* and *turned away another slap.*

The Map

I always use a map as a valuable reference. Studying it will give you ideas for your story. It may be: a real map; a fictional map; a combination of the above (with your own names for things).

If you are writing a fantasy novel with its own geography, this is an essential step. You are creating "your own world" from your imagination. When you refer to a geographical place early in the text, you want to make sure you refer to it the same way later on.

It is important that time and distance factors in your novel are consistent and "real" (even if based on fantasy geography). If someone runs from Point A to Point B, it should take the time that it takes a person to run that distance... and so forth. Use the map!

You should populate your map with references that will help you write. I mark them with distance scales. If there is a swampy area, mark where it is. It could be important to your story. If there is a thickly forested area, mark it. Do some research on the type of vegetation that grows there. If possible, visit the area or an area like it so that you get the "feel" of it and hear its sounds. If there is a heavily populated area, jot down where the key buildings are (the ones you use in the story). Again if possible, visit the area or one like it, note the types of buildings and houses and listen to the sounds.

You will need the map, the nature of the geography and its "sounds" to use description successfully in your manuscript. See Appendix B.

Action, Surprise and Shock

Surprise and shock are powerful tools of the Author in creating action. The Author may write that a character is surprised or shocked... or both. It is usually better to use dialogue to express shock or surprise. You should want to surprise or shock... or both, the Reader!

Example, Using Shock;

Chataqua rolled free, jumped to his feet and ran into the surf. He had to find a way to nullify Malapok's superior strength! Chataqua had always been a strong swimmer. Was Malapok a match for him in the water?

Malapok followed Chataqua into the surf until he waded in chest deep water. "This fight is to be on the beach!" shouted Malapok, anxiety in his voice.

"This fight can be wherever it goes!" shouted Chataqua defiantly.

<u>Malapok saw the fin in the water</u> just beyond where the surf was breaking and stepped back in fear. Was it Kakapa, the Fish-That-Eats-Men? He watched with wide and wild eyes as Chataqua entered water up to his chest near the breaking waves and beckoned to Malapok.

"Are you afraid to fight me?" shouted Chataqua. "Are you not so brave, Malapok?"

Malapok watched in fear as the fin came near to where Chataqua stood in the glimmering water. He started to shout, but fear clogged his throat and he only watched in horror.

The Reader was made to wonder how Chataqua could possibly stand up to the older, stronger Malapok. Now, a solution starts to suggest itself... fight him in the water where his quickness and strength is somewhat nullified by the water. Fight him where he is not "at home"! Now... a surprise... the fin in the water! And... a point of suspense! Is it a kakapa? This is also a good "fade" point where a scene can be ended, leaving the Reader to want to move quickly to the next scene to find out what happens. You probably want to know what happens too! Patience... patience... you will find out, just as will our Reader!

The Gore Factor

Does a novel have to contain gory description to get the Reader's attention? The answer is no... not necessarily, but you can use some of it if that's "your style". What captures a Reader is the emotion you create using the characters, situations, settings and the degree of surprise and shock! Gore for the sake of gore is unprofessional. If the use of a bloody description serves the purpose of creating emotion, surprise or shock and it is placed correctly, it can be useful.

I do not recommend detailed descriptions of gore. You can use a bloody situation described in minimum detail to trigger the Reader's imagination... and leave it up to the Reader to fill in the picture at which you have hinted.

Example, Using Gore;
When they were boys, Chataqua, Manatapac and Malapok swam in the surf at Water-That-Never-Ends nearly every day. One day, they decided to swim near the shore at dusk. The sun was sinking lower and lower and the Water-That-Never-Ends was calm and shimmering with slanting rays of the sun that colored the water purple. Manatapac began to wade ashore.

"Come out," called Manatapac. "We must return to Chesepiooc before it is dark" Suddenly, he saw a gray fin in the shallow water. "Kakapa!" he shouted in fear.

Malapok backed away from the fin as it approached him, his eyes wide with terror. The fin submerged in front of him and he felt a bump on his side.

"Kakapa!!" shrieked Malapok.

Malapok paddled furiously toward the sandy beach. Chataqua swam toward him, knowing that the kakapa would follow Malapok into the shallows. Malapok felt a searing pain in his leg. Chataqua saw the water become red with blood. He dove beneath the waves and saw a small kakapa of about an arm's length and a half pushing and biting at Malapok's leg. He grabbed the fish by the tail, pulled himself forward and began pounding it with his fist around its sensitive eyes. The kakapa released Malapok and turned, its black eyes staring without emotion at Chataqua. Then it flipped its tail and swam away. Malapok made it to the beach, his left leg ripped open at the calf. Bright red blood stained the beach.

That should be enough to let the Reader feel the horror of a shark attack and fill in the gory details in his mind. With respect to the use of gore, be sure you define your novel consistent with what "makes you comfortable" and what your intended market demands.

****

Chapter Thirteen
The Structure of a Novel

What is the structure of a novel? How do you "build it? A typical novel is made up of:

Chapters
> Scenes
>> Elements of the Scene

The structure of a novel is suggested in Figure 13-1.

Figure 13-1

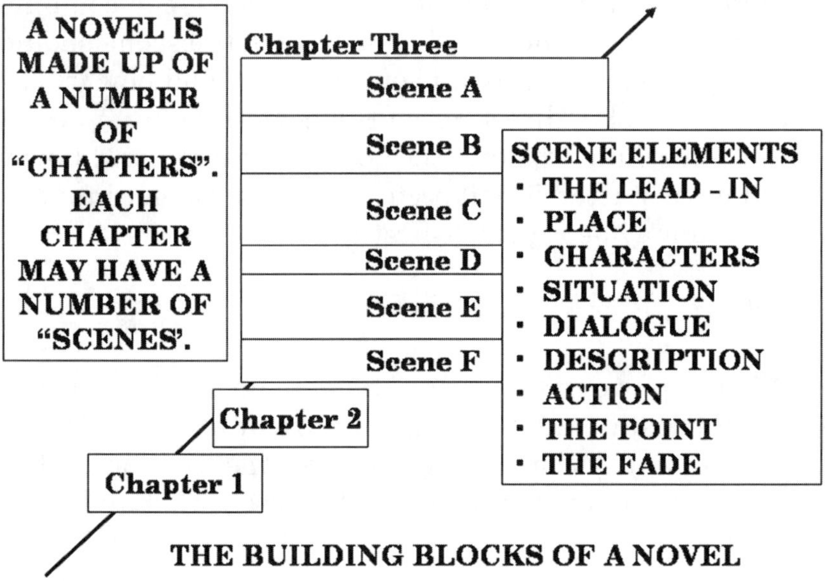

THE BUILDING BLOCKS OF A NOVEL

There are certainly alternative ways to structure a novel. You should view this figure as a guideline, not intended to stifle artistic initiative. The "scene" is the basic building block of a novel. Each scene within a Chapter should contribute to the "role" the chapter is taking in satisfying the novel's "storytelling direction". One or more "story events" take place in each scene. Scenes "logically" follow one another. This does not mean, however, that scenes necessarily pick up in time where the last scene left off. It may, but most often the Author skips to the next pont in time in which a scene can be used to "make a point" in the story. The next "point in time" follows the last point logically.

The Scene; Lead - In

One approaches the start of a scene just as one approaches the start of the novel. Each scene is a "little story" unto itself. What scenario is needed to satisfy the "role" of the scene in the novel's "direction"? What characters must be there? Avoid long descriptive lead-in paragraphs. Try to open with a character saying something.

A novel is a series of scene starts, which when combined, tell the story in the novel. The opening of the scene should in some way suggest the "point" of the scene" and how it contributes to the "direction" of the novel.

Do "something" to start the scene! Get it going... how you should have started it will occur to you as you get into the scene (you may be right the first time).

The Scene; Place

Where are we in this scene? Seldom do you start a scene with a stark statement such as "we are at place X". That's rather dull and "formula-like". Rather, the location of the scene may be defined through subtle description and dialogue.

The Scene; Characters

Who is in this scene? One does not begin with a statement that "characters X, Y and Z are in this scene". Again, too dull! Rather, one uses dialogue, description and action to introduce each character as they "appear" in the scene. The time they appear and how they appear is a part of the tempo and flow of the story. It can also provide drama, such as the sudden arrival of a character not expected.

The Scene; Situation

What situation exists in this scene that the characters must deal with? The situation is created as the scene progresses, again using dialogue, description and action. One does not "define" the situation immediately at the start of the scene... one "shapes" the situation so that Reader comes to understand it (and "discovers" as he/she reads).

The Scene; Dialogue

What dialogue takes place between the characters in this scene? A scene can be all dialogue (or all description), or better, a mix of dialogue, action and description. My style is an emphasis on "punctuated dialogue ". I believe that the most interesting parts of a novel to the Reader are the characters and their interaction, which is defined in the large part by dialogue, punctuated with descriptions of events, body language, expressions and other actions.

The most interesting part of a novel is the characters and their interaction!

The Scene; Description

How is description used to enhance the scene? As I have emphasized, a careful balance between description, action and dialogue is essential. Readers will tolerate just so much description of "the beautiful trees"... the "stimulating character"... the "rough motorcycle ride"... etc. They become impatient to "hear" the characters. They become impatient for action. In my view, description is best carried out by action and dialogue rather than story-teller ramblings.

The Scene; Action

What action takes place in this scene to progress the situation? "Action" can be inserted using either dialogue or description.

Example, Action in the Dialogue;
  "I have a knife, Malapok," said Chataqua in a threatening voice.

The example suggests action (a knife threat). It also contains description in the part of the dialogue that identifies the speaker (...in a threatening voice).

Example, Action in the Description;
  Chataqua pointed the knife at Malapok in a threatening manner.

In this example, the same action is defined by descriptive text. Which method is better? As I have said, a careful balance between dialogue and description is very important.

The Scene; Point

What is the "point" of this scene? Why does it exist in your novel? How does it contribute to the purpose of the chapter in the novel? Many new Authors make the mistake of writing a scene because it is interesting and forgetting the flow of the story... and therefore writing a scene that does not make a useful "point" in the story (even though it is an interesting scene). Be very sensitive to this.

It is easy to write a "good" scene that does not successfully make a "point" in the story.

Suppose that the scene within the chapter is designed to make the point that the villain is basically a coward.

Example, Making the Point;
  The darkness of the swamp at night was overwhelming. Chataqua couldn't see a thing, but he heard a faint noise in front of him. He knew it was Malapok. It had to be!
  "I have a knife, Malapok," said Chataqua in a threatening voice. He hoped he sounded convincing, as he was gripped with fear.

There was an ominous silence. Chataqua slashed with the knife at a tree trunk. It made a loud cutting sound into the tender wood of the pine tree.

"You wouldn't dare to attack me, Young Squirrel" said Malapok in a wavering voice that came from Chataqua's left. It sounded close.

"I will," said Chataqua in a tense voice. "I will if I must!"

Chataqua heard heavy breathing.

"I have a knife also," said the voice of Malapok in the darkness.

"Then we shall fight!" said Chataqua. "Come out of the darkness!"

There was a silence, followed by footsteps that went away.

"Show yourself, Malapok!" shouted Chataqua.

"I have no desire to kill you, Young Squirrel!" said Malapok, now further away, his voice fading "but you will regret the day you tried to take Alanoas away from me!"

Chataqua stood motionless behind the pine tree, the fear he had still gripping him. What would Malapok do?

The point that Malapok is cowardly is developed through action and dialogue... not blatantly stated ("Malapok is a coward").

The Scene; Fade

Once you get the scene going, it is hard to stop. How does one gracefully end the scene once the point is made? How does it lead logically into the next scene? How long should a scene be?

A scene should be as long as it needs to be to make the "point" successfully and artistically... but no longer. Scenes can be very short (a paragraph, even a sentence). Scenes can be long, but not too long. You don't want the Reader to feel that the scene is dragging, digressing or becoming uninteresting. Once the Reader digests the "point", he/she is ready to move on. Use only what you need to make the point.

How do you do stop (end) the scene without making it sound awkward? You do it using "the fade". Examples of several types of "fades" are;

1. A profound statement by a character (a one liner).
    "Well, Malapok," said Chataqua, "I am not yet a Brave... but I am not a coward!"
2. A humorous statement by a character (a humorous one liner).
    "You run away like a frightened deer, Malapok!" exclaimed Chataqua with a nervous laugh.
3. A hanging question.
    "So, Malapok, what now?" shouted Chataqua into the darkness of the swamp.
4. A descriptive lead-in to the next scene.
    Chataqua and Malapok stood facing each other tensely in the clearing suddenly lighted by the fire.

Format

What do scenes and chapters look like? Well... anyway you choose. Some Authors only number their chapters. Others only title the chapters. Some do both (which is what I recommend). The number and title of a chapter may appear centerline or left aligned (I recommend the use of bold font). Scenes within a chapter are normally separated from other scenes by an extra space or some type of symbol, such as:

****

How many scenes per chapter? Let chapter length be the driver. There should be as many scenes as fit into 4,000 – 6,000 words (or whatever you choose as your consistent guideline for chapter length). The scenes in a chapter preferably have some relationship to one another (same time frame, etc.), but not necessarily.

The Author should pay attention to format and be consistent. A neat, "clean" manuscript is important. Manuscripts are normally double spaced, one side only. I frequently use 1.5 line spacing to save paper. I use the Garamond (12) font. It is a space saver and is acceptable to all agents and publishers. Times New Roman and Century Schoolbook are commonly used fonts. Century Schoolbook is larger and easier to read, but will make your novel have more pages. This book uses Century Schoolbook font, as I want to make it as easy on the Reader's eyes as I can. Garamond is okay… but not for an "instructive" book. Be sure to use a "serif" font such as those mentioned (they have "little ears" at the top and bottom of the letters). Garamond, Times New Roman and Century Schoolbook are "serif" fonts. "Sans serif" fonts (no "little ears"), such as Arial, are not normally used.

A good novel is at least 80,000 words in length. An upper limit in most cases is 130,000 words. There is a small market for larger works, but these are special case novels. There is also a market for "novelettes" (50,000 to 80,000 words). At some lower point, you have a "short story". Your Rough-Through should aim for 70,000 to 90,000 words, leaving room for additions during the Creative Reviews.

How many chapters should there be? As many as you want within the total length discussed above. Some Authors like "short" chapters, believing that Readers prefer that format. A short chapter would be 2,000 words or less. I prefer 4,000 – 6,000 words per chapter. I believe that the contents of a chapter will suggest when it should logically end. If it goes more than 6,000 words, I may shorten it, or put a scene from it into another chapter. If I need only 2,000 words for the logical length of a chapter… okay. The real test is where the various scenes logically "belong". Chapters can be of differing lengths as long are none are "too short" or "too long".

Page Characteristics

It is okay to submit your manuscript using 8.5" X 11" page size. Use left and right margins of at least ¾ inches on the left and ½ inch on the right (this book), or whatever your publisher specifies. Indent your paragraphs by ¼ inch (this book) or ½ inch. Use double spacing for a manuscript to be submitted to a publisher. 1 ½ spacing is normally acceptable. Check with your publisher. Never do a manuscript in single spacing. Always number your pages (no chapter numbers in the page number). Do not try to make your pages look "fancy". The publisher is interested in your writing ability, not your prowess with software.

The Genre

Genre means the "type" or "class" of book or novel. It is a category of artistic endeavor marked by a distinctive style, form or content. Publishers and Distributors will classify your novel in some "genre". Examples of genre used are: action-adventure, comedy, drama, family, fantasy, horror, martial arts, mystery, romance, science-fiction, sports, supernatural, and general fiction.

Each genre has, over time, developed a "style" that determines "how it is viewed". For example, "romance" does not mean just a romantic novel. It has come to be associated with cheap paperback books that contain steamy love stories and a lot of torrid sex. "Mystery" usually means a detective murder mystery story, even though the word "mystery" can mean much more than that. "Action-adventure" and "general fiction" are "safe" genre.

Research

The need for research should never prevent you from STARTING!

Yes, you can start a novel without doing any research... right off the "top of your head".

You can do this because research doesn't play a strong role in "the story", unless of course it is research in seeking a Seminal Idea. Research "fills in" and makes the details of your story accurate. You eventually need some research.

Background Research

Background research means reading several books or articles about the general subject or area in which you intend to write. If you are already very knowledgeable in the area in which you intend to write (and you should be, to some degree), then background research is less necessary.

In background research, you are not "looking for something". You are establishing general familiarity with your subject area.

There is no bibliography in a novel! You aren't going to have to create a list of references as you did writing your school thesis. You are reading to get a "feel" that will help you when you start writing.

Spot Research

Suppose you start writing and you call your Chesapeake Native American character "Joe" just to get started figuring out the story. You know you'll have to do better than that with Native American names, so at some point you do spot research on names of the Chesapeake Tribe. You pause and look up key words "Chesapeake Native American Tribe" and "Chesapeake Tribe". You do it at the library and you do it on line using the internet. Spot research is done "on the spot" as you are writing.

Spot Research is looking up something specific as you are writing.

The internet is great for spot research. If you are writing along and you pen something of which you're not sure, pause and go to the internet browser. Type in a key word associated with your need and see what you come up with. If the first key word you use doesn't yield what you need, try another... and another.

In Depth Research

You shouldn't try to do in depth research "first" as it will slow you down... a writer's quagmire. I do most of my in depth research after I have completed the "Rough-

Through"… the first draft that contains the essence and sequence of the story.

In depth research is the process of filling in and validating the details.

As you hammer out the story, you will get a feel for the type of in depth research you will need. Make a list and keep it on the side for future reference. For example, if I am going to write a novel about the Chesapeake Native Americans at the time the English settlers arrived in 1607, I will have to eventually do some research into: Native American dress at the time; Native American culture; Native American agriculture; Native American weapons; the geography of the area at the time; English ships of the time; English dress, armor and weapons.

Be Organized

I won't dwell here trying to tell you how to organize your research and the material that you "dig up". Simply stated, put things where you can logically find them in a reasonable amount of time.

Writing Without Fear

As you write along, do not be afraid to assume something like a type of weapon, or a manner of dress, etc. You may have to "fill it in" later… so flag it in some way in your manuscript so you can find it later (a double asterisk works). You can "find" ** and delete it later using the "replace" function.

****

Chapter Fourteen
Perspective and Tense

Perspective defines "who is telling the story"... or "who is the Storyteller". It must be well understood by the Author and applied consistently throughout the novel.

It is easy to get caught up in a scene and slip out of perspective.

To a large degree, the story is defined by who is telling it. Examples of Author perspectives are: the hero first person; the observer first person; the third person storyteller; the omniscient storyteller; and multiple perspectives.

New Authors many times "slip out of tense". Beware of this. Be consistent with the reference tense.

The Hero First Person Perspective

The story is written as though the hero is telling it. This is a very "personal" perspective for a novel. It is also one of the most difficult ways to write.

Example, Hero First Person Perspective:
I stood at Point-Where-Great-Waters-Meet and gazed out at the horizon where the sun is born each day. I wondered how my father felt when he canoed into the unknown to the north and found a new land of abundant oysters and flat fish. Was he as fearful as I as I gazed at the unknown horizon?

Use of this perspective limits the Author in several ways: the hero becomes the Storyteller; one can only write about what the hero "sees"; the hero has to be in every scene; one can only write about what the hero "thinks"; it defines the gender of the person telling the story, which is important when considering the "type" of book and the intended Readers.

The primary advantages of this perspective are: a very personal approach that causes the Reader to closely and quickly identify with the hero; it "personalizes" the reading experience and is very useful in stories that have a few characters and a limited scenario. It is used frequently in exposés and "true life adventures".

One can also choose to use the present tense in this perspective (even more difficult).

Example, Hero First Person Present Tense:
I stand at Point-Where-Great-Waters-Meet and gaze out at the horizon where the sun is born each day. I wonder how my father felt when he canoed into the unknown to the north, and found a new land of abundant oysters and flat fish. Was he as fearful as I as I gaze at the unknown horizon?

Note that writing in the present tense does not necessarily mean that everything is in the present tense. *"Was he as fearful..."* is in the past tense because it refers to the past "with respect" to the hero first person story teller. The tense of the story teller is very important in choosing the perspective. It is the "reference tense" of the novel.

The Observer First Person Perspective

The story is written as though a main character other than the hero/heroine is telling it. This is also a very "personal" perspective for a novel. It is a very difficult way to write.

Example, Observer First Person Perspective:
I stood at Point-Where-Great-Waters-Meet and watched Chataqua. He gazed out at the horizon where the sun is born each day. I wondered what he was thinking. The sea birds circling above squawked and swooped down on the small fish beyond the waves. I wished that they would tell him how much I loved him.
I walked cautiously from behind a big sand dune. "Chataqua!" I exclaimed cautiously.

Use of this perspective limits the Author in several ways: the Observer (in this case the heroine) becomes the Storyteller; one can only write about what the Observer "sees"; one can only write about what the observer "thinks"; the observer has to be in every scene or at least, "observing" every scene; it defines the gender of the person telling the story, which is important when considering the "type" of book and the intended Readers (In the example used, the Observer is the heroine, and the Author writes from the female perspective).

The primary advantages of this perspective are: a very personal approach that causes the Reader to closely and quickly identify with the Observer, who is usually one of the main characters; it "personalizes" the story and the Reader is able to "watch" the hero/heroine through the eyes of someone close to him/her.

The present tense can also be used in this perspective in a similar way to that described in the Hero First Person perspective, though I would not recommend it.

The Third Person Storyteller Perspective

The story is written as though a detached, non-character (a Storyteller) is telling it to the Reader.

Example, Third Person Storyteller Perspective:
He stood at Point-Where-Great-Waters-Meet and gazed out at the horizon where the sun is born each day. Chataqua wondered how his father felt when he canoed into the unknown to the north and found a new land of abundant oysters and flat fish. Was his father as fearful as Chataqua as he gazed at the unknown horizon?

Use of this perspective has many advantages for the Author: one can write about what any character "sees"; one can write about what any character "thinks"; the gender of the story-teller is not relevant; the main character does not have to be in every scene; the Author is a detached Storyteller.

145

In writing from this perspective, the Author must be careful not to "jump about" too much. It is better to tell the story with a focus on the main character. Some novels are written in this perspective where the hero is in every scene. However, you can "jump" the perspective to another character when the story requires it; try not to do it in the same scene. For example, you may choose to follow the scene described above with a scene where Alanoas and Musiasas walk away from the beach. The purpose of this scene might be to better understand and develop the character Alanoas and introduce the Villain, Malapok. For this follow-on scene, the Storyteller focuses on Alanoas.

Example, Third Person Other Than the Main Character:
Alanoas walked away from the beach wondering if she would ever be able to convince Chataqua that she loved him and wanted to have his children. He was so bashful and shy that it worried her. Once behind the sand dune, Musiasas joined her. It was a short walk back to Chesepiooc along a path bordered by Cyprus trees and salt water swamps. They came to a fork in the path where one trail went to the village and the other to the Place-of-Many-Islands on the Bay-of-the-Great-White-Bird.

"Once I walked this alone," said Alanoas. "But I know better now!"

"What happened?" asked Musiasas.

"The Brave Malapok came upon me at this place," said Alanoas. "He embraced me and tried to persuade me to go with him along the path to the Place-of-Many-Islands."

"Oh! No maiden goes to Place-of-Many-Islands with a Brave... unless she is very wicked!" said Musiasas with a mischievous grin.

"Malapok held my hand tightly, but I broke away and ran down the path to Chesepiooc."

"Did he chase you?" asked Musiasas expectantly.

"He followed," said Alanoas, "but I was very mad and yelled out to him!"

"I wonder if he is in the swamp now?" asked Musiasas in a mysterious voice.

*Alanoas looked cautiously around her, but they were alone
except for the White-Bird-With-Long-Legs who waded slowly
through the swamp. They walked toward Chesepiooc,
watching the shadows in the swamp suspiciously.*

The third person perspective is the easiest to use and is
recommended.

The Omniscient Storyteller Perspective

The story is written as though a "Storyteller in the Sky" is
telling it. The Storyteller may be someone who knows the
story "from afar". The Storyteller is not "detached" as in the
third person perspective. He/she has some connection to the
characters in the story, but is not there him/her self.

Example, Omniscient Story Teller Perspective:
*I sit on the beach at Point-Where-Great-Waters-Meet and
stare out to the unknown horizon. I am Benatagua, father of
Chataqua. I was Werowance of the Chesapeake until the
battle with the Wepeneooc where I was killed by the cowardly
Opectanotak. It has been a full season of the sun since
Chataqua paddled away with the maiden Alanoas. My heart
is torn at his loss, and I wonder if he will ever return. The
men with pale skins that he brought to the Land of the
Chesapeake destroyed much of the tribe and went away in
their great canoe with wings. It is my fondest wish that they
never return, but I fear that they will. I must help the Sachem
prepare for this.*

In this perspective, the Author immediately defines an
"omniscient Storyteller" (Chataqua's father, who dies in the
story at the hands of the Wepeneooc Tribe) who will tell the
story of past events from a detached, but personal viewpoint.
This is a very difficult perspective and is not recommended.

Multiple Perspectives

The story is written from two or more perspectives. This
means just that... the narrator is detached and then first

person, etc. This is a very confusing and difficult perspective and is not recommended. But, if your story needs it, use it!

Tense

The story is "told" in some "tense". This does not mean that other tenses are not used. It means that the text that "tells" the story is in some consistent tense. All tenses in the story are referenced to the tense of the Storyteller.

Tense: a verb conjugation that indicates the time (past, present, future), as well as the continuance (imperfect) or completion (perfect) of the action or state.

The Reference Tense

The "Reference Tense" is the tense the Storyteller uses. It is the tense in which the novel is told. That does not mean that other tenses are not present. It does mean that when other tenses are used, they are used with respect to the reference tense.

For example *"Chatagua went to the old live oak tree."* The verb "to go" is used in the past tense ("went"). The past tense is the reference tense. Another tense may fit the story at this point. *"He had been there many times before."* Here, the past perfect of the verb "to be" is used ("had been"). This is the supporting tense, stated with respect to the reference tense. Don't use the supporting tense as the reference tense, i.e. *"Chatagua had gone to the old live oak tree."*

For example *"Chatagua goes to the old live oak tree."* The verb "to go" is used in the present tense ("goes"). The present tense is the reference tense. Another tense may be required in the next sentence. *"He has been there many times before."* Here, the present perfect of the verb "to be" is used. ("has been"). This is the supporting tense, stated with respect to the reference tense. Don't use the supporting tense as the reference tense, i.e. *"Chatagua has gone to the old live oak tree."*

Tense For The First Person Perspective

A story "told" in the first person may use the present tense, as though the person "is living" the story. This tense leaves the Author with a very inflexible format and is not recommended except for special stories. Here are some sample conjugations, showing the use of tense.

Simple Present: Present action or condition.
    Example (Active): I watch them.
    Example (Passive): They are watched.

Present Progressive: Action in progress.
    Example (Active): I am watching them.
    Example (Passive): They are being watched.

Present Perfect: Action begins in the past and leads up to and includes the present; continued action.
    Example (Active): I have watched them for many years.
    Example (Passive): For many years I have been watching them.

Present Perfect Progressive: Duration of an action that began in the past and continues into the present; may continue into the future.
    Example (Active): I have been watching for two hours and will continue.

A story told in the first person perspective is usually told in the past tense, as though the person is relating what has already occurred.

Simple Present: Present action or condition.
    Example (Active): I watched them closely.
    Example (Passive): They were watched closely by me.

Tense for The Third Person Perspective

A story "told" in the third person uses the past tense from a Storyteller perspective. This tense provides the Author with a flexible format and is recommended. Here are some sample conjugations, showing the use of tense.

Simple Past: Completed action or condition.
Example (Active): He and others watched the action.
Example (Passive): The action was watched by him and others.

Past Progressive: Past action that took place over a period of time; past action interrupted by another.
Example (Active): He was watching the action for three days.
Example (Passive): For three days he was watching the action.

Past Perfect: Past action or condition completed before another event in the past.
Example (Active): When he watched for her, she had already departed.
Example (Passive): She had already departed when he watched for her.

Future Perfect: Action that will be completed in the future; or before a specified time in the future.
Example (Active): By next month he will have finished the action.
Example (Passive): By next month the action will have been finished.

Active and Passive Voice

Don't try to write with an abnormal awareness of tense and conjugation! You should be focusing on the story. Usually, "what sounds right" will be correct... but not always. Be sure to check your use of tense in the Creative Reviews. In most cases in a novel, you should use the active voice.

**Active voice: The shark bit the man
(Subject performs the action of the verb)**

Passive voice: The man was bitten by the shark (Subject receives the action of the verb)

The use of passive voice tends to create awkward sentences. The passive voice is "impersonal", the exact opposite of what you want as an Author. The passive voice is more often used in non-fiction and scientific writing. Here it is has value in that the writing provides information that does not seem to be biased by individual perspectives. You should not exclude the passive voice entirely. If it fits; use it (but not very much).

Perspectives of Time and Dimensional Space

It is very important that you keep track of the dimensions as you tell the story... and that the Reader always has a sense of where and when the story is. The dimensions of a story are the same as your dimensions: when is it? Where is it (in three dimensions)? how is it moving (up, down, right left, ahead, behind, fast, slow, etc.)?

In dealing with the "when", you may be dealing in seconds and minutes, hours and days, days and months, or months and years. It depends on the requirements of the story. If you are running from a werewolf, you are dealing in seconds! If you are describing a sailing voyage, you are dealing in days and weeks.

If you are telling a story that requires you to "move ahead" to the next important part of the story ("skipping over" time), you may be dealing in days, months or years. Different parts of the novel may have different time dimensions. Don't be afraid to shift your time reference if the story in the novel requires it. Use of the Storyteller for this purpose most always works ("Two years passed...").

Remember, in telling a story, you are not accounting for every minute from story point A to story point B. In telling a story, you are recounting the important events (scenes, scene elements and events within the scene elements) that tell the story (not a chronological narrative), with a little "color" thrown in to make it more interesting. So, you must "skip" or "move ahead" from time to time. If it's a short period, you need no "fill-in". Just move on. You may even want to "move back"... a "flashback" in your story. When you use a flashback, avoid doing it all in descriptive text. As always, use a proper balance between dialogue and description.

Your Reader must know "when" in a scene to keep track of what's going on. Also remember that every "when" has a season of the year, a month, a day and the time of the day and an environment associated with it. Keep track of that too, and use the season, time of day and the environment occasionally to help remind the Reader "when" he is.

The "where" in story telling is very important. Be sure that you understand time and distance relationships and keep the Reader aware of "where" he/she is throughout the story... and how he/she got there. Make sure that the time/distance relationships are correct. There is no "beam me up, Scotty" in writing... unless of course, that's part of your story.

Keeping track of movement is also very important. Movement is related to the "where", but includes other types of description. For example, you state early in the scene that a character is sitting. At some point, this character must move to a standing position. Keep track of this sort of thing. If the Reader pictures a character sitting down and all of sudden this character does something one does not usually do sitting down, the Reader loses the picture.

Pick up one of your favorite novels and see how the Author has treated perspective and tense. Try writing in the several perspectives and practice "staying in perspective". Get a feel for which perspective is the mode in which you are most comfortable. Remember the pros and cons of the various storyteller persspectives. Give it some thought!

****

Chapter Fifteen
Inside the Creative Cave

You will need to spend a reasonable amount of time before you start the Rough-Through in earnest doing some "Creative Thinking". What is that? Well, it's sitting on the front porch (or under a tree... or somewhere like that) in reasonable isolation "thinking" about the beginning point and the end point.

Get yourself settled into your "Author's Place". Brew a cup of strong coffee... or whatever your preference. Open your "NOTES" file that contains the first Storyteller's direction you have established and any first attempts at opening scenes.

Write With the Reader at Your Side

An experienced Author will always write with the Reader at his/her side. By that I mean he/she will constantly refer to the Reader's perspective to make sure he/she is writing what the Reader will read... not just what interests the Author. My Reader's name is "Foo-Foo", an imaginary childhood playmate who I used to drive my parents nuts.

"What are you doing in the pantry, Robert?" asked my Mother.

"Foo-Foo and I are playing a game," said little Robert.

"Robert! Open that door!" said my Father in his firmest voice. "What are you doing in there?"

"Foo-Foo and I are just playing a game," said little Robert in a most innocent voice.

I turn to Foo-Foo when I am writing and ask him "What do you think of that? Is this something you want to read?"

I then become Foo-Foo and read it from that perspective. Obviously, the character of Foo-Foo has a lot to do with how I target my book. If the Readers are intended to be children, then Foo-Foo is today's child. If the intended Readers are adults who like a fast paced, emotional story, then Foo-Foo is them! Foo-Foo is very dependable. He always answers!

Foo-Foo has a friend whose name is Foo-Faa, a female Foo-Foo. Being Foo Faa is hard for me, but I think I am becoming better at it. All Authors need a Foo-Foo and a Foo-Faa.

STARTING

It's a dark and drizzly Saturday morning and you are frazzled by trying to work your "day job" and think about writing a novel at the same time! Yet, you feel good and are optimistic. Your spouse has gone shopping and the kids are at a friend's house. You enter the Author's Place, sit down at your computer, sip a good cup of coffee and stare out at the rain. Foo Foo and Foo Faa come in and sit down with you. You type the title of your novel at the top of the page, and then the Chapter number and title.

The Unknown Horizon

Chapter One
Point-Where-Great-Waters-Meet

You think about the "Point" of the first chapter in the structure of the story, and name it accordingly. You choose *Point-Where-Great-Waters-Meet* because the point of the chapter is to introduce the scenario, the main characters and their "problem". The name of the Chapter defines where the main characters are in the first scene. Do all scenes in that Chapter have to be at *Point-Where-Great-Waters-Meet*? No. The Chapter name captures the "essence" of all the scenes in the Chapter. In our story, most of the scenes in Chapter One will take place at or near *Point-Where-Great-Waters-Meet*.

Your fingers go to the keyboard of your computer. You pause, and your fingers hang there expectantly. Suddenly, your mind begins to function in a strange new mode and your fingers begin to move over the keyboard. A feeling of exhilaration comes over you as the words begin to form!

Example, Opening Scene;
    Chataqua and his father, Benatagua, paddled a long canoe with fish and sea birds carved on its sides near Point-Where-Great-Waters-Meet.

Whew! We got the first sentence into the computer. Aha! Where to go from here flows into our mind and into the computer.

    Chataqua sat in the front, his father at the rear. Both were bare of chest and wore only a loin cloth. It was a clear day in the Time-When-Trees-Bring-Leaves. The morning sun shown warmly.
    "Chataqua, you will soon be a man and seek to be a Brave," said Benatagua in his deep voice. "You paddle well and have a strong body... you will honor our family!"
    The sandy beach at Point-Where-Great-Waters-Meet glistened brightly in the sun, contrasting with the new green leaves of the forest and the evergreens behind it. Sea birds rode a soft wind current above them, searching for fish below. The water swirled with schools of small fish. It was Chataqua's favorite time, on the water with his father in the long canoe.
    "I have waited until this time... when you are to become a Brave, to tell you something very important," said Benatagua slowly.
    "What is it, Father?" asked Chataqua, a worried look on his face. He enjoyed the discussions with his father, but he sensed that he was about to hear something that would be troubling.
    "The Sachem, Chesapian, is, as you know, a friend and a wise man."
    "Yes, I have seen that the Sachem is your friend."
    Benatagua paused and pulled strongly on his paddle, looking up at the sea birds hanging effortlessly on the wind.
    "When you were a small child, Chesapian also had a son," said Benatagua. "His son died of an evil clogging of the chest before he became a small boy."
    "I am sorry for Chesapian," said Chataqua, wondering what to say that was proper.

"As you grew, Chesapian has watched you closely. He told me that he expects you to one day become Sachem."

A goal has been suggested for Chataqua that, if accepted, would change his status quo world.

Chataqua stops paddling and looks back at his Father. "How could I become Sachem?" he asked in an astounded voice.

The Sachem was to Chataqua something that always existed, a pillar of strength upon which all could rely. The thought of becoming this pillar of strength surprised and overwhelmed him.

"It is something to think upon," said Benatagua, "not something that is to be done now."

Chataqua paddled with renewed effort, the thought of becoming Sachem burning in his mind.

"I will think upon it," said Chataqua, "but it frightens me!"

"I must tell you also," said Benatagua, "when you become a Brave, beware of Maltakak, the Periku."

Chataqua was surprised. "Why is that, father?"

"Maltakak and Chesapian were rivals when they were of your age," said Benatagua in a serious voice. "Chesapian won over Maltakak and became Sachem. In the season when you were born, Maltakak tried to use an alliance with the Wepeneooc Tribe to discredit Chesapian so that he... Maltakak, could become Sachem."

Chataqua listened intently.

"Chesapian should have banished Maltakak then... but he is a kind and forgiving man, and he chose Maltakak as Periku to keep peace within the tribe."

Now we have written part of the back story using the method of having it related by a character.

"Why must I know this?"

"You have grown up with the son of Maltakak, the Brave Malapok. You may count him as friend...but I caution you... Maltakak still plots to become Sachem... and to pass Sachem to Malapok."

"Malapok was my friend...but I am not sure now that he is. He is older, become a Brave and gone a different way," said Chataqua.

We have set the seed for the relationship between Chataqua and Malapok.

There was movement on the beach. Chataqua looked and saw Masonnacok and his daughter Alanoas emerge from behind a sand dune and walk along the beach. Musiasas, a friend of Alanoas was with them.

"Alanoas is becoming a young woman very quickly," said Benatagua, waving to Masonnacok.

Masonnacok waved back and took his daughter's hand. Alanoas looked bashfully over her shoulder and turned away quickly. Musiasas skipped along beside her, saying something Chataqua couldn't hear. Masonnacok took the hand of Musiasas and pulled her along with them.

"Yes," said Chataqua, "we played together for many years, but now her Father guards her closely."

Benatagua laughed. "Yes, he is very aware of her beauty,"

"And so am I, Father," said Chataqua.

We have introduced Chataqua's love interest.

Benatagua smiled, thinking of his wife Chalata. "You will soon need to find a woman to be your wife, Son," said Benatagua. "But Alanoas is not yet of age."

"I will give it some thought, Father," said Chataqua. "But first I must become a Brave and do a great deed as you have done!"

Benatagua nodded, concerned that Chataqua felt he must equal his deed.

We have some of the opening scene into the computer! Let's continue the scene and flesh out the "problem" that Chataqua must solve. We know we have to establish "the problem" rock solid early in the novel

Example, Fleshing Out "The Problem";

"Father... tell me about your great deed... canoeing to the Land-Where-The-Cold-Wind-Blows."

"You have heard that story many times," said Benatagua with a chuckle.

"I want to hear it again!" said Chataqua earnestly.

Benatagua nods patiently. "My father, Bentaqua, always told me that there was a land in that direction," said Benatagua slowly. "He wanted to canoe there, but he died before he had the opportunity."

"He died bravely in a battle with the Wepeneooc," said Chataqua, recalling that story.

"Yes," said Benatagua in a sad voice. "It was at the time that Maltakak tried to become Sachem. My father, Bentaqua, was a great warrior, just as you will be. After he died, I built this long canoe and resolved to paddle into the Broad Waters toward the cold wind. The horizon there had always beckoned to me. Bentaqua was always with me... a part of me."

"Did you know what was there... or how far you had to paddle?"

"No," said Benatagua, shaking his head slowly. "I asked Quiacosough, the noble son of our god Okee, to guide me. I set forth early as the sun was born. I knew that Okee was with me, just as my father was. I paddled strongly with the sun on my right hand. It was a beautiful day of the Time-When-Trees-Bring-Leaves... just as now. The sea-creatures-that-smile... the calypo, played around me and I saw flat-fish-with-wings-and-stinging-tails basking in the sun near the surface. The birds of the sea followed behind me as if they knew where I was going. They reassured me that there was a land ahead."

"You were very brave, father," said Chataqua.

At some point in the story, Chataqua is going to canoe to the Land-Where-The Sun-Is-Born, and during this voyage he will face "Gitsche Kakapa", the great beast of the sea. Here at the beginning, let's set the conditions for suspense by providing a brief glimpse of this beast through the eyes of Benatagua.

Example, Setting the Conditions for Suspense;

"What happened on the way back?" asked Chataqua, knowing the answer and wanting to hear the story again.

"A strong wind from the Land-Where-The-Sun-Sets blew my canoe from the Broad Waters into the Water-That-Never-Ends. I tried to paddle toward the Land-Where-The-Warm-Wind-Blows, where our village, Chesepiooc, lies on the shore. But I knew that I was going more and more into the Water-That-Never-Ends. After the sun reached its highest point, I saw a great fin following my long canoe. I had heard of Gitsche Kakapa, the great-fish-that-eats-men, but I had never seen him. I was afraid, for I was sure that Gitsche Kakapa was tracking me across the Water-That-Never-Ends."

"What did you do?" asked Chataqua in awe.

"I made sure that my bow and spear was ready and that I had enough arrows to shoot Gitsche Kakapa if he came close to my canoe."

"Did you see more of Gitsche Kakapa?"

"He swam closer and finally to the side of my canoe," said Benatagua, looking at the side of the long canoe as if the great fish were still there.

Chataqua looked at the blue green water but saw only the reflections of the sun.

"Gitsche Kakapa was longer than my canoe," said Benatagua. "He rolled on his side and looked straight at me with an evil black eye. His mouth parted showing many long sharp teeth. I thought he would easily overturn my canoe. Tagkanysough, the evil son of Okee, held me for a moment in his arms."

Each time the picture of Gitsche Kakapa that Benatagua painted with words chilled Chataqua to the bone.

"What did you do?"

"I picked up my spear and held it ready to thrust into the great fish if I had to," said Benatagua. "But he was so large it would have been difficult to kill him."

What do we need next? Aha! We need a scene to introduce Chataqua's fantasy goal about canoeing to the Land-Where-The-Sun-Is-Born to match his Father's deed.

Example, Introducing the Goal;

Chataqua walked along the white sand beach at Point-
Where-Great-Waters-Meet, deep in thought. The sun was
rising and the pink and purple colors of dawn lingered in the
sky. Point-Where-Great-Waters-Meet was where he always
came when he wanted to think. It was so beautiful and serene
there that it allowed his active mind to wander across
everything he knew and everything he wanted to know.

Chataqua was clad in buckskin trousers and wore nothing
above them, his lean and strong body glistening in the bright
sun, his long black hair blowing in the cool sea breeze. Above
him, sea birds squawked and wheeled about, diving beyond
the calm waves where the water churned with small fish. He
sat down in the white sand, looked out to sea and wondered
what lay beyond the horizon.

"Oh Okee!" exclaimed Chataqua. "What wonders have you
made beyond that horizon? What strange people and beasts
may I find if I go there?"

A warm wind blew across him as if in answer.

"I must have the courage to canoe to the Land-Where-The-
Cold-Winds-Blow as did my Father!"

The rising sun sent a shimmering light across the Water-
That-Never-Ends, a beacon in the fresh morning air.

"Oh Okee, do you beckon to go beyond this unknown
horizon toward the Land-Where-The-Sun-Is-Born?"

The warm wind blew stronger, picking up the white sand
and hurling it at him, whistling through the sand dunes and
into the mysterious salt water swamp.

Chataqua got up and faced the wind, letting the blowing
sand sting his face and body. He knew that he must soon
prove his worth to the Chesapeake Tribe and become a Brave.
But, he had to do more! He had to canoe to the Land-Where-
The-Sun-Is-Born!

We have Chataqua's first goals in place. It's time to
provide more on Chataqua's romantic interest, Alanoas.

Example, More on the Romantic Interest;

Alanoas and her friend Musiasas watched Chataqua as he
sat on the beach. They hid behind tall green rushes growing

on a dune. Alanoas was a beautiful girl slightly younger than Chataqua. She had long black hair and a round face that always seemed to smile. Musiasas was a short maiden who tended toward chubbiness. She had a beautiful face with large eyes that matched her bubbly personality.

Note the change in the Storyteller's perspective. The Storyteller is now seeing things through the eyes of Alanoas.

"Go and tell him you love him!" giggled Musiasas.
"Oh, don't be so silly!" exclaimed Alanoas.
"You just want to kiss him and hold him," laughed Musiasas, "I know!"
"How do you know that?" asked Alanoas.
Musiasas pushed Alanoas playfully. "Because I want to kiss him and hold him, too... he is so beautiful!"
Alanoas pushed Musiasas back playfully. "You stay away from him! He's mine!"
"Then go out there and tell him you love him!"
Alanoas walked cautiously down the slope of the sand dune toward where Chataqua sat. "I have come to see you at the Point-Where-Great-Waters-Meet," she said in her soft voice.
Chataqua was startled out of his thoughts by the soft voice behind him. He jumped to his feet, turned and saw Alanoas emerging from behind a dune. He was, as always, stunned by her beauty! Her long, dark hair hung below her shoulders and glistened against the shell decorated cloth that she wore. Her intense brown eyes were fixed on him expectantly.
"Alanoas!" exclaimed Chataqua bashfully.

You made it! You are finally in the Creative Cave! The world around you, which is now oblivious to you, awaits your genius! You know you must canoe to the unknown horizon!

The Creative Cave will take you over your own "Unknwon Horizon". It is an experience you will never forget!

Four hours later, you come to a pause point and your fingers stop. Your spouse comes home and enters your Author's Place.

"Look what I bought, Dear!"

Suddenly, the Creative Cave is gone, though the euphoria of the experience lingers. You want to get back in, but you know you are in the "Doldrums".

"Oh, that's wonderful, Dear!" (or something like that)

Back to the Creative Cave

You will know you are in the Creative Cave again when you are thinking about nothing but the story in your novel. Ideas begin to flow and the wonderful feeling of creative euphoria returns. As you write, Foo Foo and Foo Faa begin to identify with the attractive characters Chataqua and Alanoas. They have an initial idea of their problem... the essence of the story. You have the "Reader Hook" dangling in front of them. You, the Author, know the "direction" that will help you tell the story of Chataqua and Alanoas! You are hooked by creative euphoria as you begin to define the universe in which the story of Chataqua and Alanoas will be told! It is your own creation!

Once you start writing the Rough-Through you are pushing toward your *Unknown Horizon* with zest and confidence!

****

Chapter Sixteen
Action and Emotional Scenes

Creation of Scenes

Now we are going to do some Rough-Through writing and practicing! When you are doing scenes and an idea "pops into your head", write it down. Better yet, follow up the idea in your writings right away, even if you have to "jump" to another part of the manuscript. The passage of minutes causes you to lose the idea or lose the thought of why it is a good idea!

We have looked at "the story" and described a series of Story Events that typically appear in most successful novels (The status quo event, the mentor event, etc.). These "events" are not "scenes". They provide "points" that should be made in one or more scenes... a potential "story line". Now we are going to look at scene construction and different types of scenes (which contain Story Events). As we write the Rough-Through we will apply the Creative Principles. We will analyze each example scene to see how many Story Events are covered and how many WOW Factors are used.

Scenes within your chapters should all contain storytelling, dialogue, description and action in varying degrees, dependent on the "point" and type of the scene. We will examine examples from:

1. Action scenes.
2. Emotional scenes.
3. Humorous scenes.
4. Mystery scenes.
5. Romantic scenes.
6. Sex scenes.
7. Innovative scenes.
8. Highly dramatic scenes.
9. Battle scenes.
10. Mourning scenes.
11. Storm scenes.
12. Fantasy scenes.
13. Peril scenes.

14. Extreme peril scenes.
15. High point scenes.
16. Multi-perspective scenes.
17. Defining scenes
18. Triumphant scenes.

Each of these scenes may have a "prelude scene"... a scene that sets up the events in the "focus scene".

Action Scenes

Below is a "Scene Summary" that you may want to use to set the idea of the scene in your mind as you begin to write. You need not follow it exactly as you get into the scene, nor should you. In fact, you don't have to use it at all... just think about it. I will not burden you with showing these Scene Summaries beyond this first one.

Scene Summary

Prelude Scene	The Periku's conspiracy
Scene	The fight between Chataqua and Malapok (The Challenge of the Brave).
Setting	On the beach of the Broad Waters, spring time on a warm day at sunrise.
Main Characters	Chataqua and Malapok.
Backup Characters	Benatagua, Alanoas and the Council of Braves
Action	Chataqua must prove his intelligence, bravery and endurance against the older and stronger Malapok as a test to become a Brave.
Point	Highlights the increasing Hostility between Chataqua and Malapok, each seeking the love of Alanoas. The outcome will determine Chataqua's status in the tribe.

Example, Prelude Scene, Establishing the Conspiracy:

Maltakak and Malapok waited in the forest near the beach where the test of bravery was to take place.

"You must humiliate the son of Benatagua," said Maltakak in a raspy voice, clutching the ceremonial pole encrusted with sea shells that he always carried as the mark of the Periku. "He must not become a Brave."

"He was my friend when we were boys," said Malapok in a confused voice, "but now he dares to challenge me for the woman I want."

Here we reinforce the "love triangle".

"Humiliate him!" exclaimed the Periku, "and you will have your woman. I will talk to the father of Alanoas, Masonnacok ... and you will have her!"

"Thank you, father," said Malapok, "But I prefer to win her myself."

"Don't be foolish! Take advantage of what you have... who you are!

Malapok wrinkled his brow and looked down. "Yes, Father."

We use dialogue to establish the subservient relationship of Malapok to his father.

"If this young boy becomes a Brave," muttered Maltakak, "he will bring more Braves to the side of Chesapian and Benatagua, and that must not happen."

"When will you challenge Chesapian again as Sachem?" asked Malapok, looking at his gray, stooped father with both love and fear.

"Soon," said Maltakak. "I must wait for the opportunity when it comes!"

The fight between Chataqua and Malapok is an early highlight of the story. Here, we begin to put it all together and provide enough detail to match the action.

Example, Focus Scene, The Fight;

"We begin the fight!" said Malapok, grinning maliciously in the morning sun.

"I am ready!" said Chataqua feeling the gritty sand of the beach between his toes as he tried to get position on his foe.

We introduce the setting of the fight using dialogue tags.

The sun was brightly low in the morning sky as Chataqua and Malapok circled each other cautiously on the beach near the Broad Waters. There was a slight breeze that rippled the water into foam as it lapped at the shore. Chataqua and Malapok were both naked except for loin cloths that held their manhood to them. Sea birds squawked and wheeled above, ready to dive on unsuspecting fish. Chataqua felt like one of those fish. He didn't know what to expect from Malapok.

Here we have a flowing mix of description, action and the internal thoughts of Chataqua, using a metaphor (the trapped fish).

Suddenly, Malapok darted in. With a strong pull, Malapok flipped Chataqua off his feet, grabbed his leg and began to pull him through the sand like the carcass of a newly slain deer.

"Aieeeee!" shouted Malapok in a mock war cry that sounded both humor and derision.

Chataqua struggled to free himself, infuriated at the humiliation being bestowed by Malapok. He rolled over, kicked violently and broke Malapok's grip on his leg. He jumped to his feet, covered with sand that clung to his sweaty body like an extra skin.

We add pizzazz... we don't say he's sweaty and covered with sand... we use a more colorful way of saying it.

As Chataqua turned to Malapok, Malapok slapped him in the face with an open palm that humiliated more than it stung. Chataqua raised his hands in defense and turned away another slap, feeling anger rise in him like a mighty storm.

The slap was insulting... as though Chataqua was not worthy of being hit.

"Hit me, Malapok," shouted Chataqua heatedly. "Are you afraid to hit me for what I may do to you?"

Malapok laughed. It sounded artificial and there was concern on the Brave's face. He swung his big fist at Chataqua. It missed by inches as Chataqua ducked. Chataqua punched powerfully at Malapok, but the blows failed to land.

"You are not so quick, Young Squirrel," muttered Malapok, swinging his arms at Chataqua in a series of rapid blows.

Malapok charged at Chataqua, grabbed him by the waist and rode him backward, falling into the sand. Chataqua struggled to free himself from the iron grip of Malapok. He rolled free, jumped to his feet and instinctively ran into the surf.

Chataqua had to find a way to nullify Malapok's superior strength! Was Malapok a match for him in the water? Malapok had never liked the water, ever since the small kakapa bit him. He wasn't sure Malapok would come into the water. He hoped fervently that he would not. He stood in the rolling surf, taunting Malapok to follow him.

We use description to provide Chataqua's inner thoughts and conflicts as he fights.

Malapok followed Chataqua into the surf reluctantly. "This fight is to be on the beach!" shouted Malapok, anger and anxiety in his voice.

"This fight can be wherever it goes!" shouted Chataqua defiantly. "Do you fear the Broad Waters?"

Malapok splashed toward Chataqua, his expression now one of mounting anger. He groped for Chataqua. Chataqua backed away and swam to deeper water, beyond where the surf was breaking.

"Fight me here, Big Squirrel!" shouted Chataqua, further taunting Malapok.

Infuriated, Malapok swam toward him. He saw the fin in the water ten arms lengths beyond Chataqua and turned away in fear. Was it a kakapa, the fish-that-eats-men? He

*watched with goggle eyes as Chataqua swam near the
breaking waves and beckoned to Malapok.*

We introduce surprise and suspense with the fin.

*"Are you afraid to fight me?" shouted Chataqua. "Are you
not so brave, Malapok?"*
*Malapok watched with wide eyes as the fin came near to
where Chataqua swam in the glimmering water. He started to
shout, but fear clogged his throat and he only watched in
horror. Chataqua saw the horror in Malapok's eyes and
turned to look behind him. He saw the gray fin of a calypo rise
and dive into the depths. Laughing, he put his head into the
water, thrust his feet high and dove deep, inviting the sea-
creature-that-smiles to frolic with him.*

This scene contains the WOW Factors Suspense (what is
the fin?), Heroism (Chataqua overcomes his fears to fight),
Emotion (antagonism between the two), Conflict (the contest
between the two), Action (the fight itself), Surprise (the
calypo) and Pizzazz (colorful descriptions and setting). The
WOW Score is 7/10.

What is a "good" WOW Score? Well, we should have at
least three WOW Factors in every scene. We should average
five per scene over the entire novel.

How about some practice? You have read this scene in my
words. Now put it aside and write your own version of it. Use
the Creative Principles we have discussed! When you have
finished the scene, look it over carefully. Did you successfully
make the "point"? Did you successfully employ some or all of
the Creative Principles we have explored? What is the WOW
Factor? Are you happy with it as a Rough-Through?

Emotional Scenes

An emotional scene is one in which the characters are
stirred by high emotion. The Reader should experience the
same. He/she should be "stirred" by the scene!

Example, an Emotional Scene:

*Chataqua waited just beyond the glow of the magnificent
campfire that burned on the beach, sending flickering yellow
light over the flat calm waters. Dancing sparks flew crazily
into the air as Sachem Chesapian walked majestically toward
the fire where members of the Council of Braves stood, their
arms folded across their bare, painted chests.*

*Chesapian wore the five feathers of leadership in a beaded
headband. Around his neck was a heavy copper chain holding
an ornament made from a cluster of shellfish, the symbol of
Sachem of the Great People of the Shellfish. His trousers and
shirt were made from the skins of deer, covered with colorful
beads from the shelled creatures of the sea. Fur trimmed the
long sleeves of his shirt. He wore a loose robe of raccoon hides
over his shirt and trousers supported on one shoulder. The
trousers were trimmed with buckskin thongs which hung
loosely. He wore long stockings, reinforced on the soles.*

Note that we have done some spot research on what a
Chesapeake Chief would wear at a ceremony.

*Two Braves came forth holding a tall pole on which was
mounted a stag's antlers. Turkey feathers hung from it. The
pole was decorated with the shells of oysters and clams
stained in red, blue and yellow. The Braves set the pole on the
earth near the fire and held it steadily. Chesapian nodded
and drums sounded. He began the sing song chant of the
Chesapeake hail to Okee and was joined by the Braves.*

*Oh Okee
Hear our wish,
We Chesapeake,
People of the Shellfish,
Oh Okee
Protect our land,
We Chesapeake,
Of earth, swamp and sand,
Give us courage,
Give us love,
As we plea,
To you, Okee!*

Where did the "chant" come from? Is it an authentic Chesapeake chant? No. I composed it for added color. It sounds like what might be chanted at a formal assemblage of the tribe.

"I am the man Chataqua, who seeks to be a Brave!" called out Chataqua

"And what has this man done to be called a Brave?" said Chesapian.

Manatapac stepped forward from among the Braves, his chest painted red with the stain of berries. He wore two feathers, the symbol of a Brave who has excelled among Braves.

"This man has done much to be called a Brave," said Manatapac proudly. "He has canoed to the Land-Where-The-Cold-Wind-Blows, to the land of the Delaware."

"Bischi," murmured the Braves, nodding in agreement.

We use the Algonquian word for "yes" to indicate that they are speaking Chesapeake.

"He has demonstrated his courage in physical conflict with the Brave Malapok."

"Bischi," murmured the Braves. There was a lesser murmur of dissent that followed from the Braves who allied themselves with Malapok.

"He has shown the skills of the forest, and remained in the wild for thirty days and nights without food or companionship."

"Bischi," murmured the Braves.

"He has shown great skill with the bow and the knife, and is among the best of the Braves in these skills."

"Bischi."

"He has shown that his body is strong, carrying the log of the Council from Point-Where-Great-Waters-Meet to this campfire."

"Bischi."

"This man who would be a Brave has accomplished the required six of the tests of the Braves," said Manatapac triumphantly.

"Then this man is to be honored," said Sachem Chesapian.

"Chataqua is a coward," shouted Malapok. "He refused to fight me."

"Chataqua showed great intelligence by challenging the stronger, older man to fight in the surf," shouted Manatapac emotionally. "He is no coward, as he took the beating by Malapok on the beach without a whimper!"

"Matta! He is a coward who refused battle," shouted Malapok shaking his fist angrily. "He would not stand beside us in battle!"

"Chataqua would stand beside us all in battle," said Manatapac strongly and evenly, glaring at Malapok. "And... he would find a way for us to win! He is Chataqua... the man with the busy and thoughtful head!"

The Sachem quieted them all with a sweep of his arm. He gazed at each Brave with penetrating eyes.

"The Brave Chataqua will join the Council of Braves!" said Chesapian loudly.

A log in the great fire collapsed and fell, throwing up a cloud of swirling sparks as Chataqua walked proudly to join the Council of Braves.

"As a Brave, I will canoe to the Land-Where-The-Sun-Is-Born!" shouted Chataqua. "I will find new lands and people to the glory of the Chesapeake!"

The scene has Emotion (Chataqua's emotion to become a Brave), Suspense (will he become a Brave?), Conflict (verbal conflict), Heroism (Chataqua and Manatapac stand against Malapok) and Pizzazz (the chant, the setting) for a WOW Score of 5/10. It is a different kind of scene than the fight scene... achieving WOW in different ways.

What could we do in the Creative Reviews to make you say WOW at least once... more than once? You can employ a computer aided trick here. Go to each emotional adjective you have used. Key in the synonym finder (Shift F7 in WORD). Pick out the best one. Make sure you are not using the same word too often. When I do SHIFT F7 on "angrily", for example, I get: heatedly, irritably, furiously, irately, and crossly. Which adjective would you use?

Okay... try the "practice" again with this scene! How much emotion can you pack into a scene? Take an idea from the novel you've been dreaming about and write an emotional scene. Don't worry about where to START, just imagine your scene, a few characters and write.

**Emotion is the most important WOW Factor.
Master emotional scenes and you're on the way!**

****

Chapter Seventeen
Humorous and Mystery Scenes

Humorous scenes are useful if properly "paced", and they contribute to a WOW book. It is good to maintain an underlying "sense of humor" throughout the book using dialogue in exchanges between the characters. As you grow to know your characters, you will better understand what they would say to one another that is humorous. It doesn't have to be a "joke"... just humorous banter will do.

The most effective form of humor in a novel is when there is a certain amount of it injected throughout (even when the novel is not a "comedy" novel). This is usually supported by the nature of the characters, which may include the following characteristics: a sarcastic view of the world, often expressed; tongue in cheek humor; a joking attitude; a ridiculous appearance; humorous mannerisms; comical personality; good natured clumsiness. Many times, the humorous character will have traits that are enduring and useful as well... a character with depth.

Humor can take visual form and the form of events. The visual and event based humor may come from: a character who is designed by the Author to be humorous (there is one of these in many novels); a ridiculous setting or environment; a ridiculous or humorous sequence of events; some or all of these.

Many times a humorous character is an animal. The animal can be given some of the same characteristics as the human characters, but of course, must "speak" through its actions (or whatever language the Author chooses to assign the animal).

Try to let the Reader "hear" some humor in each scene (the humor should fit the scene, not look "injected"). Even in scenes that are involved with danger and hardship, some humor is appropriate. Readers like a character more if he/she has a sense of humor... even the tough guys!

Example, A Humorous Scene;

Alanoas giggled at Chataqua as they stood beside his father's lodge. "I miss your hair," she said playfully.

Chataqua's hair had been cut short and gathered into a knot on the top of his head in the fashion of the Chesapeake Brave. The hairs on the sides of his head had been plucked out, as had the new hairs appearing on his chin. It was a painful process...and he missed his hair also.

"Do you love me less without my hair?" asked Chataqua mischievously, squeezing her shoulders.

"Oh no! I love you more, my Brave!" She stood on her toes, held Chataqua by the shoulders and kissed him on the cheek.

Many books benefit from having one or two scenes that are designed to be humorous. Most of us have seen the John Wayne movies where there is a big fight, usually in the mud or in some bar. People get socked and shoved around in a ridiculous, humorous way, and we laugh (those punches, if real, would hurt!). So, let's try a scene designed to be humorous. Let's also introduce a character who is designed to be a lever for humorous situations or comments.

Example, Humorous Scene;

Soon, Manatapac returned with Chalapow and Rowhatan to where Chataqua waited tending the wounded calypo.

"I hear you are saving sea creatures, now!" exclaimed Chalapow, tripping on the sand and falling beside Chataqua.

Chalapow was a young man the same age as Chataqua. He had a round face, a belly that shook as he ran and great strength. Nothing ever seemed to bother him. His usual state of jolliness made him a man that the Chesapeake treasured for that value.

"We need your strength, Chalapow!" said Chataqua.

"Yes! My strength is legendary!" said Chalapow with a grin, flexing his large, fleshy arm.

"Yes but it takes an order of the Sachem to get you to use it!" said Chataqua with a laugh.

"Chataqua!" exclaimed Chalapow with a big grin, looking with widened eyes at the calypo. "You must now change your name to Chatypo... Chataqua of the Calypo!"

With Chalapo was Rowhatan, a boy several years younger. He was thin, muscular, serious in disposition and held himself straight as an arrow. A determined look was always on his lean face. He had befriended Chalapow and the two were almost never seen apart.

Note how we have made Rowhatan an "opposite" of Chalapow.

"That's a lot of fish to carry!" exclaimed Rowhatan, doubtfully.
"We will carry it on your back, Rowhatan," said Chalapow. "I shall guide it by holding its tail!"
Calypo-Ma squeaked as if to protest. Chataqua laughed. "Calypo-Ma is worried that you may drop him."

We set up a sequence of good natured banter among friends.

Chataqua and Manatapac laughed. Rowhatan wrinkled his brow seriously, contemplating the weight of the calypo.
"Chalapow! Did you bring the herbs and cloths?" asked Chataqua.
"I have them," said Rowhatan, his face solemn as he stared at Calypo-Ma lying in the tidal pool.
They applied the herb sauce to the bloody wound inflicted by the kakapa.
"Ohh!" exclaimed Chalapow, rolling his eyes. "I feel sick!"
"Don't be a woman, Chalapow," said Rowhatan wrinkling his brow.
"But, it is a terrible wound," said Chalapow in horror. "Kakapa has very sharp teeth!"
"You should swim and let Kakapa bite off your belly!" laughed Manatapac.
"Ohhh no," screamed Chalapow, rubbing his belly. "I may never swim again after seeing this!"
Chataqua and Manatapac laughed.
Rowhatan grimaced. "You should run far with me to sweat off your big belly."

"I could run to Werocomoco to see Wahunsonacock and back... and I'd still have my belly," laughed Chalapow. "It is my friend, you see."

In this scene we have elements of a "bonding event" between the friends. It is also part of the "status quo event" depicting a comfortable world where friends depend on each other and have carefree, frivolous times. We are also "setting the stage" for events that will follow involving the animal character Calypo-Ma.

The WOW Factors in this scene are Emotion (concern for the dolphin), Suspense (will the dolphin survive?), Action (caring for the dolphin), Surprise (surprise that the dolphin can communicate), Heroism (caring for the dolphin) and Humor (banter with Chalapow). There is some Pizzazz (introduction of an animal character). The WOW Score is 6.5/10. Do you agree? How would you score it?

Try the "practice" again. What is your version of this scene? Can you inject more humor into the conversational banter? As you do these "practices", I am sure that you are finding that it takes time and a lot of "mental energy" to write a scene (even if I have given you the idea with which to practice). Don't be discouraged! A scene such as the one from which the example is drawn might take me 3-6 hours to write, including the time I sit back in my chair and let my mind search the creative heavens for more and better ideas. If you have just "read on" and not yet done a "practice", start now. It's fun!

Mystery Scenes

Every novel can benefit from some mystery... some unknown that keeps the Reader in suspense. By "mystery", I mean: a puzzle to solve; a spooky situation; suspense; some or all of those.

Giving the hero a puzzle he must solve that is related to the story is a very useful tool in writing a WOW book. The puzzle does not have to be spooky, but it can be. If it's a crime drama, it may not be spooky. If it's a haunted house drama, it demands that the puzzle be "spooky". If it's an adventure novel, the puzzle is "suspenseful"!

Example, Suspenseful Mystery Scene;

Chataqua, Manatapac, Chalapow and Rowhatan walked the beach near Break-in-the-Sand where the Water-That-Never-Ends flowed into a creek that ran inside the dunes to a salt water swamp.

"I have found many shells!" shouted Chalapow kneeling beside a small tidal pool.

The others ran to where Chalapow knelt scooping up shells and putting them into a deerskin pouch.

"The women will treasure these shells," said Manatapac.

"Ahhh..." sighed Chalapow, "Manatapac, always wanting to make the women happy... never to take a wife!"

"They will use the shells in making colorful beads for their buckskins," said Manatapac, embarrassed.

"And they will think what a wonderful Brave you are," smiled Chalapow, "and reward you nicely."

Manatapac threw a handful of sand at Chalapow, who ducked and scampered away, his belly bouncing as he ran.

"These are the shell of the shellfish-that-tastes-like-the-sea" said Chataqua picking up a shell and examining it. "It is a beautiful shell."

"Flatfish, crabs and winged-fish-who-fly-in-the-water-with-stinging-tails eat them," observed Rowhatan. "They eat the inside and cast the shells adrift."

"The tides wash them onto the beach," said Chalapow, "All for Manatapac's women!"

Manatapac threw another fistful of sand at Chalapow. "And I will have my reward!" he said with a big smile on his face.

Chataqua's eyes fell first on the plentiful shells, but there was a shadow in the pool that caught his eye.

"What is this?" asked Chataqua wading through the pool toward the shadow.

We introduce some "mystery".

Chataqua bent over and grasped a large piece of wood that lay partially submerged. He dragged the heavy piece of wood from the tidal pool.

"What have you found?" asked Manatapac curiously.

"I am not sure," said Chataqua, examining the wood carefully.

"It has a strange hard place on it," said Manatapac, placing his hand on a piece of hard material on the wood.

Now we have posed a puzzle for the boys. What is this mysterious object?

The wood was about two arms lengths long. At one end was a piece of metal that none of them recognized. They knew only stone, bone and wood as tools. The metal wrapped around the piece of wood and had a circular piece of the hard material attached to it.

"What can it be?" asked Rowhatan uneasily.

"It is a piece from a great canoe," said Chataqua thoughtfully.

"No... no," said Chalapow, his eyes wide, "no canoe can be that large!"

"This circular piece," said Chataqua, turning the wood over. "It has a piece of rope... or something attached to it."

"What is it?" asked Manatapac staring at the long piece of wood.

"I do not know," said Chataqua, irritated that he did not understand what he held.

"Leave it there," said Chalapow backing away with wide eyes. "It looks evil to me!"

"Look over there!" exclaimed Rowhatan, pointing down the beach.

They got up and ran to where Rowhatan pointed. Another piece of wood lay in the surf, moving up and down as the water foamed and rushed over it. It was longer than the first piece of wood they had found. It had the same hard material wrapped around it. Attached to the metal was more rope. The rope held a ragged piece of strange, heavy cloth. Chataqua fingered the cloth. What was it? What could it possibly be used for?

"Look!" shouted Chalapow. "Calypo! Maybe they have come looking for their friend!"

Chataqua looked to seaward and saw a number of calypos frolicking in the surf. Their dorsal fins cleaved the water gracefully, making little white ripples as they plunged in and out of the breaking surf.

"Calypo-Ma is much better," said Chataqua. "Soon he will leave the Salt Lake and join his friends in the waves."

Here we use a comment by Chataqua (an information thread) to establish that Calypo-Ma is getting better... rather than using a scene.

Suddenly a spout of water rose above the surface beyond the waves.

"Watanock is also there," said Chataqua excitedly. "The sea-creature-with-the-great-diving-tail blows his spout into the air!"

"I see it," shouted Rowhatan staring at the black mound that was the creature's back. "And there is more wood floating between the calypos and the watanock!"

"You're right" observed Chataqua. "I am going to get it!"

Chataqua walked toward the surf, flexing his arms.

"Be careful, Chataqua," said Chalapow with a mock serious face. "Kakapa, the fish-that-eats-men swims there! He will bite your manhood off and chew it up!"

"The kakapa would not find your manhood beneath your belly," laughed Manatapac. "Perhaps you should go!"

"No... the fish-that-eats-men fears the calypo," said Chataqua with authority, "they will not be here."

"What of the sea-creature-with-the-great-diving-tail?" asked Rowhatan in a serious voice. "What of watanock?

"My father says that they are gentle creatures," said Chataqua. "They are very big but very gentle."

"I will go with you to get the wood!" exclaimed Manatapac bravely.

We introduce suspense. What is the source of all these strange pieces of wood? Are there any kakapa?

Chataqua and Manatapac ran into the surf. They swam out to the breaking surf and plunged into a wave. They surfaced on the other side of the wave and swam among the calypo. One of the calypo surfaced near Chataqua, looked at him with a curious black eye, and then dove under him. Chataqua and Manatapac swam strongly toward a large object floating in the water fifty arms lengths beyond the breaking waves. They reached it and grabbed it.

We use this event to describe the nature of the calypo which is important to events yet to come.

"This is a big piece of wood!" exclaimed Manatapac.
"Let's pull it to the sand," said Chataqua, grappling with the large object as it bounced about in the waves.
They swam toward the shore. The calypo continued to break water around them, looking at them curiously with an eye over a mouth that seemed to always grin. They reached the surf and pushed the piece of wood into it. A wave took the large object and hurled it toward the sand. Chataqua and Manatapac followed, wading onto the sand. Chalapow and Rowhatan stood gazing at the piece of wood in awe.
"What is it?" asked Chataqua, striding up to where the others stood, followed by Manatapac.
"It is wood… shaped like a large woman!" exclaimed Chalapow, his eyes bugging out of his head. "Manatapac will like this wood! We had best protect it from him!"
Chalapow screens Manatapac from the piece of wood shaped like a woman.
"It is a god," said Manatapac, pushing Chalapow away good naturedly. "It is the image of a god… worshipped by someone far away."
"It may be," said Chataqua, his mind racing. "It is from a great canoe… one blown apart by the wind."
"Are you sure?" asked Chalapow, wide-eyed.
"What else could it be?" asked Chataqua.
"Maybe Gitsche Kakapa bit the great canoe into many pieces!" said Chalapow, snapping his teeth together ferociously. "Maybe Gitsche Kakapa is so large that he can do this to a great canoe."

"No kakapa could be that big!" said Manatapac, waving aside Chalapow's comment.

"Benatagua says that he has seen Gitsche Kakapa... the great-fish-that-eats-men," said Chataqua. "It was when he was blown toward the Land-Where-The-Sun-Is-Born while returning from his great discovery."

"How big was it?" asked Chalapow, his eyes wide, fear in his voice.

"Benatagua said Gitsche Kakapa was longer than his canoe," said Chataqua. "Gitsche Kakapa followed Benatagua until he paddled into shallow water."

"What did Gitsche Kakapa do?" asked Chalapow fearfully.

"It swam away to the Water-That-Never-Ends," said Chataqua. "The Broad Waters was too shallow for its liking."

"Only watanock is so big," said Manatapac "Only watanock is big enough to attack a canoe... and he does not do it."

"Gitsche Kakapa is not like the other kakapa," said Chataqua walking over to the long piece of wood with the cloth held to it by the strange metal. He knelt beside it and studied it carefully.

"Why does this wood interest you so?" asked Manatapac.

"It is not the wood that interests me," mused Chataqua. "It is the cloth."

Chataqua is known as a boy with big ideas. Will this mysterious object give him another?

Chataqua raised the pole with the cloth on it into the air and stuck it into the sand. The breeze billowed the cloth and pulled at his arms.

"The cloth has great powers!" exclaimed Chataqua. "See how it makes the wind pull at me!"

His friends watched him, strange expressions on their faces as he pulled the cloth around to face the wind.

"Where would such a large canoe come from?" asked Rowhatan thoughtfully.

Chataqua looked to the east over the blue-green ocean, the wind in his face. "From the Land-Where-The Sun-Is-Born," he said as if in a trance.

And so, a mystery is created! And the mystery of the land beyond the unknown horizon is reinforced, tantalizing Chataqua. What is the wood shaped like a woman? Where did it come from? What does it mean? What is the cloth and why is it of such interest to Chataqua? Is the story about Gitsche Kakapa true? How did the great canoe meet its end? Where did it come from? We have not "stated" these questions... we have generated them in the Reader's mind.

This is a "Bonding Event", a "Catalyst Event" and has elements of a "Decision Event". It also uses "action under cover" in a clever way (they see only the "evidence" of some mysterious tragedy at sea). It is a scene involving a mysterious event with some injected humor.

This scene contains WOW Factors Emotion (at finding the shipwreck), Suspense (what are the artifacts found?), Action (swimming to retrieve the artifacts), Surprise (that an artifact has the shape of a woman), Mystery (what is the purpose of the mysterious cloth?), Humor (banter among friends) and Pizzazz (a very "different" type of scene). The WOW Score is 7/10. Do you agree?

Note that here, as in other scenes. I have not just concentrated on the events of the scene. I have added "color" in the passages about the scallops (*shellfish-that-tastes-like-the-sea*), the dolphins (*calypo*) and the whale (*watanock*).

****

Chapter Eighteen
Romantic and Sex Scenes

A romantic scene is one where the "point" of the scene is to explore or further the romance between the main characters. It is a scene where the Author can not be "bashful".

Example: Prelude to a Romantic Scene

Chataqua sat under the spreading live oak tree outside the entrance to Chesepiooc. The great limbs of the tree waved in a strong wind from the Land-Where-The-Cold-Wind-Blows.

"Chataqua!" exclaimed Alanoas, pushing against the wind to walk toward him. "What are you doing?"

"I am thinking about my canoe," said Chataqua. "I have completed my plan and selected a tall cypress which we must hollow out."

"Where is it?" asked Alanoas coming to where he sat.

Chataqua got up and a gust of wind blew against him. A piece of bark flew through the air and hit him in the chest. Suddenly, the idea came upon him!

"Did you see that piece of bark?" exclaimed Chataqua excitedly.

"Bischi," said Alanoas. "I saw it. What is it?"

"Suppose the piece of bark were a canoe?'

"What?"

"If I had a cloth on the canoe, the wind would fill the cloth and push it along faster!" observed Chataqua.

"You have another big idea," said Alanoas with a knowing smile. "I can tell!"

"Yes... yes... maybe I do."

"Where is the cypress tree you have selected for your canoe?" asked Alanoas.

Chataqua's mind was filled with his thoughts about the strange cloth. "It's... in the Grand-Salt-Water-Swamp."

"Will you show it to me?" asked Alanoas coyly.

"Well, yes," said Chataqua. "But your Father may not want you to go into the Swamp with just me."

Alanoas took him by the hand and tugged him toward the swamp.

"Come on," said Alanoas, "before the storm comes! Don't worry about my Father!"

They ran off together.

I am using the prelude to the romantic scene to make another point in the story... the dawning of the idea of a sail... a "wind cloth"... on Chataqua.

Chataqua and Alanoas ran together out of the village past the spreading live oak tree and toward the Grand-Salt-Water-Swamp along the path that led to Point-Where-Great-Waters-Meet. The sun was low in the sky and occasionally obscured by clouds, casting mysterious shadows from the tall pine and cypress trees. Frogs croaked and small animals skittered away from them as they approached. As soon as they were out of sight of the village, Alanoas bashfully took Chataqua's hand and held it tightly.

Chataqua and Alanoas are running into the forest in the evening, probably against her Father's will. So the Reader is expecting something romantic to happen. Draw it out a little... literary foreplay!

Example, A Romantic Scene;

"You were very brave I am told... at the fight with Malapok," said Alanoas cautiously.

"I did not intend to make Malapok lose such face," said Chataqua regretfully.

"It was not your fault... it was he that lost his bravery in the water. It was he who thought that the fin was kakapa, the fish-that-eats-men and not calypo, the creature-of-the-sea-that-smiles."

"Yes... I know," said Chataqua. "But Malapok has lost face and he blames me... I am afraid that he will be my enemy."

"He already is your enemy," said Alanoas.

"You mean..."

"Yes... because he wants me."

"And you do not want him?"

"I have told you that I want you, Chataqua," said Alanoas tenderly. "I have told Masonnacok, my father, that I want you."

"Does Masonnacok want me to have you?"

"He said that is a matter for when I come of age in the next two moons," said Alanoas, "but I am sure that he likes you."

"And what of Malapok?"

"Masonnacok must somehow keep the favor of the Periku," said Alanoas worriedly. "Malapok uses the power of his father to pursue me."

We are establishing conflict and tension (drama) over the prospect of Chataqua asking for Alanoas when she is of age... which is soon.

They walked on in silence until they came to a fallen cypress tree next to the black waters of the swamp. A quarter moon was rising in the sky, even though the light of the day was still with them. Another tall cypress tree, reaching twenty feet into the sky rose above the fallen tree.

"Is that the tree?" asked Alanoas looking at the fallen tree.

"Yes," said Chataqua. "It is a mighty tree that has fallen in a storm."

"But it is a mighty water you want to canoe," said Alanoas gazing soulfully at the tree. "Is this tree so mighty that it will take you safely on the Water-That-Never-Ends?"

"Such a tree took my Father to the Land-Where-The-Cold-Wind-Blows," said Chataqua. "It will take me."

"I worry for you!" said Alanoas.

"The sun and the moon are fighting for the sky," said Chataqua, looking up.

"The moon will win... and in the morning, the sun will win," said Alanoas, "just as we all win and lose."

We demonstrate that Alanoas is a "thinking" person.

"I will win," said Chataqua. "I will achieve great things, just as my father has!"

Alanoas sat on the fallen tree and pulled him down beside her. "You will win, Chataqua," she said. "But you will also lose... some of the time."

"My father says that when you are losing, you win by showing courage," said Chataqua solemnly.

"If that is true, then you will win all the time!"

Chataqua took a deep breath. He had doubts about his courage to sail to the Land-Where-The-Sun-Is-Born... but he was in love with the challenge, and he had committed to it. A thrill of fear ran through him as he thought about it.

"Yes... it will be so with me," he said hesitantly.

"My mother, Pretioas, says that if you have real love, you will always win, no matter if times be good or bad."

"She is a wise woman."

Chataqua looked at Alanoas in the dusk of the salt water swamp. He always wanted to look at her, but often tried not to, for when he did, her beauty weakened him. It also made him happy... and lustful in a way that his mother, Chalatas, told him was natural but dangerous. Alanoas looked up at Chataqua, her eyes and lips inviting him to kiss her. Reluctantly, he gave in to his impulse and his lips touched hers ever so briefly.

"Do you have real love, Chataqua?" asked Alanoas softly.

Chataqua paused as exciting feelings ran through him from the tingle of her kiss. "Yes, Alanoas, I have real love... for you."

"I made a song for you," said Alanoas, "... for us."

Chataqua was taken aback. "Please sing it," he said.

Alanoas sang in clear, sweet tones;

> *I see the deer run, I tell the deer,*
> *We walk together,*
> *We will remember,*
> *We are forever,*
> *You and I.*

We composed this song to fit here. It adds to the romance.

"Thank you," said Chataqua, taking her hand in his.

"Now you must make a verse," said Alanoas with a smile.

Chataqua squinted his eyes and thought. Then he sang in a strong voice:

> *I see the red bird, I tell him clearly,*
> *We walk together,*
> *We will remember,*
> *We are forever,*
> *You and I.*

Alanoas smiled radiantly and a tear came to her eye. "Will you ask my father for me now that the Council has declared you a Brave?"

"I will ask for you when I have proved myself... and when you come of age," said Chataqua. "First, I must prove myself as a Brave... I must canoe to the unknown horizon!"

This example has elements of a "Bonding Event", a "Goal Event", and a "Catalyst Event". Chataqua and Alanoas further the bond established in childhood. Chataqua reaffirms his goals. He is catalyzed toward his goals by the reassurance of Alanoas. The WOW Factors present include Emotion (between the two people in love), Romance (the kisses, the song) and Pizzazz (the hesitance of Chataqua confuses the romance). The WOW Score is 3/10, but the emotion Factor is high. If we chose to "weight" the WOW Factors with a simple weighting matrix, the WOW would be higher (can you design a weighting matrix for the WOW factors?).

This romantic scene is tender and makes its point without resorting to overtly sexual events. In most cases, you don't need overtly sexual descriptions. Rather, you "plant the seeds" in the mind of the Reader and let him/her fill in the details. From this scene, a Reader can imagine the pent up physical feelings of each character as well as the emotional conflict that exists between them. You have established a tension that the Reader instinctively wants resolved, and he/she will read on until you resolve it. The Reader wants, at this point, for Chataqua and Alanoas to make passionate love and be happy together... but you haven't taken the Reader there yet.

Try the "practice" again with this scene! Oh come on now... don't be lazy! If you are to be a successful Author, you must START to do the hard part... which is to actually write instead of dream!

Sex Scenes

A "sex scene" is one that goes beyond "romance", beyond emotional and beyond just "hugging and kissing" to describe sexual acts in varying degrees. Do you need a sex scene in your novel? No. Many good novels do not "take it that far". The "degree" to which you take it is important in that it "sets the tone" of the book.

Sex scene degrees can be described as:
1. Mild   Touching gently
2. Suggestive Touching and suggestions of more
3. Hot   Emotions and descriptions of foreplay
4. Torrid   Emotions and descriptions of sex
5. Vulgar   Vivid, mechanical descriptions of sex

You should know where you are "aiming" your novel. If your target audience is a completely adult general audience, excursions to the torrid level may be the best course of action. If it is a sophisticated adult audience, you may want to stay at the hot level. For books that will be read by teens, I suggest you stay at the mild to suggestive level.

A sex scene is not just sex... you, as the Author, must create "sexual tension" between the characters to make it interesting. What are the consequences of sharing sex? What are the motivations of each partner in sharing sex beyond just that of physical pleasure? Maybe one partner seeks just physical pleasure and the other has different motivations. What are they? Does one or the other fear sex? Why?

How do feelings and motivations shape the way people come together for a sexual encounter? Sex can be a profound physical expression of much deeper emotions. Be sure to capture it all! The physical act of sex alone is only mildly interesting (unless you are thirteen years old!). Capture the profound physical expression of the deeper emotions and you will hook your Reader.

How in the world am I going to write a sex scene, you may ask? Every person I've ever had sex with will think I'm giving away his/her secrets! Well, you have to shed this kind of fear and write on. If accused, your answer is... "Oh come on, it's just fiction... I have a vivid imagination!"

Example, a Sex Scene;

Chataqua and Alanoas ran out of the village and walked together in the Grand-Salt-Water-Swamp. It had become their favorite place, dappled with sunlight filtering through gathering clouds and trees, mysterious in its smelly dark waters. The birds twittered in the cypress trees and flew merrily about. Long legged birds waded the murky, shallow waters searching for the unsuspecting fish or frog.

"We must not offend your Father with these walks," said Chataqua worriedly.

"My Mother knows that I take walks with you," said Alanoas. "She says that it is alright as long as we don't abuse the privilege."

"She trusts me?"

"Oh, she is more worried about me than you," said Alanoas, a twinkle in her eye.

Chataqua looked at Alanoas with a questioning stare. She looked back and giggled mischievously. He wanted so much to hold her... to have her, but the consequences of doing so alarmed him. How could he take a wife while he still had his great deed in front of him... his quest over the unknown horizon. How could he, a new Brave, afford to give Masonnacok a gift worthy of Alanoas in exchange for her. In the distance, dark clouds began to form toward the Land-Where-The-Sun-Sets.

"It will rain," said Chataqua looking at the clouds.

"It will not bother us," said Alanoas, glad to have Chataqua to herself for a change. He had disappeared into the Swamp every day with his friends for a full cycle of the moon and she missed him.

"When will you leave on this trip that you talk about?" asked Alanoas, anxiety in her voice. "The trip you say you must take to prove yourself as a Brave?"

"Soon," said Chataqua. "But first I must finish my great canoe!"

The Reader now understands that Chataqua is afraid of the consequences of sex.

"Can you not use your father's long canoe... the one with the fish and bird carvings?"

"Yes," said Chataqua, "I can use it, but I am building an even greater canoe... one that will stay with me in the waters beyond the unknown horizon."

"Must you do this?" asked Alanoas. "You are a Brave now... you could ask for me very soon."

"I know," said Chataqua unhappily, "but I may not return from the unknown horizon... and I would not have you without a man. It is not good for a young woman to be without a man!"

"I will be very angry should you not come back to me!" exclaimed Alanoas, her beautiful face clouding.

"I will come back," said Chataqua determinedly, "and if I am successful, I will be rewarded and be able to afford a wife."

"You are my man, Chataqua," said Alanoas, stopping and holding both of his hands tightly. "I could not belong to Malapok!"

"Yes... yes... but I must be a man worthy of you!"

"You are now!" exclaimed Alanoas, her temper creeping into her voice. "Why do you insist on being more?"

"In your eyes perhaps I am worthy...but I know that I am an unproven Brave."

"You will have a chance to prove yourself," said Alanoas. "The Wepeneooc will raid us again... and you will have your chance... though it worries me greatly!"

"I will fight the Wepeneooc," said Chataqua determinedly, "but I must also seek the unknown horizon!"

Alanoas pulled him to her and wrapped her arms around his waist. She longed for him to touch her and hold her close to him. She moved against him and felt his warm body next to hers. Chataqua kissed her and rubbed her shoulders. She loosened the deer skin cloth of her shawl, exposing the tops of her rounded breasts. His fingers passed over them, touching her briefly. Chataqua groaned and then backed away.

We show again that Chataqua is afraid of the consequences of sex. He cannot afford a wife.

"Why do you leave me?" asked Alanoas in a husky voice.

"I should not... see you, touch you," murmured Chataqua, "until I have asked and been granted permission for you to be my woman."

"You can touch me," said Alanoas, "and only we will know!"

"It would be an insult to your father," said Chataqua uncomfortably, "whether he knows or not!"

"But... I long for you so!" said Alanoas in frustration and anger.

"Walk on with me, Alanoas," said Chataqua, backing away. He pulled her gently by the hand. "I want to show you something."

They started again along the path that ran on the high ground between the dark waters of the swamp. Unnoticed to them, a dark cloud floated in the sky toward them. They approached a long cypress tree trunk. Beside it were the dead coals of fires. The log was partially hollowed out into three distinct sections. It lay among a grove of tall pine tress.

"Is this the same log we saw before?" asked Alanoas.

"Yes... Manatapac, Rowhatan and Chalapow are helping me to hollow out this log to make a canoe," said Chataqua. "See! I have carved calypos on the front of the canoe."

"The calypo are... very beautiful," said Alanoas." They will lead you on your journey."

"They will protect me and show me the way."

"The canoe is very big!" said Alanoas staring at the log.

"It has to be big," said Chataqua. "It must take me on the Water-That-Never-Ends toward the Land-Where-The-Sun-Is-Born."

"You have only burned out the log in one area," said Alanoas.

"Yes," said Chataqua. "We have much more work to do. I am going to put sapling poles into the wood and hang cloth

from them for the wind to blow."

We show that Chataqua has a solution for the lesson he and his friends learned from the wreck they found on the beach.

"I don't understand," said Alanoas.

"The wind will blow the cloth and push the canoe through the water," said Chataqua determinedly.

"Will that work?" asked Alanoas looking at Chataqua admiringly.

"It will work if you will make me the cloth," said Chataqua hopefully.

"I will," said Alanoas eagerly, "but you must show me how big it is to be."

The sky clouded over quickly and became dark. There was a rumble of thunder, followed by the crack of nearby lightning. Alanoas grabbed Chataqua and hid her head against his chest. The thunder rumbled again. They ducked behind a tall pine tree surrounded by brush. He held her close to him. He kissed her and his hand found her breasts, moving over them until she gasped in delight and rising passion. She put her body close to him and felt his strength.

"I do love you so much, Alanoas," murmured Chataqua. "More than is good for me."

She kissed him on the chest and cupped her hands over his, holding them to her breasts. "I love you, Chataqua," she said quietly. "I want you to ask for me... so that we can have this... and more!"

There was a tremendous crash and flash of light. Chataqua felt a tingling all over his body. Alanoas cried out in pain and alarm. A tall cypress tree near them fell with a grinding, roaring sound to the ground, smoking with the heat of the lightning. The smell of burning wood and disturbed ozone in the air penetrated their nostrils. Chataqua felt paralyzed... unable to move. Alanoas fell from his arms to the ground, her deerskin shirt falling open. He knelt beside her, feeling weak all over as the sky rumbled and growled.

Acts of nature are always a good way to stop something that's going on and force other actions.

"Alanoas!" shouted Chataqua, staring at her with wonder and concern.

Her eyes opened slowly and gazed at him in disbelief. "What was that?"

"Lightning... it was just lightning... the fire from the sky of Okee," said Chataqua gazing around him, feeling his strength returning slowly.

"I thought it was just you... the way you held me!"

"It was Okee and the God of the Great Skies," muttered Chataqua. "He was telling us to save our passion... that passion before the marriage is forbidden."

"No... no, it was not that," said Alanoas, struggling to her feet and pulling him up. "It was just lightning... a force equal to our passion!" She pulled her deerskin shirt over her breasts protectively.

Chataqua looked at the fallen tree. It laid smoking on the ground. It had crashed to the ground precisely next to the already fallen cypress, perfectly parallel. He stared at the two trees and a dawning of understanding came over his face.

"It is a sign!" exclaimed Chataqua. "It is what I have been waiting for!"

"What do you mean?" asked Alanoas, staring at the awe on his face.

"Don't you see?" said Chataqua, grabbing her hand and pulling her toward the smoking tree and its parallel companion. "The trees... the Great God of the Sky has told me how to build a canoe for the mighty waters beyond the unknown horizon!"

"I don't see what you mean!" pouted Alanoas, angry at the storm that had interrupted their passion.

"The two trees!" exclaimed Chataqua. "I must carve out the two trees and lash them together... just as they lay there side by side...that will make the canoe big enough for the large waves of the Water-That-Never-Ends!"

Fat raindrops began to fall through the cypress and pine canopy, making explosive splashes in the dark waters of the swamp. There was another rumble of thunder and a distant flash as the sky darkened menacingly.

"We must hurry," said Alanoas, tugging at Chataqua's hand. "The fire from the sky will come again!"

Chataqua followed her, glancing back at the parallel trees. He couldn't wait for the storm to pass so that he could return to the trees with his friends and explain to them the new idea for his great canoe.

Sex Scenes should not be "just sex". They have to other elements, such as the lightning storm and the "how to build a canoe sign" in the preceding scene. This scene contains elements of the "Catalyst Event" and the "Decision Event". The "sign" given catalyzes Chataqua further toward his decision. His decision to build a new type of canoe, what we know as a "catamaran" leads him toward the decision to embark on his quest for the Land-Where-The-Sun-Is-Born.

The scene has the WOW Factors Emotion (emotion between the two lovers), Suspense (will they share sex?), Action (the crashing tree and the "omen"), Romance (the love scene in the storm) and Pizzazz (uniqueness of the scene in blending romance and omen). The WOW is 5/10. Again, the emotion factor is high, so the WOW is 5/10+.

It is okay if writing the sex scene arouses you. You must think what the characters think and feel what they feel. If they are involved in sex, you must "be there"!

Now that you've gotten the sex scene on paper, you can go chase your mate around the bedroom! He/she will probably enjoy your mood, even if the source is unknown!

****

Chapter Nineteen
Innovative and Highly Dramatic Scenes

Innovative Scenes

An innovative scene is one devoted to the hero/heroine "figuring something out"... "innovating"... some part of his/her problem is partially solved, or at least so he/she thinks. Such scenes have "problem solving content". It may be a technical solution or a social solution... but the hero demonstrates his/her ability to solve a problem in a way interesting to the Reader.

If the problem has been properly stated and defined in preceding scenes, the solution, or partial solution will satisfy the Reader's intense desire to "know more". How in the world is the hero going to solve this problem? Does he have the smarts? The technology? The resources?

Example, Innovative Scene, Part 1;
Chataqua, Manatapac, Chalapow and Rowhatan sat under an old, spreading live oak tree just outside the village palisade. The oak sent its branches high into the sky and from them sprouted many twisting branches forming the organized chaos of the old tree. The branches hung from the high limbs almost to the ground creating a canopy impenetrable by all but the heaviest rain, the hottest sun. It was one of their favorite places, the shade from the magnificent tree making it cool and pleasant even on a hot day in the Time-When-The-Trees-Bring-Leaves.

"My great canoe is long from finished," said Chataqua staring at the moss on the ground under the old tree. "I must finish it soon and use it to go to the Land-Where-The-Sun-Is-Born and discover new things!"

"The water toward the Land-Where-The-Sun-Is-Born is unknown and very dangerous," said Manatapac. "What do you hope to find that is worth such a risk?"

"Yes," said Rowhatan, "the Water-That-Never-Ends is filled with storms and kakapa."

"I wouldn't want to go there," shuddered Chalapow.

"I must go there," said Chataqua. "As Benatagua went to the Land-Where-The-Cold-Wind-Blows, I must go to the Land-Where-The-Sun-Is-Born."

"You are, as always, very brave and very foolish," grinned Manatapac. "And filled with noble but sometimes stupid ideas!"

"Perhaps," said Chataqua with a nonchalant shrug of his powerful shoulders. "Will you help me finish the great canoe as soon as we can?"

Note here the "fade". I could have these fellows sitting under that iconic tree talking on and on… but I have made my point for the scene. Fade away and move on! By the way, that spreading live oak tree is in my back yard near the site where Chesepiooc once flourished.

Example, Innovative Scene, Part 2;
The big cypress tree lay on the ground as Chataqua and his friends chopped off its limbs with their sharpened stone axes. They were all coated with walnut oil to ward off the mosquitoes that plagued the Grand-Salt-Water-Swamp. Chalapow picked up a large limb as though it were a twig and carried it to the edge of the swamp.

"We've got most of the limbs off," said Rowhatan, swatting at a determined mosquito.

"The coals from the fire are hot," said Chalapow. "I have blown on them with my great wind!"

"You have a great wind," said Manatapac playfully, "I have felt its power!"

"His wind and his strength!" said Rowhatan seriously. "His round belly gives him great strength!"

Chalapow rubbed his belly and laughed. "The belly of great power!" he exclaimed.

"The belly the whining-bugs-that-bite-and-sting love to eat!" grinned Chataqua.

"Your great strength has its use," said Manatapac. "You should use it to become a Brave!"

"Someday, maybe I will," said Chalapow nonchalantly as if becoming a Brave had no meaning to him. "But I can fight the Wepeneooc even if I am not a Brave."

We show that Chalapow is strong and jovial, but has no ambition to be a Brave.

"The Werowance will not let you fight unless you are a Brave!" said Manatapac.

"The Werowance will allow him to help in other ways," said Chataqua. "I will see to that!"

"Being a Brave is maybe not as good as being Chalapow," said Rowhatan. "Everyone loves Chalapow...everyone does not love all the Braves!"

"You may be right," said Manatapac scratching his bald head. "I've never thought of it that way."

"But I must become a Brave," said Rowhatan. "Because I am not so lucky as Chalapow to be so loved."

Rowhatan is a complete opposite of Chalapow... serious and anxious to become a Brave.

"Oh, but you are lucky!" exclaimed Chalapow, giving Rowhatan a playful shove. "You have a friend in Chalapow such as no other!"

Rowhatan smiled. "I catch some of the love for Chalapow that spills over!"

"We will need the hot coals soon" said Chataqua standing and wiping the sweat from his forehead. "We are going to hollow out the log a little bit differently than what we are used to."

"What do you mean?" asked Manatapac curiously.

"The log will measure almost five arm lengths, "said Chataqua. "We will hollow out the log in three sections, leaving a hand length divide between the three sections."

"Why do that?" asked Chalapow. "It sounds like a lot of work to me!"

Chataqua sat down on the log. "I have made a plan."

"You always have a plan," said Rowhatan seriously. "You are a big walking plan!"

Chataqua crouched near the ground, took a stick and began to draw a picture in the dirt of his great canoe. "One arm length from the front of the canoe will end the first hollowing. Then there will be a two arm length hollowing, and another two arm length hollowing at the back."

"What is the purpose of these three hollowings?" asked Manatapac looking skeptically at the scratches in the dirt.

"I want to put a hole from the top down into the wood that separates the sections... each of them," said Chataqua drawing two lines above the sketch of the canoe, "like this... to hold strong, straight limbs we will cut... and stand them into the air."

"You have lost your mind, Chataqua," laughed Chalapow. "A canoe with a forest growing from it?"

We spend some time on the design of Chataqua's canoe. It is important to do so to establish the credibility of the adventure he will undertake... at least in his eyes.

"No... no!" exclaimed Chataqua. "Do you remember the pieces of wood we found on the beach?"

"Yes," said Chalapow, "shaped like a woman for Manatapac to hug and love!"

Manatapac swatted Chalapow playfully.

"No... no," said Chataqua impatiently. "The long piece of wood with the strange metal... and the pieces of cloth attached?"

"I remember," said Manatapac thoughtfully.

"I have thought long about it," said Chataqua. "The long pole is used to hold the cloth into the air so that the wind will blow it... and when the wind blows, it makes the canoe move through the water... don't you see?"

"You mean you won't have to paddle the canoe?" asked Rowhatan in doubt.

"Oh I will need a paddle," said Chataqua, "but when the wind blows, I will need it only to tell the canoe the direction I want."

"Suppose the wind does not blow where you intend to go?" asked Manatapac, wrinkling his brow.

"It is a problem," said Chataqua, his eyes bright with the challenge. "I will have to try the canoe and see if I can use the paddle to choose the direction... even as the wind blows."

"It is another of your big ideas that will not work," said Rowhatan with a grimace.

"Maybe," said Chataqua, his expression eager, his eyes bright with his idea. "Let's start putting the coals on the log and burning out the sections. We have much to do!"

In this scene, we have enhanced the reputation of Chataqua as a problem solver and innovator. We have engaged in further character development of the four friends. We have also performed the necessary task of making the voyage to the Land-Where-The-Sun-Is-Born credible.

This scene has elements of the "bonding event", the "catalyst event" and the "decision event". You can see from the way the "events" are building that we are not slavishly following any "outline". We are not following exactly the "story events", though we are making sure that they are addressed in some way as we proceed to make sure we have a "story" and not just a narrative. We are generally following the direction we established and writing in a free form art mode... writing a scene and asking "what should come next?"

We are also making sure that each scene has the necessary WOW Factors. The WOW factors in this scene include Emotion (the dedication to the task), Suspense (will the new canoe "work"?), Action (the innovative tasks), Humor (the banter among friends), and Pizzazz (the description of Chataqua's innovative plan). The WOW is 5/10.

As you are writing the Rough-Through and doing spot research as you go, there occurs a point at which the novel becomes "mostly clear" to you. That is, things you didn't know where to go with, or how to handle, start "shaping up". It occurs about here. That does not mean that your Rough-Through is beginning to resemble a completed manuscript. Rather, it means that the story is becoming clearer in your mind, as well as what is left to do. That's a significant milestone. Have a cup of coffee, treasure the moment, and press on!

Oh yes, here is a good chance for some more practice. Try an experimental Creative Review. Read the example in this chapter again and rewrite it focusing exclusively on "creative description". Can you handle the descriptions better? Can

you add descriptions that will make the whole scene better?
Can you maintain a proper balance between description and
dialogue?

Highly Dramatic Scenes

We need a scene that describes the situation between
Wahunsonacock and Chesapian that will lead to an attack by
the Wepeneooc. We can also use it to further explore the
rivalry between Benatagua and Maltakak. This is a
"confrontation" type scene, one of many "highly dramatic"
types.

Example, Prelude to a Dramatic Scene of Confrontation;
The meeting with Sachem Chesapian in the morning was
unusual. Most of the time, they met at night at the Council of
Braves when a roaring fire was built. It must be something
very important, thought Benatagua as he walked to the circle
of logs around the ashes of an old fire. He saw Chesapian
standing stiffly next to a tall Brave with turkey feathers in his
headband, arranged in a manner unfamiliar to Benatagua.
The Sachem motioned for Benatagua and the strange Brave to
follow him. They went inside the Lodge of the Sachem and sat
cross legged on the hard dirt floor.
"This is Mosco, a Brave of the Wepeneooc," said Chesapian
nodding at the Brave who sat across from the Sachem. "He
brings a message from Opectanotak and Wahunsonacock."
"The Great Sachem of the Powhatan Federation bids you
greetings and hopes that the Chesapeake prosper," said Mosco
carefully choosing his words. "He values your place with the
Powhatan as the dwellers most near the Water-That-Never-
Ends and wants to have closer relations with you. The Great
Sachem of the Wepeneooc sends also his greetings."
"The greetings of the Great Sachems Wahunsonacock and
Opectanotak are welcomed and are of much value," said
Chesapian solemnly.
"The Powhatan Tribes all value the oysters and fish of the
sea," said Mosco. "The oysters from your river are the biggest
and best in the land. They are a food that has redeeming
value to all. Wahunsonacock asks that you establish regular

trips to Wepecomoco, first village of the Wepeneooc, bringing oysters and fish from the River-Where-Swift-Waters-Flow. The Wepeneooc will deliver much of it to Powhatan, and in exchange will provide much corn and beans for the Chesapeake."

"The amount you have told me is far more than we can collect in a cycle of the moon," said Chesapian. "I do not know how many oysters are in the River-Where-Swift-Waters-Flow... I do not know if there are that many! If we take too many, they can not reproduce fast enough and we will lose them!"

"The amount has been set by Wahunsonacock," said Mosco, expressionless.

The seeds of the conflict between tribes are sewn.

"What say you, Benatagua?" asked Chesapian in a sour voice.

Benatagua looked at a hide handed him by Chesapian. It was marked with the amount of goods that Wahunsonacock demanded. He studied it thoughtfully.

"It is beyond our means to provide this without limiting our own food," said Benatagua. "If the Wepeneooc would send men here every cycle of the moon, they could stay in Shikiooc near River-Where-Swift-Waters-Flow and we could show them how to catch the oysters and the fish of the Broad Waters. It would help both tribes to learn to work together rather than war."

"That is not a part of what Wahunsonacock demands," said Mosco, showing some irritation. "He believes that every tribe of the Powhatan must share its wealth and provide for others."

"I will consult with my Council of Braves," said Chesapian. "We will send to you the amount that we can provide."

"You must provide what the great Wahunsonacock demands," said Mosco with a wave of his hand. "He has a taste for the oysters that come from your river!"

Chesapian nodded. "I have spoken," he said nodding his head. "Please say to Opectanotak that Chesapian is a friend *and will work with him for our peaceful existence."*

Mosco got up and walked to the door in the lodge. "I will give Opectanotak your answer," he said and left the lodge.

Chesapian sat still, a gloomy look on his face. "It's that Sachem of the Wepeneooc, Opectanotak," he said. "He has been hissing like the snake-that-rattles-and-kills into the ear of Wahunsonacock."

"Why would he do that?" asked Benatagua in a worried voice.

"He wants our land," said Chesapian, "and he plants poison about me in the mind of Wahunsonacock."

"We could never provide all that he asks," said Benatagua.

"Come," said Chesapian. "We must present this matter to the Council of Braves."

Thus we have a lead in to the highly dramatic scene... the debate between Benatagua and Maltakak at the Council of Braves regarding the demands of Wahunsonacock. Let's see how dramatic we can make it!

Example: Dramatic Scene of Confrontation;

The Council of Braves was assembled at the roaring fire that evening. There was a tension in the night air that made the Council seem like a strange place to Benatagua... a place to which he was unaccustomed. In the distance they heard howls from the dog-beast-that-runs-in-packs from across the Bay of the Great White Bird in Teme Forest. It was a bad omen.

All the Braves stood holding their spears around the fire, not taking their seats on the logs as they usually did. Chataqua had never been to a Council of the Braves where the spears were held. He knew it was a symbol that meant that there was a big disagreement to be settled. Only the Sachem, the Werowance and the Periku did not carry a spear. The Periku held his ceremonial pole covered with brightly covered shells from the water.

We spend time here bringing more "color" which serves as a background to the suspense of the scene.

*"Wahunsonacock asks too much," shouted Maltakak
angrily, addressing the assembled Braves. "We cannot bow to
his will!"*

*"This is the work of the greedy Opectanotak of the
Wepeneooc," said Manatapac, stepping forward.
"Wahunsonacock would not be so unreasonable!"*

*"Opectanotak says that he speaks for the Powhatan
leader," said Benatagua, shaking his head.*

*"Why should we pay tribute to the Powhatan?" asked
Maltakak in an angry voice. "We are Chesapeake... not
Powhatan. We are the People-of-the-Great-Shellfish-Waters!
We are different from the Tribes of the Inland!"*

*"Three Chiefs ago, the Powhatan came and displayed their
power to us," said Chesapian. "We did not have the power to
resist them... and many of our people were from the tribes of
the Land-Where-The-Sun-Sets... from the land of
Wahunsonacock... the land called Powhatan."*

*"And we agreed then to be a tribe of the Powhatan... and
pay them tribute!" said Manatapac.*

We provide some more essential back story.

*Chesapian glanced at Manatapac. He had been aware of
the big Brave before, but Manatapac had begun to exert
leadership among the Braves. That was good!*

*"Manatapac is right," said Chesapian. "We gave our word
to pay tribute to the Powhatan Federation...we do not break
our word."*

"The tribute they ask is too much!" shouted Malapok.

*"We do not have to be Powhatan," said Maltakak in his
raspy voice.*

*Many of the Braves nodded and there was a subdued
murmur of assent. Others sat solemnly with worried
expressions.*

*"We do not have the power to resist the Powhatan," said
Benatagua. "They will send the Wepeneooc against us. If that
is not enough, Wahunsonacock will send the Pamunkey
People-Who-Dig-With-Sticks... the Chicahominy People-of-the-
Gobbling-Bird...the Mattaponi People-That-Dwell-In-The-
Meadow ... and others from the River-That-Falls-Country".*

"We have the power to resist Opectanotak and the Wepeneooc," said Maltakak in an angry voice, growing in volume "and this is all his doing."

We build Manatapac's leadership characteristics.

"Perhaps," said Chesapian sadly, "but if Wahunsonacock takes the side of Opectanotak, the Chesapeake will pay dearly."

"We should negotiate with Opectanotak," said Benatagua, "and at the same time, talk to Wahunsonacock."

"Opectanotak will see to it that we do not talk to his older brother Wahunsonacock," said Maltakak. "We must resist the Wepeneooc and become an independent tribe… the Chesapeake!"

"That is not wise council," said Benatagua, his voice growing louder. "We are a small tribe, not accustomed to a long period of war."

"The people of the Wepeneooc will join us," said Maltakak. "Opectanotak is attempting to impose more tribute on them… in the name of the Powhatan Federation. He collects tribute for Wahunsonacock, and keeps half of it for himself!"

"You do not know that!" exclaimed Benatagua. "You say what your mind thinks it wants… not what is so!"

"We can make the Wepeneooc our allies!" exclaimed the Periku, his eyes wild with excitement. "I have seen Quiacosough in a vision and he beckons me to join with the Wepeneooc."

"You have seen nothing but your own dreams!" exclaimed Benatagua. "You are a traitor to our people if you think we can negotiate with the Wepeneooc!"

"You! You call the Periku a traitor?" screamed Maltakak.

"The Wepeneooc are a warlike tribe," shouted Benatagua, the veins in his neck bulging. "Their men enjoy war. You must hear the word of the Werowance!"

Malapok stood and shouted. "Braves of the Chesapeake! Stand with the Periku!"

We create a stand-off between Benatagua and Maltakak, a source of great drama.

About twenty Braves stood and began to tap their spears on the hard earth.

Manatapac stood and called out in a loud and steady voice. "Braves of the Chesapeake! Stand with the Werowance!"

The remainder of the Braves, numbering about sixty, stood and slammed their spears against the hard packed ground. Sachem Chesapian motioned for silence as he often did when he had heard enough. The noise of the spears against the earth ceased abruptly. Chesapian sat silently while the fire crackled and pondered his decision. After several minutes, he spoke.

"We will send Opectanotak what we can provide," said the Sachem. "I will undertake a journey to see Wahunsonacock and reason with him."

Maltakak's face took on an angry stare. "It is better that..."

He was interrupted by Sachem Chesapian. "It is done," he said with firm finality. "I have spoken!"

This scene provides a catalyst toward war with the Wepeneooc, "a catalyst event" leading to a "decision event". It will be in the war with the Wepeneooc that Chataqua becomes a recognized Brave and gains the support to embark on his great deed, the journey to the Land-Where-The-Sun-Is-Born.

The WOW Factors are Emotion (the embattled emotions of Benatagua and Maltakak), Suspense (will there be war?), Conflict (the conflict in visions between Benatagua and Maltakak) and Pizzazz (the setting at the camp fire, the tapping of the spears, etc.). The WOW is 4/10+.

Now it's your turn! How can we make this a more dramatic scene... with beautiful writing?

****

Chapter Twenty
Battle and Mourning Scenes

Battle Scenes

A battle scene is characterized by fast action, emotional and physical conflict set at a rapid pace. It is usually at a place in the novel that marks one or more "high points" in the pace and tempo of the story. It isn't just a "battle" for the sake of injecting some action… it is a battle that plays a crucial role in the story you are telling.

A "battle" is distinguished here from a "fight" in terms of its scope. A "battle" is usually something larger, containing more than one "fight". A "battle" implies physical conflict, but a "battle" may employ other forms of conflict (as can "fights"). A battle may be a conflict that employs only verbal weapons, or the maneuver of intrigue, or the manipulation of finances, and other such "weapons". The most dramatic battle is the one in which the primary characters are involved in a life and death violent conflict employing weapons that can kill.

Example, Prelude to Life and Death Battle Scene;
It was a dark night with only a sliver of a moon. Bright stars seemed to dance around the eerie white slice of light hanging in the sky. The campfire at the Council of Braves burned brightly and big sparks leaped into the night air, competing with the stars for attention in the sky.

"The Wepeneooc are coming soon," said Sachem Chesapian, deep in thought. "Perhaps in the morning."

"Had you honored the counsel of the Periku, this would not be happening," exclaimed Maltakak bitterly.

"Perhaps you are right," said Chesapian. "But now, we have no choice but to declare war on the Wepeneooc."

Benatagua took out his knife and cut a lock of his hair from his top knot. He took an arrow from his quiver and tied the hair to the arrow. He laid the arrow on his long bow and pulled it back, the muscles of his arms bulging and glistening in the firelight. Her aimed the arrow high and let it loose, its trajectory carrying it into the Place-of-Many-Islands toward the Land-Where-The Warm-Wind-Blows. "Let the arrows of war be placed along the trails of Opec Hap and Teme Forest," shouted Benatagua. "Let the Wepeneooc see our resolve along the path they must take!"

A loud wailing and chanting sound arose from the assembled Braves.

"The Wepeneooc will come from two directions," said Benatagua, "from the Land-Where-The-Warm-Wind-Blows through Teme Forest, across the Bay-of-the-Great-White-Bird and to the islands of Opec Hap... and from the Land-Where-The-Sun-Sets in their big war canoes. We shall have scouts in both places to warn of their approach."

"Okee has foreseen that the Chesapeake will perish!" shouted the Periku. "I have had a vision where Tagkanysough sends a fierce flying demon that breaths fire and comes from the Water-That-Never-Ends. The demon burns the Chesapeake people and all their lands!"

Here we inject a vision of the Periku that may come true... when the English explorers arrive.

"Our warriors are brave," said Chesapian, ignoring the Periku. "But the Wepeneooc will come in great numbers from the directions Benatagua has foreseen."

"We should have war parties out now," said Maltakak in a harsh voice. "We should attack now! We wait too long!"

"Our war parties would wander without purpose," said Benatagua his voice containing the wise counsel of many wars, "We attack when we can tell our Braves the direction from which the enemy comes!"

"We know where the enemy will come from," said Malapok. "They come from the land where they do not have to cross the Closed-Water-of-the-White-Bird... near the Lake-of-the-Clear-Water!"

"We do not know that," said Benatagua. "A wise warrior knows that his enemy will try to strike where he is not prepared."

"The war canoes from the Land-Where-The-Sun-Sets will be the most difficult," said Chesapian. "We must meet them on the beach and not let them come ashore."

"We can meet them in the water," said Chataqua cautiously.

We provide Chataqua's first advice to the Council of Braves. It is a precursor of his leadership to come.

Maltakak looked at Chataqua with a menacing stare. "Would you be a fish, young Brave?" he asked sarcastically.

"My friends and I are very good in the water," said Chataqua. "We swim like the fish every day when it is warm!"

"And what is it you would do?" asked Malapok with a bitter laugh.

"When the war canoes approach, Braves from Apasus Village toward the Land-Where-The-Sun-Sets can run to warn us," said Chataqua, "we would enter the water, swim beneath the surface and upset their canoes as they approach the land... then your arrows can find them easily!"

"That is a stupid idea," said Malapok jealously. "You would be lost in the water with the Wepeneooc all around you. The kakapa would have a feast!"

"We are good in the water," said Chataqua. "We can fight with our knives in the water."

"You're a fool!" exclaimed Malapok heatedly. "Our arrows would find you as well as the Wepeneooc!"

"Perhaps," said Chataqua calmly. "It is a chance we would take, because we will be for most of the time under the water."

"And who would do this?" asked Maltakak suspiciously.

"Manatapac, Chataqua, Chalapow and Rowhatan," said Chataqua.

"Hah!" exclaimed Malapok. "One proven Brave, a new Brave, a fat clown and a young boy not yet a Brave? You would attack the Wepeneooc in the Broad Waters with such?"

"They are all courageous and the best swimmers in the Tribe," said Chataqua. "Chalapow is strong of arm and Rowhatan is determined of spirit... we will succeed!"

"A waste of men!" exclaimed Maltakak. "Chalapow will be the first to have an arrow in his fat belly!"

"It is a good plan!" said Manatapac, standing next to Chataqua. "The Wepeneooc will never suspect an attack from under the Broad Waters!"

"The young Brave has a mind made of mud from the stinking swamp!" said Maltakak in a malicious tone.

"The young Brave is my son," said Benatagua, standing and facing Maltakak. "His thoughts bear discussion... not the words of ignorance and arrogance!"

Maltakak stood and faced Benatagua. "Your son is not your son at the Council of Braves," he said. "He is a young... and inexperienced Brave!"

"Each of you sit down," said Chesapian in an authoritative voice. "We will discuss the thoughts of Chataqua!"

Now we move quickly to the battle.

Example, Life and Death Battle Scene;

In the early morning mist and dim light before the sun was born, Chataqua, Manatapac, Chalapow and Rowhatan hid behind a dune covered with reeds on the sandy beach north of Shikiooc facing the Broad Waters, near the River-Where-Swift-Water-Flows. Chataqua glanced behind him and saw twenty Braves armed with bows, arrows and spears waiting anxiously. He knew that in the swamp behind them were many more Braves, waiting to fight any Wepeneooc that survived the attack from the water and the arrows. Benatagua led a large number of Braves toward the Land-Where-The-Warm-Wind-Blows to find and fight the Wepeneooc who were coming across the islands and swamps of the Bay-of-the-Great-White-Bird.

Rowhatan nudged Chataqua and pointed. "There... in the mist," he said, "there is something in the mist."

Chataqua stared in the direction Rowhatan pointed. He saw dim shapes in the mist... three of them, and then more.

"I see them!" exclaimed Chataqua.

"Chataqua," whispered Rowhatan clutching at him. "I am afraid! Is it wrong to be afraid?"

Even in battle scenes, we still work to define the characters.

"You do not have to go, Rowhatan," said Chataqua, "you are too young!"

"I will go!" exclaimed Rowhatan angrily. "I did not ask not to go...I asked if it is wrong to be afraid!"

"If it is, then I also am wrong" whispered Chataqua, undecided about allowing Rowhatan to join them.

"Braves are allowed to be afraid?"

"Benatagua says that being afraid is part of courage," said Chataqua. "Courage is when you are able to conquer the fear."

"Then... I am determined to have courage," said Rowhatan, a catch in his young voice. "I am determined to become a Brave!"

The canoes emerged from the mist. There was no time for waiting now! Chataqua waved his arm in the air and pointed at the water. Chataqua, Manatapac, Chalapow and Rowhatan crouched and ran on silent feet to the water and entered it without a splash. Chataqua and Manatapac were in the middle, Rowhatan to the left and Chalapow to the right. They swam silently with their heads low in the water.

We are taking care to describe the battle in some detail to provide the Reader with a vivid understanding of what takes place.

Chataqua saw the war canoes of the Wepeneooc coming closer. They were heading for a spot to his left. He heard the swish of paddles and made out the murky shape of Braves in the canoes. He motioned to Manatapac to his left, turned and began to swim in that direction. The others followed, carefully watching the motions of the man nearest them.

When the war canoes were about fifty lengths of foot away, Chataqua took a deep breath and slipped silently under the water. He forced himself down to about five lengths of foot in depth without breaking the surface. The others did the same. Chataqua swam toward the nearest war canoe as the rays of the morning sun began to filter through the surface above him. He heard the sound of paddles... and then he saw them, dipping regularly into the water above him.

Chataqua's lungs were beginning to hurt, but he swam on, knowing that he could keep his breath under the water for at least a swim of a hundred and fifty lengths of foot... maybe more. He saw the hull of a war canoe above him. He pulled *strongly and moved upward, timing his approach carefully. He struck the bottom of the canoe and pushed mightily with his hands. The canoe tipped and wavered crazily. Paddles splashed trying to right the canoe. The canoe tipped to one side and spilled the Wepeneooc Braves into the water.*

What would likely happen next? Are we sufficiently "into" this scene to figure it out and go on?

Chataqua surfaced amid the shouting and splashing Wepeneooc Braves. He slipped under again, unnoticed and swam toward the next canoe. He went deeper and came up under the war canoe. It upset just as the other one had. Chataqua surfaced again and drew a deep breath. Around him, Braves gasped and struggled as a rain of arrows came down upon them. Chataqua went under again, hoping that his friends were having the same success he had. He swam on, and not seeing another canoe, surfaced. He looked behind him and saw several overturned war canoes and many Wepeneooc Braves struggling in the blue-green water. He heard the sound of paddles behind him and went under again.
Sinking to five lengths of foot, Chataqua saw the hull and dipping paddles of another war canoe. This one seemed bigger than the others. He pulled strongly toward it. He swam up, barely missing a dipping paddle. He pushed at the canoe, but it was heavy and did not upset right away. He grabbed a paddle and heaved at it. There was a splash and a Brave fell into the water. The canoe rocked and finally upset.
Chataqua burst to the surface and took a big gulp of air. The Wepeneooc Brave he had pulled into the water stared at him in surprise and a look of hate and fury came over his war painted face. The Wepeneooc Brave lunged at Chataqua and grappled with him. Chataqua broke free and went under water, diving deep and kicking furiously. The Wepeneooc Brave came under the surface, gulped water and shot back up. Chataqua arced gracefully upward, drew his knife and thrust it into the Wepeneooc Brave's belly. Blood flowed from the wound in a great gush, spreading and staining the water. The Wepeneooc Brave struggled briefly and then sank into the water, his eyes glazing over.

Chataqua rose to the surface and breathed deeply as arrows whizzed into the water around him. The cries of wounded and drowning men turned the morning into a horrific kaleidoscope of agony. Chataqua went under again and swam toward the beach, diving deep so that the arrows falling around him could not penetrate his flesh. He swam by a struggling Wepeneooc Brave and thrust the knife again. More blood billowed into the water.

Blood in the water! What is the logical consequence of that?

Soon the kakapa will be here, thought Chataqua. The noise would attract them...and blood always brought them! If that happened, very few Wepeneooc would reach the sandy shore. Chataqua surfaced and looked briefly at the beach. Chesapeake Braves stood launching arrows at the struggling Wepeneooc. They shouted their war cry as they saw the black fins of the kakapa slicing toward the Wepeneooc in the water. Chataqua went under quickly and swam toward the place where the Broad Waters entered the River-Where-Swift-Waters-Flow. If he got into the river, it was unlikely that he would be mistaken for a Wepeneooc, and the kakapa seldom went into the river. He swam to the river entrance hoping that the kakapa had enough to do without coming after him. He surfaced and saw Manatapac and Chalapow swimming together. The three friends reached the entrance to the river and were swept inland by the fast rushing waters of an incoming tide.

"Where is Rowhatan?" asked Chataqua as they crawled up on a white sand beach.

"I do not know," gasped Manatapac, sitting up in the sand as the waters rushed by him.

"I hope he has survived!" exclaimed Chataqua.

"If he has, he is fighting the kakapa," said Chalapow sadly, his round belly heaving.

They sat on the beach, exhausted and thought about Rowhatan.

"He is a good boy," said Manatapac sadly. "He will make it to the beach!"

"Maybe he will appear later," said Chalapow wiping a tear from his eye.

"Okee will protect our friend," said Chataqua softly, "wherever he is."

This is the prequel to a "decision scene". It is the catalyst that leads to Chataqua's decision to conduct his adventure to the Land-Where-The-Sun-Is-Born. This is a "high" in the flow of the novel. The WOW Factors are Emotion (fear of the upcoming battle, sorrow at the loss of Rowhatan), Suspense (what will happen in the battle?), Conflict (the unique battle in the Broad Waters), Action (the torrid action of the battle), Surprise (the surprise of success or failure), Heroism (the heroism of the friends to follow Chataqua's idea and fight under the water), and Pizzazz (the unique fight under the water and the attack of the kakapa). The WOW is 8/10.

You can see that I provided the Reader with an "overview" of the battle and then shifted to the part of the battle in which Chataqua is involved. This provides a "big picture" for the Reader and allows us to concentrate on the more specific action of the fight "in the water". It is difficult to write about a big battle without it sounding like a "history", and this is a method that is useful to make the story telling more vivid. It is also part of scoping the novel and managing its length.

How good are you at writing a battle scene? Try writing the scene for the battle on the south side of Chesepiooc, where the Wepeneooc come across the Closed-Water-of-the-White-Bird and the Four Brother (Opec Hap) Islands opposed by the Werowance, Benatagua (see map in Appendix B).

Try writing the scene "from scratch", without using the example scene. Write it from the perspective of Benatagua, who, while fighting, is concerned over Chataqua's role in fending off the Wepeneooc from the Chesapeake Bay side of Chesepiooc. Include Benatagua's wife, Chalatas, and her farewell to Benatagua as he goes off to battle. It's time for you to get the feel of just how hard it is for you to muster up those creative juices "from scratch"!

Mourning Scenes

A mourning scene is one in which emotions reach a crescendo due to the loss of a friend or a loved one... or as a result of an unpleasant event. It is designed to rouse the greatest emotions in the Reader. The aftermath of the Battle with the Wepeneooc provides a perfect opportunity for a mourning scene.

Example, Prelude to the Mourning Scene;
Chataqua, Manatapac and Chalapow rested and watched the swift waters for Rowhatan. The Broad Waters were calm and there was no sign of anyone. The Wepeneooc canoes had disappeared, as had the Braves in them.

"Maybe Rowhatan swam back to the beach near Chesepiooc," said Chalapow hopefully, his face set in a miserable grimace.

"We shall run up the beach to Chesepiooc and search for him," said Chataqua, seeking to cheer up Chalapow.

Chalapow looked up at the sky and wailed. "I have lost my dearest friend!"

Chataqua grabbed Chalapow and pulled him along. They ran up the beach keeping an eye alert for Rowhatan as well as any surviving Wepeneooc. The sun climbed to near its zenith as they ran, the heat of the day upon them. They ran into Chesepiooc without a sign of Rowhatan. They found Sachem Chesapian standing near the Council Campfire. He had a mournful look on his face.

"Great Sachem," shouted Chataqua. "We are back. Where should we go to fight?"

Chesapian looked at Chataqua and heaved a sigh. "The Wepeneooc never reached the shore from their war canoes... thanks to you and you friends."

"Yeeehahh!" shouted Manatapac, shaking his hands ferociously in the air.

"The Wepeneooc from the Land-Where-The-Warm-Wind-Blows have fallen back," said Chesapian walking toward Chataqua.

Chataqua saw Braves bringing the legs, arms, and scalps of fallen Wepeneooc Braves, attaching them to tall poles around the Council fire place. They cursed the Wepeneooc in loud voices as they hoisted the poles into place. The Periku pounded on a flat stone with a club with rhythmic strokes, his voice varying from a wail to a rejoicing chant. Other Braves rattled gourds filled with small stones and accompanied the Periku's chant.

We have done a bit of spot research here as to what the Chesapeake did in celebrating victory.

"Benatagua has fallen honorably in battle!" said the Sachem solemnly.

Chataqua stared at the Sachem in disbelief. "Where... where is he?"

"He is in his lodge," said Chesapian, "but he is sorely stricken by a Wepeneooc arrow."

Chataqua walked and then ran toward the lodge, feeling a strange light headiness. He threw aside the heavy deer skin curtain at the door. He felt strange, as though he were walking in a dream, his heart heavy, his mind numb. Inside, Benatagua lay on a bed of deer hides. His wife, Chalatas, knelt over him and bathed the wound in his chest where the shaft of an arrow protruded. Chesapian was conscious, his face contorted in pain, but making no sound.

We have the opportunity to inject the strongest emotions here. Let's be sure that we do!

"Mother!" exclaimed Chataqua. "Will Benatagua live?"

"He wants to see you," said Chalatas, tears in her eyes.

Chataqua knelt next to his father and took his big hand in his. "Father!" he said, his voice choked. "You must rise up and be Benatagua again!"

"The arrow is lodged close to my heart," said Benatagua in a voice so quiet as to be unrecognizable. "The Medicine Man will push it through me and put the healing leaves of the swamp upon me... but first, I had to see you, my son."

"We... we turned away the Wepeneooc in the war canoes," said Chataqua, trying to control the growing lump in his throat.

216

"You are a full Brave of the tribe," said Benatagua proudly. "A hero of the Chesapeake!"

"No... no..." said Chataqua. "I can not be until I have the bravery of my father... and canoe to the unknown horizon!"

"I know that you will do that, my son," said Benatagua, closing his eyes briefly. "But promise me... if you find no land in two cycles of the sun, you must return to Chesepiooc... promise me that!"

"Yes... yes, Father... I promise."

"And be careful of wind and storm," said Benatagua. "The sea is mighty and your canoe is but a spot on it!"

"I know that Father... that is why your canoeing to the Land-Where-The-Cold-Wind blows was so brave... so heroic!"

Benatagua coughed and grasped at the arrow shaft in his chest. "And beware the Gitsche Kakapa... if you go too far, he will find you!"

"I do not fear the Gitsche Kakapa," said Chataqua.

"The fear does not grip you until he is close and you see his black eye... and how big he really is," said Benatagua dreamily, closing his eyes and reliving his experience.

We again build up the threat of the great sea beast.

"You must let the Periku remove the arrow, Benatagua," pleaded Chalatas.

Benatagua squeezed Chataqua's hand. "Let him do what he will. I will stand again as Benatagua... or I will join my father with Okee in the land above the clouds."

"Stay with me, Father," pleaded Chataqua fighting back the tears. "Stay with me and we will canoe and tell the old stories again!"

Benatagua grinned slightly through his pain "Wherever I go," he said, "we will always canoe and tell the old stories!"

"We will, Father," said Chataqua, tears dripping from his eyes.

"You will remember that you are to be Sachem," said Benatagua squeezing Chataqua's hand in a desperate grip.

"Yes Father," choked Chataqua.

"And to beware the Periku!

"Yes, I remember... but must he be the one to remove the arrow?"

"Go from me and let me deal with this arrow," said Benatagua weakly, grasping at the offending arrow.

Chataqua hugged his Mother and left the lodge. He went and kneeled under the spreading live oak tree where no one could see him and let his emotions burst forth. He cried without a sound and looked up into the sun as it spread its rays through the swirling branches of the tree.

"Okee!" murmured Chataqua. "Give me Benatagua. If you must take him, give me the strength to go on... Oh Okee! I pray to give me my father!"

We need to fade that scene and start another before it gets too long. If there isn't a tear in your eye after that scene, we have failed!

Example, Mourning Scene;
The next morning Chalapow found the body of Rowhatan. It washed up on the shore, missing its legs, the body penetrated by a Chesapeake arrow. The face was set in a determined, painful expression. Chalapow let out a great wail for his friend that echoed along the beach. He was in mental and emotional pain that made his chubby body visibly shake.

"My friend," wailed Chalapow, "How can I live without Rowhatan?"

"I should never have let him go with us," said Chataqua, tears in his eyes.

"You would have done him great harm had you refused him," choked Chalapow. "He wanted to go... very badly."

"He has become a Brave," said Manatapac, "even before his time!"

Chalapow, Manatapac and Chataqua wrapped the body of Rowhatan in cloth.

"Rowhatan is a Brave!" said Chataqua. "I will ask Benatagua to honor him as a Brave at the Council."

"Maltakak will never allow it," said Manatapac sadly.

"I do not intend that Maltakak have a voice in it," said Chataqua with great determination.

They picked up the cloth containing the body of Rowhatan and trudged up the sandy shore toward Chesepiooc.

Now the setting shifts and we need to fade and start another scene.

Example, Mourning Scene;
A Council of Braves was held when the sun was high. The bodies of Rowhatan and ten Braves were displayed at a ceremonial fire before they were taken to be buried in the forest. Their bow and quiver of arrows lay with them, along with their drinking cup and clothing that would be buried alongside them. Women, mothers, sisters and wives, surrounded the bodies and mourned openly, uttering guttural sounds and sobs. Men mourned by bowing their heads in sorrow and respect. They rattled gourds, chanting in mournful tones.

Benatagua lay on a mat at the feet of his lifelong friend Chesapian, wrapped in a blanket. The Medicine Man had removed the arrow and wrapped the wound in cloth. "I honor these Braves," said Benatagua in a weak voice.

"I honor these Braves and pass them to the hands of Okee," intoned Chesapian.

"I honor ten Braves," said Maltakak, "and ask Okee to bless their spirits with peace and prosperity in the world of the skies."

"There are eleven Braves to honor," said Manatapac strongly.

"I honor eleven Braves," said Chesapian in a loud voice.

Maltakak started to speak, but Chesapian waved him silent. "It was a great victory for the Chesapeake!" he exclaimed. "I honor our wounded Werowance Benatagua and ask the blessing of Okee on him."

"The blessing of Okee on the Werowance!" said the Periku with a concealed sneer.

We fade out of that scene and start another.

Example, Mourning Scene;

Benatagua died at dusk. A Council of Braves was held to honor the fallen Werowance later that night, a huge fire burning brightly. After the Council of Braves, Benatagua was returned to his lodge where he lay in rest through the night. Chalatas wept over his body.

Chataqua spent the night under the spreading oak tree, talking to his father, holding back his tears and retelling the old stories to the tree as a great fire burned in his chest. Chataqua looked up into the twisted branches of the old oak tree and chanted in mournful tones.

"Benatagua, the Werowance, First Brave of the Chesapeake, Honokaa Tu, canoed many moons ago over the unknown horizon toward the Land-Where-The-Cold-Wind-Blows! Benatagua, the Werowance, First Brave of the Chesapeake fought many battles to defend the Chesapeake and killed many enemies! Benatagua, the Werowance, First Brave of the Chesapeake was the proud husband of Chalata, the most beautiful woman of the Chesapeake! Benatagua, the Werowance, First Brave of the Chesapeake was a wise man who gave good and wise counsel to his son!"

Chataqua stopped and stared down at the ground under the tree, covered with acorns. He lifted his face to the sky and wailed, a long, mournful tone.

"Father! I will canoe to the Land-Where-The-Sun-Is-Born! I will! I will become Sachem! I will! Ask Okee to bless me as I seek Alanoas as wife and help us to have children as great as Benatagua!"

We reaffirm Chataqua's goals.

Chataqua continued his chanting and wailing throughout the night. In the morning, he went to comfort his Mother who was preparing for the traditional three days of vigilant mourning over the grave of Benatagua. Benatagua was buried with great solemnities near the spreading tree; his drinking cup placed upon the grave, and arrows planted in the ground around it. Chesapian stood over his grave with Chataqua for a full day, appealing to Okee to accept Benatagua into his realm. Men and women cut off half their long tresses in token of their love for Benatagua. During the day, the people mourned for him at dawn, noon, and twilight with a great howling.

This is the "decision event". Chataqua puts aside all his doubts and commits to the actions that will take him into a "new world". The WOW Factors are Emotion (the high emotion over the deaths of Benatagua and Rowhatan), Suspense (what will these decisions bring?), Conflict (between Benatagua and Maltaka over the number of Braves to honor), Action (the funeral ceremony), Heroism (the heroism of Benatagua in death). The WOW is 5/10 ++ (very high emotional content).

Did that stir your emotions? Is it a WOW scene? Can some more "tweaking" make it into a WOW scene? The mourning ceremonies of the Chesapeake described are from the actual rituals of the Indians of the Powhatan Federation (spot research).

The Read-Through

Every few scenes that you complete of the "Rough-Through", you should go back and do a "Read-Through". What is that? It merely means go back and read what you have written and make sure that "where you are" tracks with "where you were" and "where you want to go next".

In the "Read-Through", watch out what you call things, or name things. You may have called the Chesapeake Native American Village "Chesapeake Village" when you started writing, and at some point after some spot research changed it to "Chesepiooc". If so, you must go back and change it to be consistent. The -edit replace- function in the WORD application is useful for this purpose.

It's hard to remember everything as you proceed. But at this point in writing, you must start re-reading what you have written and bringing it all "up to date". And, every time you do a "Read-Through", you are "studying" the story and understanding it and your characters more and more. By the end of the "Rough-Through", you should be able to remember every part of the story and go quickly to any part.

The Paper Read

About half way through, and again at the end of the Rough-Through, it is a good idea to print out what you have on paper and review it in that medium. You should do this also after several Creative Reviews. You will find things from a Paper Read that you won't get from reading a computer screen.

The Visual Perspective

As you write these scenes, keep the "visual perspective" in your mind. What are the characters "doing" as well as "saying". What are they doing as they speak? What are other characters doing as they speak? You can convey a lot of meaning from a strictly "visual perspective" without a character saying anything. A good part of your scene can be descriptions of "action" and "emotion" without dialogue... but it is better that it be "punctuated" by dialogue.

Avoid a scene where all you have are characters speaking. What if this were a screenplay for a movie? What would it look like? If it's only some characters speaking without description of visual expressions of emotion, it is an "empty" scene. As an Author, you must be able to "see" and describe the whole scene, including the emotions and movements of all the characters.

****

Chapter Twenty-one
Storm and Fantasy Scenes

Storm Scenes

Storm scenes are unique in that they are a special kind of action situation in which the environment is a primary "character". Let's try one!

Example, Prelude to the Storm Scene;
The early morning mist hung low over the beach as the waves washed passively over the sand. Beyond Point-Where-Great-Waters-Meet there was fog through which the sun tried unsuccessfully to penetrate. Chataqua stood on the beach next to his great canoe with the carved calypo and the strange looking wind cloths. Chesapian, Manatapac, and many of the Braves of the Chesapeake stood with him staring out at the morning fog. Alanoas, Chalatas and other women stood behind the Braves, tears in their eyes.
"How will you know which way to paddle without the sun?" asked Manatapac.
"The fog will clear soon," said Chataqua. "The sun will burn it through."
Chataqua had waited and planned for this moment for years. Now his heart was heavy with the death of his father. He looked at the great canoe with pride. His father would be proud of him and his canoe. Its twin hulls were lashed well together, several arm lengths apart, using strong ropes woven from reeds and the fiber of trees. They were joined together by sturdy logs in three places, forward, mid canoe and aft. At the point where the log crossed at the middle, there was lashed a pole slightly taller than Chataqua stood. The pole stood upright in the left canoe, braced with several logs and set into a notch in the bottom.
Chalatas and Alanoas had fashioned cloth together that could be drawn up the pole and extended with another, thinner tree branch out over the twin canoes. There was a rope that held the smaller pole into place. Chataqua hoped that the wind would push at the cloth and move the canoes so that he

would not have to paddle all of the time. He remembered the heavy cloth attached to one of the poles they had found on the beach and how the wind had caught it and pulled at him. In the second canoe was dried meat of the deer and rawhide sacks of water. In the bottom of his canoe was a spear he had made in hopes of spearing fish should his food run low. He had a bow, a quiver made from reeds containing a number of arrows and his sharp knife in case he ran into hostile people in the Land-Where-The-Sun-Is-Born.

"In the name of the great Brave Benatagua, Father of Chataqua, we ask Okee to guard you in your voyage," said Chesapian in a loud voice. "As Benatagua canoed to the Land-Where-The-Cold-Wind-Blows and found new, rich lands where oysters and flatfish abound, so you, Chataqua will find riches toward the Land-Where-The-Sun-Is-Born... the unknown horizon. Go, now, Chataqua, to the unknown horizon and make it known!"

"Great Sachem... I go," said Chataqua solemnly.

Manatapac and several other Braves, with Chataqua, shoved the heavy canoe into the surf. Chataqua jumped into the left side of the canoe. The great canoe moved easily toward the three foot high breakers.

"I shall call my great canoe 'Seeker of Horizons'", called out Chataqua. "It will honor my Father... as my father sought an unknown horizon, so shall I... for the glory and benefit of the Chesapeake!"

On a long journey, or a long scene, you should use several "fades" such as at the end of the last scene. Don't try to account for every minute, hour or day... use the fade and move on to the next important occurrence.

Example, Prelude to the Storm Scene, Further in Time;

Seeker made its way through the water, propelled by the little wind cloth that Chataqua had fashioned. The sun rose to near its maximum height in the sky and was warm on Chataqua's skin. He didn't know how far offshore he was. He strained his eyes toward the Land-Where-The-Sun-Is-Born but could see nothing but a shimmering horizon. What lay beyond? His mind raced in anticipation of what he might find. He dozed a bit, letting the wind cloth blow Seeker along.

Chataqua awoke with a start as the horizon in front of Seeker erupted with great splashes. He sat upright in the canoe and stared ahead. The surface of the ocean was filled with jumping fish. As they drew closer, he could see that they were large fish, two to three arms lengths at least. They were brightly colored and the surface shimmered with the blue and yellow of their fins. There were thousands of the fish and they passed ahead of Seeker and to its right.

We take this opportunity to inject some "color".

Chataqua knew these fish from the tales his father had told him. They were torpak, a fat streamlined fish shaped like the tip of a spear that swam at great speeds hunting smaller fish. On occasion his father and other fishermen of the tribe would go far enough into the ocean to catch one. He remembered one that his father had brought back that was two arms lengths. They had roasted it over the fire. It tasted not like other fish. Its meat was dark red and purplish-blue. It had a strong taste, almost like venison but with a saltier taste.

The ocean around Seeker rippled with the movement of small fish. The torpak abruptly changed their direction and came toward Seeker. They jumped and swam over and under the canoe. It seemed that they would jump right into the canoe with him. Chataqua was startled at the sight and then marveled at it. He fingered his knife, thinking that if one landed in the canoe, he would kill it and save it to eat. But the torpak avoided the canoe and chased the small fish. Sea birds, seeing the disturbance, swarmed overhead, squawking, squealing and diving to retrieve the remains of the small fish left by the torpak. As suddenly as they had appeared, the torpak were past the canoe, jumping and splashing until they were gone.

"Thank you, Okee," said Chataqua out loud, "for allowing me to be among the torpak."

We use mostly description and action in this scene because Chataqua is alone and has no other person to talk to.

We know, however, that it is good writing to break the description with some dialogue, even if the character is talking to God (Okee)... or a fish.

Chataqua sat in the canoe, awed at the beauty of the water around him. The water was flat and calm, glistening like a deep azure jewel. He kept his paddle over the side, guiding Seeker to keep its bow pointed away from the sun as the glowing orb made its journey toward the Land-Where-The-Sun-Sets. The wind cloth caught the wind easily. He was amazed to find that he could choose his direction using the paddle and changing the position of the bottom pole that held the wind cloth. He pulled on the rope to the smaller pole to change the position of the wind cloth when it seemed that it was not collecting the wind. When he did that, the wind cloth would billow once again.

We have demonstrated that Seeker's wind cloth is working and set the scene for the storm. Let's get into it.

Example, Storm Scene;
As the day moved toward darkness, Chataqua saw black clouds on the horizon toward the Land-Where-The Cold-Wind-Blows. Streams of rain came down from the clouds like the long legs of a bird walking across the Water-That-Never-Ends. He put his paddle aside for a minute and uncovered the clay jars his Mother had made to collect the rain. He lowered the little wind cloth, afraid that it would not withstand the wind of a rain storm. He paddled on, the storm growing closer. The sky turned a leaden gray and he saw a sheet of rain racing across the calm ocean toward him. There was a flash of lightning in the leaden sky followed by a crack of thunder. The wind began to pick up and suddenly the rain engulfed him.
"We shall see now, Seeker," said Chataqua patting the wooden log of his canoe, "if you are a match for the Water-That-Never-Ends!"
Chataqua sat huddled in the canoe as the waves around him rose and began to toss his canoe. He paddled strongly to keep the bow into the waves which rose now to half a man's

height. The canoe began to fill with water. He grabbed a
wooden scoop he had fashioned from a pine tree and began to
throw the water from the canoe. He clambered into the other
canoe and scooped to keep the water out. Chataqua battled the
storm for over an hour before the wind subsided and the rain
became a drizzle. Then the rain stopped and the sun began to
peek through the clouds as it settled toward the Land-Where-
The-Sun-Sets.

"You have done well, Seeker!" shouted Chataqua jubilantly
into the wind.

Feeling fatigue flow into his body, Chataqua raised the
wind cloth once again and steered with his paddle. Soon, he
must see the land beyond the unknown horizon.

You should start a new paragraph whenever the "subject"
changes, or whenever someone new speaks. I recommend
that you avoid long paragraphs... but make them as long as
they need to be. When you go back and do a "Read-Through",
be conscious of paragraphing and split the long ones into two
or more if you can.

Chataqua dozed, the little wind cloth pushing Seeker
toward the Land-Where-The-Sun-Is-Born. A gray fin swam
behind Seeker, following the canoe. It swam closer and then
fell back, as if testing the strange object in the water. Then the
fin came alongside Seeker. A black eye rolled out of the water
and looked at Chataqua. There was a high pitched squeak
and Chataqua woke with a start.

"Calypo!" exclaimed Chataqua. "Calypo-Ma!"

There was another squeak and the calypo jumped out of
the water and dove back in with a splash.

"Calypo-Ma!" shouted Chataqua. He whistled in the way
he had when Calypo-Ma was being treated for the kakapa bite
in the tidal pool. Was it really Calypo-Ma, or just a curious
calypo swimming up to inspect him?

Calypo-Ma jumped again and swam away. Chataqua
could clearly see the kakapa wound on the calypo's tail. It was
Calypo-Ma! Soon Calypo-Ma returned with several more
calypo and they swam and jumped around Seeker.

"Calypo-Ma!" exclaimed Chataqua, happy to have someone to talk to, even if it was a calypo.

Calypo-Ma rolled on his side and again looked at Chataqua with an intensely black eye. He extended his flipper just as he had in the tidal pool, asking to be touched. Chataqua leaned far out in the canoe and touched Calypo-Ma. The calypo squeaked and dove under the canoe. Then as suddenly as they had come, they were gone.

Is this reality or fantasy? Well, it is a "possible reality" with some fantasy thrown in. You, as an Author can stretch reality a little to build your fictional story. What does this have to do with a storm? It is a calm interlude before what is to come.

Example, The Larger Storm;

The sun sank into the sea behind Seeker, bright orange streaks painting the horizon. Chataqua stared at the colorful display and felt lonely. Underneath that sky, Alanoas waited for him. He wasn't sure what Malapok would do while he was absent. Since Benatagua's death, the Periku Maltakak had gained in power. The Periku wanted Malapok to become the Werowance, First Among Braves. Chesapian hesitated and had not named a Werowance to take the place of Benatagua.

"Alanoas!" shouted Chataqua into the dusk. "I will come back to you!"

It made him feel better to say something, even if to the setting sun. The sound reassured him in his loneliness. Manatapac promised to watch over Alanoas while he was gone. He looked at the darkening horizon in front of Seeker and his uneasiness grew. Soon it was completely dark.

Seeker went with the wind amidst a rolling sea superimposed with a small chop of waves. Phosphorescence erupted from Chataqua's paddle every time he stroked to choose his direction. It streamed from the paddle like small spirits of the ocean, pulsing and glowing in fantastic patterns. He had seen this once before in a canoe with his father, but never in such abundance. The wind cloth caught the light wind which blew it into a delicately shaped curve. He wondered at the depths below him. What was there? How deep

was it? What lay at the bottom? What monsters lurked there?
He felt very small and alone as he paddled. He laid aside his
paddle and leaned back to rest. He dozed off.

Use the "dozing off" as a way to pass time leading to the
next important event in the story. Move to another scene.

Chataqua was awakened by the violent motion of Seeker
and the sound of the wind cloth flapping frantically at the top
of the pole that held it. Waves broke around him with white
curling foam, illuminated by a half moon that hung in the
dark sky above him. The wind picked up and he struggled to
lower the wind cloth, folding it carefully in the bottom of the
canoe. He picked up the paddle and began to pull strongly to
put Seeker's bow into the building waves. Seeker tossed about
violently and the logs that held the two canoes together began
to creak and groan.
Chataqua fought the wind and the waves as they grew
taller than a man. He had never seen the waters so angry. The
wind made a whistling sound and blew salty water into the
canoes. Chataqua scooped furiously to keep the canoes afloat.
His father had found the Land-Where-The-Cold-Wind-Blows
after paddling for one day. He had paddled and been pushed
by the wind for a day and almost a night now and had found
nothing! Panic began to grip him. He would have to go back…
go back having found nothing… go back and be seen by the
Chesapeake as a failure.
Chataqua paddled on all night, fighting the waves and
angry wind. Finally, he saw the sky to his left begin to lighten.
He changed direction and paddled toward the brightest spot,
toward the sun where it was being born for a new day. A new
day! Today he would find the Land-Where-The-Sun-Is-Born.
He had to! He stared out at the rows of large white tipped
waves that rushed toward him, tasting the salt of their spray
as the sun peeked over the unknown horizon. It rose quickly
into the clouded sky and beat down on him with its heat.

Note that this scene is not just a storm scene. Nor is any
scene "just" something. We are using each scene to "tell the
story". We must now show what the storm did to Chataqua

and Seeker in a way that sets the scene for the subsequent ordeal.

A towering wave washed over Seeker, filling both canoes with water. Chataqua struggled to remain in the canoe. Seeker's hulls sank to the upper edge of the big logs. Another wave struck Seeker… and then another! The logs holding the two canoes together snapped and the limb that held the wind cloth fell into the angry water. The canoe in which Chataqua struggled to remain broke apart from the other canoe, the thwart canoe logs dragging in the water. Chataqua watched in anguish as most of his water and dried venison washed away in the other canoe. He was soaked to the skin and paddled furiously to keep Seeker's bow into the oncoming waves. He cut away the trailing support logs.

Chataqua's decision led him into a "new world", that of the Water-That-Never-Ends. The scene we have written for our Rough-Through is a "testing event". He is reaping the consequences of his decision and is being tested by the new world.

The WOW Factors are Emotion (Chataqua's emotions regarding the beauty and danger of the sea), Suspense (what will happen when the canoe breaks apart?), Conflict (with the sea), Action (Chataqua's struggle in Seeker), Surprise (the canoe comes apart), Romance (the romance of the sea), Heroism (Chataqua as he faces the perils of the sea), Pizzazz (the settings, including the storms). The WOW is 8/10 + (strong action).

We leave Chataqua in this scene amidst building trouble. Now we have the Reader not wanting to put the book down, even though it's late and he/she is sleepy. Read on!

Fantasy Scenes

A fantasy scene is one that employs highly fanciful ideas or supernatural elements, or both. It can shift from reality to fantasy and back again. In a "fantasy" novel, the fantasy scene is reality. In a normal novel, a fantasy scene is used to produce vivid situations which represent the imagination, dreams or hallucinations of the characters. In a normal novel, it must be clear to the Reader what has caused a dream or hallucination... though not necessarily right away.

When Chataqua ventures forth in his great canoe and is alone on the ocean, there is opportunity for "mixed fantasy"... the mixing of reality and fantasy. The Author may leave it ambiguous as to which is which and let the Reader's imagination solve it, or may choose to eventually "clear it up".

Example, Fantasy Scene;
Hours passed and as the sun rose in the sky, the waves diminished. Chataqua's head ached and he felt fatigue overcome him as the hot sun shown down on him, the water shimmering around him reflecting little daggers of heat. He felt light-headed and his mind wandered to a far away place where the waters were calm and the oysters and flatfish were abundant.

"You must keep on," said a deep voice. "But after two risings of the sun, you must turn back if there is no land."

It was the voice of Benatagua. Chataqua heard it clearly. He saw the dim shape of a long canoe ahead of him, shimmering in the sun. In it sat a misty person who beckoned to him. It was Benatagua, his paddle poised, his eyes staring intensely at Chataqua.

We have returned the dead mentor figure, the father, in a mentor role resulting from Chataqua's hallucinations in the sun after the storm.

"You are courageous, my son," said Benatagua, his voice echoing across the distance between his canoe and the wrecked Seeker. "But you must have even more courage!"

"My canoe is wrecked!" exclaimed Chataqua. "How can I continue?"

"You still have a canoe!" said Chataqua. "The Great Spirit has sent me to tell you to go on... that you have the strength and courage to do it! You have a destiny to fulfill!"

Chataqua started paddling toward where he clearly saw Benatagua's long canoe.

*"You cannot come to me, Chataqua" said Benatagua.
"Only can I come to you...for I am with Okee."*

*"Father!" shouted Chataqua, tears flowing from his eyes," I
miss you... I want to fish and play in the water as we once
did!"*

*"You are a man, now, Chataqua," said Benatagua
forcefully. "Play is for the children you will have. Courage and
discovery is now for you!"*

*"How can I go on?" shouted Chataqua, his voice choking in
his throat, his chest burning with pain and sorrow. "I am
afraid to lose Alanoas!"*

*"Paddle on, my son," said Benatagua, his image fading
into the shimmering sea. "You must pursue your destiny!"*

"Father!"

"Paddle on!"

*The image of Benatagua faded and Chataqua reached out
to him... but he was gone!*

This scene is part of the "testing event". The WOW factors
are Emotion (Chataqua's desire to go back to the days of a
boy), Surprise (Chataqua's surprise at seeing his Father),
Mystery (the mystery of his Father's appearance to him). The
WOW is 3/10. This "fantasy scene" adds to the WOW.

We have used the fantasy scene to "fascinate" the Reader
and make the reading experience a bit "tingly". How can
Chataqua survive this? What would you do to make it more
"tingly"?

****

Chapter Twenty-two
Peril and Extreme Peril Scenes

Just when it seems that the hero/heroine is "in it up to his/her neck" and there is no solution in sight (peril)... that's when you want to take him/her into even more danger (extreme peril). Make your Reader say "Oh no!" Then find a way to extricate your character in an exciting, suspenseful and credible way!

Peril Scenes

A peril scene is one in which the main character, and perhaps others, are in great danger. It is a unique type of scene because it has to have the most descriptive action of all. It must have unbearable suspense and make the Reader shudder and read on. We left Chataqua in the last scene with a canoe wrecked by a storm, still paddling toward the unknown horizon.

Example, Peril Scene;

The sun was climbing higher as Chataqua tried valiantly to scoop the water out of his canoe. The waves were still half a man's height and as soon as he would get some water out of the canoe, another wave would wash in. Frustrated, he paddled on in the half submerged canoe. He had to find the Land-Where-The-Sun-Is-Born! His father had said to "paddle on". Benatagua must know that the land is only a short distance away. Chataqua was covered with sweat and crusty salt water as the sun beat down unmercifully. He chanted to himself the little song that he and Alanoas sang while walking in the Grand-Salt-Water-Swamp.

> *I see the deer run, I tell the deer,*
> *We walk together,*
> *We will remember*
> *We are forever.*
> *You and I*

In my Rough-Through, I came to this point and decided it would be good to have some song or chant that Chataqua could use to fight his loneliness and remember Alanoas. So, I conjured it up and went back and inserted an earlier scene where they sung the chantey to each other in the forest.

He could tell all the animals in the forest of his love for Alanoas... maybe that would make the Land-Where-The-Sun-Is-Born come closer. His father said that he would play with the children he would have with Alanoas... just like he and his father had played in the surf and in the sand when he was young. He longed for Alanoas. He wondered if he'd ever see her again and have those children.

> *I hear the red bird, I tell him clearly,*
> *We walk together,*
> *We will remember*
> *We are forever,*
> *You and I.*

The waves diminished and Chataqua felt better. Perhaps his fortune would change. Then he saw them coming from a distance. The black fins sliced through the water in a beautifully menacing way. They did not arc and dive like the fins of calypo. They cut through the waves in a straight line toward what was left of Seeker.

The menacing fins are the harbinger of peril. We need to make the approaching menace as vivid as possible.

Chataqua glanced down at the hull of Seeker beside him. It was barely above water. He felt like he was sitting in the water as he watched the advancing kakapa. Images of the legless body of Rowhatan raced into his tortured mind.
Chataqua could see the other part of Seeker's hull ahead of him. The sacks of dried deer meat that had been in the other canoe were now floating in the water. He knew that the odor of the dried meat would attract the kakapa. His heart beat rapidly as he saw the fins circling the hull of the other canoe. How long would it take for them to find him? He saw the

sacks of dried meat disappear one by one, floating along innocently and then jerked under the water with incredible force. He stopped paddling, grabbed the scoop and began to scoop water out of the hull as quietly as he could.

After ten minutes of quiet scooping Chataqua emptied the hull by about half of the water in it. He fingered his knife and looked to see that the spear he had fashioned was still in the bottom of the canoe. It was. It lay next to the bow and the quiver of arrows he had brought.

Slowly and carefully, Chataqua paddled Seeker around and turned toward the Land-Where-The-Sun-Sets. He didn't want to return! He didn't want to give up! He wanted to find the land over the unknown horizon! But, he didn't want to be eaten by kakapa as had been the Wepeneooc Braves after he upset their canoes and put their blood in the water. He paddled away quietly, the sun hot on his face.

Chataqua paddled for several minutes, afraid to look back. He glanced over his shoulder and his heart leaped into his throat as he saw two of the black fins following his canoe. He tried to paddle faster, but the water laden canoe was heavy and refused to move easily. He saw the two fins swim easily alongside the canoe about ten arm lengths away. Closer now, he could see that the color of their fins was a brilliant metallic blue. He could see the glimmer of darker blues and whites in the water beneath the fin. He paddled on determinedly, hoping that the kakapa would investigate him, find him uninteresting and swim away.

We have, at this point, done some spot research on species of sharks. Chataqua doesn't know it, but he has encountered some Mako sharks. Makos are a pelagic shark that is found in the deeper waters of the Atlantic from Maine to Cuba. They are fast and ferocious, and they have been known to attack boats and human swimmers.

One of the kakapa darted in toward the canoe, as if the group had delegated it the responsibility of determining just what this large object was. Their sense of smell told them that it might be good to eat! The kakapa swam straight at the canoe like arrows launched from some powerful underwater

235

bow. Chataqua was transfixed at the sight of the large fish and its ultra streamlined body. It must be as long as he was tall and weigh much, much more. He braced himself in the canoe and grasped the paddle, prepared to fend off an attack. The kakapa's fin disappeared just short of the canoe and the fish swam under the semi-submerged log, bumping it gently.

Chataqua turned to see the fin re-emerge on the other side of the canoe. It swam in circles there, as if beckoning to the other kakapa. Another fin raced toward the canoe, followed by two others. Chataqua grasped his long bow and laid an arrow across it. He did not want to shoot the kakapa, but if he had to, he would. He looked at his store of arrows... he had only four hands worth... twenty arrows. There were four kakapa... but how many more would come? The three fins disappeared as had the first one, just short of the canoe. This time there was a violent thump against the underside of the canoe that jolted Chataqua and caused him to hang on to the sides. The four kakapa swam in circles about four arm's lengths from what was left of Seeker.

What does one do when surrounded by sharks in a small canoe on the ocean? Whatever it is, we need to write about it!

Suddenly, a fin turned toward Seeker and swam at great speed. Chataqua raised the long bow and drew back the rawhide cord holding the arrow. At three arms' lengths he let go the arrow. It whistled into the ocean and struck the kakapa just forward of the fin. The kakapa rolled over and splashed violently with its tail. Red blood stained the blue waters. Chataqua watched in terror as the other three kakapa charged at the wounded fish and began to tear it apart. The ocean soon contained a spreading red stain against the turquoise blue.

Chataqua put the bow down and began to paddle away from the red stain as quietly as he could. Perhaps the kakapa would be happy to eat their own and leave him alone! Sea birds closed on the red stain squawking and shrieking and began to dive on the scraps left by the kakapa as they cannibalized their cohort.

Chataqua paddled for an hour. Several sea birds rode the wind currents above him. He did not know exactly how far from shore he was. He remembered that Benatagua had told him that the sea birds would be found two to three days from land by canoe, and not more. He figured that he was within two days canoe trip from land.

Has our hero seen the last of the kakapa? Are you wondering now how Chataqua will ever survive? Good, then the suspense is building!

The wind died down and the waves diminished until the sea was almost flat. Chataqua managed to get more water out of the hull and still paddle along. The sun climbed to its highest point and began to go toward the Land-Where-The-Sun-Sets. Chataqua continued to paddle toward where he thought he would find Point-Where-Great-Waters-Meet. His heart was heavy, as he had not found the Land-Where-The-Sun-Is-Born. All he had found was water and more water... and torpak, kakapa and storms. He felt hot and very tired. His body was encrusted with the salt of the sea and he had not slept. The sun shown warmly down on him and he began to feel drowsy. He sipped at the bowl he used to collect rain water. He put the bowl down and paddled on. He had never felt so bad in his young life.

Now Chataqua begins to wonder whether he made the right decision to venture forth in Seeker. We need to build his doubt and face him with the decision to do the courageous thing.

An image of Alanoas flashed through his mind. Warm and gentle Alanoas...the girl he was to have children with... if he survived! She beckoned to him as he followed her through the Grand-Salt-Water-Swamp, hiding playfully behind the bald cypress and pine trees. He ran up to her and she ran away laughing, her voice like a breath of warm breeze. His arms became heavy and his head fell to his chest. The paddle fell into the water. Seeker drifted along without direction.

"Uh Oh!" thinks the Reader. "Wake up Chataqua!"

Chataqua started awake and saw the paddle floating away. Fear filled his heart. He must have the paddle! Where were the kakapa? Did he have the strength remaining to swim and retrieve the paddle? He paddled with his hands, but the wooden paddle drifted away faster than he could move the heavy canoe. Chataqua knew that he had no choice. The wind cloth was no more...he had no chance to survive on the ocean without his paddle... no chance to return to Point-Where-Great-Waters-Meet! He shuddered with fear and fatigue and stared at the smooth blue waters around him. The ocean rolled gently as the sun shimmered on its surface. He could see no disturbances in the water... no kakapa fins. Chataqua eased himself over the side of the semi-submerged canoe and swam toward the paddle.

Oh No! The Reader's mind screams and he/she cringes at the thought of Chataqua swimming in water where there may be sharks! Foo Foo likes it! Foo Faa cringes... but she wants to know what will happen!

The water was cool and very salty in his mouth. The paddle was only ten arms lengths away and he easily swam to it and grasped it. Chataqua turned to swim back towards Seeker. A bolt of panic swept over him as he saw the bluish fin of a kakapa emerge behind Seeker!

This is a "testing event" scene. The WOW Factors are Emotion (Chataqua's emotion in his loneliness), Suspense (the sighting of the fins), Conflict (shooting the arrow at the kakapa), Action (the movements of the kakapa), Surprise (the arrival of the kakapa), Mystery (where are the kakapa?), Heroism (Chataqua's heroism in facing the kakapa), and Pizzazz (the bizarre occurrences in a beautiful setting). The WOW is 8/10.

Extreme Peril Scenes

Now we have to get our hero out of this jam! But... it gets even worse!

Example, Extreme Peril Scene;

Chataqua swam quietly toward Seeker, holding the paddle and keeping an eye on the fin. Another fin emerged from the water beside the first. Chataqua grasped the paddle, the only weapon besides his knife he had if the kakapa came after him. He continued to swim strongly without breaking the water, as he knew the noise would bring the kakapa to him.

Seeker was drifting away from him... he could see that. He pulled and kicked strongly and gained slightly on the drifting canoe. He submerged his head under the water and looked for the kakapa. He could see three blurred shapes behind Seeker. One of them turned toward him and came closer. He raised his head above the water and saw the fin moving at him. He submerged again and grasped the paddle.

The underwater world was surreal to Chataqua. It was a beautiful blue yet hostile world that struggled to claim him. Ahead of him, a kakapa of about three arm lengths swam slowly toward him, its large forked tail propelling the streamlined body easily. The fish came within two arms lengths and turned, staring at Chataqua with a large, inquisitive eye. Chataqua brandished the paddle at the kakapa and it moved back. Chataqua rose to the surface for a gulp of air and saw another fin approaching. Soon, he would be surrounded by kakapa. He had to do something. But what? He submerged again.

The first kakapa swam at him and rolled on its side, exposing its white belly and a large mouth filled with menacing teeth. Chataqua thrust the tip of the paddle against the kakapa's head, striking a glancing blow. The first kakapa retreated, but the second one moved in on Chataqua's side. It nudged him with its head and turned away quickly, the giant tail slapping Chataqua on the legs, spinning him downward.

Chataqua struggled to right himself, fighting panic, and watched as the two kakapa began to circle him. He swam to the surface and gulped air, observing a third fin joining the others. Seeker continued to drift away from him and was now more than ten arms lengths away. He started to swim toward Seeker watching the fins as they circled him. He mustn't let the canoe get too far away or he was doomed for sure!

We face our hero with a dilemma... swim to Seeker or stay and fight the kakapa. Either way, his chances of survival are low. In action and suspense scenes, the more dilemmas the better.

Chataqua saw the fin move toward him. Panic gripped him. He submerged and brandished the paddle. The kakapa thrust the paddle aside and lunged at Chataqua. Chataqua hit it in its large eye with his fist, but the sharp teeth grazed his side and opened a small wound. He saw his blood stain the water and a silent scream of fear raced through him. His lungs were crying out for air. He brandished the paddle, burst to the surface, gulped air and submerged again just in time to ward off the attack of a second kakapa with the paddle. He burst to the surface again to gulp air and lifted his eyes to the sky.

"Okee!" cried out Chataqua. "Benatagua... Father and protector... protect me now!"

Now Chataqua is about to die thinks the Reader. What can possibly save him from this terrible situation?

Chataqua heard a familiar sound... the piercing squeak of a calypo! He dove under the water and squeaked back, just as he had with Calypo-Ma. Squeaking and whistling sounds echoed around him, and then there were more. The kakapa continued to circle him threateningly. Suddenly, they were struck by a pod of calypo. There were more calypo than the fingers on both hands thought Chataqua as he fought his way to the surface for air.

The water boiled around him as calypos jumped and dove down to attack the kakapa. They swam at great speed and struck the kakapa with their blunt beaks. One of the calypos swam to Chataqua. It rolled over and looked at Chataqua with an eye he knew.

"Calypo-Ma!" shouted Chataqua.

Calypo-Ma squeaked his special greeting for Chataqua. Chataqua grasped the sturdy fin of Calypo-Ma. The sea creature swam toward Seeker, pulling Chataqua along beside him. They reached the semi-submerged canoe and Chataqua grasped its sides eagerly. He climbed painfully aboard, pulling the paddle in behind him. Calypo-Ma swam beside Seeker and Chataqua stroked the rough gray skin. He whistled at Calypo-Ma in the language they had created while the calypo recovered in the Grand-Salt-Water-Swamp. Calypo-Ma returned the whistle.

"Calypo-Ma," said Chataqua, "you are gitsche wingapo! You have saved me!"

Here we use the Chesapeake (Lenape) words for "great friend"... *gitsche wingapo.*

Calypo-Ma squeaked and dove into the deep blue water. Chataqua followed the path of Calypo-Ma with his eyes as the calypo swam toward a stain of blood in the ocean. He watched as the pod of calypo leaped from the water and swam away, leaving Chataqua alone on the Water-That-Never-Ends. He picked up his paddle, looked at the sun as it became lower in the sky and paddled Seeker toward the shore. He glanced back at the red stain in the ocean. Had the calypo killed the kakapa? It must be so.

"Okee!" shouted Chataqua in a hoarse, reverent voice. "Thank you for the calypo and my wingapo, Calypo-Ma!"

Ahhh... says the Reader... I feel better that Chataqua is safe. But is he?

Chataqua paddled strongly toward the Land-Where-The-Sun-Sets. Suddenly, he was no longer alone. He saw a high gray fin, much larger than that of the kakapa that had attacked him. It swam toward the red stain behind Seeker and disappeared beneath the rolling waves. Chataqua felt fear creep over him again and he paddled as quietly as he could. He wished that he had the pole and the wind cloth to carry him faster. But he didn't. He paddled on.

Chataqua glanced back looking for the large gray fin. It wasn't to be seen. He paddled on as the sun set, bringing the darkness around him. He braced himself in the canoe, expecting at any minute to be upset by a giant fish he could not see.

We are building unbearable tension for the Reader. What could be more tense than sitting in a flooded canoe on the ocean wondering what sort of monster was lurking beneath?

Chataqua remembered his promise to his father. It had been two days and he had not found the Land-Where-The-Sun-Is-Born. And, he was exhausted. His canoe was wrecked. He found a star near where the sun had set and turned the canoe toward it. The wind shifted to blow him toward the steering star, and he put his paddle down to rest. He kept glancing back, trying to see if the huge fin were there, but it was too dark. He tried to relax but the specter of Gitsche Kakapa lurking under his canoe kept him wide awake.

This is a "testing event" scene. The WOW Factors are Emotion (Chataqua's emotion in his loneliness), Suspense (the sighting of the fins), Conflict (the fight between Chataqua, the calypo and the kakapa), Action (the movements of the kakapa), Surprise (the arrival of the kakapa, the arrival of the calypo), Mystery (what is under the canoe?), Heroism (Chataqua's heroism in facing the kakapa and the unknown), and Pizzazz (the bizarre occurrences in a beautiful setting). The WOW is 8/10+.

Write your own version of this scene. When you re-read what you have written does it build anticipation in you?

****

Chapter Twenty-three
Turning Point and Multi-perspective Scenes

Turning Point Scenes

A turning point scene is one in which a major change in direction occurs in the story. Chataqua's encounter with the white explorers is a "turning point".

Example, Turning Point Scene;
Chataqua rubbed the dried swamp-root-that-smells-like-bad-mud onto the wound in his side inflicted by the kakapa attack. The wound burned from the salt of the water that encrusted his body. He managed to get most of the water out of Seeker's remaining hull and it rode high in the water, the waves lapping at its sides.

Chataqua slept fitfully as a half moon rose high in the sky over the Land-Where-The-Sun-Is-Born. The paddle was clamped between his legs where it was safe from falling over the low side of Seeker. Moonlight streamed across the Water-That-Never-Ends making little silver ripples on the undulating sea. Unseen by Chataqua, a large gray fin slid above the surface of the water twenty arm lengths behind Seeker and followed the canoe as it drifted in the moonlight. The wind was from seaward of the Land-Where-Warm-Wind-Blows and it blew Seeker almost directly toward Point-Where-Great-Waters-Meet.

What is this "large fin"? It is the fin of a Great White Shark. The calypo (dolphins) attacked and killed a Mako, and drove the others off. The Great White Shark arrived on the scene, drawn by the blood of the Mako. The calypo fled. The Great White Shark contented itself with consuming the Mako. It then followed the wake of Seeker, curious about the canoe, though not on the hunt, having consumed the Mako.

Here is an example of "action under cover"... action the character in the story cannot see, but action that nevertheless is a part of the story. The character in the story sees only "evidence" of the "action under cover".

Chataqua slept fitfully, unaware of the large fin that followed him relentlessly. The wind picked up slightly as the first dull grays of the morning approached in the sky toward the Land-Where-The Sun-Is Born. He awoke and stared behind him, wondering if the morning would bring higher winds and storms. As long as the winds blew him toward the Land-Where-The-Sun-Sets, it was good, providing of course that they did not bring the storms that would fill his canoe with water and toss him in great waves. In the dull gray morning light, he saw the large gray fin behind Seeker and a wave of revulsion and disgust ran through him. Not again! Surely not again!

We are preparing to take our hero into ultimate peril.

Chataqua paddled on, ignoring the fin, hoping it was just a hallucination and that it would not be there the next time he looked. He turned occasionally to see if it was still there. It was, though it did not approach more closely. The sky toward the Land-Where-The-Sun-Is-Born began to turn yellow, then orange with a pink hue. The sun peeked over the horizon and cast its rays across the rippling water. Soon the sun was fully above the horizon, which was alive with flickering images that could be anything one would imagine. Chataqua thought he saw the silhouette of land rising from the unknown horizon and was tempted to turn Seeker about and paddle toward it. He watched the image intently, not noticing that the gray fin began to come closer.

"No," he said out loud, "do not be a fool! The canoe is damaged and you almost lost your life to the Water-That-Never-Ends... you must return to the shore!"

We are treating the sighting of the ship Discovery by Chataqua in a way that builds suspense.

Chataqua kept, however, gazing back, wondering if his eyes were tricking him. There was definitely something just to the right of the rising sun... something that seemed to be blazing white in the bright rays. Was it a mountain of white sand? He glanced at the gray fin and knew that it was a foolhardy thought. Would he have to fight the kakapa again? Was this the fin of Gitsche Kakapa?

We are still among the "testing scenes". The turning point is his sighting of "something" on the unknown horizon. The WOW Factors are Emotion (Chataqua's emotion at finding the trailing gray fin), Suspense (what will Gitsche Kakapa do?), Mystery (what is it that Chataqua sees on the unknown horizon?), Conflict (Chataqua's conflict in having to choose to turn back). The WOW is 4/10.

Multi-perspective Scenes

We are now going to examine what I call a "multi perspective event". This is an event seen or described from the perspective of two or more characters in several scenes, leading to a merging of the perspectives in the finale of the event. It continues the "turning point" sequence.

Example, Multi Perspective Scene, Part 1;
Eight bells sounded, echoing over the sunny, rippling water of the morning. Nathan Smythe, having just relieved as the Officer of the Watch, stood in front of the sailor who manned the tiller on the main deck of the two masted pinnace "Discovery". The sails were filled with a twelve knot wind from the southeast and the ship was making, by his estimate, a good five knots toward the east. Discovery rolled slightly in a gentle swell from the south-southeast. The morning air was cool, but Nathan knew that the sun would soon warm the air. To the northeast, he saw a gray cloud and the telltale lines beneath it that identified a rain squall. It was four to five miles away and headed to the east. The sky to the west in front of Discovery was clear. The ocean was marked with one to two foot waves that provided no obstacle for the heavy wooden hull of his ship.
Sir John Ratcliffe, the Master of Discovery came up the ladder from the 'tween deck. His blue coat was rumpled from the cramped quarters below. His eyes were a penetrating deep blue with the intensity of the sun.

"Well, Mr. Smythe," said Sir John in a deep voice, "what shall we see this morning?"

"I suspect we shall see more of the ocean, Sir," said Nathan trying to sound in complete control. "But anything is better than those terrible storms of the past days!"

"Have optimism, young man," said the Master. "A sailor must believe he will find fair seas and fair lands over every horizon. If not, why would he venture forth at all?"

"Yes, of course, Sir," said Nathan, "I have optimism… I just don't have any facts… yet!"

"Ah, the brutal call of reality," said the Master, smiling. "Reality is the fly in the soup of the dreamer, you know."

Nathan smiled. Sir John was known as a tough man, and he could be just that. Nathan also knew him to be a romantic, a man who aspired to the heroic and occasionally found it.

"Any sign of Susan Constant and Godspeed?" asked Sir John.

"They are, I believe, still behind us, Sir," said Nathan. "The storm has confused our navigation."

"I trust that they have not encountered bad fortune," said Sir John a bit worriedly.

"I trust God that is so, Sir," said Nathan.

"Many ships have been wrecked in these waters, and I do not intend to join them!"

"I shall keep a good watch, Sir John."

"We should take in sail and allow them to overtake," said Sir John. "We must not remain separated too long."

Note here that I am taking a bit of time to develop these characters further.

Example, Multi Perspective Scene, Part 2;
Chataqua watched a rain cloud skitter across the ocean to the northeast of where he paddled Seeker. He hoped none would come his way. With the breeze behind him and hard paddling, perhaps he would see the shore before the sun was lost below the horizon this day.

Chataqua heard a rush of water and felt a strange rising of the canoe. He was startled to look to his right and see a huge gray fin extending over an arm length above the water. It

*slid by Seeker only two arm lengths away. Chataqua could see
the great fish through the clear water... its dark gray back, its
white underbelly and the large pectoral fins like underwater
wings just behind a massive, pointed head. The great tail
broke the water with a splash and Gitsche Kakapa turned
away from Seeker, apparently satisfied that it was an object of
interest.*

Now we have "converging" incidents that must be
satisfactorily resolved... the oncoming *Discovery* and
Chataqua's encounter with Gitsche Kakapa. Note that
Nathan and Chataqua both saw a rain squall... the same one.
These visual oservations serve to "link" the multiperpective
event.

*A thrill of terror coursed through Chataqua's body as he
watched Gitsche Kakapa swim away. What a magnificent
fish! He had never seen one of these monsters before, and
certainly not up close. Such a fish could chew him to pieces
and swallow him quickly, but he was more in awe than he
was terrified. He watched the kakapa swim behind Seeker
and take up a position to follow.*

*Chataqua glanced back toward the rising sun. The
mountain of white sand that he had fantasized as the Land-
Where-The-Sun-Is-Born had changed shape! He looked at it,
puzzled, not sure it was a real object or a trick of tired eyes in
the sun. Had it moved? It was now to the left of the sun, where
before it had been to the right. Or had the sun moved?
Chataqua shielded his eyes from the bright sun and stared at
the shape. It now seemed like a great white sea bird, with
wings that moved in the wind. Alarm shot through him. What
was this strange object?*

*"Okee! Great Spirit!" shouted Chataqua hoarsely, his
throat parched from the salt water and sun. "Great father
Benatagua! What is this you have sent toward me?"*

*The ocean around him was silent except for the lap of the
waves against the hull of Seeker. The fin of Gitsche Kakapa
still followed relentlessly. Suddenly, the fin moved toward the
canoe. Chataqua saw it, reached for his long bow and laid an
arrow across it. The huge kakapa came straight toward the*

247

canoe. *Chataqua loosed the arrow and it hissed into the blue water, striking Gitsche Kakapa between his head and the huge fin. The arrow bounced into the air and fell harmlessly into the ocean. The kakapa turned away and swam by the canoe. Chataqua laid and released another arrow. It struck the kakapa in the body near the fin and lodged itself there. Chataqua saw a trail of blood as Gitsche Kakapa swam away with a violent thrust of his huge tail.*

We return to the other perspective, which aids us in keeping the suspense high!

Example, Multi Perspective Scene, Part 3;
    Nathan Smythe stared ahead of the ship bracing his legs to the roll. He wondered if the sun on the sea were playing tricks on him. About a half mile away he saw a young Savage in a small boat of some kind loosing arrows into the ocean. He shook his head hoping it would clear, and stared at the ocean again. He saw the young man kneeling in a log canoe. Suddenly the canoe was jolted and seemed to rise in the water. The young man held on and the canoe settled into the water with a visible splash.
    "You there," shouted Nathan to a sailor standing near the tiller. "Please request the Master attend the bridge."
    "Aye, Sir," said the sailor and ran down the ladder to the 'tween deck to the after part of the ship.
    Soon Sir John was on the bridge, pulling on his tunic as he approached. "What is it, Mr. Smythe?" he asked in a gruff voice.
    "Sir, one point on the starboard bow at about two miles distant, I have sighted a Savage in a small boat," said Nathan carefully. "I believe he is in some sort of distress."
    The Captain turned his eyes on the ocean ahead of Discovery. Edward Bollingham came up the ladder from the 'tween deck to where they stood and gazed in the direction the Master was looking.
    "What is it, Mr Smythe?" asked Bollingham impatiently.
    "A Savage in a small boat," said Nathan.
    "Yes, I can see the man," said Sir John.

Bollingham stared intently. "Yes, I see the man," he said. "It appears that there is a shark of some kind there also."

"Really?" asked Nathan in horror.

Nathan saw more clearly now a young Savage in a small log boat. He watched as the man laid an arrow on a long bow and loosed it at something in the water. Then he saw the fin. It seemed huge! He couldn't imagine what it looked like to the young man in the canoe.

"He is being attacked by a very large shark!" exclaimed Nathan. "May I proceed to pick him up?"

"What is a Savage doing here in a small canoe?" asked Bollingham. "I say leave him be! He may be dangerous!"

"Sir, the Savage is in great danger," said Nathan. "We are honor bound to intervene!"

"For a Savage?" sneered Bollingham. "I think not... he is just a Savage, after all!"

"If the man is here in a canoe, we must be nearing land," observed Sir John, thoughtfully, rubbing his bearded chin.

"If we help this man, it may assist us in dealing with the Savages," pleaded Nathan.

"The only way to deal with the Savages is to kill them before they kill you!" exclaimed Bollingham in a furious voice.

Test the resolve of your characters and show their "character" in reaction to an event... every chance you get.

The Master walked slowly to the starboard side and watched the Savage in the canoe. He watched for several seconds and paced back and forth across the bridge.

"Mr. Bollingham," said the Captain, "take the watch and lay the ship alongside the savage's canoe. Mr. Smythe, muster the crew to rescue this man."

In the next scene, we pick up the action as seen from Chataqua's perspective.

Example, Multi Perspective Scene, Part 4;
Chataqua watched the giant gray fin of Gitsche Kakapa as it trailed astern of Seeker. He turned to see the great white object behind him take form in the shimmering sunlight. He

gasped, forgetting for a brief moment the threat of the kakapa. As it came closer, the object became a great canoe. He could see the wood of its hull. Above it were wind cloths like the ones he had found on the beach.

Suddenly, the huge fin started closing on Seeker again. Chataqua snapped out of his trance, picked up his long bow and laid an arrow across it. He launched the arrow at the charging kakapa and saw it lodge next to the other one just ahead of the fin. Gitsche Kakapa turned away at the last moment before he would have struck Seeker. His passage left Chataqua rocking in the waves. Chataqua watched as the fin disappeared behind him.

The great canoe with the wings of a giant sea bird was coming straight toward him. What was it? Was it alive? Or were there men on it? If there were men on the giant canoe, what would they do to him? He gritted his teeth and held on to his courage. He must face the teeth of Gitsche Kakapa and the unknown fury of whatever demons were aboard this great canoe!

Suddenly Chataqua's canoe was thrust upward. He grabbed the sides and hung on, balancing to keep the canoe upright. He fell to one side and shifted his weight to the other trying to stay out of the water. He saw the great fin and the two arrows in the broad gray back of Gitsche Kakapa rise under him. The great fish smacked the side of the canoe with its mighty tail, sending a shudder through the frail craft and through Chataqua. Chataqua righted the canoe and grasped his long bow, straining his eyes to see where the kakapa would next emerge. Could he kill it with arrows? The arrows in the beast's back seemed to not have telling effect. Where could he shoot it? In the side? In its mouth? Where could an arrow penetrate this huge fish that would kill it? Could he strike it with his spear and kill it? Or, would it pull him into he water to face a huge mouth with sharp teeth?

The great canoe was so close now that Chataqua could see that there were men aboard it. They wore strange, colorful clothes. He heard them shouting at one another as the great canoe came directly at him. It seemed to Chataqua to be tremendous in size, its brown colored sides rising the height of

*a man above the water. He glanced back and saw the fin of
Gitsche Kakapa coming again at Seeker, trailing blood.*

*The strange canoe approached and suddenly, the wind
cloths above it came down with a crashing noise and it glided
beside Seeker, turning into the light wind. Chataqua looked
up at the great canoe in fear. A young man with very pale
skin, a large blue hat and hair on his face shouted to
Chataqua. He was afraid to answer. He was afraid of what
these strange men might do. The strange canoe came very
close to Seeker. A rope ladder fell down its side. The young
man in the blue hat shouted at him again and motioned to
him. They wanted him to get into the strange canoe! Should
he? Could he?*

*A jolt from below sent Seeker violently up, throwing
Chataqua into the air. He fell with a splash into the water. He
felt the wound in his side rip open, and he knew his blood was
in the water. The rough side of Gitsche Kakapa rubbed past
him, flailing his skin. The giant tail thrashed and thrust him
underwater. He struggled to get back to the top. He heard a
strange noise that startled him. It was a loud, cracking sound,
muffled by the water. Chataqua surfaced, gasping for air and
saw blood in the water all around him.*

We are now at that point where we must begin to describe
the things the English have (such as a musket) as Chataqua
would see them.

*The pale young man with the hairy face plunged into the
water near Chataqua. He swam toward him, gesturing
toward the strange canoe. The noise came again, this time
very loud as it was not muffled by the water. Chataqua had
never heard anything like it. There was a flash of fire from the
side of the great canoe and the air filled with smoke. The pale
young man with the hair on his face grabbed Chataqua and
pulled him to the rope ladder. Chataqua was too weak to
resist. The hairy faced man pointed upward. Chataqua
grasped the ladder and climbed slowly up the side. Hands
reached down and grasped him. They pulled him into the
great canoe. He fell to the deck between two towering poles
held in place by many ropes.*

The young man with the pale skin and hairy face came over the side of the great canoe and knelt beside Chataqua. Chataqua trembled in fear, his side bleeding from the Mako bite and where the rough hide of Gitsche Kakapa had scraped him. The young man pulled Chataqua to his feet and to the side of the great canoe.

Chataqua saw Gitsche Kakapa turn toward the strange canoe, the huge gray fin leaning over at a crazy angle. A trail of blood followed the great fish as it propelled itself at the canoe. The loud sound with fire and smoke came again. Chataqua flinched, shrinking away from the noise. He saw a man pointing a strangely shaped stick at the water. The men on the deck of the great canoe made loud sounds, apparently happy about something. He peered over the side and saw the water stained with blood. Gitsche Kakapa sank into the clear blue-green water, blood spiraling up from the huge body. The pale men had killed Gitsche Kakapa with a stick-that-made-fire!

Chataqua stared at the pale men. They were big men with blue and white striped shirts and hairy faces. Their large noses made them appear very ferocious, and Chataqua feared that he would be made a slave, or worse, be eaten by these strange beings. The young man with the pale face put on his large blue hat, bent over Chataqua and looked at his wounds. Chataqua held himself very still and wondered at his fate.

Now, the action in the scene has been described from two perspectives, each overlapping the other. We must now "merge" the perspectives in a new scene.

Example, Merging the Multi Perspective Scene, Part 5;
Chataqua got to his feet and stood defiantly, determined to not show fear amongst this strange tribe. A terrible man with a scar on his forehead glared at him, and Chataqua saw that one of his ears was missing. A very fat man came toward him with a scowl on his round face. He wore strange, colorful clothes that ballooned at the sleeves and trousers.

The fat man coughed loudly. "A foolish display of courage, Mr. Smythe," he said shaking his head.

The man with the scar shook his head in agreement. "Better that the shark eat both of 'em than bring the savage aboard!"

"You do not value your honor, Sir," said the young man.

"Watch the Savage carefully Mr. Smythe," said the fat man. The fat man pointed at Chataqua and the man with the scar and missing ear took a strange looking metal object from his trousers and pointed it at him.

A tall man with hair on his face and strange blue eyes walked to where they stood on the rolling deck. He wore a dark blue hat like that of the young man, but trimmed with a bright color that shown like the sun. Chataqua shrunk back. This man with the ghostly blue eyes must be their Sachem.

"Well done, Mister Smythe," said Sir John.

"Thank you, Sir John."

"Mr. Bollingham, I would be pleased to be underway... course due west."

The fat man moved away and began bellowing to the other men. They rushed to the tall poles and the wind cloths rose into the air. The ship began to plunge as it gathered speed toward the setting sun.

"How do we communicate with this Savage?" asked Sir John in his deep voice.

"Be kind and patient and he will respond," said Nathan worriedly.

"Kind and patient?" asked Bollingham harshly. "Bind him and put him below in the cargo hold... or he will try to kill us all... just as those Savages in the Canaries tried!"

"He is wounded," said Nathan anxiously. "Can't you see?"

"It's too bad the bloody shark didn't eat 'im!" exclaimed the man with the scar.

"Please...Sir!" exclaimed Nathan. "I will take him below and post one of my men with him until we find the shore and can return him to his people!"

"You heard me, Mister Smythe," said Bollingham, irritation in his voice.

"Wait," said Sir John. "Mister Smythe, take him below and see if you can find out how far it is to the shore... and what we may expect there."

"Aye, Sir," said Nathan, gratitude and relief in his voice.

253

*Nathan put his hand on Chataqua's shoulder and
motioned with his other hand to follow him. Chataqua
followed him reluctantly, staring uneasily at the strange men
and ship that surrounded him. Bollingham and Cutlass
followed their progress with scowls.*

Chataqua pointed to Sir John with a questioning look.

"That's the Master, Sir John," said Nathan.

"Mata?" asked Chataqua trying to form the words.

"Master, Sir John!"

*"Mata-ser-jon," said Chataqua shaping the syllables
carefully.*

This is a good point to shift to another scene.

*Nathan and Chataqua went below to the 'tween deck
where Chataqua had to bend his head to keep from hitting it
on the deck above. There were a dozen or more people there
living in extremely cramped conditions. They stared at
Chataqua. The deck was smelly and Chataqua gagged and
tuned pale. Little tables sat in front of rough, white colored
curtains that masked pads on the deck where the people slept.*

*Nathan motioned to Chataqua to sit on a bench at one of
the little tables. He did so, looking uncomfortable. The ship
rolled and Chataqua began to feel sick.*

*"Nathan," said Nathan pointing to himself. "I am
Nathan."*

*Chataqua looked at the strange, pale faced man curiously,
wondering if he should fear him or not. He sat reluctantly,
feeling the motion of the great canoe as it moved through the
water. He shuddered involuntarily, still weak from his
encounter with the Water-That-Never-Ends and Gitsche
Kakapa.*

*Nathan smiled. "Nathan," he said again, pointing to
himself.*

*Chataqua understood. He tried to form the strange word
on his lips. "Na-tank," he said.*

"Who are you?" asked Nathan pointing to Chataqua.

*Chataqua paused. He understood what the man wanted.
Should he give him his name? Maybe if he did, they would not
eat him. "Chataqua," he said pointing to himself.*

"Shaw-tak-gwa," said Nathan pointing to Chataqua.

Chataqua nodded. Nathan poured water from an earthenware pitcher and handed it to Chataqua. Chataqua took it and drank, thankful to have water after his ordeal in Water-That-Never-Ends. He kept his keen eyes on the strange young man with hair on his face.

"Eat," said Nathan handing Chataqua a piece of moldy bread. He made eating motions with his mouth.

Chataqua took the bread. He was very hungry after three days on the Water-That-Never-Ends. He ate the bread. It had a strange taste, but it made him feel better.

This is a sample of how to handle a scene in which the people involved speak different languages and are of different cultures. This is a place to "move ahead in time" to another scene.

Chataqua spent the night sleeping on a pad on the deck next to Nathan. He slept fitfully. Early the next morning Chataqua and Nathan walked together on the deck of Discovery.

"I'm surprised to see ya alive, Mister Smythe," said the man with the scar... what with that Savage being with ya!"

"The Savage is a human being... and seems a nice fellow," said Nathan.

"He's just waiting to slit your throat and cook ya in his pot!" said Cutlass with a leer.

Nathan walked on, ignoring Cutlass and the stares of the seaman on deck. Chataqua watched Cutlass carefully, fearing that the man might attack him at any time. He began to understand that Natank was protecting him against the others.

"English," said Nathan pointing to himself. "We are English."

Chataqua thought about the word and then tried it. "Ing... Ingel-e-sez," he said pointing to the men and to Nathan.

Nathan nodded. This man is not a Savage, he thought. He learned so quickly and there was the gleam of intelligence and humanity in his eyes.

Chataqua looked behind the great canoe and was astounded to see two more great canoes even larger than the one he was in. Nathan saw his surprise.

"Susan Constant and Godspeed," said Nathan watching Chataqua closely.

Chataqua stared in awe at the two ships as their wind cloths billowed and pulled them through the water. It was amazing. There was much to learn from these Ingelesez.

We have completed a "resulting situation event". It is a result of Chataqua's decision to pursue his goals and surviving the "testing events". The WOW Factors are Emotion (Chataqua's emotions at being saved by the strange pale men), Suspense (would Chataqua survive Gitsche Kakapa?), Conflict (with Gitsche Kakapa), Action (the fight with Gitsche Kakapa), Surprise (the arrival of the great canoe with wings), Heroism (Chataqua's struggle against overwhelming odds), Humor (the initial exchanges between Chataqua and Nathan), and Pizzazz (the vivid descriptions of the sea and the ship). The WOW is 8/10 +.

Oh yes... your homework. This time, take a portion of the examples provided and, rather than writing your own version, take the writing as it is and "tweak it"... make it better! Also... analyze it with respect to the Story Events.

****

Chapter Twenty-four
Defining and Triumphant Scenes

Defining Scenes

A defining scene is one that further defines an important "turn of events". Chataqua's safe return from over the unknown horizon with the White Explorers requires a series of such scenes.

Example: Prelude to Defining Scene;
"What is that?" shouted Manatapac as he pulled in the fish net. He looked back at Chalapow who was staring at the horizon toward the Land-Where-The-Sun-Is-Born.

"So... you see it too?" asked Chalapow. "I thought my eyes were as crazy as I am!"

Manatapac hauled the net ashore. Inside were hundreds of small silver fish, wriggling and jumping. Three larger fish of about an arm's length thrashed about, held in the web of the net.

"You have blue-fish-that-snap-with-strong-teeth!" shouted Chalapow rubbing his belly. "We will have a feast tonight!"

"Never mind your stomach!" shouted Manatapac. He hauled the net well up onto the beach and stared to seaward. "What is it that we both see?"

"It looks like a great bird," said Chalapow. "It is a giant bird that skims the water!"

"No... it is not a bird," exclaimed Manatapac. "It is a canoe... a canoe with wings!"

"How can it be a canoe?" asked Chalapow in awe.

"Look... look beneath the white wings!" exclaimed Manatapac. "There is a great log holding the wings!"

"I can see two more!" exclaimed Chalapow.

Again, we use the multi-perspective situation to give depth and balance to our story. We shift to Discovery.

Example, Prelude to Defining Scene;

Chataqua stood uncomfortably at the railing of Discovery with Na-tank and watched as the great canoe approached the beach near Point-Where-Great-Waters-Meet. It came very close to the white sands. Chataqua wondered how many arms lengths the great canoe descended into the water, for he knew the water depth where they were to be less than a man's height.

Chataqua snuck a look at Na-tank as the young Ingelesez stared at the land that spread in front of them. It was a land of deep green foliage. Pine, cypress and walnut trees sprinkled with the white of dogwood and laurel spread along the coastline. Patches of red and violet wild flowers could be seen growing beyond the white sand beaches.

There was a rumbling noise. A large forked piece of wood fell from the front of the great canoe into the water. It was affixed to the ship by a piece of rope. The ship slowly swung around, the rope stretching out to the large piece of wood, holding the ship in place. Chataqua stared at the rope. Every minute he learned more and his mind raced with new ideas. He watched as the larger canoes of the Ingelesez anchored further offshore. Chataqua's heart leaped as he saw a large number of his people on the beach. He saw two canoes put forth into Broad Waters.

"Shawtakgwa, these are your people?" asked Nathan.

Chataqua looked inquisitively at Na-tank. The young gentleman pointed to Chataqua and then at the people on the beach. He had a questioning look on his face. Chataqua understood.

"Chataqua... Chesapeake," said Chataqua pointing to the men in the oncoming canoes and then to himself. "Na-tank... Ingelesez.

"Chesapeake," said Nathan pointing to Chataqua. It was clear what the Savage was trying to tell him. His people were called "Chesapeake".

Now we have established understanding of the two terms "Ingelesez" (English) and "Chesapeake".

Chataqua nodded and smiled. It was the first time Nathan had seen the Savage smile. He wasn't sure until that moment that they could smile.

"Chesapeake!" said Chataqua pointing at the people on the shore.

"Yes…Chesapeake!" said Nathan.

Chataqua nodded. As the canoes approached, Nathan saw that each contained six Savages, each with a paddle, three to each side. The canoes were hollowed out tree trunks much like the one from which they had pulled Shawtakgwa. They approached to about twenty yards and stopped, staring at the ship and the strange men in it.

Chataqua stared at the canoes. His face flashed with recognition as he saw Manatapac in the first canoe. Then he saw Malapok in the second canoe and a worried look spread over his face. He turned to Na-tank and pointed at the first canoe.

"Manatapac," said Chataqua.

"Manatapac?" said Nathan trying to understand what the Savage meant.

"What is the Savage saying?" asked Bollingham gruffly.

Chataqua shrunk away from the big Ingelesez with the gruff voice. He did not like this man who stared at him as though he were an animal to be hunted.

"His name is Shawtakgwa, Sir," said Nathan. "I believe he is telling me that a man in the canoe is named Manatapac."

"Come now, Mister Smythe," said Bollingham coughing into a lacey white handkerchief, "these Savages don't have names… like people do."

"I assure you, Sir," said Nathan impatiently, "that they do."

"These Savages in the canoes have bows and arrows and spears," said Bollingham, looking at the canoes. "They must be hostile!"

"I don't believe that they are," said Nathan worriedly.

"Sir John," said Bollingham, "these Savages are hostile. Perhaps they are cannibals. At your pleasure, Sir, I will fire into them and destroy them."

"Hold your fire, Mr. Bollingham," said Sir John. "Don't be a fool!

Bollingham's face turned red.

Remember, good novels are about conflict, violent and otherwise. Here we are establishing conflict between Bollingham and Nathan.

"Mr. Smythe, if you please, try to get your Savage to be seen by the ones in the canoes," said Sir John.
"Aye Sir," said Nathan.
"And give him this," said the Master.

Note the several ways of referring to Sir John in the dialogue tag.

Ratcliffe handed Nathan a leather pouch. Nathan took it, opened it and looked inside.
"Give it to the Savage as the Master has declared, young man," said Bollingham. "You need not cast your eyes upon it!"
"Sir, I must know what I give this man," said Nathan with irritation, "if he is to trust me!"
The leather pouch was filled with necklaces and bracelets of brightly colored glass beads.
"Tell the Savage we will bring them more in exchange for food and water," said Sir John.
Nathan motioned to Chataqua to step forward.
"Allow the Savage to swim to his people," said Ratcliffe. "That will show them that we mean them no harm."
Nathan motioned to Chataqua again. Chataqua stepped cautiously to the railing. Nathan handed him the leather pouch. Chataqua took the pouch cautiously. Nathan pointed to him.
"This is for you and your people... for the Chesapeake," smiled Nathan.
Chataqua looked at the pouch with questioning eyes. He opened it and looked at the glistening beads inside. They shown in the sunlight as none he had ever seen before, and were of many colors. He looked down at the blue-green water. He looked at the Chesapeake canoes and waved his arm over his head. Manatapac saw him instantly. He shouted Chataqua's name and waved happily.

Nathan made an inviting gesture with his arm, indicating that Chataqua was free to swim to his people. Chataqua watched uncertainly. Nathan made the gesture once again. Chataqua took the cue. He climbed over the railing and jumped feet first over the side, landing with a splash in the warm, salty Broad Water. He went under the water, surfaced, looked up at Nathan, waved and began to swim toward the canoes grasping the bag of beads.

This is another among several "resulting situation events". The WOW factors are Emotion (Chataqua's range of emotions as he encounters the Ingelesez and finds that they intend to let him go), Suspense (What will the Ingelesez do with Chataqua?), Conflict (between Chataqua and the Ingelesez besides Nathan who see him as a "savage"), Heroism (Chataqua as he comes home a hero having survived his adventures). The WOW is 4/10.

Try your hand at "fleshing out" the improvised conversations between Chataqua and Nathan. Can you think of more things they would have tried to communicate to one another?

Triumphant Scenes

A triumphant scene is just that... a scene where the hero/ heroine triumphs and is recognized. It is an opportunity to build to a "high" in the tempo of the novel, from which you can generate a new "low" in the emotional swings of the story.

Example, Prelude to Triumphant Scene;
Chataqua and Manatapac stood near the lodge of Benatagua. Beside it was the long canoe in which Benatagua had canoed to the Land-Where-The-Cold-Wind-Blows. It was covered with leaves, the ornate wood carvings of fish and sea birds on its bow caked with moss.

"We are glad to have you back!" said Manatapac. "We worried that the Water-That-Never-Ends had eaten you."

"It nearly did," said Chataqua, now rested from his ordeal. "But I found the strength..."

"You always have the strength, my brother," said Manatapac, a twinkle in his eye.

"I have your friendship," said Chataqua. "I draw my strength from you!"

"I thank you for that," said Manatapac, putting his hand briefly on Chataqua's shoulder.

"You must soon be Werowance," said Chataqua. "You will be First Among Braves!"

Manatapac laughed. "Chalapow told me that, also," said Manatapac. "How can I be Werowance when the son of the Periku seeks it?"

"You have the strength!" exclaimed Chataqua.

"And so do you," smiled Manatapac.

"I am but a new Brave," said Chataqua.

There was a silence between them as they stared at Benatagua's canoe.

We raise the issue now of who will replace Benatagua as Werowance. The Sachem's choice will be very important in the continuing competition with the Periku.

"Benatagua's canoe requires your attention," said Manatapac.

"Seeker was lost," said Chataqua, "so my father's canoe will now be mine."

Chalatas came out of the lodge and busied herself with a stack of maize outside the lodge.

"Have you told him?" asked Chalatas impatiently.

Manatapac shifted his weight nervously. "No, I have not told him," he said.

"It is time that he knows," said Chalata grimly.

"What?" asked Chataqua. "What is it?"

"Malapok has asked Masonnacok, the father of Alanoas, that she be given to him as wife," said Manatapac worriedly.

Chataqua stared at Manatapac and then at his mother in amazement. "It cannot be," he said. "She will not be of age until the time of the hot sun on the next cycle of the moon!"

Our hero has returned triumphant, but is now faced with a new problem.

"He has asked Masonnacok anyway," said Chalatas
irritably.

"She is to be the mother of my children!" moaned
Chataqua.

"I didn't want to tell you," said Manatapac, a worried look
in his face.

"What did Masonnacok say?" asked Chataqua. *"He knows
what is between me and Alanoas!"*

"I do not know," said Chalatas with a shrug.

"I will challenge him!" exclaimed Chataqua. *"Alanoas can
choose who she marries... it is the law of the Chesapeake."*

"She can choose, yes," said Chalatas, *"but her father must
agree."*

"Now that I am back, he will not give her to Malapok,"
anguished Chataqua.

"Have you asked for her, Chataqua?" asked Chalatas.

"Well, no," said Chataqua sadness in his voice. *"I had to...
seek the unknown horizon!"*

*"You will be rewarded for finding the Great-Canoes-With-
Wings"*, said Manatapac. *"You will have enough to present
Masonnacok for his daughter."*

"You are very foolish to wait," said Chalatas. *"Ask for her!"*

With that interlude to further the situation between
Chataqua, Alanoas and Malapok, we turn to the triumphant
ceremony marking Chataqua's return.

Example, Triumphant Scene;
*The ceremonial drums sounded and Chesapian walked to
the center of the Council of Braves and faced the symbol of
Okee, the stag's antlers, eagle feathers and the shells of oysters
and clams stained in red, blue and yellow. Chesapian
chanted:*

Oh Okee
Hear our wish,
We Chesapeake,
People of the Shellfish,
Oh Okee
Protect our land,

We Chesapeake,
Of earth, swamp and sand,
Give us courage,
Give us love,
As we plea,
To you, Okee!

Chataqua stood at the fire of the Council of Braves. It was
dusk and he could still see the ships of the Ingelesez in the
Broad Waters through the palisades of the village. The nearest
ship seemed to be stationary there, a short distance from the
sandy beach. Manatapac stood before the Council of Braves
and looked reassuringly at Chataqua.

"Chataqua has canoed toward the Land-Where-The-Sun-
Is-Born and found the Ingelesez Tribe who live there!"
exclaimed Manatapac. "He has brought gifts from the men on
the Great-Canoe-With-Wings."

Manatapac pointed to the shiny glass beads that lay on a
deerskin in front of the fire, glistening in its light.

"What are these?" shouted Malapok. "They are no better
than our own shells... they shine with an evil glow."

Chataqua rose from where he sat and turned to the
Council. His side was still cut and raw from his encounter
with the kakapa. He gathered his breath, as he knew he was
to tell his story, and it had to be told dramatically and with
emotion, as befitted a Brave of the Chesapeake.

Storytelling is viewed as an art among the Chesapeake,
an art that every Brave should master.

"I canoed toward the Land-Where-The-Sun-Is-Born hoping
to find riches that would make the Chesapeake great," said
Chataqua in a loud and firm voice. "My canoe was wrecked by
a great storm that threw me about and filled my canoe with
water. My father, Benatagua, came to me in a vision and told
me to paddle on... paddle on!"

Chataqua paused and gazed around the Council. All eyes
were on him, waiting for him to speak. "I was attacked by
kakapa and received the wounds you see."

"You tell a story we cannot believe," shouted Malapok.
"You have brought evil men and evil things among us!"

"Malapok speaks as he always does," said Chataqua
looking at Malapok with fiery eyes, "with only the knowledge
of what he thinks should be... not the wisdom of what is."

We see here that Chataqua is not afraid of Malapok any
more.

Malapok's face turned furious. "Chataqua is a danger
among us," shouted Malapok. "He brings us only lies."
Malapok started toward Chataqua, raising his fist in a
threatening gesture. Chesapian held up his hand, and with
that small gesture stopped Malapok in his tracks.
"Let the Brave Chataqua speak," said the Sachem sternly.
Malapok stepped back, his expression sullen.
"I was saved from the kakapa by my friend Calypo-Ma and
his friends, the calypo," said Chataqua. "Okee answered my
plea and told Calypo-Ma of my battle with the kakapa.... and
he came and killed the kakapa."
"Okeetaka! Okeetaka!" shouted Manatapac, using the word
for "brave and determined man, blessed by the god Okee".
"I paddled on, determined to find the Land-Where-The-
Sun-Is-Born," said Chataqua with paddling motions, entering
a trance-like state with a determined look on his face.
Other Braves of the Council picked up the chant in low
tones. "Okeetaka! Okeetaka!"

This is a multi-character scene, one of the most difficult to
write. The chant helps to provide action from characters who
are in the background.

Chataqua spoke in a loud voice over the chants. "I endured
a night in my damaged canoe. I turned back toward the
Land-Where-The-Sun-Sets, discouraged that I had failed.
Come the dawn I was stalked by Gitsche Kakapa. I could see
the huge fin of this beast following my canoe. I paddled on."
"Chataqua is Honokaa Tu, as was his father," shouted
Manatapac, using the Chesapeake words for "honored one".

"Matta," shouted Malapok, his voice sounding hysterical. "Only the Sachem may declare Honokaa Tu."

"Someone of courage who has accomplished a great deed is Honokaa Tu," shouted Manatapac, "and Chataqua has done this! It is so. The words of Malapok cannot change this!"

Chesapian stood and folded his arms across his chest. He glared at Manatapac and Malapok. "Chataqua will be heard!" he said in a booming voice, raising his hands high.

A silence came over the Council of Braves as Chesapian glared around the circle that enclosed the crackling campfire. Chesapian sat down.

"It was then that I saw the Great-Canoe-With-Wings," said Chataqua, the strongest emotion in his voice, looking skyward. "It seemed to me a dream... a vision of a great white bird with legs long enough to reach the bottom of the great sea... but it was not that. As it came closer I could see that there was a very large log beneath the wings of the bird. And the wings were not wings... they were very large wind cloths, wind catchers... like the kind on my canoe, but much bigger."

"Okeetaka! Okeetaka!" chanted the Braves, except for Malapok, Stakto and their followers.

"The great canoe with the wind-catchers like wings came close to me in my canoe," said Chataqua. "Inside were strange men with pale skin and hair on their faces."

Now we will establish conflict between those in the tribe who do not welcome the Ingelesez and those that do.

"Evil! Evil!" shouted Stakto. "We all know that to let the hair on one's face grow long is a sign of evil!"

Chesapian glanced at Stakto and the young Brave became quiet.

"Gitsche Kakapa swam strongly into my canoe and threw me into the water," shouted Chataqua, making thrashing motions with his arms. "I went under the water and tried to see where Gitsche Kakapa was. I could not see him... and then I heard a terrible noise... like the lightning and the thunder of the skies. I came to the top of the water and there was smoke... a terrible smell in the air, like the smell after the fire-from-the-sky! I looked and there was blood in the water all around me!"

Chataqua paused and looked around the Council of Braves as he had seen others do when telling a story. He had come to the point where he must hold them in suspense as to what happened. They all sat silently as the fire crackled and snapped, its light flickering dramatically over the face of Chataqua.

"Suddenly, one of the pale men in the great canoe jumped to me in the water. He pushed me to the side of the great canoe before Gitsche Kakapa could strike again. I climbed the side of the great canoe which was more than a man's height above the water. Strong hands gripped me and pulled me from the bloody water," said Chataqua in a whisper that built to a shout. "I found myself in the great canoe with the pale men with hair on their faces. I thought that I was to be killed. Then I saw a man raise a long stick and point it at the water. There was a terrible noise and fire shot out of the stick! Smoke and the same terrible smell swirled around the great canoe. I thought I was dead, but after awhile I breathed and knew I still lived!"

"Okeetaka! Okeetaka!" chanted the Braves.

"I was in the great canoe with the wind-cloth-that-looks-like-wings," continued Chataqua. "I thought I would be eaten by these strange men... or beaten... or made to be a slave, but they did none of this."

Chataqua paused and paced back and forth dramatically. "These strange men made the wind-cloth gather the wind and we moved toward the Land-Where-The-Sun-Sets... moving through the water so swiftly that I could only stare at the waves as they rushed by. Then they took me into a lodge beneath the great canoe and gave me food...a smoked meat and a grain made into a kind of gruel, as we do with maize."

"There is no lodge beneath a canoe," spat out Malapok contemptuously. "You must all see now that Chataqua is a teller of things that are not... he tells them only to make himself sound brave... and he is not!"

"Oh, you are wrong, Malapok," said Chataqua. "All things I have said are true... as Okee and my father with him will witness."

"You dare to call on Okee to commend your lies?" asked Maltakak, the Periku.

*"Okee will know that I tell the truth," said Chataqua
earnestly. "He will cast me into the sea for the kakapa if I do
not tell the truth!"*

*"And what are these bright objects that the pale men with
hairy faces, these Tagkanokoc, have given you?" asked
Maltakak.*

Maltakak fears the rise of Chataqua to the status of hero
in the Tribe. We build that tension further.

*Chataqua was concerned that Maltakak used the name
Tagkanokoc for the pale men. Tagkanokoc meant "hairy evil
ones, disciples of the Great Evil Son Tagkanysough".*

*"These men are not Tagkanokoc, Great Periku," said
Chataqua emphatically. "They are Quiacokoc... the kind ones.
They saved me from Gitsche Kakapa! They call themselves...
Ingelesez... they are Ingelesez."*

*"What does this mean... Ingelesez?" asked Chesapian
suddenly.*

*"It is the name of the land beyond the unknown horizon,"
said Chataqua, "a far away land where they live with their
great canoes and wonderful treasures. They are Ingelesez...as
we are Chesapeake!"*

"And how do you know this?" asked Chesapian.

*"The young one, Na-tank...the one who came to me in the
water... he told me. He made me wingapo!"*

We know that the Tribe is split between those who favor
Chesapian and the followers of Maltakak. We exacerbate
that split with a split on how to treat the English.

*"Wingapo" shouted Stakto wildly. "Chataqua is now
wingapo with the Tagkanokoc!"*

*Malapok stirred from where he sat. "The Periku has
declared that they are Tagkanokoc," he shouted. "The bright
objects are the evil symbols of the Tagkanokoc!"*

*Chesapian shook his head impatiently and held up his
hands for silence. "We do not know these men in the great
canoe with the wind-cloth that looks like wings," he said.*

"How can we call them Tagkanokoc... or Quiacokoc? We do not know them!"

"We should welcome them," said Manatapac in a strong voice. "Then we can decide what they are!"

There was a murmur of approval from the Braves in the Council.

"What are the bright objects, Chataqua?" asked Chesapian.

"I believe, Great Sachem, that they are only rich decorations given to show the good will of the Ingelesez."

"How do you know this?" asked Chesapian looking at Chataqua curiously.

"I have studied the objects and found what I say to be so, Great Sachem. They are harmless but valuable decorations."

Chesapian looked at Chataqua admiringly. "You have the head that thinks... the ability to find knowledge."

"Thank you, Great Sachem."

Chesapian rose to a standing position and faced the Council. "Chataqua has honored us in battle against the Wepeneooc. He has shown great courage in braving the Water-That-Never-Ends beyond the unknown horizon."

"Chataqua has courage," chanted the Braves.

"Chataqua has found the Ingelesez, who have sent us valuable objects in tribute!" exclaimed Chesapian.

"Chataqua has wisdom," chanted the Braves.

Chesapian withdrew an eagle feather from his cloak and held it aloft. "Chataqua is an honored Brave of the Chesapeake," he said wrapping the second feather into the top knot on Chataqua's head.

"Chataqua is honored," chanted the Braves.

"Chataqua has completed a deed worthy of Honokaa Tu," said Chesapian in a deeply emotional voice. "He is honored with his father."

"Honokaa Tu! Honokaa Tu!"

Chataqua stood proudly in the firelight, his heart beating wildly in his chest. Chesapian took the colorful beaded cape of Honokaa Tu and held it over his head. The cape was covered with the shells of oysters and clams stained red, yellow and blue. He draped the shawl around the shoulders of Chataqua.

"Wear the symbol of Honokaa Tu, Chataqua, the honored one of Great People of the Shellfish!"

269

"I wear it and remember my father, Benatagua!"

"Tomorrow," said Chesapian turning to the Council of Braves, "We welcome the Ingelesez and see what other wondrous things they may have."

And so, we have a scene of triumph. This is another "resulting situation event". The WOW factors are Emotion (the emotion of triumph), Suspense (what will happen in the continuing confrontation with Malapok and the Periku?), Conflict (the continuing verbal conflict between Chataqua and Malapok), Action (the ceremony, the chanting), Heroism (the recognition of Chataqua's heroism with the honor of Honokaa Tu). The WOW is 5/10 +.

When you read a scene like this, it should put you right into the skin of the main character and allow you to feel his/her emotions. How did it affect you? Does it need more work? Can you do better? Okay... for homework, give it a try!

****

Chapter Twenty-five
Endings

I'm going to stop the examples here, because I want you to read "The Unknown Horizon" when it is available...so I can't give it all away! Let's explore several possible "endings".

Ending A: Short Novel, Happy Ending

1. The Periku secretly creates reason for conflict between the Chesapeake and the Ingelesez.
2. Chataqua and Manatapac succeed in exposing the Periku. The Periku is discredited
3. Malapok kills Chesapian. Chataqua kills Malapok.
4. Chataqua and Alanoas are married.
5. Chataqua becomes Sachem.
6. The Chesapeake Tribe thrives under Chataqua.
7. Nathan visits and helps to resolve the problems with Wahunsonacock.

Ending B: Longer Novel, Happy Ending

1. The Periku secretly creates reason for conflict between the Chesapeake and the Ingelesez.
2. Conflict erupts. In a battle, Malapok kills Chesapian with a stick-that-makes-fire and makes it look as though it was done by the Ingelesez.
3. Maltakak assumes Sachem with Malapok as Werowance.
4. Malapok claims Alanoas as wife.
5. Chataqua rescues Alanoas and flees with Manatapac to Teme Forest.
6. Many Braves follow Chataqua into Teme Forest (about a third of the remaining Braves).
7. Chalapow remains in the village under the guise of his timidity and good nature. He is really on the side of Chataqua.
8. The Chesapeake fall on hard times under Maltakak.

9. Malapok seeks Chataqua and Alanoas in Teme Forest. Chataqua and Malapok meet in a personal battle. Malapok is killed.
10. Chataqua overthrows Maltakak and resumes his rightful place as Sachem.
11. Chataqua and Alanoas are married.
12. The Chesapeake Tribe thrives under Chataqua.
13. Nathan visits and helps to resolve the problems with Wahunsonacock.

Ending C: Longer Novel, Bittersweet Ending

1. The Periku secretly creates reason for conflict between the Chesapeake and the Ingelesez.
2. Conflict erupts. In a battle, Malapok kills Chesapian with a stick-that-makes-fire and makes it look as though it was done by the Ingelesez.
3. Maltakak assumes Sachem with Malapok as Werowance.
4. Malapok claims Alanoas as wife.
5. Chataqua rescues Alanoas and flees with Manatapac to Teme Forest.
6. Many Braves follow Chataqua into Teme Forest (about a third of the remaining Braves).
7. Chalapow remains in the village under the guise of his timidity and good nature. He is really on the side of Chataqua.
8. The Chesapeake fall on hard times under Maltakak.
9. Malapok seeks Chataqua and Alanoas in Teme Forest. Chataqua and Malapok meet in a personal battle. Malapok survives and escapes.
10. Chataqua overthrows Maltakak and assumes his place as Sachem.
11. Chataqua and Alanoas are married.
12. The Wepeneooc attack to enforce Wahunsonacock's demands. They are aided by a few Ingelesez with muskets.
13. Nathan tries to bring peace between the tribes.

14. Malapok comes out of the forest and tries to kill Nathan. Chataqua saves Nathan and kills Malapok.
15. Nathan tries to get Chataqua to acquiesce to the demands to keep the peace.
16. Chataqua will not give up his honor and refuses.
17. The Wepeneooc attack again. There is a great battle and the Chesapeake are defeated.
18. Nathan helps Chataqua, Alanoas and some of the Chesapeake to escape by canoe, canoeing to the Land-Where-The-Cold-Wind blows.
19. Chataqua leads the remaining Chesapeake to a new and happy life.
20. Chataqua and Alanoas have children. He tells them the "old stories".

Ending D: Stop Where the Story is.

We could stop where the examples end, making the climax Chataqua's triumphant return from the unknown horizon. This would allow us to "fill out" the events to that point.

Ending E: Your Ending.

How would you do it? Thinking about it in this example will help you with your novel.

Thinking about the Endings

Endings A and B are the "happy" ones. Ending A is a shorter novel, which can be an asset. Ending B has a more complex plot which provides potential for a more exciting novel. Ending C is the tragically romantic and longest story.

Endings A and B will make people "happy". They will "feel good" when they finally put down the book. Foo Faa likes Ending B. Ending C is a tragic romance with lovers canoeing off toward unknown horizons seeking a better life. This is the one Foo Foo likes. The Reader will be "emotionally stirred" by the tragedy of this ending... yet still be "happy" for Chataqua and Alanoas. Ending D is a very short novel, but one compact in its story and plot. Which ending has the most Reader appeal?

Consider the WOW Factors again. How can we use them in our ending?

WOW Factor: Emotion

Of the WOW Factors, the most important is EMOTION. Emotion is what hooks the Reader more than anything else. You must mix joy, sorrow, jubilation, despair, love, anger, greed, generosity, etc. into the story in generous doses. You must take the Readers to a "low" filled with sorrow and despair and then bounce them to a "high", filling the entire spectrum of emotion... and then do it again!

WOW Factor: Suspense

The second most important WOW Factor is SUSPENSE. The reader wants to be kept in suspense. He/She wants to wonder about things and discover the answers when you choose to reveal them. The Reader wants to feel and be stirred by the drama of conflict and tension.

WOW Factor: Conflict

The third most important WOW factor is CONFLICT. Most stories are based on some kind of conflict; violent conflict, romantic conflict, business conflict, emotional conflict, etc. You must weave the conflict into the story and highlight it in some way in most scenes.

WOW Factor: Action

The fourth most important WOW factor is ACTION. The Reader wants to be stimulated by the action that takes place. Your story must be told with a pace and flow in which action ebbs and flows but never disappears for very long.

WOW Factor: Surprise

The fifth most important WOW factor is SURPRISE. Surprise goes hand in hand with suspense, but is different. Suspense is the unveiling of information to the Reader that "keeps him/her guessing". Surprise is "an unexpected and shocking turn of events". It is the turning point in the "twists and turns" of our plot. You should have at least one good surprise in the plot... preferably more.

WOW Factor: Romance

A good "boy meets girl" story serves emotion, suspense, conflict, action and surprise. Importantly, it serves that most important WOW factor, emotion, extremely well. Some novels have the romantic theme as the main story. For example, the main character's goal is to win the affections of the boy/girl and he/she is transformed by the experience of courting him/her, etc. In other novels the romantic theme is a subplot that is interwoven with the main plot.

WOW Factor: Mystery

Mystery is related to suspense and surprise, but is not the same. Mystery is suspenseful and can involve surprise (things jumping out at you). It also implies a certain eerie, different environment and the need to "solve" a complex problem for which you have only "clues".

WOW Factor: Heroism

Everyone likes and admires a hero... and so having effective heroism can often make or break a novel. Many times, the story in the novel is about the transformation of a normal person to the status of "larger then life" hero.

WOW Factor: Humor

Humor is very useful even in books not intended to be comedy. In creating emotion, you want to make 'em laugh, then make 'em cry. Humor can and should be injected into every story to some degree. The Author should write with a controlled sense of humor.

WOW Factor: Pizzazz

The dictionary definition for pizzazz is "flamboyance", "zest", "flair". In the right places, you should write "with a swagger", with pizzazz! Some of your characters should be flamboyant and irreverent. Your main characters should have a "zest for life" and the action and dialogue you write should show that.

The Climax Scenes

Whichever ending we choose, we want to lead toward an exciting sequence of "climax scenes". These scenes should all be high tempo, emotional scenes involving peril and finally triumph. They should gradually "bring together all the loose threads".

How Will it End?

The success of the novel depends heavily on the "ending". We have spent the whole novel creating conflict and tension that will allow a dramatic ending. How do we cause the reader to say "WOW, What a book!"? I'm still thinking about how to end "The Unknown Horizon". Think about it with me. For homework, write your own version of an ending. Then describe why your ending will produce a WOW novel! Put it away, read it later and see if you still believe it! Later, when The Unknown Horizon is published, you will see what "storyteller's direction" I took!

****

Chapter Twenty-six
The Rough-Through and the Creative Reviews

We have completed looking at the Creative Principles and examples of how they are applied. We have used the Rough-Through to "get the story down"... that is, we now know the whole story (with options for the ending) and the rough sequence of events. We know our characters much better than we did when we started.

Writing the Rough-Through is the most difficult chore of the Author. Making words... the right words, in the right place at the right time... is creative art in its most demanding form! At times it is pure drudgery to "get something on paper". But, it must be done! At this point, you should go back to the beginning and read your Rough-Through to see if the story and the sequence of events "make sense" to you.

As you do this, feel free to add or subtract... you are looking for whether or not the Rough-Through has the essence of your story on paper. Remember, in your Rough-Through, you were "bulling" your way through, getting words on paper and capturing the essence of your story. You were not stopping to iron out details... that can come now. You were not stopping to do research... that can come now (see your notes regarding where you need research).

The Creative Reviews

The Creative Principles and WOW Factors are applied to the Rough-Through by conducting a "Creative Review". We make sure that all of the necessary Story Events are present. This is not a "process". It is not a "check-off list". Rather it suggests to the Author how to artistically "shape" the Rough-Through to produce a WOW novel.

Let's review the characteristics of a WOW novel;

1. A 100% WOW novel is one that arouses the strongest emotions of the Reader. When he/she finishes reading it, he/she says "WOW... What a book!"

Key Word: "Emotion"; Does the novel contain enough gripping emotion? Does it stir true emotions in the Reader? Does he/she identify sufficiently with the main character(s) such that he/she shares their emotions as if he/she were "there"? Does the ending stir gripping emotion that will be remembered?

2. A WOW novel puts the Reader in a state of euphoria.

Key word: "Euphoria"; Does the novel, when finished, leave the Reader in a state of euphoria? (Euphoria: A state of great happiness or well being). Is the Reader happy that he/she read the novel? Do the "pictures" painted by the novel linger on in the mind of the Reader?

3. A WOW novel captures... indeed imprisons... the Reader in an exciting fictional universe that seems real, but allows the Reader to escape reality.

Key Words:
   a. "Exciting fictional universe"; have you created a "fictional universe" in the novel that is so real, so impressive, and so memorable, that the Reader will always think back to it? Did the Reader feel that he/she was "in it"?
   b. "Escape reality"; have you caused the Reader to escape reality in a fictional universe that seemed real to him/her?

4. The memories of a WOW novel linger with the Reader, as do the emotions it stirs.

Key Word: "Memories"; will the Reader remember this novel "forever"? Will the reading of it be an experience that he/she will use in his/her lifetime and hark back to?

5. WOW novels are always enthusiastically recommended to others.

Key Word: "Others"; will the Reader enthusiastically recommend the novel to others? Will he/she do so in glowing terms, describing it as "an experience to never be forgotten"? Will he/she "demand" that their friends read it (a simple "you should read this" is often not enough)?

6. WOW novels are reread, and reread again.

   Key Word: "Again"; will the Reader enthusiastically read the novel again after some time spent thinking about it? This is a key test of a WOW novel. All WOW Novels are read more than once by the same Reader!

7. WOW novels don't always make the best seller list... but they should!

   Key Word: "Best"; will the Reader think of the novel as one of the several best he/she has ever read?

A Creative Review is a complete read of the Rough-Through with a focused, specific objective. For example, the focused specific objective for Creative Review Number One could be "logic and flow". The second could be "scenario embellishment"; the third could be "beautiful writing"... and so forth. If during the Creative Review you have a new idea, go ahead and pursue it... "loop back", rough it into the text, and then return to your Creative Review. Then on to the next Creative Review... and so forth. Your "new idea" will get smoothed out as you go along.

Figure 26-1 pictures the "rough idea" of Creative Reviews.

Figure 26-1

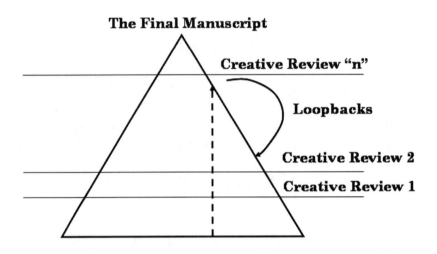

Use the WOW Factors in each creative review. Keep a list of them in front of you and constantly think about whether or not you have them, and enough of them. A suggested list of Creative Review Elements is as follows:

1. Creative Embellishment
   a. Can it be said in a better way?
   b. Can I add adjectives and metaphors that make it more real... more dramatic?
   c. Can I cause my characters to speak in a dialect that makes it more real? Where should I use slang and where not?
2. Grammar, Tense, Syntax and Spelling Review
   a. Have I made mistakes in grammar? Use of words?
   b. Where can I replace awkward sentences?
   c. What has been misspelled?
3. Plot and Scenario Review
   a. Where can I enhance the plot?

    b. Have I left out important scenes that would give the plot better continuity?

4. Logic, Flow and Perspective Review
    a. Is the flow of the text, scene to scene logical? What should be added to improve the logical flow?

5. Research Review
    a. What scenes can be improved by more research?
    b. Did I do all the research I noted as I wrote the Rough-Through?
    c. Have I "guessed" at things I really need to research?

6. Character Review
    a. How vivid have I made each character?
    b. How can I improve the "feel" for each character that my Readers will have?

7. Dialogue Review
    a. Does my dialogue sound "real" as I read it all again? Does it sound "stilted"? Artificial?
    b. Does each character say things that are "in character"?
    c. How is my dialogue-description-action balance?
    d. Am I comfortable with the use of curse words I have chosen?

8. Description Review
    a. How is my dialogue-description-action balance?
    b. Is my description vivid? Does it conjure up vivid images for my Readers?
    c. Do I rely too much on description... does it "drag"?

9. Action Review
    a. Are my action scenes fast paced and dramatic?
    b. Are there gaps in my description of the action that need to be filled in?
    c. Does my dialogue fit the action?
    d. Is the action described in enough detail?

10. Romantic Review
    a. Are the romantic scenes realistic?
    b. How much emotion is created in each romantic scene and where can I enhance it?
    c. Am I satisfied with the sex scene "levels" I have chosen?

11. Emotional Review
    a. I want my novel to create emotional highs for my Readers... do I do it?
    b. Where can I enhance the emotion through action, description or dialogue?
12. Humor, Fantasy and Mystery Review
    a. Have I succeeded in injecting some humor into the novel? In the right places? Where can I enhance this?
    b. Have I succeeded in injecting some fantasy into the novel? In the right places? Where can I enhance this?
    c. Have I succeeded in injecting some mystery into the novel? In the right places? Where can I enhance this?
13. Climax Review
    a. Have I successfully kept the Reader in suspense through the climax scenes?
    b. Have I brought all the issues I have introduced together in the climax, and resolved the main ones?
    c. Is the climax dramatic and action filled?
14. Storyteller Review
    a. Have I used this tool well? Too much? Not enough?
15. Special Review
    a. Defined by the Author and specific to the manuscript.
16. Format Review
    a. Do I understand my format and have I applied it consistently?
17. Final Review
    a. Am I ready to stop the Creative Reviews and move on to editing, or are there more Creative Reviews I want to perform?

More than any other thing, how did we treat the main character? Did the Reader quickly identify with him/her? Was the goal he/she had to achieve clear? Did he/she "transform" in the process of seeking that goal? Was he/she dynamic and interesting in seeking the goal? Was it clear that he/she achieved his/her goal and was rewarded for it? What "new world" resulted?

As one goes through the Rough-Through over and over again, further ideas are catalyzed... and the story is shaped, even changed. The story becomes better and better! With each read, the Author more and more understands the story, the characters that populate it and the situations that pace it. Thus, the Author is, in each reiteration, better able to tell the story.

The Final Manuscript

When you feel that you finally have a WOW novel... you must take the final, very important step in making it "publishable". You must edit! The Author is always the best Editor... if he/she can keep the focus. Hiring an Editor is expensive and puts another set of "eyes" on the work... but a hired Editor does not have the same interest as the Author.

Editing is not "artful" work, but it is very necessary. A novel without good editing is like a painting that uses inferior paints; music played by unaccomplished musicians; a sculpture using concrete instead of marble.

You may, if you are published by a large publisher, have a good Editor review your material. Even so, he/she does not "know" your material as you do. He/She is good, but he/she is not the Author! If you are published by a small publisher, the quality of the editing is mixed... from nonexistent to "a little". You can't count on them finding and correcting errors with a high degree of confidence. You, the Author, must do it!

It is embarrassing to find typos and flaws after the book is published. Your friends will surely detect them! The picky Reader may get a poor impression of the novel based on the flaws in editing without seeing how "good" the book really is! So... edit! Do it over and over!

"I've read this thing so many times I just can't do it again!

You are bound to say this sometime in your editing efforts. Keep at it! Remember, edit word for word, comma for comma! If you skim it because you "already know what it says" you are guaranteed to miss something that may embarrass you later (and, once you submit it to a publisher, that publisher may charge you extra to fix mistakes you later discover!). In editing, you are not focused on "what it says"; you are focused on spelling, syntax, punctuation, paragraphing and formatting.

As you edit, you will get "new ideas". For the most part, save them for the next book! At this point you have been through this novel so many times that it should be approaching quality… a potential WOW book. New ideas mean additional length, and you want to manage that carefully. You don't normally want to have a "long" book (More than 130,000 words).

Readers are impatient with "long books". They want a slam dunk emotional roller coaster ride in a package they can read in less than a week… or in 2-3 "sittings" for the Reader who can devour the pages (and if they do, good for you, as you have their focused interest!).

As you come to the end of the editing effort, you should obtain at least one "Test Reader" if you can. A Test Reader is not an Editor. Do not depend on a Test Reader to find typos, misspellings, syntax errors or errors in format. A Test Reader is a person, preferably one you know and trust, who will read the book and give you:

1. His/her "gut" reaction
2. Comments on where the novel is strong or weak.
3. Suggestions

Should you hire a Test Reader that you do not know who will give you a harsher critique that someone you do know? Perhaps. I prefer Test Readers I know, since I then understand where the Test Reader is "coming from", which helps me to evaluate his/her comments.

If you have a "Book Coach" (see Appendix A), he/she is usually a good Test Reader. He/she may be able to "edit". This is someone you know and have worked with. It is someone with whom you have a professional relationship who will give you a good critique.

When should you "stop"?

1. When you have digested what your Test Reader has to say, and made any final corrections based on that input that you feel are appropriate (don't be bound by what a Test Reader tells you. Evaluate his/her comments carefully and use them professionally).
2. When you can read the whole novel through and not have a "hiccup".
3. When you can read the whole novel and feel the emotion, even though you've been through it a zillion times.
4. When you have a WOW novel... at least for you!
5. When it is fully edited!

Editing Tips

Here are a few editing tips that I have found useful.
1. Look for redundancy and edit it out. For example, as you are composing, you may write "It is very interesting to write a very interesting chapter..." (A redundancy I found in one of my editing sessions). There are clearly too many "verys" and "interestings". Take one of each of them out!
2. Editing is not "reading". When you read, you are free to skim over word and punctuation and concentrate on absorbing the essence of what is written. When you edit, you must be in a different mind set than when you read. You must have the energy and will to focus on every word and every punctuation.
3. Edit for 1-2 hours first thing in the morning when you have the most energy and focus. Then put the editing aside and do something else until the next morning.
4. Search for common misspellings. Use the -edit-find-replace function in the WORD application on your computer. For example, a common error is to type "form" when you really mean "from". So, search for "form" and if that's what you meant, keep it... if not, have the word "from" in the replace cell and replace "form" with "from". "Feel" is sometimes typed in as "fell" by mistake, and vice versa, etc.

5. A common mistake is to put two spaces where there should be one. Use the -edit-find-replace function in WORD. Using the space key, type "space space" in the -find-cell- and "space" in the -replace-cell-. Then execute –replace-all- and the computer will take out all the double spaces and replace them with a single.
6. Every Author has "favorite" words that he/she uses. When writing, these words tend to pop up frequently. Use the -edit-find- function in WORD to search for the "favorite" words. If you have a 200 page manuscript and a "favorite" word appears more than 50 times (25%), it is too many.
7. How many edit reads should you do? I have done as many as ten on a final manuscript until I declare it my "submission" manuscript. Even then, when the proofs come back from the printer, I still find ten or more things that need correction before printing.

If "Sally" is printed as "Silly", you must endure the consequences, no matter your intent!

8. At the end of each editing session, type the word "placemark" (or anything you want) in the text where you stop. When you come back to it, search for the word. It's important to always know what has been edited.
9. When you have accomplished enough editing sessions, save your file with a name that indicates that this is the one you are going to "go with" (my novel submission version.doc).
10. When your publisher or printer sends you back the "proofs" of the manuscript, edit it all again very carefully.

Once it's printed, you live with it!

****

Chapter Twenty-seven
Getting Published

This book is mostly about how to write a novel. How to get it published is another complete story. So is how to sell it! However, I want to briefly explore with you the most important aspects of publishing and selling. For, while the act of completing a good novel has some satisfaction, it is not complete until the publishing and selling is accomplished. I encourage you to read several of the many good books available on these subjects (See Appendix C).

Figure 27-1 shows a flow diagram of Author to Reader and all the "in betweens".

Figure 27-1

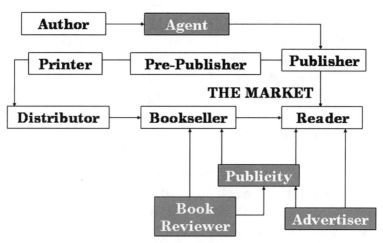

Indicates an "option", though all are necessary for success.

Agents

Do you need an Agent? Unless you are incredibly lucky in approaching publishers... yes. Some small publishers will review your work without the recommendation of an agent. Try some of these. But also look for an Agent.

You should have a quality product before you try to get an agent... or approach a publisher. You are wasting time and money if you go to agents before your manuscript is "publishable" (See Appendix A). The competition between publishable manuscripts is torrid. If your manuscript has not been reviewed and declared "publishable" by someone qualified to make that certification, it has near zero chance. There are of course exceptions... but they are very, very rare.

Good agents are hard to find! And if you find one, it is very difficult to get one to represent you. If you are a beginning Author, look for an Agent outside of a major metropolitan area. The "big guys" are the ones who will likely shun you, whether you have a good book or not! Look for an Agent in smaller cities, preferably one near you. Contact them personally if you can and "sell" yourself.

Have the following ready to provide to an Agent:
1. The Premise and Controlling Idea.
2. A two page synopsis of your story.
3. A capsule synopsis (half a page or less).
4. A short biography of the Author.
5. Several sample Chapters.

Agents make money by receiving a percentage of your profits if they get the work "placed" with a publisher. So, if an Agent agrees to work with you, it should cost you nothing up front. Read the contract carefully. If you are not familiar with contracts, you should get familiar... lawyers are very expensive for this sort of thing (you don't normally need one).

If an agent wants some small "up front money" for mailings and telephone expenses, I do not object, particularly if the Agent is not associated with one of the larger companies. But, if the Agent wants a large sum of money to represent you, or wants to charge you "by the hour"... avoid them. Such agents seek profits from your naiveté, not through representing you.

A good listing of available Agents can be found at the "Literary Market Place" (www.literarymarketplace.com). Like many such web sites, there is a cost associated in "joining". If you don't have an agent and need one, it is worth the cost. There are places on the internet that list available Agents that do not charge a fee. They usually provide incomplete information. But, it's worth "searching around". Go to the internet and type in the key words "literary agent". You will get a field displaying many choices. You have to experiment with one or two and "get smarter" about agents as you do.

Pre-Publisher

There is more than meets the eye to writing and publishing. There are companies out there that provide what are called "pre-publishing services". Normally, as an Author, you will not have to deal with them unless you decide to self publish… but your Publisher will, unless he has the required talents in house.

Pre-publishers provide services such as:
1. Cover design
2. Editing
3. Formatting
4. Computer formatting of text for printing
5. Obtaining an International Standard Book Number (ISBN)
6. Obtaining a Library of Congress Number
7. Bar Code service (for price scanning)

Some of these are discussed in subsequent paragraphs.

Go to the internet and type in the key word "pre-publishing". You will get a field of choices similar to the previous example.

See the following websites:
www.booksjustbooks.com
www.bookmasters.com

Publishers

Publishers are interested in producing a book that will provide profit and enhanced reputation. They are highly selective in what they agree to publish, being very sensitive to the market and the quality of the book (story, cover, font, quality of printing, quality of binding, etc.). It is very, very difficult for a new Author to be accepted by a large, well known publisher... unless the Author has a "big name"... or is well known for his/her accomplishments or notoriety. If you are a new Author, look for a small publisher who will take the time to evaluate what you have done.

"Vanity Press" is a name given to publishers who will publish almost anything to satisfy the "vanity" of the Author. They make money from charging Authors large amounts to publish their books ($10,000 - $20,000 per book typically). They also put your book out to sell, but they already have their profit (from you) before they sell any books. Booksellers usually avoid books published by these companies. Books published by these companies usually sell to the friends and relatives of the Author, and not to many more. If you have the money and you just want to see (and have your friends see) your name as the Author on a book, go for it. But, in most cases avoid a "Vanity Press". They are clearly identifiable because they want a lot of your money up front.

Small publishers will often offer new Authors a "shared risk" or "new author" contract in which the Author is asked to share with the Publisher in the publishing costs. The Publisher will then print a limited number of books (200-1000) and see if it sells. If it does, you are in business! If it has only limited sales, you can at least claim to be a "Published Author", which is a valuable title to be able to claim. Publishing costs for a 300 page book will range from $8,000 to $20,000 dependent on the book type (hard cover, perfect binding, etc.). Of that, about 50% will be printing costs. Other costs derive from cover design, formatting, placement with distributors, etc. The price varies with the Publisher.

If you are a new Author, I consider going with a "shared risk" publisher to be a worthwhile venture. Such a publisher will not accept your work if it is "junk" or not considered marketable. This type of publisher wants you to have a best seller, but wants you to share the risk of publishing a new author in a highly competitive market (because small publishers seldom have the capital to fund the publishing of many books). That is a reasonable approach.

I used a "shared risk" publisher for my first book. It gets your "foot in the door". As a "Published Author", your resume will be more attractive for your next book! Books published by a "Vanity Press" will not count toward gaining the title "Published Author" (except perhaps among your friends).

"Print on Demand" (POD) publishing means that the publisher does not print many of your books. Rather, the publisher will print a small batch of books when there is "demand", that is, when someone actually orders some books. Distributors and booksellers generally do not like "print on demand" books because their availability is not always timely. Books that "can't cut it" in the traditional market are typically published by "print on demand" publishers. Avoid them if possible. Be careful... POD publishers often disguise themselves as traditional publishers. Having a "print on demand" book may be a solution for you... if so, go for it!

"E-Books" are another form of "print on demand". They are basically manuscripts that can be downloaded from an internet web site after paying a fee. This format was initially popular, but has trailed off in popularity in recent years. Avoid this format if possible.

Self Publishing is an alternate to finding an agent and publisher. You essentially have to become a publisher. It is time consuming, expensive, and requires development of talents you probably don't possess, at least at this time. But, it can be done!

A publisher "owns" a number of International Standard Book Numbers (ISBNs). The ISBN is a number used to identify and catalog all books that are offered for sale. If you own ISBNs, you are a publisher... if you can get yourself through all the pre-publishing hoops and successfully get a book to distributors and booksellers.

Go to the internet and type in the key word "publisher". You will get a field of choices for that key word.

See the following small publisher websites:

www.powerfulpublisher.com
www.fourseasonspub.net

Cover Design

Your cover provides the Reader with a first impression. Many books are sold on the basis of the appearance of the cover! If you do not have art and graphic skills, I suggest you hire a cover designer. You can obtain a well designed cover for $300-$600. You should be very specific about what you want in a cover, even to the point of sketching out your vision of a cover (even if you can't draw)! Go to the internet and type in the key words "cover design" for more information.

Editing

Editing is a tough task! If you are good, patient, persistent and have a realistic knowledge of the language, you can be a successful editor. If not, hire one. Go to the internet and type in the key words "novel editing".

Formatting

Book formatting is very important. It must "look" professional. Everything must be in the right (traditional) place. All good book pre-publication companies and printing companies have a recommended format, and it is usually available on line. Go to the internet and type in the key words "novel formatting" for more information.

International Standard Book Number (ISBN)

The ISBN (International Standard Book Number) is a ten digit number that identifies one title or edition of a title from one specific publisher. It is unique to that edition. This number will expand to a thirteen digit format in 2007. For a full explanation, go to:
National Information Standards
www.niso.org/standards/resources/isbn.html

The official ISBN Agency for the United States, R.L. Bowker Company is responsible for assigning the ISBN Publisher Prefix to those publishers with a residence or office in the U.S. who are publishing their titles within the U.S. Your publisher will assign the ISBN number to the book. ISBN numbers are bought from the R.L. Bowker Company. Go to the internet and type in the key letters "ISBN".

See the web sites:
www.bowker.com
www.isbn.org.

Library of Congress Number

Your publisher will normally assign the Library of Congress (LOC) number to the book. Some publishers may not do this. Ask them to. It is not "required" but it is a good idea. Go to the internet and type in the key word "Library of Congress".

See the web site:
www.loc.gov

Copyright

Your novel is protected by U.S. copyright laws as you write it. These laws make you the "owner" of the "intellectual property" that you create. At some point you should apply for a copyright. It is simple to do and not costly. I recommend doing it at the same time that a publisher accepts your work. Some publishers will do this for you, which is okay... just get a copy of the copyright from them, and make sure they do it in your name, not theirs! You should have the copyright in hand by the time the novel is "on the street" if possible.

See the web site:
www.copyright.gov

Bar Code

A bar code is a label that can be scanned by a computer to identify your book. It contains your ISBN number in code that can be scanned by a computer. Look on the back of any book, usually at the bottom, and you will see its bar code. A bar code must be placed on your novel. Your publisher will take care of that. There is bar code software. Type "bar code" into your browser and you'll see some offered.

Pricing

What should the sales price of your book be? Whatever you want it to be! Your publisher will recommend a unit price to you. Go with it! The price is a function of:
1. Number of pages.
2. Trim size (physical size of the book, such as 6"X9").
3. Cover type.
4. Paper used.
5. Number of colors used in the cover or text.
6. Number of pictures and diagrams (if any, color or black and white).
7. What the market will accept.

You don't want your book overpriced, or it won't sell. At the same time, you want to price it so that a sale produces a reasonable return. Look at what books similar to yours cost. Hard cover is more expensive to produce than Perfect Binding (a soft cover with a quality between that of hard cover and paper back) or paperback. A 300 page novel produced in hard cover sells in 2006 for about $23.95. The same novel in perfect binding would sell for about $15.95 to $19.95. A paperback copy would sell for $9.95 to $12.95.

Types of Covers

"Hard covers" are the most prestigious and expensive. They usually come with high quality paper "dust covers". These are used for high quality novels (coffee table books).

"Case Covers" are hard covers without dust covers, and are usually used for books that are not novels (picture books, children's books, etc.)

"Perfect Bindings" use a quality paper cover that is hardy and presents a very good appearance. These are used for many novels and are "perfectly" good, though not as hardy or prestigious as hard covers.

"Paperbacks" are smaller books with paper covers of less quality. These are often referred to as "Pocket Books". Novels of lesser quality or "niche" novels such as "westerns" or "romance" usually come in paperback form. First run hard back or perfect binding novels may appear in paperback after a period of time.

The Market: Readers

Finally, your market "hears" about your novel... at least some of them. Will they buy it? Well, you have to get these folks interested enough to go to a place they can buy the book... a bookstore, or on the web. People "go out" to get bread and milk... but seldom just to "buy a book". People surf the web, but seldom just to "buy a book".

The general rule is that if a hundred people see or hear something about your book, and are in a place to buy a book, ten of them will give it some attention, and one or two will buy it. What causes a person to buy a book? Some of the frequent reasons are:

1. They know the Author and are curious.
2. The book has been recommended to them by a friend as a "must read".
3. They have heard of the Author and want to "check it out".
4. The cover design looks exciting.
5. The subject matter is something with which they closely identify.
6. They are looking for a WOW Book... something that will really get their juices flowing.
7. They have seen the title on some "Best-seller List" or the equivalent

Please note that only number six of these reasons is because "it is a good book!" You've got to have some kind of "external hook" that causes them to buy it... something that has nothing to do with whether or not it is a WOW book!

Once you get them to buy it, you've got to "hook" them to read it all... and enjoy it! And tell their friends!

Readers pay more attention to the Author than the book.

If the Author is a "household name", the Reader will assume that the book is good and worth reading. People will say, "I think I'll go down and pick up Clancy's latest book!" Not only do they want the book, but the name association with the well known Author will, at least in their mind, give them "good taste" points with their friends. If you are a new Author, you have a long struggle ahead of you to become a "household name"... if ever. So, your book must sell for one of the other reasons. Pay attention to them all! Remember, no matter how good the book, it will not sell unless your potential Readers hear favorably about it!

Being "The Author"

What kind of Author are you? Here are some I suggest you don't want to be:
1.   The Lazy Writer
2.   The Narrative Focus Writer
3.   The Writer With a "Cause"
4.   The Writer Who Loves What is Written
5.   The Hurried Writer
6.   The Discloser
7.   The Arrogant Writer

The Lazy Writer

The Lazy Writer avoids the passages that are "hard to write". Most beginning writers start writing without a firm idea as to where they "are going". That's okay... but beware the "NEED Point!" The NEED Point is where the Author becomes aware, as he/she writes along, that there is a NEED at the point where they are writing for additional background to make something in the story "happen".

NEED Point:

There is a need to show why a character acts the way he/ she does. The character had some traumatic experience, or meets some yet undefined character, or as some horrific experience that forever affects him/her... and this experience is a part of the story because it defines the character.

The Lazy Writer will at this point, stick a piece of narrative in with regard to this character's experience. The accomplished writer will write out the experience in some detail, using the proper mix of storytelling, description and dialogue. He/she will then restructure the novel as necessary to insert this "experience" in the right place. It can be done as a part of the time line of the novel... or it can be treated as a flashback. Use the proper place in the time line rather than a flashback if you can. Too many flashbacks destroy the continuity of a novel.

The Narrative Focus Writer

For most people, narrative and description are easier to write than storytelling and dialogue. A chronology is "easy" for someone who experienced it... a story is much harder. What people "say" is hard to write and make sound real. Yet, it is what the characters say to each other in their interactions, the setting and the action that is taking place that is the most interesting... for most Readers. DON'T write a story that is primarily narrative and description. Learn how to write interesting dialogue... and write for the best mix of storytelling description, action and dialogue as outlined in this book! A good Author writes descriptively. An outstanding Author also writes dynamic dialogue punctuated by description and action!

The Writer With a "Cause"

The Author who wants to write for a "Cause" believes that because he/she is so passionate about the cause that what is being written must be a "good story". It becomes a "sermon". The "Cause" can be the basis for a good story if it is written right, following the principles outlined in this book. It is not a good story if all the Author is doing is getting it off his/her chest!

As you are writing, don't throw in an emotional thought that has little to do with the story... "war is stupid". If you want to make the point in a well told story that "war is stupid", you have to show both sides of "going to war" and show why it is "stupid" using characters, description, action and dialogue.

DON'T just write for a "Cause"... tell a good story!

The Writer Who Loves What is Written

An experienced Author knows that a certain percentage of what he/she writes is either "junk", "doesn't fit" or is unnecessary to the telling of the story. This Author never... NEVER... "falls in love" with what has been written. A good Author is analytical in rereading the manuscript and sorting out the parts that fit the above description. An inexperienced Author believes fervently that anything he/she has written "must be good" and is very reluctant to discard any of it! DON'T "fall in love" with what you have written. You MUST be capable of discarding parts that, upon analysis, are "junk", or are unnecessary to the story.

The Hurried Writer

The Hurried Writer is one who is impatient to tell his story. He/she doesn't understand that each sentence, each piece of dialogue, each description... must be a work of art and is due the time it takes to make it so. DON'T rush on. Each time you sit down to write, it should not be to "write the book". Rather, it should be to write the "scene of the day"... the piece of the whole story you can write in one time "in the cave". You must put every ounce of skill you have as an Author into that "scene of the day", share the emotions of the characters and live the action taking place.

The Discloser

The Discloser is one wants to tell the "whole story" right away. He/she has no sense of timing and suspense. He/she doesn't understand that the Reader must be held in suspense and "find out" things only gradually... or you won't set "the hook". DON'T "give away" everything. You, as the Author, must understand the "whole story" (or most of it, depending upon where you are in the process)... but you must build a puzzle for the Reader to slowly assemble as he/she reads.

The Arrogant Writer

The Arrogant Writer believes that anything he/she writes is good and "should be enjoyed by the Reader". More than that, this type of writer believes that his/her story is good in the first version. This type of writer will put out a "stream of consciousness" that makes sense and is interesting to him/her... but not necessarily to the Reader (the 30 day version). This type of writer is not an "Author"! An Author has to do many rewrites. He/She has to have a thick hide and experience many rejections, analyses, comments and criticisms... and be able to successfully react to them.

The Author You Want to Be

You want to be published! You want to be published by a traditional publisher (in hard cover if possible, but "perfect binding" is okay) and have your books available on line and at book stores. Whether you sell a lot of them or not is not as important as the "fun" of being an Author!

Being "The Author" can be a very rewarding experience! So... enjoy it. Everyone will think you're rich. Only you will know how poor you are! If you hit it big, you may become rich... but that's not likely. What is likely is that you will know you wrote a good book, a work of art that many people will enjoy. There is a lot of satisfaction in that. So, buy a tweed jacket with leather elbow patches and smoke a pipe... or a flowered dress and floppy hat and smoke cigarettes in a long gold holder... or whatever. Better not to smoke at all and just be a little bit of a character!

Most people view writing a novel as an awesome task that they could never accomplish. For that reason they will look up to you and admire you. So be a good guy/gal! Respond to them... humbly of course. You know that many people who think they can't write a book really can... if they're willing to spend the time and effort learning how.

Most people only dream of writing a book.

You did it! You wrote a novel! You went through the frustrations of learning and the long hours of pouring over your manuscript. You had fun writing it! Now you are <u>The Author</u>. Keep writing until you hit it big!

****

Chapter Twenty-Eight
After Publishing

After you publish, you will encounter many new things. I will describe some of them to you here.

Distributor

Distributors are the publishing "middle man". They also soak up a large hunk of a publisher and Author's profit. But, they are necessary within the "system" as it now exists. Many book companies will only buy from a large, recognized Distributor. They do this to ensure that the books that they do buy have been screened and have a reasonably high probability of sales in sufficient quantity to be profitable.

Distributors demand and get very restrictive criteria for accepting books. The most important rule is that the Publisher is not paid for a book until it is distributed and sold by a Bookseller (and the Bookseller and the Distributor get their "share"). For example, a publisher might have a hundred books at a distributor that he hasn't been paid for (and therefore, the Author has not received royalties).

After three months, five books have been sold (which is deemed an insufficient sales rate). The Booksellers take the remaining books off their shelves and return them to the Distributors. The Distributors determine that they can no longer provide warehouse space due to low sales rate and return the books to the Publisher. The Publisher is paid only for the five books sold (less the Distributor and Bookseller share). The Publisher must now warehouse the remaining books or find another way of distributing them. Hopefully, your novel will "hit it" and all hundred novels will sell quickly and the Bookseller and Distributor will recorder!

Go to the internet and type in the key words "book distributor". You will get a field of choices similar to the previous example.

See the following websites:
www.ingrambookgroup.com
www.ipgbook.com

www.btol.com

Bookseller

There are a great variety of booksellers out there, from the small "Mom and Pop" bookstore to the giants such as Amazon, Barnes and Noble, Borders and BooksaMillion. There are also the "afterthought" bookstores such as supermarkets, drug stores, airports, etc. All of them have one thing in common; they all use the catalogues provided by the major distributors such as "Ingram" and "Baker & Taylor". The distributors, to a large degree, determine what appears on the book shelves of book stores through their marketing (which is different from "publicity"). To be successful, a publisher must have a good distributor with the right connections!

Marketing

A Distributor will "market" your novel to some extent. That means that he/she will catalog it and represent it to as many Booksellers as possible. The Distributor will try to "place" as many books as possible with as many Booksellers as possible. This does not mean that the Distributor will "advertise" it to the public or generate publicity regarding the book and it's Author. The publisher, and usually the Author, have to advertise to create "demand". Some of the best books have little demand because the Publisher/Author can't afford the steep advertising prices. Some books of questionable quality have high demand because they have a "name" Author and are widely advertised.

Book Reviewer

A desirable, but not always necessary part of the book system is the Book Reviewer. This is a person who reads, reviews and critiques the novel and provides this information to newspapers and other information sources. Anyone can be a book reviewer. You can also review books on web sites such as those operated by Amazon and Barnes & Noble.

The best bet to obtain a professional Book Reviewer is to contact your newspaper (Book Section) and request a review. Of course, like many other places I am discussing, they will want a free promotion copy of the book (these add up... you must be prepared to provide 25-50 promotional books to reviewers, agents, distributors and bookstores... not to mention all the friends who expect a free book!).

See:

www.bookreview.com

Advertiser

An Advertiser is someone the publisher (or Author) pays to provide publicity for the novel. There are many different kinds of Advertisers:

1. Newspapers
2. Magazines
3. Radio
4. Television
5. Web Sites

Advertising, in general, is very, very expensive. Because it is, you as an Author must not depend on any publisher or distributor to advertise your work to a high degree (some will, but never enough). You, the Author will probably have to pay for advertising if it is to happen. A 2 X 3 inch advertisement in a local paper can cost as much as $1,000 or more for a one day appearance. For a national level advertisement, increase that by an order of magnitude ($10,000). Ouch! Not many Authors can afford that. And, in many cases, the sales generated by such an advertisement will not pay for it.

Radio advertising can be reasonable if you use a small, local station. As soon as you move up to a station with wide coverage, or a national station, it gets very expensive. The cost is based on "coverage", i.e. how many people will "hear it" (the output power of the station).

Television advertising is "out of sight" for the average Author and Publisher, except for the largest Publishers.

Will people who hear or see an advertisement buy a book? Maybe. Nothing is guaranteed. I have found from doing book signings in malls that perhaps 10% will "listen" and 1% will buy.

You, the Author definitely want to set up your own web site. Don't rely only on your Publisher's web site. You'll have some fun setting it up and maintaining it. It isn't as hard as you may think. If you are not conversant in HTML language, see some of the software that "does it for you", such as Microsoft "Front Page".

Publicity

The preferred way to get your book "seen" by the market (Readers) is to generate "free" publicity. This can take many forms, among them:
1. Book Signings.
2. Talk Show Appearances (Radio and TV).
3. "Interest" Articles in local and national periodicals and newspapers.

I'll describe these events in paragraphs that follow.

Book Signings

A Book Signing is where the Author spends 2-3 hours at a Bookseller store talking to Readers and signing books that they buy. It's not as easy as it sounds!

If you go to a Bookseller and offer to do a Book Signing, the first question you will get, is "where do I get the books?" If it's a big Bookseller, they will want to order the books from one of the big distributors (Ingram or Baker & Taylor, for example). This is to your advantage, providing your books can be obtained that way. Know about this before you see your bookseller and propose a book signing. You want to generate sales "in the system" so that your reputation and sales record is enhanced. If you, the Author or Publisher, just provide books to the Bookseller for the event, you are not generating reputation and sales record.

If you are a new Author, or for that matter any kind of Author, do book signings. They work in your favor. But, do them right! Contact key book stores and make the offer. They will usually be glad to do it… IF your books are "in their system" (through a distributor that your publisher uses). It benefits them! If they tell you that the book is "not in their system", ask them how to get it there and contact your publisher. Many of them will not order the books unless they can do it from one of the recognized, big distributors. They do that because, in ordering the book for the Book Signing, they want some guarantee that some of the books will sell (they may lose money on shipping costs if the books do not sell). It is more likely that the book will sell if it is stocked by a recognized distributor (because it has gone through a significant review process).

Now, you finally have some books in a bookseller store due to your offer to do a Book Signing. But will they stay there? "Shelf Space" is a critical factor for a bookseller. He/She must keep only books that have a reasonably high sales rate on their shelves. Space on their shelves costs them overhead money! If they don't sell, they'll be sent back to the distributor. If the distributor does not distribute enough books at a reasonable rate, he/she will send them back to the publisher. And remember, the publisher is paid only for the books that are sold!

So, you have successfully scheduled a Book Signing! Make a sign that advertises it and provide it to the Bookseller in advance. It's easy to do with modern computer graphics and materials you can get at your office supply store. Have "Author" business cards made up. Make "flyer" handouts. When the Book Signing occurs, don't just sit there… get up, walk around and talk to potential Readers. Hand everyone a brochure (they may read it). Talk to them… they want to see if you are interesting enough that they might enjoy reading your book. Be a little bit of a "character"… that's what they expect from anyone crazy and artistic enough to be an Author!

Talk Show Appearances

If you can get on a radio or TV talk show, it will likely help your sales a lot. What? Too bashful? Well, it's true that you have to be able to talk… and you have to have something to say. You can talk about your book, or talk about being an Author, or talk about something else you are "expert" in and then fold it into some talk about your book. Give your talk show host a list of things to ask you, but never expect them to ask you exactly what you have provided!

Talk shows go on anywhere from a five minute "clip" to several hours. The shortest I have done is ten minutes… the longest is two and a half hours. How do you get on a talk show? You request it directly from a radio station or talk show host using the telephone or Email. Or, you may advertise (yes, it costs you more money). There are numerous magazines and web sites which advertise your availability as a talk show guest. If you advertise, put some thought into what you will talk about that will "grab" the host's listeners. Just saying "I'll talk about my new novel" is never enough! There has to be a "grabber", something that will "grab" the audience (I was a teenage werewolf… etc.).

Go to the internet and type in the key words "talk show guest". You will get a field of choices similar to the previous example.

See the following web site for Radio TV Interview Report (RTIR), a company that advertises to talk show producers.
www.rtir.com

Interest Articles

An "interest article" is something you can convince a newspaper or periodical to do about you… free of charge, particularly your local newspaper (local interest story). There are lots of folks out there who write for newspapers and magazines and provide "local interest" or "hometown boy makes good" types of articles. Take advantage of this! Call your local newspaper or any other periodical that does this type of article and suggest that it be done. In most cases, they'll eventually do it, complete with picture (have one ready).

Web Sites

If you are an Author, you should have your own web site! You can hire people to set up and do your web site, as well as maintain it. But, it's much more cost effective to do it yourself. Another advantage of this is that you can update it at any time without having to "go through" someone else (who will charge you). There are software programs out there that make it easy for you to set up and maintain a web site. Spend some time learning to use these. You won't regret it.

You will have to obtain a company to provide your "server" and a web site name. There are many companies that can do this for you at minimum expense;

See the web site:
www.bizland.com

See the web site:
www.microsoft.com
and read about the "Front Page" program

See my Author and Publisher webs page:
www.robertcpowers-author.com
www.powerfulpublisher.com

On Line Marketing

Many companies are engaged in on line marketing to assist your sales. Be careful here... they can cost you a lot of money, so be sure you are getting the sales in return!

See the web sites:
www.websitepros.com
www.google.com
www.yahoo.com

On Line Sales

As a new Author, the easiest listings for your novel will be through "on line" sales". The biggest on line sellers are:
1. Amazon
2. Barnes and Noble
3. BooksaMillion
4. Borders

There are many others. You can have decent sales through this method. You and your publisher should pursue them with vigor. However, don't give up on getting your book "on the shelf" in a book store. When that occurs, you are on the way to selling profitable quantities of books and becoming a recognizable Author.

See the web sites:

www.amazon.com

www.bn.com

Analysis of Book Profit

How much are you going to make on your book? Well, the answer is "not much" considering the time and effort you have put into it... unless you have a very good "niche" book and are very lucky.

A typical hard cover book may be priced at $20.00. The table below shows an <u>approximate</u> distribution of costs and profits.

Table 28A

Item	Per Cent	Amount
Book Sale Price	---	$ 20.0
Publisher Costs	30%	$ 6.00
Publisher Profit	5%	$ 1.00
Distributor Costs	10%	$ 2.00
Bookseller Costs	35%	$ 7.00
Bookseller Profit	10%	$ 2.00
Royalties to Author	5%	$ 1.00

You priced the book at $20.00 per copy. That does not mean that it will sell for $20.00. Booksellers, particularly on line book sellers almost always offer "specials". So your book may sell for $15.00. You must adjust Table 29 A for the changed price. You say, "Can't I control that?" Usually not. Distributors and Booksellers in many cases will not take your book unless they can sell it for "what will sell".

Note that when a publisher quotes "12.5%" royalties to you (or whatever per cent), it does not necessarily mean 12.5% of the sales price. It may mean 12.5% of what the publisher receives after distributor and book seller costs. Be sure to understand "per cent of what" when a publisher quotes a royalty in a contract. This is illustrated in the following table:

Table 28B

Item	Amount
Book Sale Price	$ 20.00
Distributor & Bookseller Costs	$ 12.00
Amount Publisher Receives	$ 8.00
Per Cent of Amount Publisher Receives	
Paid as Royalties to Author	12.5%
Author Royalties	$ 1.00

As you can see, you are going to have to sell a lot of books to pay for the time and energy you put into writing a successful novel. A goal for the $20.00 book used in the example is to sell 3000 copies a month (royalties of $36,000 in a year). This is seldom achieved. A reasonable expectation for a good book with excellent publicity would be 30 copies a month (royalties of $360 in a year). In the beginning, until the book is well known, if you sell one copy a month, you are fortunate.

Books do not sell, regardless of their quality, without a lot of publicity! And... publicity is not free! Publicity comes from two places... the Author and the Publisher. Distributors and Book Sellers seldom provide publicity (advertising) except locally for a book store. Advertising campaigns and various kinds of promotions have to come from the Publisher or the Author. Publishers have a budget for advertising, but the amount available is proportional to the size of the publisher (usually small). A small publisher will tell the Author that advertising is "up to the Author". So, what part of that $1.00 per book royalty are you going to spend on advertising?

So, given the dismal financial projection I have painted for you, why would you want to write a book? If you are a "big name", that is, you are widely known because of "something", the financial projection is better. But, for Joe Author out there, it's a tough road. Don't plan to make a living at writing novels... unless you "luck out" right away due to genius level talent or notoriety. Keep your day job! If you write a novel, do it for the pure joy of creativity. If it sells, that's a bonus. You will derive great personal satisfaction from writing a novel even if it sells only a few copies. The novel will exist even after you are gone... a legacy for your heirs.

Screen Plays

If you want to really get some attention drawn to your novel, have someone make a movie of it! That said, it is a very difficult and drawn out process... and highly improbable, even for a good book. How to write and sell a screen play is worth a book itself (See Appendix C).

First of all, you need an agent who has the connections in the film industry to represent your book. Some times, a producer may buy the rights to a book and hire someone to do a screen play. It helps to sell the book as a film if you already have a screen play associated with the book. Screen plays based on your novel can be produced with computer programs that provide you with screen play format (though it requires considerable time and effort).

Screenplays are different from novels in that you are using images and action to portray your story rather than "telling" a story. Screenplays are very "action" oriented (what you see, what you hear). That's an important difference and should be considered carefully if you decide to embark on writing a screenplay. Also, screen plays are typically written in the present tense, while novels are usually in the past tense. So, there's considerable work involved in converting the text of a novel into a screen play.

While a novel may be 300 pages of prose, a screenplay is typically 120 pages of tightly written, action oriented script. Writing a screenplay is a different adventure than writing a novel. But... it's a lot of fun!

As in selling a novel, selling a screenplay is best done through an agent. See the web site:

www.hcdonline.com

Go to the internet and type in the key words "screenplay software".

See the web sites:

www.sophocles.net

www.screenwritersfederation.com

There are many books about writing screenplays. Go to amazon.com and query "screenplay".

The Predators

Beware! The land is filled with predators with slick schemes to prey on aspiring Authors. In all the areas I have written about, there are numerous companies ready to assist you, some good, some bad. They will populate your Email "in box" with their "pitches". When you venture near one, take some time checking it out. Ask the right questions. Be very careful what you sign up for! The counsel of a book coach or some experienced author is invaluable (See Appendix A).

A lot of money is made from people trying to be Authors.

Knowing When to Stop

I keep thinking of more things to add to this book that you should know. I've done a partial Rough-Through example for you. The content is good if not complete on this exhaustive subject. Anything longer may begin to defeat my goals; to show you that writing a novel is freeform art, not a mechanical formula; to suggest to you ways to accomplish your goal of writing a novel; and doing it as concisely as possible.

I go now to my Creative Cave... to my own universe... the one I have created for my novel... and enjoy the beautiful people, the horrible beasts and villains, the heroic deeds, the conflict, the drama, the surprise and suspense, the mystery and throat choking emotions. For, after all, in my own universe, I am immortal!

****

Appendix A
Book Coaching for Authors

You have gained an idea herein that writing a novel is doable... but not easy! Most beginning Authors think they know how to write a novel... that it is a natural talent that they have. Most beginning Authors think they don't need any help learning the art of writing a novel. And also, they have neither the time nor the resources to spend learning more. Why do they need any help when they already have the talent? And... they have written other things already... essays for the church news letter, etc.

All beginning Authors need some level of coaching in writing their first several novels.

When I began trying to write a novel in 1986, I knew I had the talent. But, I wasn't getting anywhere toward getting published. So I paid a well known publisher to review my material and provide me with critical comments. It took me about a dozen rewrites based on that publisher's comments before I had a manuscript that was "publishable".

If you are a beginning Author, you need a Book Coach!

If you were planning to learn to play the piano, you would hire a piano teacher, even if you already had an inherent musical talent. If you are planning to be an Author, you should hire a Book Coach to help you get to the point where you have a "publishable" manuscript.

Most people who think they know how to write a novel, don't.

Of course, having a "publishable manuscript" doesn't mean that it will be published. So much depends on timing and need! But, your manuscript will now have a chance!

When you submit a manuscript to an agent or a publisher, don't expect them to provide you with useful critical comments. Most do not. They will accept it, or simply tell you that "it does not meet their needs at the time". Translate that to mean:

1. It is not a publishable manuscript.
2. It really doesn't fit their "needs" at the time (or both).

If it is a good manuscript, chances are a publisher will find a way to make it fit his/her needs.

A good Book Coach will:

1. Spend time with you discussing your ideas.
2. Help you get over the first obstacle; the "I wrote it, it must be good" hurdle.
3. Teach you how to use the Creative Principles discussed in this book.
4. Review your material and provide critical comment and recommendations.
5. Help you produce a publishable manuscript.
6. Tell you when your work is "publishable".
7. Help you get published (but most of this is up to you).

What about attending Writing Seminars and using DVD Tutorials? They are usually worth the investment involved. But they are not a substitute for a Book Coach. When you hire a Book Coach, plan to thicken your hide!

Having a good Book Coach is an ego bending experience that will toughen your hide for the experiences that are ahead!

All Authors, particularly beginning Authors, tend to be "in love" with what they have written and how they have written it. They don't know what they don't know about writing a novel! But... it is theirs! It is a work of art... a labor of love! I understand that completely. I've "been there".

Most people think they can write a novel... until they learn how. Then it takes longer!

Many beginning Authors want to tell all their ideas to the Book Coach. That's okay, but you have to be able to slip out of "transmit" mode occasionally and go into "receive" mode. You are paying your Book Coach to suggest to you how to do things... be sure to listen! And, you must be willing to "go back" and try what the Book Coach suggests and see if it works! Don't expect instant approval. You have to love the "rewrite".

A good Author must be capable of accepting criticism and applying it to rewrite after rewrite! If you can't do that, don't hire a Book Coach, as it will be money poorly spent. If you can do that, hire a Book Coach! It will be money well spent.

You will treasure the day when the Book Coach declares that you have a "publishable manuscript". BUT... be prepared for the hard work that is involved!

Many folks decide they are going to write a novel and plunge into it with good ideas, good intentions, potential and inherent talent... and fail! They fail because they don't know how to write a novel (A "book" is not necessarily a "novel". A novel is a unique art form!). They fail because they do not have someone who can tell them when they have a publishable manuscript... or how to produce one! And, they are frustrated by the innumerable rejection slips that result.

Would you go sky diving without an instructor? Diving?

You must do what you must do to learn that which you wish to do!

Hiring a Book Coach does not mean spending your life's savings. But, be careful... hire someone who has written published novels! There are a lot of folks out there who will take your money but lack the credentials to give you good advice.

Hiring a Book Coach is an investment, just like hiring a piano teacher, or a diving instructor, or any other kind of teacher or instructor.

I had a Book Coach. It worked for me. It will work for you, and the cost is comparable to any other kind of teacher.

****

Call 757 621 6846
Or see
www.powerfulpublisher.com
to investigate
Book Coach Services

Appendix B
Map for use with "The Unknown Horizon"
Figure B-1

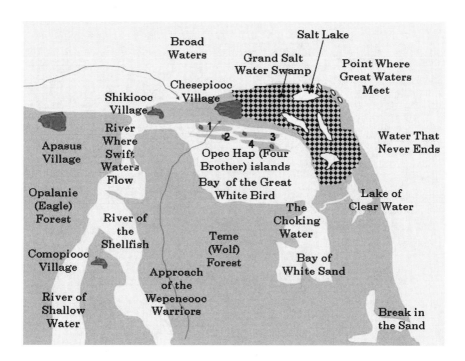

The map shows Broad Waters (Chesapeake Bay), Water-That-Never-Ends (Atlantic Ocean), Point-Where-Great-Waters-Meet (Cape Henry), River-Where-Swift-Waters-Flow (Lynnhaven River) and various fictional names for places in "The Unknown Horizon".

Appendix C
Bibliography

There are many books and video courses for Authors and Screenwriters available. The ones listed here are the ones I have found to be useful.

Vogler, Christopher, <u>The Writer's Journey</u>, 2nd Edition, Mythic Structure for Writers, Michael Wiese productions, 1998

Trottier, David, <u>Screenwriter's Bible</u>, 4th Edition, Silman James Press, 2005

Brogan, Kathryn S., Ed. Brewer, Robert Lee, asst. Ed., <u>Writer's Market</u>, Writers Digest Books, 2004

Johnson, Robert Bowie, Jr., <u>Publishing Basics</u>, a Guide for the Small Press and Independent Self-Publisher, RJ Communications LLC, New York, 2000.

Callan, K. <u>The Script is finished, Now What Do I Do?</u>, Sweden Press, Studio City CA

McKee, Robert, Story, Regan Books, New York 1997

Go to <u>www.amazon.com</u> and enter key words (for many more references)
    How to write a novel.
    How to write a book.
    How to write a screenplay.
    How to write a story.

I recommend that the aspiring Author read more than one book on writing a novel or screenplay and acquire an up to date library of at least six books on the subject. Every one of them will give you a new idea, every time you read it or look up a subject of interest.